almost REAL

MORE BOOKS BY NICOLE SNOW

Almost Ever After

Almost Pretend

Almost Real

The Rory Brothers

Two Truths and a Marriage

One Big Little Secret

Three Reckless Words

Bossy Seattle Suits

One Bossy Proposal

One Bossy Dare

One Bossy Date

One Bossy Offer

One Bossy Disaster

Bad Chicago Bosses

Office Grump

Bossy Grump

Perfect Grump

Damaged Grump

Dark Hearts of Redhaven

The Broken Protector

The Sweetest Obsession

The Darkest Chase

Knights of Dallas

The Romeo Arrangement

The Best Friend Zone

The Hero I Need

The Worst Best Friend

Heroes of Heart's Edge

No Perfect Hero

No Good Doctor

No Broken Beast

No Damaged Goods

No Fair Lady

No White Knight

No Gentle Giant

Enguard Protectors

Still Not Over You

Still Not Into You

Still Not Yours

Still Not Love

Marriage Mistake Stand-Alones

Accidental Hero

Accidental Protector

Accidental Romeo

Accidental Knight

Accidental Rebel

Accidental Shield

almost REAL

NICOLE SNOW

Published by Montlake, Seattle

www.apub.com

EU product safety contact:
Amazon Media EU S. à r.l.
38, avenue John F. Kennedy, L-1855 Luxembourg
amazonpublishing-gpsr@amazon.com

ISBN-13: 9781662535338 (paperback)
ISBN-13: 9781662535345 (digital)

Cover design by Logan Matthews
Cover photography by Michelle Lancaster PTY LTD
Cover image: © Casey Horner / Unsplash

Printed in the United States of America

almost REAL

1

DOG DAYS

(LENA)

This job is bittersweet.

You don't sign up for this business unless you live, sleep, and eat challenges.

Because no girl in her right mind dreams of spending her Friday evening cleaning up puddles of puppy pee.

I mean, it's not that I *mind.* The puppies are adorable, bouncy little balls of golden floof, still finding their paws when they're not mouthing everything in sight. Who am I to judge them for not knowing how to hold their bladders yet?

At their age, I probably couldn't either.

But I love my job, urine and all.

Maybe I'd skip janitor duty if I could. But you don't get the sparkle in life without taking out the trash.

So, here I am, mopping and disinfecting until my arms hurt. It's just before closing, and I'm doing my very best not to eavesdrop on Dr. Ezzie's conversation like the shameless rat I am.

Easier said than done when her office door is cracked open.

And I was born curious. Came out of the hospital wanting to know everything about everyone, so yes, my ears perk up at the concern in my boss's voice.

Not good.

I can't quite make out the words, but I don't need to when her tone gives away so much. That sad, clipped edge in her voice says the news she's getting isn't sunshine and rainbows.

I finish cleaning and flush the dirty water from the bucket down the sink in the back room. Even from here, I can hear the way Dr. Ezzie's tone rises and falls in the background, this nervous rhythm with a slight hush that hints she's trying so hard not to overreact.

My heart hurts.

It has to be about her folks again.

Last week, her elderly father had a nasty fall and broke his hip.

That's what happens when people get old—just like animals—but it doesn't make it suck any less. Dr. Ezzie came in frazzled this morning, straight from the hospital, trading one bone-white center for sick creatures for another.

Straight from looking out for her dad to looking out for us.

As for her mom . . . well, I guess the jury's out on whether she's still all *there*. The last time she visited, her mother didn't recognize her.

The thought hits me with anxiety.

It makes me worry for my own mom one day, and mourn the way I'll never get a chance to face love and frailty with my dad because he's already gone. But that's not the only reason I'm worried today.

Why does this feel like a bad omen for Pawsome Hearts?

We're a small clinic. One of those scrappy family-run businesses that put the well-being of our furry, feathered, scaly patients above all else. Dr. Ezzie drives the whole operation.

She's the entire reason I applied for a position here, and I've loved it ever since.

But if she has to quit to play full-time caregiver or just because the job becomes too much when she's got so much on her plate—

I don't know.

I don't have a clue what that means for the clinic without its owner.

And honestly, that scares me.

There's no one standing by to swoop in and fill her shoes, to give us a fighting chance in a crowded Seattle market.

Without Dr. Ezzie, Pawsome Hearts won't exist.

Not without a buyout from one of those big corporate places where they count dollar signs more than healthy animals. I can only pray that doesn't happen.

Having our supplies and every hour I work micromanaged to "streamline" efficiency is not what I signed up for.

I glance at my smartwatch. It's eight o'clock now—closing time.

Finally.

I head to the door to flip the sign and make sure it's locked, pausing at the window to glance over the property.

Across the courtyard, on the edge of the parking lot, there's the building for the kennels that backs up to the park, where dogs are bedding down for the evening. Keith, our lone night shift boarding guy, gives me a friendly wave as he circles back inside to check on them.

For Seattle, Pawsome Hearts is a unicorn. One of those rare overgrown green spaces bursting with small-town vibes in the big city, where people still know each other's names and greet you with a smile.

No, I wouldn't dare change a thing, even if our daily operations demand it.

When I first hired on, we had more kennel workers for boarding. We had larger kennels too.

It's been a tough year. Even without Dr. Ezzie leaking deets about her finances, I know that.

It's pretty impossible to miss when we've had to make cuts left, right, and center.

I suppose I should be happy, though.

I still get to work here.

I still get to help awesome pets and mend their owners' worried hearts. All in a day's work for a tireless vet tech who runs on iced lattes and ginseng tea.

Hopefully that won't change.

I'm still mulling that over when I see people approaching the door. Just before I can reach them to say we're closed, the bell jingles.

Great. I was so distracted I left it unlocked.

I instantly know this won't be an easy job.

Not because of the dog but because of the people bringing it in.

They're picture perfect, like they were built from the ground up with Olympian genes and born to make cameras smile. They look like they know their best angles better than their own names.

The man—he's a giant.

Insanely tall with thick, dark hair pushed back off his face and flashing blue eyes that stop me in my tracks.

Pretty boy doesn't do him justice.

Not when he's *billboard pretty*, all short, trimmed beard and sculpted muscle and this big lopsided smile that suggests he's used to getting his way.

Late twenties or early thirties, I'd guess.

Although he looks casual, dressed down in a crisp T-shirt and shorts, his outfit has that timeless quality that tells me everything he's wearing drips money.

Not to mention the Apple Watch with the designer wristband on his arm. That gold looks real, and it's totally not the default rubber wristband those watches come with.

There's something else too.

The way he carries himself has an aura. Something like raw confidence except sharper, more intense—pure command, maybe.

Or maybe I'm just that helpless against staggering good looks that practically give him a glowing head like an Orthodox saint. He's the kind of visceral handsome that punches you in the face.

Beside him, the blonde is also tall, though she barely reaches his shoulder height. *Statuesque* would be a good description. She has severe pouty features that look like they've been carved from marble by a sculptor intent on capturing resting bitchface in grim realism.

By the way she holds herself, hip out and breasts pushed up, I'm almost certain she *is* a model.

She's also sneering at me before I've said a single word.

Bad move. It's way too late for this kind of client.

But there's a wiggling corgi in the man's arms with a floppy pink tongue and sad whale eyes that say he'd rather not be here.

Me too, little guy.

I feel for the corgi. I'm already no fan of his owners, and they've been here for ten seconds.

Although I have to admit: The man is hot.

Like, not just a little bit hot. The blow-your-socks-off, every-woman's-dirty-secret kind of hot. Rugged and piercing like he makes workouts and stern glares his whole personality.

I wouldn't be surprised if he did.

But in my experience, I know guys like him. Too good looking, made from old family fortunes and tech money. They don't have much else to fall back on.

At least he's smiling, though.

I can't say the same for Miss Scowlypants.

"Hi," I say, plastering on my own fake smile. "I'm sorry, but we just closed. If it's an emergency, there's a local animal hospital over in—"

"We need a quick look." The man dials his smile up another notch while his eyes harden. Oh God. I practically need shades. "We found this little guy while we were hiking, hiding under a stack of driftwood. He seems dehydrated—he's been panting like hell, anyway."

Hmph.

I catch myself nodding before I can grimace. I *just* said we were closed, but here I am, ready to come rushing to the rescue.

Wow, he's good.

"The air's pure soot today. All the smoke from the wildfires," he continues. "With the heat, I wanted to make sure his lungs are good. You know, just in case he's having an allergic reaction or something to all this crap in the atmosphere."

Ugh.

He has a point.

There *is* a lot of smoke dusting Seattle lately—a pattern that keeps repeating way too often during our summers. Today it's that hazy, slightly grey smog hanging around that makes your nostrils burn like you've just inhaled seawater.

The fires up in British Columbia haven't spread down to Washington, thank God, but the smoke has drifted south.

Usually does, but this year it's hitting earlier and it's lingering.

He's also right—animals can suffer plenty from breathing it. The poor dog's tongue is hanging out, meaning the little guy probably *is* dehydrated. His sides keep rising and falling with each breath, a little more than they should.

I bet he's hungry, too, especially if they don't know how long he was lost out there.

Blondie McScowlyface rolls her eyes like a cheerleader in a '90s sitcom. She's wearing winged eyeliner that looks so dramatic it practically reaches her ears.

Catlike, definitely.

It's a look, for sure.

"She said *no*," she whines, and to absolutely no one's surprise, her voice is as grating as her sour pout. "God, Brady. Why can't you ever take no for an answer?"

Brady, huh?

It feels oddly good to put a name to his ridiculously handsome face.

"Because I want him checked out," Brady says firmly, flashing her a pointed look.

"Yeah, but how is this dog *our* problem?" She folds her arms, tapping the toe of her designer boot on the floor. "Just drop him off with animal control and be done with it."

Yep, it's not just the face.

Raging bitch confirmed.

I have to bite the tip of my tongue and choke down my disgust.

Customer face *on*.

Even when the customer has a lump of coal instead of a beating heart.

Even when Brady isn't much better, barging in after hours and demanding we do something. But at least his heart's in the right place.

If I could throw this woman out on her butt, I would, but I can't do that to the little guy squirming in Brady's arms, and I can't give Dr. Ezzie a lawsuit either.

One of these days, my soft spot for animals will get me into trouble. But that's the whole mission at Pawsome Hearts—healthy paws and claws first and always.

"Hold on, I'll go ask my boss," I say, leading them to the closest exam room. "If you guys can just wait here for a second, I'll be right back."

The blonde rolls her eyes and immediately sinks into the single available seat, making a face like its plastic coating feels offensive to her skin. Her boyfriend sets the dog down on the table, smoothing a hand gently over its big ears.

His ears, I correct myself.

The dog's coat looks a little matted, but his butt wiggles as his tail wags and he licks Brady's fingers. For some reason, I linger on the scene.

His hands are big. Easy to notice from the way they span the corgi's back and neck, but they're affectionate too. Soft and soothing.

The dog clearly loves the attention, leaning into his palm.

I'm oddly transfixed.

Look, it's not like I'm doubting he can be nice to animals. Most people are—I like to think of it as a baseline morality test.

Either you're kind to the innocent beings we share the planet with, or you're a shitty person.

Easy.

But that also doesn't mean you're an angel if you show some basic human decency. It just means you're probably not a demon.

Brady gives me another high-voltage smile.

"Thank you. I appreciate it," he says, like he's expecting me to curtsy.

Bitchface rolls her eyes to the ceiling again and huffs loudly.

Obviously I'm nothing but another nuisance in her oh-so-rough existence.

It must be so *terrible*, strutting around the world when you're rich and beautiful. I wonder what fancy dinner reservation the corgi rescue interrupted.

Considering dog-whisperer Brady is with Possessed Barbie in the first place, he can't be your normal, everyday upstanding person, regardless of how much this corgi adores scritch-scratches behind the ear.

"Sure." I nod, smile, and close the door behind me.

Dr. Ezzie's door is still cracked. I rap on it gently, trying to ignore the heavy silence inside her office.

"Hey, Doc?" I call. "We have a couple here with an abandoned dog, and I wondered if you'd be okay giving the poor thing a quick look? The air's pretty rancid today, and he doesn't look too comfortable."

Although if that tail was any indication, he's not feeling too awful.

Dogs aren't like people—if they have any serious issues, they usually show it. Lethargy, lack of enthusiasm, lack of appetite. Lack of responsiveness to affection.

Still, it's not my place to say.

But I don't get a response.

I push the door open, revealing Dr. Ezzie, and I do a double take. Her mouth is pressed tight, and her eyes are red.

Guilt punches me in the stomach.

I was right: Whatever was on that call wasn't good news.

And now I've gone and dragged her out of her cave before she was ready.

But I don't let my face reveal my guilt. Maybe she knows it looks obvious she's been crying, but that doesn't mean I need to stare and make her feel worse.

I don't need to look shocked.

Dr. Ezzie never cries.

In the years I've worked here, I've never seen her shed a single tear. Even yesterday, when she got the call about her dad's fall and rushed to the hospital, there was nothing but strong determination on her face.

The guilt in my belly tightens into a knot.

Something must be horribly wrong.

But she forces a smile anyway, though it doesn't reach her eyes. "Certainly, Lena. Thanks for showing them in. Anything I can do to help."

She stands.

"They're in Room B," I say too brightly.

Yeah. No one will hand me an Oscar anytime soon for my acting.

I just try to cling to my calm even though I'm stressing like crazy. My boss so doesn't need this today.

She follows me to the exam room, though, where Blondie scrolls TikTok with the volume cranked up while her obscenely hot boy toy strokes the dog's back.

"Hello, I'm Dr. Ezzie," Dr. Ezzie says coolly, her professionalism snapped back in place. "How can I help?"

Brady glances at me before saying, "We found this boy on a hike down by the beach, stuck under some driftwood and panting like mad. Don't know how long he was there. I figured it was long enough with the bad air."

I can't help it—I look out the window, staring at the evening haze painting gloom over everything.

It's a minor miracle the dog is even here.

What kind of man goes hiking in *this* black lung environment? A masochist? Some health freak who puts muscle and endurance over long-term lung capacity?

Then again, judging by his build, I shouldn't be surprised.

"He was whimpering when I tried to coax him out. He wouldn't come," he continues, "but my driver had some beef jerky, and we caught him eventually. No collar or anything. He's a friendly pup."

His *driver*?

I have to stop myself from snorting.

Seattle money is annoying.

Young Seattle money is fucking infuriating.

Oh, I'm sure he feels like he deserves a Purple Heart today, courageously taking precious time away from living like a prince to breathe some smog and help a lost corgi. All with his hired help stepping in, because God forbid he do *anything* himself.

For a second, I try imagining what that must be like. Having someone there to wait on you hand and foot.

Nope. Can't picture it.

I've worked hard for everything I have. That doesn't make me better than him, no, but it sure as hell doesn't make him better than me.

"Let's have a look and see if he's chipped," Dr. Ezzie says, once she's given the corgi a quick inspection. "Ah, here we are. Lena, can you grab the owner's info, please?"

I step up to the computer as she scans the dog's chip, clicking through the database as Dr. Ezzie advises Brady and Blondie what to do.

As we suspected, our boy is a little dehydrated and his lungs are irritated, but otherwise he's unharmed.

I'd bet my bottom dollar that Ice Queen over here doesn't have any intention of caring for the corgi a minute longer than necessary. She must be counting the seconds until they can leave.

It's a little impressive, to be honest, to be that heartless and self-centered. God must've missed her when he was passing out empathy.

As if she can sense what I'm thinking, she glances at me, her mouth pinched in a frown. On anyone else, it would be unflattering, but she somehow manages to pull it off.

Pouty. Picture perfect. Evil.

I give back a little smile.

Just a tad patronizing, because if she thinks her looks will do her any favors here, she's dead wrong.

"His lungs sound okay," Dr. Ezzie says, checking the corgi again. "Though he should stay indoors until the air clears up." She checks her watch. "If you'd like, you can stay another hour for observation."

"Yeah, thanks." Brady sounds grateful. "I'd definitely like to keep him here as long as you can give us—or until his owner comes to pick him up. I'm happy to pay for that too. Just send me the bill."

Blondie huffs loudly.

Holy shit, if she keeps that up, I *will* punch her.

How can anyone be so dismissive with an animal in need?

"His name is Charlie," I announce from the desk. "I've got his owner's number here—I'll just step out and give her a call."

Dr. Ezzie gives me a proud smile. "Yes. Thank you so much, Lena."

It's just my duty.

Regardless of who brings in a pet, I'm always at my best. It's the least they deserve—just like how Charlie needs to go back to his family.

"We'll be out of your hair soon," I hear Brady saying. "Thanks again for taking us in. We appreciate you making sure he's okay after normal business hours."

"Of course."

He's making it harder to hate him.

Sigh.

I shut the door and block out the rest of the conversation so I can make the call.

Our receptionist, Trish, has gone home for the evening—and given how quiet it was, I said she could head home early if she wanted and I'd help cover the phones.

Friday evening and all.

So many companies give that spiel about how they're family, but that's genuinely how it is here. My colleagues are more than coworkers.

My heart lurches when I think about Dr. Ezzie and her bad news again. Whatever it is, the odds are stacked against any big improvements. For Esmerelda Serena and her family, there's just a long way down.

Tick tock, the empty room announces.

Mom always said I had a morbid streak. Always prone to stressing about worst-case scenarios and black-swan disasters.

I suppose that's true, but what's the harm in being aware?

Just *knowing* what the worst might look like.

Just in case, y'know.

That's one life lesson I learned the hard way, and one I'll never forget.

"Hello?" The owner has an elderly quiver in her voice as she answers.

"Hi, is this Mrs. Hernandez?"

"Who is this?"

"This is Lena from Pawsome Hearts veterinary clinic over on Edmunds Street in Beacon Hill. I'm calling about your dog, Charlie."

"Oh, you've found the little Houdini?" The relief in her voice is palpable. "Thank you! I've been worried sick. My niece was out walking him yesterday, and he broke off his collar and escaped. We were sure something dreadful had happened—and it was so out of character for him!"

"He was found down by the beach, from what I know. We'll make sure he gets some food and water. Any dietary restrictions?"

"No, and thank you, dear. My poor Annie, she was so distraught. She's walked him hundreds of times and there's never been any trouble. But all it takes is once. Is he truly okay? He wasn't hurt?"

"Nope, just a little dehydrated. Plus some lung irritation with the bad air. He should stay indoors overnight until the sky clears up. When would you like to pick him up?"

"Oh shoot." She speaks to someone else on her end, her voice muffled. "We'd come tonight, but we're out of town—that's why my niece was looking after him. And tonight she has a night shift, I'm afraid. Is it possible for you to keep him? Just for tonight?"

Oof.

I really should say no.

We're a small clinic with limited kennel space. It's already crowded with our regular dogs, and Keith is running himself ragged. But there's nowhere else for Charlie to go.

I can't bring myself to turn her down.

"Can I call you back? I'll check with the owner and see what I can do," I say instead. "You said you can grab him tomorrow?"

"Yes, yes, absolutely! Thank you so much." Her voice breaks. "I wasn't sure we'd ever see our baby again. Thank you so much."

"You're very welcome. I'll be in touch."

She thanks me again, and I smile as I end the call.

This is what the job is really all about. Making a difference for the people and pets who need it most.

The right owners—the good ones—they're always grateful.

As for the bad ones . . . well, I don't like to think about them. I tell myself there's a special place in hell with their seat reserved.

I scoop up the card reader as I head back to the exam room. At least they're paying customers. God knows the clinic needs it with how tight things have been.

"Good news," I say as I open the door. "We've found—"

I stop in my tracks as I see Brady holding up his phone, posing with Charlie, who's slumped on his side, tired but happy and wagging his tail.

What the hell?

Heat turns my blood into lava.

I should have known.

You go and find an abandoned dog, then bring him in just so you can flaunt your heroics on social media. Because *that's* what the world needs right now.

Apparently, all good deeds are transactional for earthworms like Brady McMoneybags.

More rich virtue signalers, measuring their morals in likes.

Oh my God.

Charlie doesn't even know he's a prop, of course.

The corgi looks up lovingly and licks his face. Brady laughs, and I have to admit—even though I'm pissed enough to spit nails—it's a charming laugh.

That doesn't mean this whole thing isn't *gross*.

It gives me massive ick, just watching it unfold.

He's not a good person. He's not altruistic or kind or selfless.

He's one more ginormous prick in a city crawling with them, turning a good deed into a spectacle.

No, it doesn't matter if he's built like Hercules with an Instagram filter.

As far as I'm concerned, he's a first-class asshole.

I have plenty of experience to know. After you've dated the king of abusive predators and lived to tell the tale, you don't forget.

He glances up at me with a small smile like a cobra watching its prey.

"Is it good news, Lena?"

I hate that he knows my name.

I inhale a long, slow breath.

Paying customers.

Paying.

Smile, bat your eyes, and shut it.

There's no way I can unload on him now, especially if I want to get them out of here ASAP.

"I managed to get in touch with the owner, yes," I say coldly. "She'll come tomorrow morning, but she can't take him until then because they're out of town."

"Damn. They left town without their dog, huh?" Brady's smile drops.

"Their niece was looking after him, I think. It's a whole thing." I wave a hand, because the owners' situation hardly matters when I just caught him making a big stinking hero spectacle right in front of me.

Calm, calm.

It's not easy when Blondie sighs. "What's the problem now? Why are we still here?"

"Nancy, enough." Brady shoots her an annoyed glance.

"What? She found the person, didn't she?"

"The *problem* is we don't have enough kennel space," I clip, cutting them off before they get into it. I like my toxic relationships to stay on Netflix, thank you very much. "We recently had to downsize, and there just isn't room for Charlie there. There's one spare kennel in the observation room. But it's not the most comfortable place for a dog who isn't sick."

Brady scratches the dog's head idly as he thinks. I watch the movement, knowing I shouldn't.

His hands are so nice. Neat, but not too sculpted.

He probably climbs with them or something, but there's a rhythmic quality to his movements. It looks poised and elegant even if it's just the way he rubs behind Charlie's ear.

The corgi closes his eyes and leans his head back with a satisfied grumble.

I can relate.

It's been years since anyone touched me like that.

"Why don't I take him?" Brady says suddenly.

I look up, annoyed that I do a double take.

"I can look after him for the night and meet you back here tomorrow to hand him off," he explains.

Blondie—Nancy—makes a noise that can only be disgust.

She's a charmer, all right. I can totally see why he likes her.

"I have the perfect place for Charlie boy. Here." He pulls out his phone and scrolls until he stops on a picture of what must be his house.

It's enormous, of course, and right on Lake Washington. That picture-perfect blue water is a dead giveaway.

There's even what looks like a mini sculpture park by the water.

Obviously.

What person doesn't need their own private art walk?

"Plenty of grass," he continues.

Like I need more convincing.

It's almost worse than I imagined. The entire property looks like it's within spitting distance of the billionaire estates perched in the hills. I bet he waves to household names and tech CEOs while their landscapers mow the lawns.

Maybe they get together and talk about tax loopholes and exotic stock options.

Hell, maybe they have cocaine binges on the weekends.

Whatever it is people do when they're loaded and they don't have to get up at five every morning just to make rent.

Another reason to loathe his entitled ass.

Then again, this *is* the answer I was looking for, even if I hate it. Also, he seems sane, if spoiled rotten, and Charlie likes him.

The stay would save us the headache of finding another kennel to board the dog this late or cooping him up in the sick room.

Whatever.

"Sure. That would save us a lot of trouble, assuming you don't mind," I say.

"Not at all. I'm a dog guy," he announces proudly.

"But it's clinic protocol to follow up, just to make sure Charlie gets reunited with his owner," I warn.

He smiles. "I'll be here bright and early. Just name the time. When do you want me to meet you?"

Oh goodie. An invite to deal with him again.

If he can sense the laser beams of frustration blasting from my eyes, he doesn't show it.

"Brady, c'mon. Let's go!" Blondie whines, taking his arm and tugging.

Yes, please leave.

"Awesome. Now we'll have to cancel the reservation for sure," she says as he scoops Charlie back into his arms. The dog, exhausted but at ease, just wags his tail a few times and settles in for the ride. "Now you'll have to take that smelly dog. What will your dad say?"

"He won't know tonight," Brady says calmly, giving me a nod as he strides out to the parking lot.

The car waiting for them is a sleek, newish upscale SUV. No surprise.

And *obviously* an older man in a suit—the driver, I assume—steps out and opens the door for them.

Honestly, I'm surprised they didn't send the driver to do all their dirty work. Or maybe he's not authorized to use the prince's credit card.

No, I doubt that.

Someone like him has at least six credit cards, most with no limit, and he's not going to get fussy about who uses them for company expenses.

And when you're rich, everything is a company expense.

Yes, I'm glaring as they leave.

Jealous much? I am.

Like I said, this job is bittersweet.

The animals are awesome about a hundred percent of the time. It's the people who suck way more often.

But at least we did our duty.

We helped solve one more case of lost paws tonight.

I wish it made me happier.

As I watch the SUV pull away, shaking my head at the way Brady waves through the window, I wonder how long Pawsome Hearts can keep the rescues going.

How long do we have left?

II

DOG TIRED

(BRADY)

I wear responsibilities like an old scar, intimately familiar with the pressure.

They keep you moving as much as they keep you in line. They can be your biggest carrot or a stick that bludgeons you to death.

Today, they have me working on my laptop early in the morning, sitting at the long table in the old family library while a big lump of corgi dozes at my feet.

Charlie slept through the night, and he's still tired. He's also part of the reason why I've forced myself to become a morning person. You can't fix the world's pet food problems if you're crashing out at 4 a.m. and rolling out of bed past noon.

Still, just because it's necessary doesn't mean I enjoy it. I take another pull off the huge mug of black coffee at my side. It's already halfway down.

The latest report from the lab blurs together in front of my eyes. I've damn near needed a crash course in veterinary nutrition to make heads or tails of these things, but I'm getting there.

By my feet, Charlie finally groans, sits up, does a big stretch, and pads over to where Mom sits, reading the morning news on her tablet.

He yips.

Mom looks up over her glasses and smiles.

My mother's at her best in the morning, before the day's obligations come crashing in.

Later, she'll put her contacts in and change into something more stylish. Kerrigan Pruitt's image is her main commodity, and she's all about being perfectly put together.

In her opinion, failing eyesight is an unacceptable weakness, and she's already had laser surgery twice.

Charlie barks again, his fluffy rump wiggling as he bounces around Mom's chair.

I swallow a laugh, happy as hell to see him gearing up to play.

I idly wonder if the latest stuff my people are coming up with would ever appeal to an energetic beast like Charlie. It might make him happier and healthier, but only if his owner can afford it.

There's the fucking rub.

Mom saves me before I glue my eyes back to the screen. She puts down her iPad and laughs, reaching down so she can cup Charlie's fox-like face in her hands.

I'm glad he's a well-behaved boy and his antics aren't pissing her off.

Yesterday, when I brought him to my parents' place from the vet, she was delighted.

My father never let me have dogs, growing up, but that doesn't mean she doesn't adore them.

Charlie was cute enough to warrant an overnight stay in my old room, which opens up to the spacious yard leading down to the summer shore of Lake Washington.

That's the real reason I brought him here, rather than my place. High-rise condos aren't much for a dog to run around. Plus, I didn't want to risk overexerting him at a public park before he's truly rested.

"Is he annoying you?" I ask, glancing at the time. "I'll be taking him to the clinic soon."

"Hardly, he's a dear." She smooths her hand over his head, smiling. "You should take a break and enjoy your morning. It isn't every day you wake up with a puppy."

I grunt reluctantly.

"I mean it, Brady. You're an investor, not a scientist. You won't magically conjure the world's best organic dog food out of thin air by staring at reports until your eyes melt."

"I'm the CEO, Mother." I run a hand through my hair. "It's my money on the line and my responsibility to be on top of everything."

"Careful. You sound like your father." Goddamn, that stings. "Does that mean working yourself into an early grave?" She examines one hand, the one with the diamonds glinting on her ring finger.

My parents have been married for a long time now, but she's never stopped staring at that ring.

They have their faults, sure, but there's no denying they love each other.

That, or she just loves the way it sparkles in the light.

Sometimes it's hard to tell.

"There's a gap in the market, and we're going to fill it. I'm sure we can bring the prices down. Keeping more pets healthy with the good stuff people can actually afford will make everyone happier."

"Yes, darling, I've read your mission statement several times." She glances back at her tablet and continues, already distracted as Charlie settles at her feet.

To her, my achievements aren't the important thing and the details hardly matter. She's too used to snapping her fingers and letting someone else make miracles happen.

But for me, that's the entire point.

Principles are God.

Adopting a pet for life is fucking hard. Giving them what they need while you're on a shoestring budget—especially in an expensive city like Seattle, where food and housing for people is a constant issue—that's harder.

That's also why someone needs to make it happen, and that someone is me.

I've done my market research. There's space for high-quality, *healthy* food for dogs and cats that doesn't bleed bank accounts if it's just sourced right and formulated wisely.

I'm going to prove it's possible, even if it makes me want to tear my hair out sometimes.

Hell, *often*.

Mom puts her iPad back down again with a sigh, looking at me over her glasses. "I know you have your heart set on this. But I wonder if dog food is really the right direction for you right now. You could always develop another app."

"Been there, done that. Key word being *done*."

I have to fight to keep from snarling.

Being a prisoner of your own success is too real.

My first start-up went terrifyingly well. So well, it's left everyone who matters staring at me impatiently, waiting for me to work digital sorcery again.

"You have talent. We both know it," she continues. "You could do something more exciting—and better for your image—than that dating app you sold last year."

"Something better for *your* image, you mean?"

I know her real worry. I'm practically the face of Pruitt Brands, ever since my father couldn't be.

"Well . . . dog food doesn't have a whiff of scandal, but it's simply not"—she pauses and catches herself—"not very dignified."

My eyes bounce to the clock on my computer. Damn, it's still not time to head to the clinic yet, which means I'm stuck in this conversation.

This must be the hundredth time she's brought up my reputation. There's no denying the app made money and proved I can live off more than the family name.

If it were just about money and success, she'd be thrilled.

In her own way, she is, I suppose. Success is one language my parents know by heart.

What she doesn't like is that the app revolutionized online *dating*. As far as she's concerned, it fuels the playboy sins the press won't let me shake.

She's not wrong.

Still, I couldn't give a flying shit about my reputation as long as it doesn't interfere with what I *want* to do.

The app was about getting serious and mastering business. The pet food project is about getting real.

Like everyone else with a pulse, I want to do something meaningful with my life. More than just coming up with new ways for horny young people to hook up. Unlike everyone else, I've got nine figures in my bank account to make it happen.

"If it's a choice between dignity and meaningful action, you know what I'll pick every time," I say.

She purses her lips together as she pushes her glasses up her nose.

Then the door swings open and a human bull storms in. Dad just missed a conversation that would've left his face red.

Even in his motorized wheelchair, flanked by his nurse, he's an imposing figure. He still dresses in a designer suit and tie daily, unchanged since his heart attack.

It takes him all of two seconds to look at Charlie and turn his nose up like he sees a ratty raccoon caught tracking mud into his house.

"Is this what you're doing with your life now?" he demands, his voice quivering. "Blowing off family friends to pick up stray dogs?"

Fuck, here we go.

I slam the laptop shut. No point in trying to accomplish anything now.

My father never allows much room for multitasking. As far as he's concerned, everything I do should require one hundred percent of my focus.

If that's another conversation from hell, fine, I need to give him all my attention. I can already predict every word he'll say, so I start the debunking.

"It made sense for me to bring him somewhere he could touch grass without a long trek down the elevator and two blocks to the nearest park. My penthouse isn't the most comfortable place." I shrug. "Also, Nancy's parents aren't 'family friends.'"

No, they're more like future in-laws I'm not remotely interested in having.

Ever since I had to take over Dad's media footprint, my parents have been driving the marriage freight train full speed ahead, trying like hell to set me up with Nancy Loomer. Like it's totally normal to behave like we're eighteenth-century socialites who do arranged marriages.

You'd think the world would move past that shit.

"Well, you're damned right about that. You've proven you're not taking this seriously." Dad leans back in his chair, his big hands folded on his lap, glaring with an energy his failing body lacks. "Nancy won't wait around forever, you know. Neither will her folks. She's a nice girl and high IQ."

It hurts not to laugh in his face.

No one who gets to know this girl would ever describe her as *nice*. She isn't particularly bright, either, but it doesn't matter when Dad's IQ assessments operate on image and ambition rather than real accomplishments.

"Alec," Mom cuts in sharply. "Must we start the day like this?"

"We must, considering how he's behaving. I need my son to think harder about his life instead of filling in for animal control."

Prick.

Behind him, his burly nurse, Freddy, coughs awkwardly. Poor dude's lived through enough Pruitt family spats to know what's coming.

I inhale sharply. "We found a lost dog stranded outside with the shitty air. What was I supposed to do in your view, Dad? Leave him there to suffocate?"

"You could've left that stray at the vet. As far as I'm concerned, you went above and beyond simply by taking him there. Time is your greatest asset, Brady. Start acting like it."

Charlie stands with a disinterested yawn. Yeah, he's got the right idea.

"The tech told me their kennels were filled to capacity."

"And that's your problem why, exactly?" His brows descend in a stormy expression I recognize too well. "If you won't get serious with your career, you *will* get serious about your relationship with Miss Loomer."

"Alec," Mom says again. "You can't be mad at Brady for looking out for this little guy. He's sweet." She strokes Charlie under the chin as he stands up to her knee height, the entire back half of his body swaying as his tail wags.

"I've already told you." It's an effort to keep my voice down, but I try. "I'm not participating in an arranged marriage from the last century. If that's what you think I want for a public face, no thanks."

"Arranged marriage? Stop being childish and—" He pauses for a brief coughing fit.

They've been getting worse lately, and I see Freddy eyeballing the oxygen tank on the back of his chair with concern. Dad wipes his mouth angrily and points at me.

"Like it or not, you've inherited this legacy. You're the public face of our family *and* our business. When people think Pruitt Agriculture, they see your face first, especially when you plaster yourself over social media."

Shit, I wish he didn't have a point.

Having a public-facing figurehead is important for any big business like ours, especially the boring ones that mostly run in the background. We've always sold ourselves as a family business going back generations—only now that means half the world ogling at you online, never mind the institutional media.

Dad knows this too well, and so do I. Not that it stops him from throwing it in my face whenever he thinks he needs to grind me into shape.

He folds his arms until he looks like a muffin, all chest exploding out of his suit.

"We've put up with a lot from you, son. We've even indulged your costly little sideshow with dog food, built on our resources and supply network."

"You have, and I'm grateful," I bite off, trying to keep a lid on my temper.

Dad holds up a finger. "But I've warned you—if any of your online fluff causes even a whiff of bad press, I won't stand for it. None of it, Brady. You'll find your own damn farmers and specialists, right after you shut down your social accounts."

Mom winces before I can say a word.

"Your father has a point," she urges gently. "You just need to be more *careful*."

"Careful. What the hell does that mean?" I demand.

In answer, she holds up her tablet with a thin smile. The Instagram Reel I posted last night plays. I walk over, take it, and scroll through the comments.

Adorable dog! one comment says.

Love the way he's helping out, another says.

Holy pissy missy! Look at that mad bish staring him down, someone else says. Several people agree, making it the top comment.

A few more make jokes about my next hookup with the girl shooting daggers out her big brown eyes.

Like I was trying to be anything else than charitable.

Like I ever do anything else with my account these days.

Even so, the sight of the vet tech's glower makes me smile. The camera caught her when she wasn't paying attention.

Lena, wasn't it?

The brunette was pretty in that soft, demure way I've started to prefer because it's more authentic. Little to no makeup and surgical enhancements. No flashy tattoos done by a guy with an art degree, and no lip filler slowly turning her face into a plastic doll's.

Her amber brown eyes look bright here and narrowed, right above a soft mouth that curves at the corners when she's pissed.

Under other circumstances, she might be more used to smiling than scowling.

Definitely not here.

At the time, I thought it was Nancy's stupidity winning us the stink eye, but playing the video back, it's clear the girl's rage is aimed at me.

Damn.

So maybe I didn't make the best impression.

I just wanted to make sure Charlie got checked, but I guess I didn't go about it as well as I should have. I could've waited to show him off to the world, after I had him back at my parent's place for the night.

Not cool when the clinic went out of its way to help us.

I should've been more apologetic about barging in there after hours too. Hell, maybe I should've even tipped them.

Dad sighs roughly, sinking down into his wheelchair.

"We need you to start turning your life around, son. Wake up. Be more aware." His frown looks tired this time, like my antics have aged him. "No one's getting any younger."

For a fraught second, we lock eyes and I see vulnerability behind his usual incoherent anger. He's not the same man he was a few years ago before his brush with death, before the heart attack left him hollowed out.

"Understood." I swipe away from the video and hand it back to Mom.

"I don't need to tell you large brands are more online than ever," Dad growls, his humanity vanishing. "We can't have an unmarried thirty-year-old son playing tabloid prince that fucks everything that moves."

"Alec!" Mother gasps, shaking her head.

Whatever flicker of sympathy I had for him a second ago dies.

The rush of anger is explosive.

I should've known it would come down to this—I should've fucking *known*—but it doesn't make his words cut any less.

All this high-and-mighty hand-wringing over my organic pet food brand, and this is his real problem.

My sex life.

No, not even that—the public's *perception* of my sex life.

The fact that I wasn't a damn Boy Scout in my past life.

Bullshit.

And I've smelled it enough for today.

I snap my fingers, and Charlie's ears perk up. He follows my silent instruction to come join me, then sits.

"You're supposed to be retired. Find a better hobby than my damn dating life," I snarl. "It's beneath you, old man."

I snap my fingers again for the corgi, and we're already moving. I barely remember to grab Charlie's leash before I slam the door.

"Now look what you've done . . ." Mom says miserably as I leave the room.

I ignore them both and take the long, winding staircase two at a time to the entryway, waiting for Charlie to catch up on his stubby legs.

Luis, my assistant, is walking in through a side door. And Luis being Luis, he immediately notices the look on my face.

"Again?" he whispers.

"Yes. Selfish fuck." I pinch the bridge of my nose and take a deep breath.

The truth is, Dad's an old-school jackass, but he's not entirely wrong. That almost makes it worse.

"What was it this time?"

"The usual lecture I've heard a thousand times. I need to get my shit together and stop fucking everything that moves." I snort.

Luis rolls his eyes.

"You'd think they'd find better things to get on your back about."

"Yeah." I sigh. Assistant or not, there are days when Luis doubles as my best friend. We've known each other for years, though Dad likes to call him my "handler."

Because he's such a comedian.

"I should've kept hooking up with that model last year just to throw it in his face," I say.

"Can't argue with that. She was a baddie," Luis says with a laugh.

"To you, horny asshole."

"You said it first."

I blow out a long breath. The fact is, I know I've fucked up, and I don't get the luxury of living down my mistakes.

At the time, I was doing well. I hadn't partied for years or flaunted actresses and models hanging on my arm.

I thought it was casual enough. No big deal, a couple nights without consequence, but she misread the situation.

Then she went nuclear on social media after I said I wasn't interested in anything more serious. I became the techbro YouTuber heartbreaker king of assholery every young woman in America loved to despise overnight.

It was the usual social media flash in the pan, sure, instantly forgotten once the next drama bomb exploded. But it was enough.

Bye, reputation.

My parents were livid.

"Nothing wrong with a little fun," Luis says. "But you should probably vet their history first. Background checks, NDAs . . . that chick was slamming her exes like a psycho since she was seventeen. Did you know?"

"No, Luis. Didn't think I'd need to get a shrink's assessment for a damn hookup."

He chuckles and shrugs. "Man, that's what you get for being rich and famous. Everything has a cost."

He mimes fishing.

"Goddamn, remind me to never let you moonlight as my wingman."

"Since when do you need it? Is there a raise for protecting you from crazy chicks?"

"Oh, fuck off." I laugh, though, because he's not wrong.

Fallout aside, I've never struggled with finding dates, hookups, whatever I please.

Money makes up for whatever I might lack in the common sense department. The second a girl hears my name is Pruitt, they're interested.

I could have a face like a vampire bat, and they'd still queue up around the block for their crack at landing a ring from Prince Charming.

Sometimes, it's depressing.

Mostly, it's just a distraction. A biological urge like scratching dry skin so I can get the hell back to work.

Luis claps me on the shoulder. "All set to take the best boy home? I've got the car waiting."

I nod, following him outside and helping Charlie into the back seat next to me.

"Image management doesn't have to be pure torture, you know," he says, glancing at me as he adjusts the rearview mirror.

I shake my head. "Tell me you haven't spent time with Nancy Loomer without telling me you haven't spent time with Nancy Loomer."

He wags his eyebrows. "You think I'd mind? She's hot enough."

"Dude, if you knew her personality was hot trash, you'd reconsider." For all his joking, I know he likes girls with more substance.

Nancy wouldn't know substance if it beaned her on the nose like a softball. She'd care more about having to fix her makeup.

"I might," he agrees.

"Easy for you to say. You're not the one under the gun to propose to her."

"Jesus, is she really that bad?"

"Worse," I say flatly. "It's not like I didn't give her a fair shake. Hell, the last four or five times we went out, I gave her every chance to prove me wrong. Show me there could ever be a spark."

Instead, all she proved was that she was spoiled rotten.

Everything had to be just so, or she'd freak.

Tapas and wine menus. The cloud cover on a chartered day cruise out of Lake Union. No greyhounds at the dog rescue event I sponsored from a local shelter because they "freak her out"—and you'd best believe I vetoed that one.

Greyhounds were half my world as a kid.

Every time, the same. No grace, no humility, and no respect for people or animals. I also never missed the way she'd check herself out in every mirror we passed.

One time when I didn't immediately compliment her dress, she sulked through dinner.

I don't have the time or patience to deal with an overgrown teenager.

I'm definitely not putting up with that shit for the rest of my life.

I'm not stunting whatever progress I've made escaping the black hole of ego and entitlement just to settle for someone who thrives in it.

"Yeah, man." Luis winces in sympathy. "Gotta say, I'm glad I'm not stuck in the billionaire dating pool. It's not all it's cracked up to be. Too bad you can't find a decent girl to buy yourself some time so they'd get off your ass."

I laugh, but then—

An idea.

A wild, wicked, workable idea.

What if I *could* buy a little time to derail my parents' marriage-from-hell train? What if I broadened my options to include a girl who's actually palatable—even if it's just for appearances? Even if it's only fake and temporary?

"What now? What's with that look?" Luis says, staring at me in the mirror. "Why are you smiling?"

“Your fault.” I grin, scratching Charlie’s shoulders as he licks my face. “Thanks for the inspiration.”

“Oh no.”

“You might’ve just saved my life, Luis.”

He groans nervously. “I don’t know what that means, but I know you, boss. Whatever you’re scheming, it won’t be good.”

III

CAT GOT YOUR TONGUE

(LENA)

Here comes this idiot again.

I pause what I'm doing just to glare out the window as the sleek black SUV pulls up in the parking lot and idles like a tank.

"Does this man ever drive himself?" I mutter to Trish, the receptionist.

"Who cares? He's cute. And rich." She taps the keyboard and cackles loudly as she stares out at Brady and the young Latino man climbing out of the car.

"Seriously, Trish?"

"What? I ain't as young as you, but my eyes still work just fine," she drawls in her East Tennessee accent.

She must have brought a Southern appetite for men too. I definitely can't understand it.

"Well, don't get too attached. He's a total piece of work. I wonder if he would've picked up that corgi at all if he didn't have social media brownie points to gain."

I purse my lips sourly, hating that I regret those words.

The fluffy dog looks happy.

Charlie bounces out the second Brady opens the passenger door, a ball of energetic fluff who delights in pulling on his leash.

Brady almost loses his grip and catches it again with a grin. His shirt strains across his shoulders.

Seriously, this man is built like a statue come to life.

He drags a hand through his thick dark hair as he gives his chauffeur slash babysitter a wry look.

Another car pulls up then, a Volkswagen, and a little old lady jumps out of the driver's seat, practically screaming.

Charlie yips with sheer excitement, barking loudly even through the glass. He almost goes airborne as he leaps, testing Brady's leash grip all over again.

I'm *not* smiling.

I promise you I'm not.

"Look at you! All smiles," Trish says like an annoying mind reader.

"He's a cutie—the dog, I mean. Look how happy he is to see his mom."

"Adorable," she declares, but her tone leaves it ambiguous who she's describing.

I huff a breath.

Whatever.

Yes, Brady Pruitt is fine in that hypermasculine, hyperaware way guys are when they know they're attractive and they have the resources to strut around like gods among us mere mortals.

But that's not something that turns my crank.

Not even a little.

And little old Mrs. Hernandez lowers herself to the ground to greet Charlie properly, rubbing his back as he licks her face.

Adorable is right.

Brady turns and reaches into his vehicle—is it even his car if the other man drives?—and pulls out a heaping basket of treats and dog toys.

Oh my God.

I wrinkle my nose.

Why does he have to do it? Blow all my ugly expectations to pieces by being so nice?

I'm half expecting him to pull out his phone and make a big scene, but he doesn't.

He's a grade A prick, yeah, but at least he's a generous one. That's slightly less horrible.

I feel like I'm betraying myself by even admitting it.

But Mrs. Hernandez beams like it's Christmas morning. She gives him a big, heartfelt hug.

"See?" Trish says sharply, drilling her gaze through my face. "Cute as hell, inside and out."

"You better be talking about the dog."

"Uh-huh." She giggles again.

Sigh.

With one last wave, Brady turns and heads into the clinic.

My guilt eases quickly, knowing he's here to make my day worse.

Trish rivets her eyes to the screen again, typing an email as she grabs her headset. "I'd better give you guys some space. Y'know, so you can talk out your feelings. Back room's open if you need it." She winks at me.

"Traitor," I hiss.

Then the bells on the door jingle as Brady steps inside, something clasped under his arm.

"Lena," he says with another look that snips my soul in half.

Holy hell. Is this man trying to start a fire with those eyes?

And when he smiles—I'm gone.

There's a slight tilt to his smile—not quite the rehearsed look I expected.

Unexpected and, somehow, almost worse.

That doesn't change anything, though.

"Special delivery," he says, holding up the box under his arm. "Consider it a thanks to the clinic for all your help after hours. Lots of quality dog treats for your visitors."

I don't want to accept the box, but before I know what's happening, he's shoved it into my arms. The thing must weigh more than ten pounds.

"I also want to apologize," he says.

"Apologize? For what?" I adjust the box in my arms, keeping my feet firmly planted on the ground.

His gaze flicks to my stance, and a smile tugs at his lips. "For not making a solid first impression. I regret it."

Oh, so he picked up on the obvious, huh?

Fine, whatever. I don't want to spend more time here gabbing with him than I need to.

"Don't worry about it," I say flippantly. "I'm glad Charlie could crash with you until his owner could pick him up."

He meets my gaze with those flashing blue eyes that feel more piercing than they have any right to be.

"Actually, I was hoping I could thank you personally. How about a drink later?"

A. What.

My brain shuts down.

Is he seriously asking what I think he is?

"A drink?" I repeat numbly.

"Whenever you're off shift." He shifts his weight as he waits for my reply, like he's certain I'll leap into his arms.

I don't even know how to respond.

Not with every muscle in my body locked up.

Some distant part of me screams that I need to stay professional, but I've just lost every desire I ever had to be nice because he's basically asking me at work to be his sidepiece.

Smoking-gun proof he's every bit the asshat I imagined.

"Absolutely not," I spit. He blinks in surprise. "I don't date guys who are taken—crazy, I know—and I'm not interested in men who turn decent human behavior into a spectacle."

Trust me, I'm being nice, even if I sound like the rudest bitch on earth.

The shock that flits across his face makes the crack in my professional mask worth it.

Dr. Ezzie might have my spleen for spouting off at work, but no one needs spleens, anyway.

"Taken?" His voice loses that smug, almost flirtatious edge. Then he chuckles deeply and shakes his head. "Oh no, you think—I'm not taken at all."

"Really? You're telling me you're not with Miss Attitude?"

"Nancy? Nah, fuck. We're just friends. And barely." He shakes his head again, maybe for emphasis, but it just makes me think of Shakespeare—*he doth protest too much.*

"Friends," I clip coldly. "She was pretty bossy for a friend."

"We're not together," he insists. "And I'm not—what do you mean, making a spectacle?"

I shrug. "What would you call taking a video of poor Charlie for internet points? You must've posted it online."

A muscle ticks on his jaw, even as keen awareness sweeps across his eyes. I hate noticing how that makes them look. How the color deepens.

"I get how it looks," he says firmly. "I only took a few clips on my phone so I could post about Charlie to my followers. I've got a good-size presence on Instagram and YouTube. I asked them to donate to a charity that helps lost dogs."

How convenient.

"Great. But even if I believed one iota of that, you are so *not* my type."

As in, I would rather go out with a bowl full of worms.

He seems to get what I don't say from my expression, a thin line appearing between his brows, but before either of us can say more, the door's bells chime again.

There's a deafening bark, and a familiar dog explodes inside.

Sherry, a very mildly named Doberman with a huge hyperactive streak and a strange love for visiting the vet. She's here for a follow-up on a knee scrape, and she's predictably escaped her owner's leash.

The deer-dog launches herself at me full force.

I yell as Sherry's weight hits and sends me spinning, my arms still full of that stupid box of treats that ruins my center of gravity.

My life flashes before my eyes. I see an ER visit in my future. An expensive co-payment. Maybe a potential concussion.

But just when the world tilts and I'm about to hit the hard tiled floor, two strong arms catch me, pressing me against a slab of pure warm stone.

Brady's chest.

Sherry hits the ground with a loud bark.

And I'm stunned, staring up into Brady's mesmerizing blue eyes, the concern in them unmistakable.

Oh.

Oh shit.

He smells good, too, all subtle cologne that doesn't blow my nose off. Fresh sea breeze and citrus and something more primal underneath.

Not deodorant, not laundry powder, but *man*.

Something in my belly flips over.

Not the reaction I need.

His face is so serious, but the light in his eyes shifts. There's no unseeing the heat flare.

Oh no, no, no.

Absolutely not.

I am so not going to let this cheesy meet-cute thing happen to me.

And Trish is standing up, forming an audience with a couple grinning clients, watching me defying gravity in this handsome stranger's arms.

I snap back into my senses and struggle to my feet, taking a large step back to give us both some much-needed breathing room.

"I have to get to *work*," I snap, putting the box on the reception desk and brushing myself off. Trish can deal with it later. I start walking.

"You're welcome!" he shouts after me.

I don't dare look back.

I don't need to see how the heat in his eyes dies.

My ears are still ringing as I stop moving, burning like they're a hundred degrees. Sherry's owner, a stocky man in his fifties, bursts through the door, bellowing, "Oh God! I'm *so* sorry! She just got away from me."

"That's all right." I keep my back turned on Brady, pointedly ignoring him. "Let's go get her settled in, shall we?"

After the dramatic near-face-planting incident, I thought this day couldn't get worse.

I thought wrong.

It's just after close. I'm finishing up my shift and closing down the clinic when I hear a voice that walks needles up my back.

Harry Jay?

It can't be.

It's been years since I last saw him, since he smashed my heart with a sledgehammer. But I'd recognize that smarmy, radio-perfect voice anywhere. And somehow he's here, standing in the lobby, announcing to Trish that he's here for a meeting with Dr. Ezzie.

I do the only sane thing a girl in my position can—I dive into the cleaning closet.

Not my finest moment, I'll admit. But there's no way I want to risk Harry getting a good look at me.

He doesn't know I work here, and ideally, we'll keep it that way.

My heart starts pounding. My hands go slick with sweat.

I finally reached the point where I didn't think about him for *months*. Maybe longer. Life has been perfectly great without him haunting my memory.

But good things don't last when you're Lena Joly.

Deep breath.

I hate how he still has the power to turn my stomach inside out, even after all this time. All the anxiety, the humiliation, the panic, comes rushing back.

Footsteps. He's heading to Dr. Ezzie's office, I think.

I wait until I hear the door close before I slip back out of the closet and shut the door behind me.

Crap, that was close.

But I can't run. As tempting as it is to get the hell out of here, I have cleaning to do and supplies to unpack. Trish gets to head home once we close to the public, but techs don't get that luxury.

Calm down.

Who cares if he's here? Maybe he's a client now.

But I didn't hear anything about an animal. And there was nothing on Ezzie's schedule about an appointment this late.

That's so unlikely, it hurts. Harry Jay never showed the slightest interest in animals.

Pretty typical when you're the bastard son of a slime mold and a scorpion.

Pure scum of the earth disguised as a charming young man with an old-timey mustache who can talk anyone into massive trouble.

At least, that's how he was in college, when I knew him—and I seriously doubt he's changed. If anything, he's probably gotten worse.

I scowl as I disinfect the table, scrubbing in anger.

How am I dealing with him again? After I blocked him and his scumbag friends years ago.

I had no good reason to ever see him again.

And too much reason to think about him, to hate myself for ever falling for his crap.

Trouble is, you don't just shrug and get over a bad relationship like that. Not after what he pulled.

My hands are shaking, and I stare at them, unsure if what I'm feeling right now is anger or embarrassment or just pure adrenaline stabbing through my veins.

But there's only one raw emotion closing my throat, and that's the one I won't acknowledge.

Fear.

God, I *hate* the way he makes me feel so cornered. My brain doesn't recognize that I'm at work and totally safe.

I force myself to finish up so I can get out of here, but about half an hour later, just as I'm grabbing my last box of supplies to bring to the back room and unpack, a deep voice calls my name.

"Lena?"

One word, half question and half hungry predator.

My body locks up. He knows I'm here.

No time to dive into a cleaning closet now.

I don't dare turn as he stalks closer, herding me against the door with an oily smile I'd love to rip right off his face.

I can see his reflection in the glass door. Still just as tall and handsome as ever with that coppery hair brushed back off his forehead and those laser-green eyes. Still wearing his trademark mustache, this ridiculous thing from the 1900s that's shaped and waxed until it's almost wider than his face.

I thought that facial hair made him fun and easygoing once. Now, it's never made me feel more like I'm being hunted.

It takes me back to when I was a teenager, young and impressionable.

Back when I thought he wasn't a terrible guy.

Back when I would have done *anything* for him.

Back when I was a ginormous idiot.

Now, the only thing I want to do is run at him full force and throw him through the door.

But my lungs tremble, and I can feel my heart skipping dangerously.

A smirk flits across his face, telling me he can see my confusion and maybe my fear too.

I've never hated another person like I hate him.

But he just stands there, watching it pass over my face without caring in the slightest. Why hasn't he come closer yet? At least then I could kick him in the balls.

It's a real shame physical violence is frowned on in service jobs.

He folds his arms and leans against the wall like he owns the place.

He's shameless arrogance stuffed in a suit.

I won't be falling for it again.

"Harry," I bite off, mustering the courage to finally turn and face him.

"Small world, LeeLee." His smirk looks carnivorous. "Nice seeing each other, huh?"

No. If I never saw you again before I died, it would be too soon.

It's only respect for Dr. Ezzie that keeps me from saying it.

And knowing I have bills waiting. Plus, I love my job. Even more than I hate him.

In a way, it's nice knowing he isn't the biggest force in my life right now. Even if it feels like it in the moment, standing face-to-face with a monster.

When I don't say anything else, the smile slowly melts off his face. That mustache tilts down like a pitchfork with his frown.

Then he pushes off the wall in one quick movement.

"Cat must've ripped that little tongue right out. Pity, there's so much to catch up on," he mutters. "Be like that, baby doll. We won't have to meet again if your boss is as smart as she looks."

Without another word, he brushes past me and slams both hands on the back door, throwing it open.

I hold my breath, shaking like a little girl with a mountain lion stalking past.

Then I collapse against the wall in a heap, the box of gauze I was holding clattering to the floor.

What the hell is going on?

Why was he talking to Dr. Ezzie?

IV

BARKING UP THE WRONG TREE

(BRADY)

So much for an easy catch.

Maybe I should've thought this through. I shouldn't have put her on the spot in her workplace like that, then and there. That was my bad.

But I'm not giving up.

I scroll through Lena Joly's social media accounts, flicking between Instagram, X, Facebook, and LinkedIn. None have much activity.

Damn. All I need to know is how to make a pitch that will seal this deal. I need a hint of her interests, her dreams, her situation.

What am I missing?

Some old LinkedIn posts liking professional articles about breakthroughs in veterinary medicine. Her Facebook and Instagram are private, but she's left some old posts up for a dog rescue place.

When I search Pawsome Hearts, she also appears in a few staff photos.

And that's it.

Barely any followers. No pressure to post. No expectations from hungry followers waiting for you to boast about amazing deeds and show off lovable animals.

Jealousy knifes me hard.

What the hell is that like? A normal life? The only time people will accept a lack of presence from me is if I physically *can't* post.

Those times are getting rarer now, especially with Dad's health. I damn sure don't have much time to take off work.

Would my life be easier if I didn't have to look so perfect? If I didn't need to reinvent the playboy idiot who blew himself up too many times when he was young and stupid?

Still, seeing a few scraps about Lena's life leaves me more convinced that she could be my answer, a way to stall my parents' ridiculous demands.

A way to meet them on *my* terms, or at least to give them the illusion.

She's the kind of fresh, normal girl I need.

Passionate about dogs, bare-bones online presence, and damnably cute.

There's no hiding her soft curves completely under her scrubs. My eyes feasted, everything from her chestnut hair on down through ample tits and a peach of an ass I'd kill to bite.

The menacing looks she gave me promising instant decapitation take nothing away from her appearance.

I just have to persuade her to make the craziest deal of her life—agree to date me long enough to take the pressure off.

Agree to fake date me for pure optics.

Agree to lie to my folks and the Seattle press so I won't have to waste time with empty succubae like Nancy.

But what's in it for *her*?

As I sip my coffee, I consider my plan.

She hasn't warmed to me much, but we have animals in common. If I could just get her to understand that I mean it when I say I care about them . . .

But I already know that's a massive challenge. Even my parents don't think I'm being serious.

They think this pet food project is some stupid phase, a temporary bridge between their son's first rave success and settling into the calm, moneymaking triumph of adulthood. Right at the head of Pruitt Ag.

Just like they think I'm destined to be hitched to Nancy Loomer.

Fucking shudder.

On paper, it's good for our brand, and her parents were always close to mine.

In practice? The concept makes me want to climb out of my skin.

Fuck, I still don't see how it means roses for our brand either. An arranged goddamned marriage?

Why can't rich people just be *normal*? Why do we still have to marry for money when we're already goddamned made of it?

Of course, if I did marry her, people would assume it's purely political and all for the money. Anyone who knows this woman can instantly write off the personality factor.

Ridiculous.

Thanks to the dating app, even without my parents' wealth, I have more than enough cash to power my life.

Nancy, on the other hand . . .

She must realize our parents are setting us up. For all she pretends in public, I don't think she's wild about me either.

Not really.

She loves the Pruitt name. She likes what I represent. She doesn't mind my looks, and she adores the thought of landing exclusive rights to a hot, eligible bachelor commodity, like a bee covets honey.

I'm sure she respects my fortune, too, though it's not like she doesn't have her own.

We were both born to big money most people would consider obscene.

For her, it comes down to status.

In Seattle, my last name means a lot.

I'm the ideal prop in Nancy's world—rich husband from a good family who will look good on her arm.

Count me the hell out.

My mind flips back to Lena as I click on her picture. Big, soulful brown eyes, and mahogany hair falling in ripples around her face.

Vintage pretty. Not Instagram-famous good looks.

Lovely in a distinctly natural way.

Frosty. Feisty. Begging to be thawed.

I reach up and slap myself, clicking back to my email tab. Regardless of how pretty she may or may not be, this shit isn't about attraction.

This is about practicality. Freedom from annoying fucking obligations to focus on what matters, even if it's just a brief stretch of peace.

I only need time to get my dog food formulated and out the door.

Snarling, I push my laptop back and head into the kitchen for coffee. I'm pulling an espresso shot through the machine when my intercom pings with a visitor.

"Brady, it's me. Let me up," Nancy's voice sings through the screen.

I groan, burying my face in my palm.

The woman has a talent for showing up at the worst possible times. I don't have the patience to deal with her today. Not when I'm cooking up a scheme to kick her to the curb.

But I also don't have any good reason for turning her away. She knows my habits and my schedule too well.

Swallowing a sigh, I press the button to let her up and make an extra coffee heaped with sugar and frothed cream. Normally, she likes to go out and be *seen* with her coffee, but I'm not giving her that today.

When she walks off the elevator and through my door, she's dressed in some leather and tartan outfit. It's short and revealing and probably high fashion, but it's the most boring try-hard shit I've ever seen.

Nancy doesn't care much what look I'm into as long as she's into it. Not a big deal when it's just about clothes.

But we both know it isn't.

Another reason we would never work, never mind the most forced friendship in the world.

"Coffee?" I say, handing her a mug. "I was making some when you dropped in."

Because it would've been too convenient for her to call ahead. It also would've given me a prime opportunity to say "Fuck no."

Two things she knows.

One of the many downsides to our family history is Nancy thinking she has a God-given right to breeze in and out of my life whenever she pleases. Whether I want her around hardly matters.

"Thanks. Is this oat milk?" She eyes the mixture with healthy disgust.

"Would I poison you with anything else?"

"Well, no. You know I don't do dairy." She giggles and takes a sip, scrunching up her face with delight.

I hate my life.

If it was an actual dietary restriction, whatever, fine. But Nancy's selectively gone dairy-free because it makes her trendier. I don't bother asking about the late-night fondue she scarfed down practically solo just a few weeks ago.

She seems to think dairy-free begins and ends with liquid beverages.

"What do you want, anyway?" I throw myself back in front of my laptop at the marble island.

"Oh, nothing. I just thought we could talk, y'know? We didn't get much chance after that stupid dog ruined our last date."

Stupid dog.

I grit my teeth.

"What do you have to say?" I can't hide the scorn dripping from my voice.

"I dunno." She shrugs. "Like, talk-talk, Brady. What's going on in our lives? What's up with you?" She throws herself down, resting her elbows on the island and leaning forward so she flashes her cleavage.

It's so transparently ridiculous I almost laugh in her face.

"Don't have much going on right now, Nance. Just work. The usual."

"Oh?" She doesn't sound like she cares. There's a long pause, and I realize she's waiting for me to ask about her.

"What are you up to lately?"

"I'm *so* glad you asked!" Her smile widens. "You remember I told you about Tahiti?"

"Tahiti," I repeat. It's vaguely familiar, though I can't remember any details. "You're going to French Polynesia?"

"Dude, do you *ever* stop working long enough to pay attention? Never mind, I'll forgive you this once." She rolls her eyes, wagging a finger. "Anyway, remember how I said I was going for a shoot?"

"Sure." I don't remember shit.

"It's gonna be more of a work-and-pleasure thing, and it's coming up in two weeks!" Her eyes flick up suggestively. "Such a fun opportunity. Prettiest water on the planet. You can post stuff from there without any people and still get ten thousand likes on Insta."

"Yeah. I get why you're pumped," I lie.

"It's a *gorgeous* hotel, all expenses paid. You know the five-star resorts where they pamper you all day long?"

"Yep." Been there, done that. Luxury overload gets old fast.

"But there's one little problem." She pushes out her lip in an exaggerated pout. "It's lonely. Wouldn't it be so nice to have someone with?"

Obviously, I know what she's trying to do—I'd have to be blind to miss it—but no.

No fucking way.

There is *no way* I'm flying out there willingly for some kind of pre-proposal BS trip where she'll probably be expecting a ring. Even if all expenses are paid.

I can afford to pay for my own luxury travel, and when I do, it won't be some sparkling hotel rising from Pacific paradise like a fairytale castle.

I open an email from the lab I'm working with and say bluntly, "Maybe you should ask one of your friends."

"They're busy," she rushes out. "Don't you think it would better if—"

"That's a shame," I cut her off. "Hopefully you'll have a fun time solo."

"Brady! It would be *so much* better with my boyfriend."

My face hurts from the effort it takes not to wince.

Goddamn, she's relentless.

Silence is my answer. I hope it pisses her off enough to take the hint and walk away, but that feels too easy.

"I was *hoping*," she says, layering so much emphasis on the word I almost cringe, "that *you'd* come with me."

There it is.

Shot between the eyes.

I hoped she wouldn't outright ask, when I'm clearly not interested, but now that she has, this won't end well.

"You know I have work, Nance. Critical phase with the lab working on the formula." I gesture at my screen. "They're almost ready with some new test samples. I have to be around to see how that goes."

Almost immediately, her eyes glaze over. The second I mention details, she switches off.

"You always have work," she says bitterly.

"All part of the process. Nobody ever said start-ups are easy." I stare at her, wondering why I bother to take the edge off. "It won't always be like this. Once we're in the pilot phase, I might be able to take my foot off the gas a little before the full launch. But that's a year out at least."

"A whole year," she echoes miserably. "All for fucking dog food."

"Scientifically formulated, ethically sourced, organic, and affordable for the masses, thank you." I flash her an exaggerated smile, beaming it through the knives etched on her face.

Work is an excuse to get out of a trip to hell, but it's also *true*.

"What did I do to you?" she asks sharply.

"What?"

"We've known each other since we were kids. So why am I not *enough* for you?" She darts up and stalks closer, rounding the island until she's next to me. "Why haven't you ever tried to kiss me? Touch me? You know you could have it all . . ."

Fuck.

Her eyes are hard and sharp. This isn't hurt speaking but entitlement.

She's always been gorgeous, yeah, but there's something pointed and weaponized about her beauty now. Get too close, and you'll eviscerate yourself on those curves.

"Are you still fucking a new girl every week? I know your history," she whispers, too close to my ear now. "It's not like you don't have needs. And I'm cool with your appetite, it's all part of the package, I get it. I'm not asking you to be exclusive. Not yet. So . . . why haven't we fucked?"

I clear my throat, wishing I could suffocate. She's the last person I want to be talking about this with. Maybe the second last, after my old man.

"Those days are behind me," I say carefully. "I'm not like that anymore. Those times caused me grief, Nancy."

"Whatevs." She rolls her eyes, snorting. "Jesus, just tell me you think I'm ugly. It'd be a lot more believable than this horseshit."

"I'm not the same man I was a few years ago. I don't like casual sex, Nancy. No more than I like you rubbing it in my face," I growl.

"Why?"

Because I don't fucking like you.

I could say it, and to her, it's probably not good enough.

"Time for you to go," I snap, standing and waving at the door. "Come on. Don't make me drag you."

"Leave?"

It's like a foreign concept she can't understand.

Enough.

I start walking, and she finally moves. I escort her all the way to the door, one hand on the small of her back.

"It's not going to happen, Nancy. Help me let you down easy. This doesn't need to get ugly."

"What isn't, Brady?" Her breath hitches like she truly doesn't get it.

"*Us.*" I stop and stare at her. "Look, I know it's what our families want, but sometimes what they want isn't always what we need. We're grown-ass adults. We don't need to follow a plan drawn up when we were kids."

"What *you* need, you mean."

She's right. That's exactly what I mean.

For the first time, I see something like real hurt on her face, and I'm not happy. But this is the route she chose.

"We can be cordial," I tell her, though I don't know if that's something she can ever wrap her head around.

At this point, I'm prepared to say anything that will get her out of my condo before she bashes me in the face with her designer purse.

"Whatever. Fuck you, Brady Pruitt," she spits, turning so abruptly I almost crash into her. "You've made your choice, but let me tell you something. I'm *not* covering for your noncommittal playboy ass anymore."

I should've known she wouldn't go down easy.

"What the fuck is *that* supposed to mean?"

"It means that next time your parents drop hints and ask how things are going, I'll tell them the truth. All the gory little details." She lifts her chin with a terrible smile. "I'll tell Mommy you're too immature, playing with animals and chasing one-night stands like you're eighteen. And Daddy, I wonder what he'll think when I say your dick doesn't work? Seriously, Brady, why can't you *grow up*?"

Fuck. This.

I stare her down, refusing to engage in something so high school petty.

Maybe she wants a fight. She wants me to roar and scream and give her more leverage to skewer me, but I'm the bigger person.

I'm not giving her a damn inch.

I'm also not going to break down and sleep with her just so she'll play nice and show some basic decency.

No, this bullshit only ends one way, and it has everything to do with Lena Joly helping me buy breathing space.

V

WOOF!

(LENA)

I am not upset.

I will not get upset.

I *definitely* can't afford to get upset, because that upsets Dr. Ezzie.

Just in case my body betrays me, I repeat the mantra two more times.

Doing it, that's easier said than done, especially considering my hands are still shaking after that awful encounter with Harry every time I think of it.

Yes, even though it was a couple days ago.

Ugh.

Years have passed, and it still feels like a trauma response. My body's still hardwired to reject him in the most visceral way possible.

Smarmy, soulless asshole.

It's embarrassing that I ever thought I loved him. Me, Lena—the girlie who hands out tough love advice every time a friend panics over a guy.

God, the way I held Elle's hand last year during her whole fake-engagement-turned-real with billionaire hottie August Marshall . . . Where would my bestie be without me?

I have a good head on my shoulders and a heart wrapped in barbed wire. I can forgive my younger self for a lack of judgment.

It's going to be okay. I'm older and wiser and determined to never let a man like Harry walk all over me again.

Sighing, I suck in a deep breath and knock gently on Dr. Ezzie's door.

"Come in."

I am not upset.

I step inside her adorably cramped office, closing the door carefully behind me. Dr. Ezzie sits at her computer. The usual laser focus gleams in her eyes, but her shoulders are slumped.

Crap.

This doesn't look good already.

"Hi, Lena. Is everything okay?" She gives me a tired smile.

"Um, mostly. I actually just wanted to talk to you about a man you met with a couple days ago. Harry Jay."

"The investor, yes." Her brows knit together. "You know about that? Do you know him?"

"I—" My mouth clamps shut. Where do I begin? "I knew him in college. He's a big-time real estate investor now, right?"

I've done some googling, and I know the answer.

"Yes," she says.

"I just—I have concerns. About whether or not he's right for Pawsome Hearts. His local track record seems pretty cutthroat." I looked into him the second I got home. It's no surprise Harry made a splash in the years since he smashed my heart—and not in a good way.

Not if you have a moral compass in good working order. If you have no standards, then Harry's record of pure rat fuckery in business probably seems like a good thing.

Cutthroat can be code for *efficient.*

With him, it proves his cruelty to the core.

That's not just my personal experience talking. That's every reason why I need to warn my boss before it's too late.

"Look, I know it's not my business. You can yell at me for that." I raise my hands defensively. "And I know things are crazy tight and you have a ton on your mind, but . . . I feel like getting him involved won't end well for us. Surely, there must be better options more aligned with our values, if you're looking to inject some cash?"

Dr. Ezzie's face looks so sad my heart lurches.

"I hear you, Lena," she whispers. All I can hear is *But it's not enough to convince me.*

No, of course not.

If she's at the point of bringing Harry in, doesn't that mean she's seen his reputation?

"Have a seat," she says kindly. "I appreciate your concerns. Unfortunately, we're at a crossroads where we can't be too choosy."

". . . Is it *that* bad?" I whisper.

"Worse. Our position is dire, Lena. I don't mean to scare you, but even if I didn't have to take care of my parents, we'd still be in a tough place. With them, I've had to take out personal loans for their care, and the clinic counts as collateral."

My heart spirals.

"The truth is, you know the boarding staff was downsized last year and kennel capacity reduced. We just don't have the clients anymore, never mind the repairs coming up to keep everything in working order. We can't keep up with all the shiny corporate places that have exploded over the past ten years. We certainly don't have ball pits and pools for dogs to splash around in."

"But they're not the same, Doc! We have people who *care*." I have to bite back the words *We're better than them.*

We are, though.

The big corporate places are understaffed and usually can't keep up with individual dogs, even if they have better toys and entertainment. But Dr. Ezzie needs me to stay calm.

I can't lose my shit, no matter how tempting.

"It's a matter of style, perhaps. People want sleek and fun," she continues. "They also want the full package, groomers and special play options, but we just don't have the funds to hire more staff or renovate. It's a pipe dream. Plus, we own a bigger piece of property than the other places around. I've had this practice since before the real estate boom. The property taxes on our land just keep ballooning, and without the clients to bring in enough bacon to make it financially viable . . . You're a smart girl. You can figure it out."

Oh, I know what she's saying, but it still makes my heart implode.

My priority has always been animals and clients first. Making their experience as good as possible. *Helping* as many people as possible.

But I'm not stupid. Every word she says holds true in a shifting business where boarding can pad your revenue a lot.

Numbers are ugly things. They're real, merciless, and they have teeth.

"And that's not even getting into the roofing and insulation work due on the old building." She sighs, looking down gravely. "Frankly, it makes me sweat just thinking about it. We'll have to shut down for that, at least for a few weeks."

Unfortunately, she's right, and we know what that means.

Money dries up fast.

She rubs her face as she looks up, showing the exhaustion lining her eyes.

"So, to answer your concerns, yes. When I made a few queries in a small business group and Mr. Jay came calling with a very fair buyout offer, I had to hear him out. I had no choice. The moral high ground is a bigger luxury than it seems. Would you slam the door on opportunities when they knock?"

When it's Harry Jay, hell yes.

Absolutely.

Without question.

Ideally, closing the door to trap him inside with a napalm fire raging.

"Dr. Ezzie, I get it. But he won't be any good for Pawsome Hearts," I say weakly. "You know he's only after the land. The minute he thinks you'll sell and close up shop, he'll be on you like a hawk. Doesn't keeping the clinic going mean *anything*?"

Too far.

Ezzie's eyes start misting, and I instantly regret my words.

"Only the whole world." Her voice cracks, and guilt drags me low. "But I'm just one woman, Lena. I'm so tired of swimming."

"Let me help! Whatever you need." So long as it's not number crunching. She needs to keep her CPA for that.

"I appreciate that, really, but I'm afraid you can't. Not with this. I've always loved how you're so willing to fight, but sometimes hard decisions are inevitable. I suggest you brace yourself, and so will I."

She slumps back in her chair, looking like any fight she ever had has drained from her already. I douse the feeble protests burning on my tongue.

She's right that she's only one woman stretched to her breaking point. You can practically see the boulder on her shoulders and her spirit buckling under it.

No, revealing the full horror of who and what Harry is won't help today. Not when her mind is made up.

I just don't have the heart to pile more guilt on her brittle shoulders.

"I should go." I gesture to the door with my thumb. "Good night, Dr. Ezzie."

"Good night, Lena."

Time to get home, take a long soak in the tub, and figure out my next move.

Dr. Ezzie was right about one thing, though. I am a fighter, and I have no intention of giving up, even if I have to go it alone.

Sighing, I grab my bag and jacket and head out into the rainy evening.

At least, I *try*.

What actually happens is I face-plant into a massive wall of a chest.

When I look up, it's Brady looking down at me.

His easy, disarming smile disappears when he gets a good look at the pain etched on my face.

Nice knowing I must look as grim as I feel.

"Lena," he says, taking my shoulders and steadying me like I weigh nothing. "You look like you could use that drink today."

Oh, this boy has a death wish.

"Holy shit, take a hint. I really don't think—"

"Just one drink. Hear me out." He holds up his hands. "No BS, no hookups, I promise. We can even just do coffee if you want."

My first instinct is to smack him in the face. My second instinct is to smack him harder.

I'm so not in the mood for an awkward bar hangout with a stranger frenemy treating me like a piece of meat.

But he's cute. I'll give him that.

And I don't know how truly bad he is inside.

I also don't know what's waiting for me at home besides another lonely evening where the highlight is ordering three days' worth of Thai takeout to eat my feelings. Granny Lark, the old lady up the street, isn't around to bother me this week because she's hanging out with her granddaughter.

Would it really be so atrocious to just humor him? To get this persistent, grandstanding gold monkey off my back?

"You know what? Fine. You win." My teeth clench with regret.

"You're serious?" His eyebrows shoot up. "Damn, I thought I'd have to bribe you or something."

"You do. When you buy me a cocktail, it better have the top-shelf stuff."

"Noted." His eyes flash like the winter sky.

"Also, I looked you up after our last—" *Meeting* isn't the right word. More like *disaster*. "Our last interaction. Your channel's kinda fun, and I appreciate you trying to rake in money for animals."

"All the time," he tells me, a whisper of a smile pulling at his lips. Not the spotlight charm he switches on when he wants something. This looks more real. "So you're a new fan, huh?"

"Hardly. Wasting hours on YouTube isn't my thing," I say quickly, shifting my bag on my shoulder. "But I'm glad you give a damn sometimes. You only use your channel to puff yourself up about fifty percent of the time."

"Flattering. I'll work on raising that up to an even seventy."

I glare at him, second-guessing my state of mind.

It's a terrible idea to get involved with him at all, I'm sure. Tomorrow Lena is already side-eyeing me hard, demanding to know what the hell I'm thinking for even *considering* this.

But an evening out still feels better than moping over my nightmare ex and a business deal I can't control. I'm due for a distraction, and a free drink or two feels like the ticket.

Even so, there's no way I'm going out dressed like this and covered in dog hair.

"Two hours," I say. "We'll meet at Benny's. I'll Uber."

Benny's is a local wine and espresso bar, which gives me the option of keeping it cool and getting a small coffee flight or yielding to temptation with alcohol.

I know which way I'm leaning, but I'd be stupid to let my guard down around him too soon.

He doesn't smile, but there's a smug, delighted glint in his eyes as he says, "Wish granted, Lena. See you soon."

◆ ◆ ◆

This is *not* a date.

It's so not a date that I settle for a casual dress, nothing showy. Blue, summery, soft, and warm—something that screams modest comfort and not *I'm going home with you later*.

Because that's not happening with half a dozen drinks. Not even ten, and I'm a lightweight who can't pound it back like I used to.

The only reason I agreed to see Brady Pruitt is *not* his smoking hot body or the way his eyes felt magnetic when he asked me out.

Nothing to do with his mile-wide shoulders or the softness of his thick, dark hair or the scruff of shadow around his lips that could melt any red-blooded woman with a single scrape.

Still, I hate that I even had to think about what to wear to my next mistake.

When I get there, he's on time, seated and waiting at the bar with one hand raised as soon as he sees me.

The place is crowded. More than usual for a breezy Wednesday evening, but then again, I don't usually go out midweek. Not since Elle married herself off to a god and my other friends fell into careers where they live at the office.

In the corner, a few college guys hoot about something, clustered around one guy's phone. Work colleagues in their business wear gather around another table, slowly swirling their wineglasses in idle conversation.

The best part is the smell: vibrant coffee and the subtle twang of wine.

Weaving my way through the crowd, I make it to Brady's side. He helps me up onto the stool with a hand.

An actual gentleman.

Dangerous.

"You made it. Gotta admit, I wondered if you'd ghost," he says over the low, thudding music.

"And look like I'm scared of what? You?" I snort. I nod toward the group of ladies in their thirties and forties. "Someone had to save you from those wine moms. Total cougar pack over there."

His deep chuckle should be lost in the noise, but it vibrates through me. I watch his throat bob with the overwhelming sense that I've already sealed my doom.

When he leans in, I do my best to ignore his scent, that citrusy sea cologne again mingled with testosterone. It's *unfair* how he smells like he just swaggered off a warm beach in Maui.

He's dressed up for the occasion, I think, wearing charcoal slacks and an off-white button-down shirt rolled up at the sleeves.

I hate that I'm a sucker for rolled sleeves when men have muscles to show off. Especially when half the single men around here either don't lift or still dress like they're teenagers.

This man has guns. Sculpted, intense, and accented with a hint of a Celtic tattoo weaving up one bicep that makes him look even bigger.

Eyes on his face.

His face, Lena. Now.

This is the twenty-first century and I'm a sensible girl. We're not animals fresh off some cheesy sexting conversation from an app.

I *have* standards.

It's just entertainment—something to take the edge off a long, beastly week.

"So how about that drink? I've got you covered tonight."

"Only if I take the next round." The words are too aggressive, but I can't help myself. He might be inhumanly rich, but that doesn't mean I'll skimp on paying my way, outside the obligatory top-shelf drink he promised.

"Sure." The corners of his eyes crinkle.

"Espresso martini. That's their signature thing here," I decide.

Best of both worlds. Who needs sleep, anyway?

"Good plan." He gestures to the bartender and orders. While we're waiting, he props his elbow against the table and looks at me again.

How does he do it?

Making me feel so small with just a glance?

I can't lie—it's a little unsettling.

Also a lot disconcerting when men this fit usually aren't strong in the subtlety department. They're prone to getting grabby rather than stripping me down with bedroom eyes.

Is this a thing rich guys practice? Flirting with just the eyes?

"Thanks for bringing Charlie home last week," I say. "And, um, for saving me from getting knocked down by Sherry. Her owner swore he'd work on her manners for the last two years, and it still hasn't happened."

"She was just enthusiastic." A small smile, but he shrugs. "You handled it well. I just broke your fall."

"Mm." Our drinks arrive, and I take a large sip. Sweet perfection. The coffee, vodka, and sugary liqueur go down like water. Too easy. "So how many pets do you have? Any purebreds?"

He pauses mid-sip and stares at me before he swallows.

"None. I'm too busy to invest the time, and my parents never allowed it, growing up."

I can't hide my surprise.

"Wow, really? With the fundraisers and animals on your channel, I guessed you'd have a whole menagerie."

"Not yet. Maybe that's why I care so much for everyone else's pooches and cats." He sips his own martini, reflecting, and I watch the way his throat moves.

"But they wouldn't let you have one dog? Don't tell me it was a money thing?"

"It was an optics thing. Image is law when you grow up like I did. We had all the resources in the world to have a few dogs, sure—hell, even a small hobby farm a few hours away. But my mom wouldn't dirty up the house with a puppy, and Dad won't be seen showing a single human crack in his armor."

Interesting *and* complicated.

The more I learn, the more I want to know, and that's not good. It shows the lack of excitement in my life.

Hanging out with him feels more interesting than a lonely bath at home, though. The bar is so low it's basically a flooring pipe.

But it doesn't *mean* anything.

Yet I still find myself leaning forward, my body language open. *Tell me more.*

Maybe by the end of the night, he'll spill some dark secret that would bring his family's entire empire crashing down.

Or maybe he'll offer me a ride home on a unicorn, but a girl can dream.

He gives me that sharp, spearing glance again, like he's looking at the most interesting woman in the world.

"You really do love animals, don't you?"

I blink. "I mean, that's kinda a given, considering where I work. With you, it's more interesting because you don't have to love them to make rent. Where does it come from if you didn't have any pets, growing up?"

"I was big into greyhound races when I was young. My grandfather's hobby. He'd take me out to the tracks pretty often. He'd usually lose a bundle on his bets, but he loved it to death. I loved hanging out with dogs on the side, and Gramps had the weight to get us VIP access. My mother hated me when I kept begging her to open a racetrack in Seattle three Christmases in a row, even after Gramps was gone. I wanted her to name it after him."

Oof. That's a big, heaping ask I can't begin to imagine. The kind that only comes with money. But it's also an adorable one for a little rich boy.

"Oh wow. Greyhounds are fascinating. We have a couple who come to the clinic." I don't have to fake my enthusiasm.

Too many people think these gentle giants are ugly with their lanky bodies and oversize snouts, and it pisses me off all the time. Especially when you'll never meet a bigger sweetheart in your life than a lazy lump of a retired racing dog.

He takes another drink, but the warmth in his eyes fades as he looks past me, into the distance. "Honestly, I think my interest truly took hold later."

"What did? Your crush on greyhounds?"

"Dogs in general." He meets my eyes, and they're serious. "I did a few years in the US Army. Mostly my father's idea, to make me fly right and keep me out of trouble. It was trouble, all right, but fuck getting into that."

I bite my lip so I don't smile.

"Anyway, I wound up in Syria at a really chaotic time," he says.

The confession stuns me a little. I never would've guessed he's an army vet, but that helps explain the Instagrammable physique. Another piece of the Brady Pruitt puzzle I don't know what to do with yet.

How much trouble was he in? Men like him don't usually serve abroad. They don't give up time and risk their neck for their country if they don't have to.

"Surprised?" he asks. "Can't say I blame you. Money shields you from a lot of bullshit in life. In my case, I'm glad it didn't here. I had a lot to learn when I was nineteen."

"That's a wake-up call, for sure," I admit. "What does it have to do with dogs, though?"

"A brave K-9 attached to our unit saved my life." His voice grows serious. A bit low, slightly gritty, like the memory burns his throat coming out.

I can relate.

Some memories just do that to you. They burrow through your grey matter with hooks and claws, and every time you rake them out from the back of your mind, they draw blood.

But it's not always bitter. There's some sweetness too. And I can see it in the way he smiles.

Not with his mouth, but this tiny, half-hidden light swirling in his blue eyes.

My stomach flips. I'm suddenly worried it's not just the espresso martini making my cheeks heat.

Oh boy.

"There was a small town outside our base. The people were good to us, always sending intel about terrorists, so we protected them. One day on our routine patrols, there was a hidden improvised explosive." He pauses, watching how I stare before his eyes return to his drink. "I had no clue—my unit would've walked right into the damn thing if we didn't have Oscar with us. Big old Belgian Malinois, friendly as hell off duty, more focused than a lot of people when he worked." He smiles. "Oscar smelled the bomb, and if he hadn't . . ." He trails off, but I can fill in the gaps.

"So scary," I say softly.

"It's what lit a fire under my ass. Dogs aren't toys. They're real companions. Sometimes, they save your life. That's why I'm pouring energy into my current project. Working on a good, organic dog food that doesn't cost more than the processed stuff. I want dogs like Oscar to eat well and live as long as possible."

"Dog food? I thought you made your money with some kind of dating app?" At least, that's what the internet said.

"I'm out of that game. Sold my entire stake off to a bigger company last year."

"Why?"

"It got my foot in the door and let me make my own money and make connections, rather than resting on the family business. Still, it's not what I care about. Another round?" He gestures for two refills. "But what about you?"

"What about me?" I shake my head. "I'm sick to death of dating apps, and I barely remember to charge my phone. I'm overworked at a small clinic and undersocialized. My friends are getting married to superheroes and living their best lives. I'm stuck with my bad self because my last date wouldn't shut up about his fifty-dollar investment in a crypto coin with an anime logo. Blah."

Too honest?

I wonder when I see the way he cocks his head.

"Never asked about your dating life, Sass."

My face heats. It's in the way he says it—no silly nickname should be that devastating.

"Hey, you asked for a briefing. That's my messy, boring life. Stay away if you're smart."

"I'm more interested in today, woman. You going to tell me why you always leave work looking like you've had your heart split in two?"

Holy ouch.

The memory comes sweeping back, all sharp claws. The wound reopens in my chest, gushing fresh sorrow.

I think about Dr. Ezzie. Her defeat and despair, the sad way she's resigning herself to being eaten by a shark before we ever put up a fight.

God, the way she *has* no fight.

One meeting, and Harry's sucked that much life out of her.

"That face," Brady rumbles, sipping his new cocktail and setting it down with a *clink*. "That's the one I'm wondering about. You're wearing it now."

"It's a long story."

"I'm in no rush."

I grab my drink and down half of it in one gulp that almost makes me choke. Not how anyone should relish a thirty-dollar craft cocktail, but hell, I needed a boost.

"A couple days ago, my boss had a meeting with a man. Harry Jay," I say. "He works in property investment."

Brady tilts his head. "Think I've heard the name. Made a big splash in real estate, didn't he? I remember he was involved in that pier renovation along the waterfront. I never wanted to touch that game."

"That's smart."

"So, what about Harry Jay and your boss?"

I try—I really do—to keep my fury under wraps. But it's impossible, because my ex gives me that imminent-spider feeling.

"He wants to invest in our clinic. It's a high-risk situation with debt, and he's the only kind of investor my boss could find," I say. "But really, he's not looking to help us keep the lights on. I think he just wants the land Pawsome Hearts is on. You've seen it—this big piece of property that's gotten rare. Very few small businesses own a plot like that outright. Dr. Ezzie bought it back when things were cheap. But it's been a struggle the last few years. She's having a hard time keeping up for personal reasons. I just know that shithawk's swooping in while we're wounded and bleeding to—sorry." I catch myself, taking another violent swig of my drink.

"Shithawk. I like it."

"It's true. The land is—I don't know how much it's worth, but it's valuable."

"A pretty penny," he offers with a nod.

"Right. And Harry, he's—he's the worst kind of creep. A freak who enjoys humiliating people." There it is: my anger boiling over in hot, vicious words.

At this point, I don't know when I'll ever be over him, and that's embarrassing. Even on this not-date.

Brady's eyebrows go up.

"Forget the last part. There's a reason I don't normally do the mid-week-drinking thing," I lie.

The clear blue of Brady's eyes hardens into ice as he stares at me.

"You know him," he growls. It's not a question.

". . . We might've dated in college." The confession comes out in a rush. My face is *burning*.

"Shit," he rasps.

"It's whatever. Let's just say it didn't end well. He's a raging asshole. It was years ago, and I thought I was done with that chapter, but now he's coming in hot to ruin my life again. So yeah, it's personal and I'm a little bitter."

I don't realize I'm almost breathless until Brady lays his hand on my arm. He orders a couple glasses of water from the bartender.

"Have you told your boss about him?"

My breath shudders on its way out. "I tried, but she's hard up. Desperate almost."

What is happening?

I didn't think Brady's thick palm could feel this good on my skin. He still carries himself like a massive prick, but tonight he's being human.

"Hey." He's suddenly moving closer, his fingers twined with mine, and that's when I realize I'm crying. My hands are trembling.

My vision blurs, and I suck in another shaky breath.

Holy hell, I'm ready to shrivel up and die from shame.

If only I'd stuck to coffee.

"Come here," he says gently, and it's so easy to let him tilt me forward until I'm in his arms.

That musky ocean smell is a welcome distraction. It teleports me to a peaceful place with clear blue skies, far from the ugly grey clouds of bad memories hanging over Seattle.

My face stays pressed against his shoulder, his arms around my back, his hands rubbing soothingly.

It's so much nicer than anything I'd expect from him—and it feels so *good.*

His heart thuds slowly and strongly. The drumbeat vibrates through his body into mine, like he's loaning me something I didn't know I needed.

Steadiness. Calm. Courage.

It's shocking how human he is, and maybe it shouldn't be.

I feel bad for being so shallow, so jaded and quick to judge.

He's made of flesh and blood, after all. Not emotionless metal and rubber, like some kind of AI robot powered by money.

My breathing slows to match his.

"Pawsome Hearts is more than just a job," I whisper against his shoulder. My mouth moves against the fabric of his jacket, and I briefly imagine it against his skin. Salty sweet.

What the hell are you doing?

Stop.

I pull back, and he lets me, sliding away to give me space.

This would be so much easier if he was the ridiculous caricature I imagined.

I dab under my eyes. Of all the things I could've done in front of him, I just had to turn on the waterworks.

"What I really need," I say shakily, searching for a lighthearted tone, "is a billionaire sugar daddy. My best friend married one, and she's set for life."

"What?" Brady stiffens like I just insulted him.

"My best friend, Elle. She's awesome. Super-talented illustrator, sassy bitch, partner in crime. I love her to death. But she met this guy, August Marshall, and he paid her to be his fiancée. It was this whole drama arc, but now they're married and she's living out her dreams, illustrating stories. You know Inky the Penguin?"

"Who doesn't? I used to have Inky pajamas when I was five. Must've wrote that penguin a hundred letters growing up." His words are light, but there's no humor in his eyes.

Dude, why is he looking at me like that?

Brady watches me like a hunting hawk and clears his throat before he drains the rest of his drink. The glass comes down with a loud clink.

"Actually, Lena, that's the reason I brought you here tonight. I have something to ask you."

What?

". . . To be my sugar daddy?" I am so confused.

"Not quite, but when you put it that way, it's not so different, I suppose." He spreads his hands flat on the marble bar. "We both have problems we could help each other with."

I almost snort espresso liqueur through my nose.

For real? What the hell can I do for Brady Pruitt, heir to billions and social media prince?

"I'm serious. Listen." He leans in again, catching my hand, his eyes dancing with an energy that's as intoxicating as my cocktail. "If you've stalked me online, you know I had a rough reputation growing up. Too many rich-kid parties and girlfriends I went through like eating grapes. Since then, I've been working overtime, getting my shit together. I promise you that shit chapter's closed now. Only, my family's been riding me hard to settle down. Get married. Look responsible. My father can't be the public face of our brand, not since he wound up sick. They made me take over, and they want me to do it right. All for the almighty optics again."

"So that's it," I whisper. "That's why you're with Blondie McBrat."

"Nancy, yes. I'm sure you can guess they think we're a match made in heaven—but you saw what she's like."

"Holy shit, yeah. I thought you guys were dating." I make a gagging sound.

He chuckles roughly. "Fuck no. I'll never be that hard up."

The roughness in his voice rumbles through my bones.

I don't like where this is going.

"Sooo, what are you suggesting?" I ask.

"I need to buy time. Enough to keep my family from climbing up my ass before I'm ready to launch my product line, find my footing, and rebuild my reputation with old-fashioned grit." Those big blue eyes are midnight now, dark with determination. "I need a ruse. You need money. That makes us perfect partners, if we team up and—"

Panic.

I throw my hands up.

"Whoa, *whoa*. How about no?" I lean away from him. "No way, Brady. If you think I'm signing on to some wacky fake-engagement thing with you, count me out. Sorry, I'm not your girl."

A slow, inappropriately sexy smile spreads across his lips. "Not even for a million dollars?"

A million—

Oh. My. God.

My vision starts spinning with zeros.

I'm glad I'm not the fainting type like poor Elle, or I'm pretty sure I'd be sliding off this stool boneless and face-planting on the marble bar.

"Nope, I—" I stop, staring at him. "Did you really say a *million*?"

"Seven figures. Count them, Sass. I told you: This can be a mutually beneficial relationship."

Holy shit, I can't do this.

That's crazy money. Certifiable. And it comes with strings attached that originate in hell.

Worse, his offer tells me I should have listened to my instinct.

I knew I should never have gone out with him.

Does he seriously think he can *bribe* me into some sleezy romance arrangement worthy of a bad reality show?

Woof.

My instincts were right.

Brady Pruitt is a giant selfish dickprint.

"No thanks," I strangle out. Then I start digging in my purse, thankful I have a few bills to throw down on the bar for my partial tab. He can figure out the rest for this humiliation. "Absolutely no fucking *way*. I'm out of here."

And I'm moving like a bullet, bolting through the crowd as I hear him call, "Lena!"

This is so not my day.

Now, instead of moping around at home, I get to drag myself back with my tail between my legs.

And I'll spend the night wondering why every man in this city really is a selfish psycho, and when I became a magnet for bad intentions.

VI

A DOG'S DINNER

(BRADY)

Under ordinary circumstances, the lab lights me up like nowhere else.

It's the place where the future unfolds, and that makes me feel more at home than—well, *home*.

No matter how nice my condo is, everyone thinks they can drop by and interrupt my flow. Ungirlfriends (Nancy Loomer), my mother, old friends, and cousins who pop in a few times a year.

If I don't want to be seen, there's nowhere to hide.

My parents' house hasn't felt like home, either, not since I came back from serving Uncle Sam.

It may be beautiful, but it's stuffy, all old-world money and suffocating obligations. Imposing as hell and cut from an age where the wealthy in Seattle rubbed it in with the biggest castles and flashiest cars imaginable.

It's also the place where their rules and expectations reign.

If I don't follow them to the letter of the law, they bring consequences crashing down on my head like an avalanche.

It's easier to avoid it entirely, unless I have a good reason for showing up.

Then there's the lab.

It's this small local place, looking more like a college lab than a state-of-the-art facility for world-class R&D. I contracted them with my vet nutritionist to help formulate my test products a few months back, and ever since, I've found myself damn near living there some days.

Luis is with me today, too, frowning over the notes we've been given.

"Any questions?" The lab tech, Grace, a lanky brunette with serious eyes and a ponytail pulled tight across her head, looks at me expectantly.

"Heirloom grains?" Luis asks.

"Mostly barley. A little goes a long way for a dog's gut health, supposedly," I say shortly.

"It also pads the calorie content and possibly balances the flavor profile. Anything packaged for storage inevitably loses a little." Grace smiles, but I note the missing confidence in her voice.

Great. Nice knowing she thinks we're making progress.

As I said, under *normal* circumstances, the lab is my favorite place.

But when we've been pushing our brains to their limits to make the pet food affordable, palatable, and marketable, it's a tight balance. It feels like a place where dreams go to die.

Maybe that's a little overdramatic, but it's exactly how I feel.

Without warning, Lena crowds my brain.

The way she felt in my arms as she buried her head in my chest—this iron woman suddenly a naked cactus without her thorns.

Then I had to open my dumb fucking mouth and shit up everything.

The raw anger in her eyes.

The ugly emotion boiling out behind her beauty.

The scorn I deserved after I betrayed her trust.

What was I thinking?

She's combative by nature and guarded as hell. Maybe if she wasn't so standoffish to begin with, I wouldn't be so bothered.

Hell, I like the way she fights for her passions. The clinic means a lot to her, and the second after its dilemma broke her in front of me, I put my entire shoe up my ass.

Those eyes.

Those big, brown, beautiful eyes, spinning with disappointment.

That fucking *hurt*, and yes, I'm keenly aware there's no one else to blame.

I wouldn't pretend to date me for a million dollars either.

Jackass idiot.

I deserved far worse than the way she stormed out like I lit her on fire. Plus, the awkward looks from the bartender and the patrons around me.

Maybe they saw a clueless donkey sooner than I did, bleating selfish promises at a woman he barely knows like he's the miracle in life she's been waiting for.

Luis looks at me sharply and clears his throat.

I forget he can read my mind. He's the only one who knows about that disaster, and he's spent enough time around me to know how fuck-ups eat me alive.

"Right," I tell Grace, my brain filling in the parts of the conversation where I zoned out. "If they're ready, bring the dogs in. We're not getting anywhere if they don't like it."

"Coming right up!" She heads for the door to the back room, and I lean against the chrome table.

"Bad date still got you down?" Luis asks dryly.

I shoot him a dirty look.

"You can always come back another day," he adds.

"No. We have to see if this works."

Goddamn, I hope it does.

"The sooner we can check off our formula, the faster it goes into production."

He nods, looking unconvinced. He has a sixth sense for a hell of a lot more than just driving and organizing my life. Somehow, he always knows when I'm bullshitting.

Although this time, I'm hopeful. We're teetering on the edge of a breakthrough.

Like Grace, though, I'm not sold on the heirloom grains being our missing piece.

But before I can mull over that too long, the door opens and three happy dogs pile in. They're all golden retrievers with enormous appetites. If this works, we'll extend our taste trials to some other breeds.

After the dogs sniff my hand and settle in, they cautiously eye the bowls placed down for them.

There are three small bowls for each dog in separate wooden holders. Two of the three bowls contain food from established organic brands, and the last is ours, arranged for each dog in a different order.

I'm breathless, watching their mouths go to work.

The first dog is a machine, wolfing down two bowls—until he's left with the third. He slows down and sniffs forever before taking a bite.

Fucking great. I have a nasty suspicion it's ours, even if I can't see the markings well from here with the dogs in the way.

The other two retrievers eat slower, stopping when there's one bowl left for them. Their tails wave slowly, like they're unsure but happy because it's food.

Dogs. Gotta love their simple emotions.

Despite everything, I smile.

But that smile slides right off my face when the two uncertain dogs stop eating after two bites and walk away with the last bowl half full. Meanwhile, the big girl who scoffed down all her food starts hacking.

Shit.

Swallowing a growl, I drag a hand through my hair. "Since when are dogs such connoisseurs?"

"Since they were born to eat the same stuff twice a day." Grace smiles kindly.

"It's the protein content, isn't it? Still too low, and it saps the flavor. Possibly makes it too dry too." I walk over to the hacking dog, now licking her chops, and gently pat her back. "Sorry, girl. You'll get some chicken treats for your trouble when they take you back."

"Yes, well, it might add flavor, but it would add to the cost. I'm sure you know," Grace says with a sigh. "I'm not sure there'll ever be an easy way around adding more protein to make it more appetizing, Mr. Pruitt. And that's bad news for the cost analysis and your pricing targets."

Dammit, she's right.

I feel like I'd have an easier time solving the world energy crisis than inventing a dog food formula that's tasty, cheap, and healthy. When I got into this game, I didn't think I'd need superintelligence to solve it.

Then again, that's why there's the gap in a very crowded market. No one else has figured this out.

"Okay," I say. "As always, thank you for your time."

"We'll keep at it, Mr. Pruitt. I'll touch base with the nutrition team again, of course. That's what you pay us for."

"I know you will. Thank you, Grace." I give her a quick wave as she leads the dogs out, then Luis and I head back to the parking lot.

"That went well, man. I thought that poor dog was about to barf on your shoes," Luis says with a laugh.

"Noted. Add an interview for a new assistant to my schedule," I throw back.

He laughs harder. "What will you tell your folks about how it's really going? Or do you want me to help cover?"

"They'll ask, but you can keep yourself out of the fire this time, Luis."

Dad always demands updates.

I hate that he has good reason, because I'm leaning on his farms.

Still, that's not why the man is a bulldog, demanding to hear about the latest tests and scowling *I told you so, you damn idiot* without uttering a word.

Sometimes he erupts, threatening to send me packing as much as he's threatening his damaged heart. He swears it's a good business lesson or some shit, but I know it's all petty outrage.

He also knows he needs me to give up on this gig on my own, without them pushing. Then I can settle into being the full-time, pristine face of Pruitt Ag with two kids for background and a wife I can't stand in between sunset cruises on the yacht.

Just like he wants.

Just like his boring damn life.

"You can stall them out, you know," Luis suggests.

"Not for long. Dad owns a huge chunk of the organic farming sector in the Pacific Northwest. Lots of smaller farms answer to him too. If I don't tell him why I'm changing the formula again, he'll call up any farm I'm working with and ask. Hell, he might do it anyway for spite." I kick at a rock and dig my phone out of my pocket, buzzing with notifications.

Instagram DMs.

Not unusual, but the face on one profile hits me right in the gut.

Lena.

You stupid selfish prolapsed asshole, her latest message reads.

Accurate.

But there's more—a long chain of messages as I skim down, each more vulgar than the last at a glance.

Damn.

I don't know what I've done to make her madder since last night. I figured I'd never see her again after that.

"Hold up," I mutter to Luis as we wait for the car.

He scrolls his emails as I dig through the full chat, trying to catch up.

There's more name-calling. A lot of name-calling.

Tons of newly invented curse words that would make a fifteen-year-old gamer blush, followed by demands to know what the hell I've done.

I don't understand.

You want to enlighten me? What's going on? I text back.

Corbin Daniels, my auxiliary driver, pulls up with a Suburban and parks on the curb. As Luis and I climb in, I show him the messages.

"I don't get what I've done to make her so livid."

"You don't already know?" He looks at me, almost wincing.

"If I knew, would I be asking?" I stare back flatly.

"Here. I've been watching it unfold all morning. I didn't want to say anything before the test. Don't shoot the messenger." He passes me his phone with an article pulled up.

So, Benny's wasn't the best place to meet, after all. I thought it'd be fine and we'd melt into the crowd, nice and anonymous.

But I still have times where I forget some people just can't get enough of Brady fucking Pruitt. And somehow those people found me, which means they found Lena too.

My gut sinks as I flick through the photos.

There's me on the barstool, leaning into her with a smile and an espresso martini in my hand.

Her taking a sip from her drink. Gesturing.

And then the moment where we're hugging and she's crying out her soul.

Fuck.

There are so many pictures of that. One single point of contact, and it's everywhere.

People thrive off making assumptions if you're attractive and the least bit famous. When their own lives don't have enough excitement, they need to borrow mine.

Whatever the motives, the result is the same.

That damn heartfelt hug is plastered all over social media now.

Not just Instagram, but TikTok, X, everywhere.

There are even videos with a so-called body language expert analyzing everything, and three bad lip readings.

I'm so fucking cooked.

"Buddy, this is bad," I whisper as I scroll the rest with my lip curled.

"Yup."

I squint at him, wondering at the last time his bluntness was useful.

Then my phone buzzes again, probably with Lena's reply.

There's nothing I can think to say. There's truly nowhere in this city safe from prying eyes.

I hate that a devious little devil on my shoulder sees opportunity. If I were every bit the bastard she thinks I am, I could use it to draw her in, to shoot my shot one more time.

This is the push she needs to really consider my offer when half of Seattle already thinks we're together.

But I can't.

I fucking won't.

Waving a fat paycheck in her face while she was hurting was bad enough. A movie-villain, dick move.

Doing it after I've made her infamous?

No.

Luis has been with me long enough to read my face. He drums his fingers against his knee, thinking.

"You're not going to ask her again, are you?" he finally says.

"I'm not a monster."

"So, what will you do, boss? There's more to worry about now than your folks pushing Nancy on you."

Sighing, I pull out my phone. She's sent the worst of the pictures directly to me with a series of emoji and question marks.

"I'm going to meet her. ASAP, on neutral ground, like a local park," I snarl. My fingers punch the screen as I type a message. "Somehow, we'll dig our way out of this. I just need a chance to make it right."

Somehow.

Luis's heavy sigh tells me I might have an easier time moving Mount Rainier.

VII

THE BARK SIDE

(LENA)

I almost don't go.

Right up until the minute I arrive, I'm thinking I'll turn back.

And I look ridiculous, walking into another ambush. It's clear they could be anywhere—clout chasers on social media, armed with their phones. Waiting to spot Brady and anyone he's with to photograph their every move.

I've gone out of my way to look inconspicuous, but it's turned me into a slob.

Instead of my usual jeans-and-tee off-work combo, I've gone for an oversize hoodie and sweatpants.

Hair in a bun, hood pulled down over my face.

The biggest pair of shades I own. I think I only wore them once to a bachelorette party where we dressed up like a group of old ladies going out for bingo night.

Honestly, I look like someone *trying* to hide.

Ugh.

Why bother? At some point you have to ask yourself.

There's a decent chance I've stepped over some invisible line. Maybe vaulted over it, and there's a minefield waiting on the other side.

But the last thing—the very last I want—is for some jerkoff to see me with him and think we're dating.

All because he gave me a hug.

Because I let myself cry all over him.

The sad part is, I still *liked* the hug. I mean, who doesn't enjoy a little comfort when they're coming apart?

If he's got enough heart to rescue a dog, he has enough to give me a hug.

Or so I thought.

But that was before he offered me a deal with the devil. Before the pictures dropped.

Just thinking about them makes my anger boil over.

How many times have I gone to Benny's before? And the *one* time I go out with Brady, against my better judgment, it's a setup.

I think back to the crowds and busy tables there. So many people who could've taken advantage of the buzz and snapped a few photos.

I haven't decided yet if he planned this whole thing. I can't dismiss the idea, knowing he only wanted to take me out in the first place to ask me to be his prop.

How far would he go to get his way?

How many affluent fuckboys like Brady Pruitt never learned how to comprehend *no*?

And if he did, he's not getting his way. I don't forgive and I don't forget.

I've already been through far worse than anything he can do to me.

Even so, I glance over my shoulder to make sure no one's following me with a camera right now. Thanks to the social media flap, I'm now "Sad Girl," the latest love interest for a man this city obsesses over.

Whatever. It won't help him convince me to be his pawn.

Somehow, despite every bitter voice in the back of my mind telling me I should just head home and forget Brady exists, as the sun drops behind the horizon, I find myself waiting where he told me.

Logical? Hell no.

I'm leading with my one vulnerability.

Despite the drama, I still want to think the best of him. At least, I want to give him a chance to apologize and fix this like a man.

The rich clown owes me that much.

Even Dr. Ezzie asked about it earlier, which was doubly humiliating.

She had to confirm if the woman in the picture even was me, after Trish showed her everything, of course. They recognized Brady from our stint with Charlie.

I'm stewing more by the minute when I finally spot Mr. Jackwagon himself, a few minutes late, striding up the path.

Like me, he's dressed down today. He doesn't stand out as one of the most eligible playboys in the city, I guess.

Sure, he still looks like he could've stepped out of a photo shoot, but I figure that's a common style for him. It comes with the territory when you're naturally gorgeous enough to bend the world to your will.

And is he walking like he's a man with a little humility in his veins?

Nah.

He strides through the park with that loose, easy stride I've seen before, graceful and strong. He should be *crawling*.

His eyes flick to mine immediately.

Guess my disguise isn't nearly as good as I'd hoped.

We're not alone in the park, but no one gives us so much as a second glance as he reaches me and stops, this conflicted and lopsided smile hanging on his face.

"Glad you came, Sass."

That makes one of us.

"Oh, no. Think hard before calling me that." I fold my arms. "I hope you had time to rehearse. Start groveling."

His eyes widen, and he shakes his head.

"Didn't come here to do anything else." His charming smile drops, and he looks so serious. Disarmingly so. I wonder if he's practiced that sad-puppy look. "Look, I'm sorry as hell. This isn't close to what I intended."

"You mean you *weren't* trying to force me into a pretend relationship?" The acid in my voice hurts.

He winces. "No, hell no. I get why you're pissed—you have every right to be. And I know it looks bad, but I didn't know we'd get dinged all over the damn internet. I'm not planning to pressure you into anything. If the photos hadn't dropped with a dozen big Seattle influencers weighing in, you never would've seen me again."

"What a relief," I hiss.

He sighs. "You deserve a way out from my problems, Lena. I'm here to help you find one. This was my fuckup for not being more careful. I should've remembered how impossible it is to catch a break. Reinventing yourself takes years, apparently, when everybody's dead set on reminding you what they see."

Annoyingly wise words.

Despite myself, I feel a twitch of sympathy.

If he's sincere about changing, it would suck to have the whole world making it harder, I guess.

"This happens a lot?"

"You have no clue." He snorts.

The way he rakes a hand through his dark hair looks genuinely tormented. The kind of genuine I thought I saw back at the bar when he smiled like I meant the world.

Backstabbing, rich fucknugget.

God, I wish hating him was *simple*.

"I never should've offered you a drink. Never mind anything else. It's my fault, and I'm not denying it." He chuckles, short and dark. "I must have been out of my fucking gourd."

"You got that right."

"Which brings us to today and why I invited you here." He pulls out his phone and waves it at me. "I want to set the record straight. This isn't about you, and I'm not leaving you hanging, spinning in my net."

That little grain of sympathy sprouts.

Damn him. Having to deal with so many rumors must get exhausting, especially when he's trying to avoid some twisted arranged marriage with Miss Congeniality.

But I can't bring myself to care.

It will only make the whole thing even worse.

I'm annoyed that I imagine Nancy reacting when she hears the news. She acted like she had some kind of claim on him.

Plus, his stuffy, image-chasing parents. He hasn't said much about them, but I'm not stupid. I know the implications.

Then I wonder about Harry.

What if he recognized me in the photos?

God.

He'll almost certainly come stalking around Pawsome Hearts again, armed with a way to embarrass me to death. Pressuring Dr. Ezzie until she hands him the keys to the kingdom.

All so he can demolish the clinic and build an ugly new stack of gentrified condos.

Holy hell, no!

Before, this dilemma felt hopeless. Going up against Harry with my limited influence felt like throwing a bucket of water at a wall and praying for erosion.

But if I had Brady's help . . .

Stupid, I know.

Reckless.

Self-destructive.

When I came to the park, I was ready to throw his offer back in his face, and maybe any stray coffee cups I could find littering the ground. To laugh at the idea that he *ever* thought he could bribe me into being his flipping girlfriend.

Now, though, I see the offer for what it is without the personal outrage.

It's more transactional.

One million dollars isn't anything to sneeze at either.

Yesterday, I fled because the thought of lying to the world for money made my skin crawl. And he threw it in my face two minutes after I thought I could trust him.

Today, I'm reassessing my memory and my morals. What I'm prepared to do to save Pawsome Hearts.

"What's your plan?" I ask, leaning up on my toes so I can see what he's typing into his phone.

"Shoot this situation dead. I'm posting the truth for my followers. Everything. I'll deal with the shitstorm it'll bring down later. Almost done," he grinds out, glaring at the screen like it's biting him.

"Wait, don't post it yet," I say.

He stops and looks up. A fraught line appears between his brows. "What?"

"I said don't post."

He shakes his head.

I inhale slowly. "If I wanted to be your fake girlfriend—*if*—I'd need the money up front."

"The money . . ." His face clears. Those blue eyes blaze. His mouth loosens just a fraction before it tightens again. "The money I offered yesterday, you mean?"

"Duh. Do you think I'm beating back rich guys who want to pay me to kiss them?"

"Lena, I—" He blinks and then buttons his lips like he knows he's about three seconds away from blowing it again. "Go ahead. Talk."

"I don't like being forced into anything." Understatement of the century. "But a small part of me *might* see how this could benefit us."

He looks like he's biting his tongue, but he just nods.

"The thing is, I'd need to convince Dr. Ezzie I'm her other option for a buyout," I say. "I'll also need to find a new vet doc to partner with. I can't run the clinic without doctors."

"Sure." Brady looks out across the blue-grey water, his eyes sharp. "We'd just need a contract outlining the terms."

A contract. Yikes.

So official.

But maybe that's exactly what we need to keep this from getting too stupid.

It's not that I necessarily think Brady will take advantage of me. Not intentionally. Not deliberately.

But I do think this situation is delicate and requires rules engraved in legalese.

"The contract would state I'll relinquish my right to continue our arrangement after one year," he continues.

"A whole year? Holy shitballs." I stand with my hands on my hips, legs splayed.

Yeah, it's a power pose. I once read about them helping in social situations, but today it helps keep *me* from feeling like I'm helpless here.

Even while I'm giving up my soul.

From the way Brady looks at me, it's working. Or *something* is working for him.

"It has to look authentic," he says.

"A whole year of my life. Awesome."

"This has to work for me too," he says gruffly. "A one-year gig for a million dollars up front—that's more than fair, Sass." He stands loosely yet firmly, a statue carved in raw emotion.

I hate that it looks so good on him.

Then again, he's got the jawline and the soul-stripping eyes that look good with everything.

"One year," I muse. "I think I can handle that."

For Pawsome Hearts, I will. Really, what's one measly year of my life when it could keep the clinic alive?

It might even give us a fighting chance to revive its former glory. Dr. Ezzie had the love but not the energy. If new people come in with passion and heart, there's no telling how we could turn it around.

"So, let's hear it. What am I in for?" I ask.

"Your obligations, you mean?" He stops to think. I do my best not to notice the sharp way his gaze flicks across the water, watching a huge cargo ship pass by. "We'll need to make some public appearances. Mandatory and tightly controlled, especially early on. We'll want the shit-stirrers and local media to see us on our own terms."

Sensible. Unfortunately.

I breathe through stabbing anxiety.

The attention can't be much worse than the current mess, and this time I'll know it's coming.

"You'll have to meet my parents too," he says carefully. "I'll keep them the hell away as much as possible, but to really sell it on my end, you'll have to play girlfriend." He pauses, and his eyes lock on mine. "At some point, we'll probably have to be engaged."

Engaged.

Deep breath, Lena.

I don't know how I ignore the sheer panic ripping through me, but somehow I manage not to freak.

This is what high-paid fakery involves. And if I want to save Pawsome Hearts, I need to commit now.

It won't be forever.

"Okay, understood."

"We should also discuss physical boundaries. Better now than later, to clear up any misunderstandings." That razor-sharp gaze slides back to me, weirdly gentle behind his intensity.

If a shark could apologize before snacking on a fish, this is what it would look like.

"Physical boundaries," I repeat numbly.

Why does it feel like it's ninety degrees outside?

"What you're comfortable with, specifically. Obviously, there has to be some touch."

Some touch.

Oh my God, stop.

There's only so much my heart can take before it shorts out.

". . . What are you suggesting?"

"Holding hands, for one. Hugging, kissing, nothing too scandalous. About what you'd expect for public affection."

"Kissing?" My voice squeaks.

Sit down, you prude. You've kissed men before.

But I've never fake-kissed them.

And I've certainly never wrestled lips with a man descended from the Olympian gods of this city.

I've just bitten off way, way more than I can chew.

"That's what couples do, yeah. Don't tell me you're that clueless?" Brady's smile returns, more wicked than ever.

"I *know* what lovers do, idiot. Spare me the birds-and-the-bees lecture."

"Good, then you get why it's nonnegotiable."

"Right." I clear my throat. "That's . . . fine, I guess. I can kiss."

"Can you?" He narrows his eyes.

"Yes! I mean, it would be weird if we didn't, right? People would talk."

"They would." His devilish grin slices me in two.

"Cool, then it's settled."

Good thing I'm not trying to get him to date me for real.

I looked into him thoroughly when I did my Google stalking. So much spilled tea that causes him so much grief today.

Scorned models.

Dicey hookups.

Public spats.

Casual affairs with women whose appearance is their livelihood and who owe enough in taxes to make me pale.

I am so not in his league. Not even in the same zip code.

I mean, I clean up okay.

But there are levels to social value. And what's the point of getting your nails done pretty when tomorrow you might be cleaning up puppy barf?

"Well, if that's the nitty-gritty, I guess we're done. You should get going before people notice us together," I say.

"Isn't that the point now?" Brady's eyes spark.

Ugh, it is.

"But not until we have a contract in place." I hold up my hand. "Thanks for the apology, though. And for reassuring me you're not a pile of tapeworms in a suit."

Snorting, he looks at the hand I extend, then my face.

His lip curls, feral and sensual in a way that sends shivers down my spine.

Then he steps closer, knocking my hand away, and catches my face in his hands. His palms feel so warm against my cheeks.

But it's nothing like the hellfire when his lips meet mine.

Holy flaming shit.

For a second, I'm too stunned to react.

I'm not sure I *can* react.

My knees lose their structural integrity as he hits me with high-voltage Brady Pruitt passion.

Blazing breath.

Teeth. Lips. Tongue.

All *him*.

We haven't signed a thing yet, but he's looting my mouth.

And there's no prayer of pointing that out, because his kiss is too searing to stop. His tongue flicks at my bottom lip, and my mouth opens without meaning to.

This man is a master conductor, and right now my body feels like the whole orchestra, singing for him so sweetly, just as he commands.

And oh, this is music.

I'm clinging to him, one hand on his arm and the other fisting his shirt at his waist. Both his hands are still on my face, gentle yet firm as he tilts my head slightly, fitting us together at a better angle.

Fireworks.

Literal fireworks.

My stomach leaps in a way I've never experienced. Like I've swallowed a whole summer's worth of butterflies.

Super cheesy. But super real.

Is this what kissing is supposed to feel like?

Or have I just been kissing the wrong men all my life?

Or maybe—the thought irks me, though I don't know why—he's just kissed enough women that he's an expert in the dark arts of sex.

That's the most likely explanation.

I tell myself I don't care as his tongue roams mine and his fingers press into my cheek, adding this roughness I shouldn't like.

I definitely don't mind that he's turned my body liquid.

That shameless surrender spreads from my knees to the rest of me too soon.

If he didn't have another hand on my back, holding me up, I'd be so screwed.

Pretty sure I still am, because I've forgotten how to breathe.

If he wasn't so good at this, I'd also say I've just forgotten how to kiss. Because this kiss tells me I never knew.

But his lips move slowly and suggestively—all sharp, silent words—until only primal instinct remains.

When he moves away, I follow him before I catch myself and jerk back.

No way. I can't be doing this.

I can't seek his warmth, dick-matized by a near-stranger I wanted to strangle half an hour ago.

Right now, I'm nothing but bad instincts, and most of them are lodged in my lower belly. There's an ache between my thighs I haven't experienced in ages, pulsing so intently it scares me.

Holy *shit*, this is bad.

And that was quite possibly the best kiss of my life.

Speechless.

"Practice, Sass. Don't look so shocked," he tells me.

My mouth opens, and I fully intend to say something witty and harsh, but all I can manage is "What the hell?"

Clever. That'll show him.

"I'll have my people send over the paperwork soon. Tell me you get it when it comes through." He has the audacity to salute as he walks away.

Looking utterly unaffected.

And I think I'm back to hating his smug, arrogant ass, even if he's converted me to the dark side.

Just not like before.

Not when it's also possible that I'll never forget this shredding, world-tilting kiss for as long as I live.

And that's the worst part.

There'll be more kisses like that coming, and soon they'll fill my head until I forget how to keep my guard up.

VIII

BARKING MAD

(BRADY)

Some days, I forget I'm the son of one of the richest business magnates in Seattle.

Today is not one of those times.

Dad's favorite breakfast spot is a Filipino American diner, and like usual, he buys it out for a couple hours so we can eat in peace and privacy.

Usually, it's such overkill I laugh. He loves to pretend he's more famous than he really is. Even if he isn't far off the tech titans you always hear about, he doesn't have anything close to their media footprint.

Today, though, I don't mind.

His face is already cherry red as he glowers at me from his wheelchair.

"I can't believe you'd do this. After you insisted you were done screwing around," he snarls. His big hands hold his coffee mug like he's on the verge of hurling it at me.

"Now, Alec." Mom puts a hand on his arm. "We haven't even eaten yet. Let's take it down a notch."

"That's the damn point. We haven't even had our coffee, and he's ruined breakfast with his alley-cat bullshit exploding across the internet. What the hell were you thinking?"

"Thanks." I look up and smile at the poor server who finishes filling my mug.

"Brady!" Dad barks, crashing his fist against the table. "Are you listening?"

"Yeah. Everyone in a three-mile radius can hear you too." I add a splash of cream to my coffee and stir.

I knew he'd react like this, yes, but it's so fucking infantile I have trouble keeping my temper in check.

"Explain yourself. And you better have an excellent excuse for humiliating the Loomers and the entire Pruitt brand with this nonsense. The money we've had to shell out on those damn reputation managers over the years to bury your antics . . ." He shakes his head.

Never one to mince words, my old man.

"First of all," I say, "I was never *with* Nancy. You guys kept pushing her on me, yeah. I went out of my way to give her a chance. It just didn't work, Dad. You can't hold a gun to my head and make me like her, especially when I have better options. Like Lena Joly, for one."

"Lena." Dad snarls her name, slamming his mug down again until coffee sloshes over the cup.

"Alec, calm down," Mom says. "Drink your coffee, and listen to Brady, honey."

"Frankly, it was electric, Mother. I felt it right from the start." I pin on a smile. "The first time I met her months ago, we were inseparable."

Lie number one. A particularly insane one because Lena hated my guts the first time we met, and that wasn't even a month ago.

Call it necessary. No one's going to believe I'd sacrifice everything to be with a girl I barely know.

"Electric," Dad rumbles.

"Why didn't you bring her up sooner, darling?" Mom asks.

"Because I know how you guys are. We had to keep it private, taking it slow—and no, I didn't tell Nancy. I consider her a friend, and once I was sure about Lena, I let her down easy."

"Easy," Dad mutters, his face inventing new shades of red.

"Alec, please," Mom warns when she sees his eyes twitching. "Remember what the doctor said about your heart."

Yeah, I wonder why.

As horrible as his heart attack was, it wasn't a huge surprise for a man intent on working himself into an early grave.

I take a satisfied gulp of my coffee—the perfect mix of bitter and sweet to take the edge off this nightmare.

The sooner I can escape this travesty of a breakfast, the better.

"Obviously, I didn't announce it to the world. Or you guys," I say. "No point feeding the media circus if it was never going to work out. I had to be sure. Plus, Lena isn't used to this kind of frenzy. I had to give her fair warning, ease her into it."

That much is true.

I won't forget the way she looked at me with such hot betrayal when I met her in the park, like she thought I'd orchestrated the entire damn thing.

This craziness isn't her life.

At least, it wasn't until she signed up to play charades with me.

"I'm still concerned about that. We can't afford to have people photobombing the clinic where she works."

"Clinic. For animals?" Dad grumbles. "That's all the family needs. A damn veterinarian."

"A veterinary nurse, actually—and she's a damn good one." Pride slips into my voice. "She'll be part owner of a long-established Seattle practice very soon."

"Ridiculous." Dad's scowl deepens.

"Worse than an artificial marriage, you mean? With someone I barely like? Why wouldn't you want me to marry a woman I can show the world I truly love? *That's* good branding. That's authenticity."

Mom smiles at me. "He has a point."

"He has a sickness. He's thirty years old, and he's handling romance like a goddamned kid."

"If they feel that deeply about each other, how is that bad? It's time he settled down. We both know it." Mom's eyes flash with empathy, the same blue shade as mine.

"Only if he settles down with someone good for him."

Good for us, he means.

It takes titanium self-control not to snort in his face.

"There's no one better than Lena," I throw back. "Think how it'll look. I'm not shacking up with some spoiled supermodel or a girl who's spent her life on a leash in DC with the secretary of agriculture. Most of Seattle hates Nancy."

"Don't disrespect her," he snaps.

"Are you seriously telling me you don't know her reputation? I've tried to ignore it, but it's everywhere. Lena isn't like that. And people will see how much I care."

"You must introduce us," Mom says cheerfully.

"Kerrigan!" Dad looks at her in disbelief.

"What? You think I don't want to meet the young lady who's put a sparkle in my son's eyes?" She smiles at me. "This is the most enthusiastic I've seen you get in a long time, Brady. Especially for anything besides work."

Fuck.

I knew an in-person meeting was coming, but I didn't know they'd want it so soon. She'll be thrown face down in the frying pan before she's really gotten started with this sham.

Dealing with my parents makes the media maneuvering look easy.

"Sure, Mom." I force a smile. "Wouldn't dream of keeping you waiting. We'll set up something soon."

Meanwhile, I'll have to remember how to walk through a minefield again without blowing myself to pieces.

◆ ◆ ◆

Brand first.

Mom would glow with pride if she knew what I was doing to make sure my public image looks sharp and polished.

Technically, she'd still look down on me for debasing myself with pet food, but I think she'd appreciate the aesthetic.

Luis and I head over to a big dog show in Bellevue today, one of those high-class events where tech bros and rich grandmas show off their pampered pooches. I lean my head back against the seat as he drives.

"I have something to tell you," I say.

"Let me guess. The girl again?"

"Lena. She has a name, dude."

"Glad you can remember this one." He shoots me a sideways glance. "I'm happier the girl isn't Nancy, though."

"Yeah, fuck that. Here's your update on that—I told Nancy we're never hooking up. She took it about as well as you'd think."

"Shit! Mad respect. And you walked out with all your fingers and toes?"

I laugh.

"It gets more complicated."

"For Brady Pruitt? Never," he says dryly.

"Come on, stop busting my balls. You know the rumors flying around about me and Lena?"

"For God's sake, Brady." He rolls his eyes and changes lanes, pulling ahead of a large truck. "I'm the man who *showed* you those rumors. What's this about? You said you weren't going to use them to push her into anything."

"Oddly, I didn't have to."

His eyes bulge, and I smile to myself.

"She's the one who brought it up," I say. "I met her at a park. I was typing up a post to debunk the rumors right there. Then she decided she wanted the money."

"Interesting. So, you've solved the fake-dating riddle." When I don't say anything, he looks at me. "What's eating you? You're talking like it's bad news, when it's everything you wanted yesterday."

"At first, I was excited as hell. Now, I'm not sure if I've thought this through. My mom wants to meet her. Sooner than I thought."

"Well, yeah. What mother wouldn't? If I slip up and admit I even looked at a girl, my mama starts cleaning the whole house and cooking a feast. You basically told them you're about to get engaged."

Holy fuck. When he says it like that—

What *am* I doing?

"I think I just bought myself an entire universe of shit. Galaxies and all."

"Yeah, probably." Luis chuckles.

"Thanks for the reassurance."

"Just facts, my man. Face them."

"What? Like the fact that my folks will lose it if they ever figure out the truth?" I grimace and drop my hand. "Or the fact that I agreed to fund her business-buyout plan? She wants the clinic, and her boss is selling."

"Tough situation," he admits. "You were born to be a diplomat, though. When you started in on the dog food gig, I never thought you'd talk your dad into letting you source straight from the family farms."

"Yeah, that was a coup." I grin. "Don't know why I got stuck with you, though."

"I'm like your grand vizier. You need an adviser to avoid any traps," he says wisely.

"Right. So if you were me, what would you do?"

"Go big!" He looks at me before riveting his eyes back to the road. "If you can fool the world, you can fool your parents. And you can use everyone else's opinion to help convince them."

"You want me to fool the world first?"

"I want you to man up and make an engagement announcement. Right after you give her a ring. Like I said, go big or go home."

My gut churns.

This is getting way too real, but he has a point.

"Now?" I planned on waiting just a little while before going in hot with the ring. I don't know why I feel a live current in my nerves.

"Now," he echoes. "Commit to the ruse. Your fans will eat it up, especially all the ladies who love a wedding, even if they're turning green. Feed the happy people your happily-ever-after."

"Easy for you to say," I growl.

"Your parents will buy it if a million people do." He smirks. "They'll see what they want to see. If you look like you're happy and in love, they'll see you with a girl and a big ol' ring, and their mind will put the rest together."

"Apart from the skeptics, you mean. And the unhinged types. Do you know there are stalkers online who fixate about everything? Shit, I had two nutjobs in my comments the other week telling me the corgi we picked up was AI and wasn't real."

He laughs. "You'll always have those, no matter what. But people *want* to believe in the happy endings, boss. Give them their show."

Damn, he's right.

What I told my parents was right too. This will be good for our brand.

People want proof I'm not a raging asshole or some infantile playboy who changes models like socks.

Lena's a vet nurse. Relatable and sexy and strong. The perfect partner for the biggest crime of my life.

It's why I chose her.

I can't get cold feet now when I have a reputation to unfuck. And Lena—she doesn't strike me as a quitter. She might regret signing on to this, but she won't bow out.

As long as I can pull this off.

As long as she's on board.

It's bizarre to shove this entire deception into the public eye, but maybe it's exactly the kind of weirdness we need.

I pull out my phone and start texting Lena, asking when she can meet me.

"Remember, you said it first. I'll need your help."

Luis groans. "Where would you be without me?"

"She'll meet us soon. Let's expedite the announcement."

IX

STRAY CAT

(LENA)

I've never felt so out of place anywhere in my life.

Brady lives in a two-floor penthouse suite that looks over half the city, which shouldn't surprise me as much as it does.

Yes, the place is *nice*.

I mean, bonkers, off-the-wall fancy with sleek marble, natural wood finishes, and these artsy light fixtures that look like they're straight out of a museum.

The kind of place where a girl might relax in a classy red dress and sip champagne as she lords over Puget Sound through the floor-to-ceiling glass walls masquerading as windows. Or at least *lord* over it vicariously through Brady.

But the place isn't sterile like so many luxury caves on Instagram. Somehow, he's made the place feel homey.

Expensive, yes, but homey, nonetheless. The overstuffed furniture doesn't hurt to sit on, and the tasteful wall art with abstract nature scenes and Japanese-inspired calm don't make my brain panic, trying to decipher what it is.

My mind is racing for another reason: I have no clue what I'm doing here.

Except deep down, I do, because my dumb ass just signed a contract. My willingness to lie to total strangers—that's why I'm standing in this man's elegant condo, listening to his assistant talk.

His *assistant.*

Luis looks like he's around Brady's age, handsome and relatable, like he knows how to have a good time and when to get down to business. No accent, but I hear him curse in Spanish under his breath a few times.

I know the feeling.

Pretty sure he wants to be here for scheming up illusions about as much as I do.

At least he doesn't have as much riding on it.

"Camera ready?" Brady asks once Luis fills me in on the assignment, which is pretty simple today.

A basic introduction.

Smile, act like we're in love, and he'll take a video to document it in 4K that will probably show every blemish I've had since I was fifteen. Then Brady will make an official post announcing our engagement.

Official.

God.

Again, not a shocker. I literally signed up for this.

My stomach still dives like a hawk with a broken wing.

Engagement. As in, we're going to be engaged.

Obviously, we know it's fake, but nobody else does, and we'd better keep it that way.

It's like having a wish I never made granted. This fast track into the kind of fame I've happily avoided until now.

That little taste of notoriety I had with Harry Jay was more than enough to leave me queasy.

Not that this will be like that. That's what I keep telling myself.

My arrangement with Brady isn't *sleezy*. No one's being duped or tricked into anything against their will.

"All set. Lighting might be better outside," Luis announces after checking the camera. He waves us out to the balcony.

Of course, Brady has a balcony bigger than some Seattle apartments, spacious seating area and fire pit included.

Pinch me. I need to stop gawking.

As we step through the double doors, the wind slaps my cheek, stirring my hair. But the sun feels lovely on my skin. This is one of those dreamy summer days that makes up for months of slate grey skies and constant rain.

Oh, and the view.

No wonder Luis wanted us outside. I actually recognize the scenery from looking at a few old Insta posts on Brady's account, but seeing it in person is something else.

Behind us, the whole bay churns with ships, cargo and ferries mingling with sailboats under the gentle watch of the distant mountains.

"We'll keep it simple, Sass. Straight to the point," Brady assures me with a gentle hand on the small of my back.

"If you say so. I have no experience with cameras in my face."

As long as I don't barf over the railings . . . and how bad would it be if I do?

"Oh, hell. Hang on, I almost forgot." Brady smacks his forehead.

I turn to him as he stands, staring in disbelief as he pulls a small box from his pocket, kneels, pops it open, and offers me the unspeakable.

A giant sparkling stone attached to a shadow of gold. Large and square and bursting with diamonds.

Holy shit!

Every bit of me should hate how gaudy it is, but instead I feel adrenaline.

"Lena." He smiles like the cocky madman he is as he looks into my eyes—definitely not the expression I ever imagined on a man confronting me with a ring.

My lungs stall before he says those four fatal words.

"Lena, will you marry me?"

So fricking *weird.*

I have to resist the urge to laugh brokenly in his face. The worst part is, I don't know why.

I just feel the metric ton of emotion dropping me on my face, squeezing my life out.

My very first marriage proposal—the *only one*—and of course it's a total fraud.

We're just doing this to pull one over, and he had to turn it into a more depraved joke than it already is.

That slight gurgle in my stomach since I woke up this morning intensifies into a cramp.

But there's no way I can crack. Not when I've already embarrassed myself in front of this man.

". . . Real gold, huh? I'm impressed." I genuinely am as the pretty ring catches the light, breaking the light like glitter dust.

"Would I give my fiancée anything less than the best?" He gets up to sit next to me again. "So, will you?"

God, why? Why is there a boulder in my throat?

As he holds it out for me—guess no one ever walked him through a proposal before, like how you're supposed to slide it onto the woman's finger—I lean forward and whisper, "If you have my check, I'm yours."

"Of course." He grins and pats his pocket. "Now put it on so we can see how it fits."

Fantasy ended.

After fumbling around, I slide it on my ring finger.

A little too easily, almost. It's a hair too big, but it's nothing a quick resizing won't fix, and it'll work for this cringe video.

"Are we ready?" Luis asks behind the camera, frowning at our little sideshow.

Absolutely not.

But Brady turns to him and nods. "Start rolling when she says okay. Ready, Lena?"

Not for a hundred years.

But my ego could never survive panic-running now, so I just beam back this flimsy smile.

"Yep. Let's make a few suckers," I manage.

"Great!" Luis adjusts his camera. "Live in three . . . two . . . one . . ."

Am I ready now?

Not even a little bit.

But just before Luis gives us a thumbs-up, I tack that smile on until it hurts my cheeks. I hope my face doesn't look too much like a Halloween mask.

I'm not expecting it when Brady wraps his arm around me, though, swift and easy. It's too natural, like we've done this a thousand times before and we're totally not two strangers faking the most meaningful relationship of our lives.

"Hey, party people," he says casually, like he's catching up with an old-school friend. Like he knows his followers personally—and they have a right to know about his life. But I guess that's why he rocks this media thing. "As you know by now, I've got a secret."

He looks down at me with a breathtaking smile, and . . .

Am I still breathing?

There's a decent chance I'm not.

All I'm thinking about is the way he kissed me dizzy last time.

Until now, I've been repressing the memory, but there's no squashing this.

"Today, I'm announcing I've found the love of my life—and she's *everything*," he growls reverently.

Holy hell.

Weirdly, my smile doesn't feel so forced anymore.

So, not only am I not breathing, but I'm blushing, the heat turning my cheeks into frying pans.

This man has hijacked my pulse.

"She's smart, she's gorgeous, and she's just as passionate about animals as I am. Honestly, she only has one flaw—she's camera shy. Good thing you've still got me." He takes my hand, squeezing my palm, holding the ring up to sparkle for the camera. "Ladies, you'll be happy, even if I know a few of you might be disappointed. I'm officially off limits."

He doesn't fake the enthusiasm in his voice.

For Brady Pruitt, this is the dream. The only rich man in Seattle who wants to run *away* from women.

Luckily, no one will be chasing me anymore.

I wave, but the movement feels awkward as hell. Sixty seconds in, and I'm already blowing it.

No one will buy that I'm madly in love with this guy.

No one will even buy that I was born anatomically human.

I look like I've forgotten how my limbs work.

"Say a few words, Lena?" he urges.

His fingers fold tighter around mine.

I want to drop thirty floors into screaming traffic.

Brady makes this look so easy, but it's actually worse than talking down one of those rude clients who blames you for their cat shedding a claw sheath after fighting them back into their carrier.

"Hi, I'm—I'm not very good at this. But I just wanted to say I'm thrilled to be the next Mrs. Pruitt. Brady, he's—he's *incredible*, really. Amazing and famous and so intelligent. He could work on his people skills—"

I stop cold as Brady stares me down.

"But we're in it together! I'm coaching him all the time. Honestly, he's so good it's a little overwhelming, but . . . I wouldn't trade this for anything. You're looking at the luckiest lady ever, Seattle. Thank you and good night."

There. Hack job complete.

"We're both lucky. It's a hard chase, finding your soulmate, but when I met you, Sass, I knew."

Oh boy.

He's using that nickname in public—and he makes it sound affectionate.

But it's his eyes that take me down.

Brady's gaze drips with so much honest gratitude I'd choke if I wasn't riveted in place. He's too good at this show, and it's quietly killing me.

"Get used to that pretty face, folks. You'll be seeing a lot more of her in my videos soon," he says.

A lot more.

I blink. Maybe he's expecting me to nod along and agree, but I feel like a deer caught in the headlights.

What is he planning?

There's no time to wonder when he turns my face to his, gently slides one finger under my chin, and kisses me breathless.

Just like before, it starts off searing and only gets hotter. Like sliding into a hot tub, the heat soothing and blanking my brain.

I don't know how he manages when we're both standing still. My eyes flutter closed, and I bring my hand to his wrist.

Just touching him. Fingers on skin.

A million of my worries against his wall of muscle.

Mouth against mouth.

Tongue against—

Oh God, his *tongue.*

It explores my mouth like he knows it belongs there.

Searching, claiming, teasing me to mush.

Every frenzied brushstroke sends more fire to my belly.

My head tilts back. I sure as hell hope it looks like I'm lost in his kiss, because it's not fake. It's the realest thing I've felt since the camera started rolling.

Terrifyingly true.

Tingles race up and down my spine, and I'm boneless in a matter of seconds, my breath stalled in my lungs.

Good thing, too, because the world-ending way Brady kisses leaves zero room for breath.

Soft lips, demanding.

Rough fingers pinching my skin, gentle but intense.

Catastrophically romantic.

How, I don't know.

But somehow, I know he's playing me for optics. He knows this is exactly what people love, selling a princess dream come true.

Perfect couple.

Perfectly happy.

Perfectly in love.

"All right, that's a wrap," Luis calls, looking up from the camera.

Brady breaks away.

He's wearing this whisper of a smile like there's a secret I'm not in on. All I can see are his lips.

Bladed. Lush. Deeply sensual.

Is this what it feels like when you're losing your mind?

"You did it. Still feeling okay?" he asks.

There's no way I can answer that question in a way that doesn't make me sound psycho.

"Yep. Easy peasy," I lie.

"You were amazing, woman." He releases my chin like he's only just realized he's still holding it.

I step away.

Seriously, I need distance, space to catch my breath. But if he notices and thinks there's a problem, he doesn't look like it.

Maybe he feels the need for a breather too.

It can't be easy mustering up that much passion to power-kiss a woman he'd never touch without this goofy arrangement.

Really, it makes sense that he kissed me and played it up for the cameras. We were making an *engagement* announcement.

The kissing was kinda mandatory to sell the big lie.

The trouble is, nothing about kissing Brady Pruitt feels fake.

Yes, I'm well aware that's all in my head and it shouldn't be.

I can't let this man make me forget this isn't real, not even for a few seconds. He's mastered the black art of kissing, and I'd better find a defense fast, before he leads my heart to the slaughterhouse.

He reaches past me to take a folder from Luis and then holds it out to me. "It's all in there, your copy. Any questions, let me know."

The money, he means. The legalese.

We're right back to business—or did we ever leave it? The worst part is, I barely care about dollar signs anymore.

Scary.

Sure, Pawsome Hearts comes first and last, but in the inferno of his kiss, everything fell away.

I cared about the paycheck more before he kissed me.

Before he started a fireworks show in my chest.

Before he ignited chain reactions much lower in my anatomy and made the cameras seem phonier than that ginormous ring on my finger.

Even scarier.

I don't understand why I'm unraveling and how he's so good at pulling on every thread.

Pretending to care about Brady was supposed to be the hard part. The improv act I just had to grit my teeth to get through.

When I showed up at his condo, I was certain it would be.

I felt out of place. Awkward.

But after his kiss demolished me twice, everything feels like it's spinning into uncharted territory.

Ten billion dollars wouldn't make this any easier.

Not because I can't stand him.

No, because I don't know what to do with him baiting my heart like a stray cat, when I know full well it's just one night by the fire.

He's keeping me warm and fed and happy to get what he wants, and tomorrow he'll dump me back on the street.

THE THREE F'S

(BRADY)

Mission accomplished.

Now it's time to figure out if this damn illusion will take flight.

With all the notifications flooding in, I swipe my phone to silent. I'm a veteran at this, and it's better to wait a few hours after major news for the ground to settle. Even when a few million strangers online have an opinion about my fiancée.

It's almost too calm in my condo. Anticlimactic.

"See you tomorrow, boss." Luis waves as he lets himself out.

I walk Lena to the sofa, urging her to settle in.

Although she's smiling, she's gone pale enough to worry me. I don't want to turn her loose just yet, though it's probably her biggest wish.

"Drink?" I ask. "Lots of reason to celebrate after that performance. You were fucking Oscar worthy."

"No need to lie." She laughs numbly and shakes her head, playing with the hem of her blouse nervously. She's dressed in what I'd call business chic.

Luis suggested she dress up, but I prefer it this way.

Just her, without any artificial glamour to throw her off kilter.

If we're going to play this game, then we should cling to the truth as much as possible to avoid complications.

She's agreed to move forward with my bullshit, and she deserves a seamless experience.

"I'm going to order some dinner," I say casually from the kitchen, pulling a few water bottles from the fridge.

Then I change my mind and grab two beers instead.

Hell, we deserve them.

Lena's gaze flicks toward me. She's always had a frosty look, like she's ready to judge me then and there.

A little unsettling.

I also must be all over the damn place from kissing her. I can't help noticing the way her lips purse, begging to be claimed like a treasure.

I hate that it makes carving the mental distance I need harder.

The softness of her mouth, the way she whimpers, the shy and willing flutter of her tongue on mine.

I'm lucky that video ended when it did. Two seconds longer and the wrong angle, and some joker on the internet probably would've noticed the hard-on I couldn't hide.

"Takeout? What are you having?"

"Mm." I scroll through the list of restaurants. "I was thinking Thai, but we could do whatever you want."

She tilts her head as she thinks, her hair piling over one shoulder. That chestnut hair looks like pure velvet, a few natural red highlights coming through as the evening light catches it.

I think I'm fucking jealous of the light for the first time in my life. I want to thread my fingers through her hair instead.

Ridiculous.

This is all an act, and I'd better remember it.

"Thai's good," she murmurs.

"Great." I pull out my phone, open the delivery app, and toss it over. She catches it right before it smacks her in the face. "Sorry. Bad aim. Get whatever you want."

The beer foams as I crack it open, and I try not to down it in two gulps.

Shit.

I know it's a summer evening, somewhere in the eighties for temperature, but it's never this hot in here. I normally don't crank the AC up unless it's really oppressive. At this rate, I feel like I need a cold shower to avoid turning into a sticky mess.

I can't blame it on summer. Having her this close does terrible things to me.

Until the park, I didn't know how soft Lena Joly could be.

Who knew that a woman who spits fire daily could be all silk, her curves supple and wickedly proportioned to make the barbs on her tongue worth it.

Yeah, there's more to her than most of the women I've dated. This natural look pairs with a take-no-shit energy that hounds me to do diabolical things to her.

I can't.

I can't lose my head and make this a thousand times more complicated.

The ring shines nicely on her finger too. I try to keep a lid on my pride, seeing how it fits.

Lucky guess.

Now, I just have to distract myself until I stop daydreaming of kissing the woman wearing it. Pretend or not, it's a primal impulse I didn't expect.

This caveman shit warns me there'll be hell to pay if I don't check it ASAP.

The way she chews her bottom lip when she thinks doesn't help at all.

"Here." After what feels like an eternity later, she passes the phone back.

I punch in my usual order for spicy drunken noodles with shrimp and pretend to check my text messages. The silence yawns between us like a thick blanket.

I almost regret asking her to stay.

Then again, I don't.

We *need* to learn to tolerate each other if we're going to make this work. If we're going to get past her urge to scratch out my eyes, or my temptation to carry her off to the bedroom over my shoulder.

We need to act like sane people.

There's too much riding on this deal to blow it now.

"You know, I researched you more last night. Pretty deep dive before I agreed to something totally crazy." She glances across at me.

"Yeah? I'm not surprised. You don't just jump in and fake-marry a dude without knowing something."

"Why pet food?" she asks.

Unexpectedly blunt. But she's still just staring, waiting for an answer.

"Why pet food," I repeat.

"You mentioned it at the bar. When I looked it up, I found your website. Pretty well put together. I wasn't expecting a whole white paper linked to the mission statement." She smiles curiously.

"I didn't write it. I have a couple nutritionists who roped their peers into helping me refine my plan."

"Well, obviously. You don't get to add *scientist* to your skills."

I snort. "If you didn't sound like such a smart-ass, I might think that was a real compliment."

"It was. You're welcome."

"Shit, Lena. I'd hate to hear what you sound like when you're insulting someone."

"Usually I'm happier than this," she assures me as she sips her beer.

Biting back a smile, I drop down on the sofa, my bottle hanging loosely in one hand. "I know it's a crowded market. I've heard a hundred reasons to bail out before I blow a ton of money and wind up with nothing to show for it. But it's important to give everyone a fair chance to help their pets live long, happy lives. That shouldn't just depend on money."

"Fair. Guess you really meant it when you told me that story about the army dog." She pauses, and I nod. "That's admirable for Daddy Dollars. If you're not careful, you'll lose the nepo baby label with your haters."

My gut quakes as I snort and shake my head.

"Tragic. How would *you* hate me, then?" I growl, trying to look unaffected.

Honestly, I fucking hate being told my efforts only mean anything thanks to the family name. Especially because it's true, minus my stunning success with the dating app.

"It would be a little more convenient," she says, idly twirling a strand of her hair in the evening light.

"For pretending you're in love with me? I could see that."

Her cheeks brighten, and she looks down. "I thought you were a mammoth asshole the first time we met."

"And the second. Am I down to dwarf elephant yet?"

That thin smile returns, igniting her eyes. They look almost golden in the light.

"Don't push your luck. You weren't too great the third time, come to think of it."

"Only at the end."

"And the next day."

"Until we met in the park," I say, my voice dropping to a whisper.

I kissed her then. Sprang it on her so thick it surprised me, her shock and awe delighting me.

The price was instant addiction.

Fuck, there I go again, thinking about kissing Lena's soul out.

She's too damn beautiful, splashed in gold sunset, a stark contrast from the first time I took her lips.

I hadn't noticed so many details then. Sure, I thought she was pretty with her curves and classic beauty, set in a face that doesn't smile enough.

But back there, in the park, with her chin lifted and her eyes glowing, I think I already knew how royally screwed I was.

I never could resist a challenge, and she's handing them out like fucking candy.

For a moment, we're silent, lost between words.

She curls her legs up under her as she finally relaxes. "I do have a question . . ."

"Shoot."

"Why me?"

I frown, taking another pull off my beer.

"I mean, why me, specifically? Couldn't you find someone way better? Like an out-of-work actress?"

Good question. The beer bottle almost cracks under my fingers as I grip the glass, thinking what to tell her.

What the hell. We're friends, right?

"If you googled me, you must've counted how many times I've fucked up," I say carefully. "Needless to say, my past hurt my image and limits my options. Bringing in anyone too desperate—especially from Hollywood—it just didn't seem wise."

"Your dating history, you mean?"

"Yeah. Once you're stuck with the playboy image, it's impossible to shake. My antics as a kid and a few times after I came home from the army stalled my career. It's not just the family name that gets me a business meeting. For too many people, it's the only reason." I suck down the rest of my beer. "If I could give up my money and comfort to take it all back, to start over, I'd push the button. No hesitation."

"Is that what you're hoping with this? Besides buying time with your parents, I mean. To have this sham make the old Brady disappear . . ." Her mouth purses and tilts to one side as she looks at me, her brown eyes softer than ever.

"I want it to bury him alive." My voice is thunder, low and intense.

"Wow, you're serious. The prince wishing he could just be a peasant—that's classic myth stuff. Was everything about your old life so bad? Most guys would kill for your edge with women. If you didn't have the media blowback, I mean."

I pause.

"What life? What edge? The one where I've screwed myself out of having a chance with any decent girl? Where I'm stuck dating women from rich, insular families so close they feel like cousins?" I shake my head. "No, fuck that entirely. Any woman I'm going to be with has to be authentic going forward. I need chemistry beyond the looks and a love for world travel."

"Apart from me, you mean."

"Apart from you," I echo, though how inauthentic is it, really? The engagement, definitely. But the chemistry?

It's burning the air like a flame to paper as we speak.

"What about you?" I ask. "Since we're trading regrets, it's your turn. Don't tell me you're still single thanks to one bad prick?"

She hesitates, taking a long drink from her beer before setting it down. "I haven't dated for a while, really. Not seriously. Too busy with work, and I like it that way. It's just easier."

I wait, letting my silence press her for more.

"There was a guy, a few years ago." The words are quieter now, spoken to her hands instead of me. "We were . . . serious, I guess. At least, I thought he was. Then he wasn't."

She doesn't say who, but she doesn't need to.

She's a god-awful liar.

It doesn't take much to know it's her ex, the heart-wrecking asshole who's coming for her clinic.

Damn, what did he *do* to her?

My blood boils as I reach for her hand and squeeze it too hard, looking at her intently.

"Don't talk about it if you don't want to. You don't owe me everything."

"Thanks."

It must be the light painting her like an angel that's crossing my wires.

"Just know there's always another chance. I don't know how he hurt you, but there's no reason that has to be the end of the line. Even if this isn't real, you and I, it's a reset. For my reputation and yours."

"*My* reputation?" She blinks. "I don't have one. Not like you."

"The one in your head, Sass. You start letting ugly mistakes define you, you can't learn to forgive, that's when you're sunk." I smile, stroking her fingers. They're strong from her work yet still so delicate. "You can buy Pawsome Hearts now. Take the wheel, do all the things you've ever dreamed of. Best of all, you can take it and spit in that fucker's eye."

She laughs roughly, like she's barely holding herself together.

"Brady, I—" Her throat bobs, and fuck, it's so easy to lean in, tugging her closer, tangling up her warmth with mine.

She doesn't resist.

It's even easier to tilt her face up.

This woman is a broken dove. Proud, strong, determined as hell, but unable to heal and take flight.

Tears cling to her lashes, mirroring the tiny freckles dotting her cheeks like constellations.

This time, I'm not sure who moves first.

Maybe both of us at the same time.

I just know we collide like a volcanic blast, falling to a hunger that's mindless. Needy. Rampant.

This isn't like the staged kiss for the cameras at all.

Then, I lost myself in her for a few heady seconds, but I was constantly aware of the camera, my fans.

I was focused on making it look like this wasn't new for either of us.

Now, I don't care how it looks.

The urge consumes me, and there's no one watching.

Just us.

Just *Lena*.

She's so impossibly warm it hurts not to kiss her.

Her hand curls around the back of my neck for support, and I trace her curves with one palm.

A small sigh escapes her mouth, passing from her lips to mine. Over her clothes, I find her breasts. Even through her bra, I can feel the hard nub of her nipple, aching to be sucked.

Moaning, she arches into my hand.

Forget restraint.

You couldn't hold me back if I was chained to a mountain.

One more flick of her tongue, and I'm hard enough to split rock.

"Brady." The faint gasp of my name has me seeing myself tugging those jeans down her slim legs and discovering what's between them.

Then she slides up and perches on top of me, her lush hips rolling against mine like waves calling me to dive in.

Fucking madness.

Her cheeks are still damp, reeling from that harsh confession about her ex ruining her for other men—and it makes me want to find him and kick his nuts through his skull.

This isn't real.

It isn't supposed to be.

But every kiss, every moment, every scalding breath can't lie.

My fingers dip down, diving under her jeans, toying with the lace underneath, pulling until she whimpers. She inhales so sharply there's no resistance.

If I want to rip her panties off and mount her right now—

But what's that sound?

Somewhere in the distance, there's a sharp *thud*.

I'm so sex-drunk I almost ignore it.

It can't be important when I have Lena Joly on my lap, her mouth fused to mine. If it's some lost maintenance guy or building security making the rounds, they'll find their way out.

I slide my hand through her hair, and it's just as soft as I imagined.

Sweet perfection.

Then another sound. The chime of my doorbell this time.

Lena breaks away.

"Brady?" Her rosebud lips are flushed, and her eyes are mad marbles.

"Ignore it. They'll go away." I move in to kiss her again, but she turns her head.

"I don't know if she will," Lena whispers, twisting away.

She?

For the first time, I hear my name in an incoherent screech.

"Brady Pruitt, you answer this door right this fucking second!"

Goddamn, so much for paradise.

Why did they let her up?

Lena slides off my lap, rushing to fix herself, running her hands through her hair and over her clothes to smooth everything back into place. "I think you're going to have to answer."

I wish I didn't, but there's no point delaying the inevitable. And with the announcement, it's not like Nancy Loomer's dropping by for an ice cream social.

"What the hell?" I snarl as I walk over and rip the door open, but Nancy bolts in without waiting for an invitation.

I shouldn't be surprised.

"Oh, good. She's still here," she snarls the second she sees Lena.

"Watch it," I warn.

"Seriously, Brady?" Nancy whirls around and jabs me in the chest with one long nail. "*This* is what you picked over me? This . . . this nobody? This budget bitch who can't even look happy for a three-minute Insta Reel?"

"Enough, Nance. Walk yourself back out. Right the fuck now," I growl. Lena's on her feet behind me, her face flushed with anger. If I'm not careful, I could have a brawl on my hands. "I told you how it had to be the other day. Made it clear we're not right for each other. Now it's time for you to accept that like an adult."

"That." Her laugh is more of a cackle, high pitched and grating.

"I let you down gently. I tried," I say, folding my arms. "But hell, Nancy, if you keep barging in here with your insults, I won't be gentle at all."

She staggers back like she's been shot.

In another setting, it might be amusing. But when she straightens herself enough to look at me, her eyes are seething.

Whatever. She thought she had me in the bag.

She wanted our arranged mismatch to work from the first time my mother set us up, but until now I could never figure out why she was so damn invested.

"Okay, Mister Man. Fine. Enjoy it when the shit-talkers come calling to rip your balls off. I'll tell them you're a two-pump chump too. Gladly. You'll regret walking away."

I swear I can feel my blood pressure spiking.

I'm on the verge of picking her up and throwing her out by those fake-ass hair extensions when I feel two small hands winding around my waist, hugging me from behind.

"Sorry you're salty. You lost," Lena says with the sweetest venom in her voice. "But honestly, can you blame him when you're such an entitled freak?"

"Entitled? Who do you think you are, you little—"

"Wasn't done yet. The *only* thing Brady should ever regret is every second of misery he wasted with you. He's found better company now." The acid in her voice should be criminal. "We're in a happy mood today, and that's why I'm going to give you a choice—pick yourself up and go crawl off to lick your wounds, or we'll have you in handcuffs. And not the kinky kind. You're not welcome here, bitch."

Holy fuck.

Nancy doesn't even blink. Two screaming red blotches surface on her cheeks.

It's like Lena just repeatedly slapped her across the face.

And she did, without lifting a finger.

Nancy's a self-propelled ego. I have no doubt this isn't how she imagined this conversation going.

I also have no doubt she's about to start swinging, so I step up, lodging myself between the two women.

"You heard her. Get out," I order, pure violence in my tone. "Get the *fuck* out! And if you know what's good for you, don't ever show your face again."

I regret nothing, even if this causes a hurricane-grade shitstorm.

After all the times she's barged in like she lives here, like she has a right to me, this feels glorious.

Cutting Nancy loose—that's a huge win.

When she still doesn't move in her paralyzed state, I turn, wrapping Lena in my arms and pulling her in for a kiss until the other woman stumbles back.

Then the door slams in Nancy's face.

I don't stop when she's gone.

Neither does Lena, attacking me but staying where we are. Almost like there's this unspoken agreement binding us from moving to the sofa.

You can't go there, no matter how fucking tempting. Here, there be dragons.

"She's gone." Lena's soft mouth curls into a smile under mine.

"She's smoldering ashes. That was you, hellcat." I kiss her again, my arms locked around her waist, bending her body into mine. She doesn't resist. "Do we always need an audience for this?"

"*This* is supposed to be fake."

"Doesn't mean we can't have real moments." I groan raggedly, taking her mouth again.

This wasn't what I intended.

Hell, if anything it reminds me why kissing a beautiful woman like her is so recklessly dangerous. Still, I can't bring myself to regret it, much less to stop.

"Nancy Loomer had that coming since the day she was born," I mutter. "I'm just glad you were the one to dish it out. You're tough as nails, Sass."

"You aren't pissed I didn't save you the honor?" Her eyes dance as she leans back, holding my hands.

"Hell no. I enjoyed the show." Reluctantly, I release her and step back. "I haven't said this enough, but I'm glad I chose you for this adventure, Lena. Imagine having a partner in fakery without some teeth."

She laughs until she's red in the face, and I just stand there, gobsmacked.

It feels deceptively ordinary, having this girl slam my heart across the Milky Way.

At least there won't be much trouble faking chemistry.

With Lena Joly, I only have a hundred other problems.

XI

BAD DOG

(LENA)

Dr. Ezzie's office always looks so tidy in the morning. I think the first thing she does when she gets in is clean up the mess of papers left the evening before.

Throughout the day, it gets progressively messier. By closing time, her desk looks like the aftermath of a buffalo stampede.

Luckily, I'm here first thing. But judging by the shock on her face, she's half a beat away from tossing the stacks of papers on the floor and letting them stay there.

Hello to you too, anxiety.

I didn't think I'd be this tense, coming to her with a buyout offer when it should be a dream come true, but here we are.

My brain spins, horrified at what will happen if, after all this, she still refuses and goes with plan A.

Plan A means my gross ex gets his grubby paws on Pawsome Hearts and its days are numbered. He'll have it leveled in a matter of months to make way for more soulless high-rises aimed at multimillionaires, and he'll be laughing all the way to the bank.

Maniacally.

So maybe it's the stress dunking me in pessimism today.

Sue me. There's a lot riding on this.

Dr. Ezzie pushes her glasses up her nose. She sighs and takes a sip of her coffee. Lately, I notice she's running on extra caffeine and fumes of kindness.

Not healthy. Especially for a lady who used to skip out on her midday lunch breaks to jog two miles.

When she said she needed to take a break and focus on other priorities, she wasn't kidding.

Which is exactly why I need to convince her I'm the miracle she's been waiting for.

"I hate to ask, but you're being absolutely serious, Lena?" She fixes me with a stare so intense it worries me.

"Serious as the grave, Doc."

"You have the money? In your bank account? Or is this contingent on selling something else—"

"I do. All liquid cash." I smile. "I had a bit of a windfall recently. It's a long story, but the point is, I'm loaded."

That gets me a tired laugh as she sits back and clasps her hands. I can't blame her for being skeptical.

I'm the girl who had to ask her two or three times over the years to advance my pay early just to make rent when I had a nasty, unexpected car repair or major plumbing work.

"And you're prepared to take on Pawsome Hearts as is? With all its known issues? With its debts and liabilities?" Her large brown eyes seem duller and bleaker than ever, like she's begging me to walk away while I can. "Tell me you have a cash cushion beyond the asking price. This place will eat you up fast if you don't, and I'd never forgive myself if I let you get in over your head."

Yes, I planned for that.

"Doc, relax. How many times have you told me I'm a stubborn badass? You know I'm prepared to dig in my heels and fight like hell for this clinic." I lean forward, resting my elbows on the desk—for once, there's a patch of bare wood for me to lean on. "I mean it. Everything I have is going into the Pawsome engine. I even brought along a written proposal."

I reach into my tote bag and dig around for an embarrassing minute before I free the folder with the pages I printed off this morning.

I thunk it down on her desk with a grin. "It's all there. You can comb through my financials with a grooming brush."

"My, you are prepared," she murmurs cheerfully as she flicks it open.

"I want this. Badly. I won't let our clients down, or you, Doc."

Her eyes swell with empathy. "You certainly have the gumption, and I believe you have the money. Of course, you know you'll need another vet to—"

"Already on it. I've started looking, and I have a couple prospects for a partner. We're meeting later this week." I'm practically fizzing in my seat.

Is it bad that I'm obsessed with my work when ninety percent of my social life consists of a fake relationship?

Even if I didn't love animals more than my next breath, I'd need a distraction from those kisses that shouldn't keep happening.

Brady won't leave my brain. Not even when I'm here, negotiating the biggest win of my life.

"Give me some time," Dr. Ezzie says gently. "Frankly, I didn't expect to have competing offers. Yours is a nice surprise, to put it mildly."

"No rush. I'm just glad to have a chance. I'm going to make this work, Dr. Ezzie," I assure her.

Her smile looks worn but genuine. "If the financials didn't matter, Lena, I'd hand you the keys tomorrow."

It's pretty late by the time I get home.

My feet ache like usual, and I smell like wet dog meets fishy canned cat food. It's been one of those days where the long shower will be mandatory.

But first, hot drink or microwave dinner?

No one ever said I'm a good cook.

I've just put the kettle on the stove for tea when there's a loud knock at the door.

Oof.

Normally, that's Granny Lark, the sweet old lady up the street and my bestie's grandmother, wanting to catch up with me. But it's late, and she's normally bedding down after eight o'clock.

This weird psychic sense in my brain tells me not to open the door. Turn the lights out. Pretend I'm not home.

But what if it *is* Gran and she needs a hand with something? Wouldn't be the first time she had a few bags of soil or mulch delivered and she needs my help to lift them due to her knee injury.

I'm not feeling sensible tonight. I'm tired and grouchy, and my feet are barking like angry huskies. It doesn't sink in that it could be dangerous until I throw the door open and see my worst nightmare.

Effing Harry.

Just as tall and obnoxious as I remember. That long waxed mustache that should've stayed in the last century gives him a cartoon-villain vibe.

"Lena." He bares his teeth in what might be considered a smile on another planet.

Not here. Not now.

My body stiffens, bristling to face the threat before my brain catches up.

"What are you doing here?" I spit, making sure I sprawl out to block the doorway.

"Hello to you too, doll. Aren't you going to invite me in for old times' sake?"

What is he, a vampire?

"No. What do you want, Harry?"

"Aw, jeez. I'm just here to talk." His grimace-smile widens.

"Then talk." It takes monster restraint not to add *asshole* to the end.

Maybe that's why he stares at me like he wants to feed me into a wood chipper.

Believe me, it's mutual.

When he sees I'm serious and I'm not budging, he folds his arms and lets the plastic smile drop a little. A good thing, so I'm not blinded by his overwhitened teeth.

I blink, a little too fast.

"I spoke to our friend Dr. Ezzie earlier," he says. My bravado deflates like a dying old balloon.

Crap.

I should've known the only reason he'd show up is to pressure me or rub his disgusting triumph in my face.

I frown. "How'd you even know I'd be here?"

"Oh, let's not worry about that. You're a smart girl, and it's your mom's old house. Wow, you haven't changed a *thing*, have you?" He leans in closer.

I get a whiff of his cologne, so strong it knocks me back.

Or is it the past sweeping in like an ice-cold wave?

God.

There's a reason people say scent provokes the strongest memories. I think this smell throws me through time and space. Even if he's older and meaner and richer now, he still wears that same damn fragrance.

Suddenly, I'm nineteen again, serving ice cream at Raven Swirls, my mom's summer pop-up shop, and getting painfully shy when the best-looking man on earth shows up twice a week.

He always tips more than the cost of his cone. He makes me laugh with his crazy, antiquated mustache and his backward ballcap that says "Give A Damn."

I'm twenty, my heart racing in his arms, listening to him tell me he loves me and he's sorry if it hurt when he took my virginity. He just needs it "a little rough" to get off.

I'm almost twenty-one, and he's outside my apartment, hurling a rock at my window. It scares me when it hits and cracks the glass. Telling me how “fucking brain dead” I am to get worked up over something so stupid. He always gets black-out drunk on his father’s yacht with his friends because he knows “how to live,” and I need to just deal with it.

I’m twenty-two and still anxious. I’m expecting to come home to his ridiculous mustache twitching as he screams at me and breaks another plate in my house, even though he’s long gone.

I find one of his old shirts in the back of my closet. It still smells like him.

I burn it in the old grill out back, crying.

The full force of emotion almost makes me slam the door in his face, and I have to remind myself to breathe.

He doesn’t have that hold on me anymore.

I’m not the same dumb college girl, and I’m sure as hell not his little “doll.”

“Dr. Ezzie,” I mutter, playing dumb. “What about her?”

“She told me you want to buy her out. At first, I laughed my ass off. Then I realized she was serious.” He spreads his hands and inhales sharply. “So, yeah. Let’s not make this personal, okay? I bet you weren’t planning on dropping your life savings on that dump until I showed up with the funds and an actual plan.”

He would make the bet. Harry never saw a pull tab machine at a dive bar he could turn down.

Then he’d bellow and kick the machine when it inevitably ate his cash until they threw him out.

But I don’t remind him what a spoiled, raging demon he is. I don’t say anything.

My feet stay glued to the floor. My heart jitters in my chest like a trapped bird, desperate to break out of its tiny cage.

“I’m serious about the buyout, Harry. Frankly, you’re better off moving on. You must have other projects?”

“Serious.” He snorts loudly. “Yeah, sure you are. So am I. C’mon, why don’t you let me in so we can sit down and talk like civilized people?”

Oh my God.

I can't help my face turning red.

But finally, when I can take a step forward, I block his path more firmly, staring him down in his dead green eyes. The only way he's getting in here is if he shoves me to the floor.

Which I wouldn't put past him.

But then I can nab him for assault and maybe breaking and entering. It's a quiet neighborhood. Someone will call the cops if I scream.

Only, he just falls back, throwing his hands up. "Fine, we'll have it your way. But listen to me, LeeLee, and listen *good*."

I wince.

Out of all his pet names, that one's the worst. I can't hide the disgust contorting my face.

"I've heard enough," I throw back. "If you want the clinic, make another bid and let Dr. Ezzie decide. Isn't that how this works?"

"Fuck no. You might know animals, but you don't know real estate." He smirks. "Just hear me out—five years of your salary in exchange for dropping your offer. That's six figures, easy. You can walk away and go back to Mommy in Port Townsend. You never were a big-city girl at heart."

Until now, I always thought *vibrating with anger* was just a phrase. But suddenly I'm living it.

Is this man for real?

"Go to hell," I bite off, putting every ounce of venom I have into staring back. "Also, it's a little late for professionalism or whatever. This *is* personal, Harry, and you made it that way. You're not taking my career too."

"Too?" He lifts a brow, and his ugly smirk widens.

He knows exactly what I mean.

"You're not going to get your way this time," I say. "You're not turning Pawsome Hearts into another ugly, overprice commercial turd that sits vacant when MicroDick Incorporated lays off half its Bellevue workforce thanks to AI."

Any trace of amusement leaves his face as it firms into a vicious scowl.

"Funny you should say that. And funny that you've got the funds to buy me out *now*. We both know you're shit with money, LeeLee. You could never afford lunch without bumming a few bucks off me after you left my place, less mouthy and satisfied. Say," he growls, slamming his hand on the doorframe next to my head. "I wonder who's fucking you now? Is that the real problem? Seeing how you've got microdick on the brain and all."

"Harry, get out. Leave me alone," I hiss.

I am so entirely ready to scratch his face.

Screw the consequences.

"It reeks. That's all I'm saying. Or maybe that's just you after a long day of blood and cat piss. Whatever you're doing—and I know you're doing something—your story fucking sucks. You wouldn't live in this shithole house if you had the coin to live somewhere decent. So where did the windfall come from, huh?"

Brady flashes in my mind.

The way we teamed up in front of Nancy. The way he turned feral at the end, the delicious scrape of his teeth and his stubble.

Jesus, I can't let him down.

I can't let this brute threaten a man who's the only reason why I have a chance to save Pawsome Hearts at all.

If Harry acts on his threats, we'll both be so neck deep in crap, we won't be able to breathe.

I can't let him find out.

"Your boss might not be able to do her homework, but I will. I'm going to dig real fucking deep, LeeLee. I'm going to find the real story," he taunts, leering in, drowning me in that wretched cologne until I gag. "What are you hiding, I wonder?"

"Last chance," I whisper harshly. "If you don't leave now, I'm calling the cops."

His smirk widens until it's too big for his face.

"You won't. We both know you'd be wasting precious city resources, pulling cops away from real crime. I haven't done shit. I'm not hurting you. And I'm not dragging you out by the hair and chucking you in a drainage ditch. Shit, LeeLee. We *know* each other. You had my dick in your mouth."

I can't breathe.

The implied threat in his voice chokes off the righteous fury in my throat.

"It's sad, really. I thought you'd get over it eventually. Looks like you didn't." He reaches out, trailing his finger along my jaw. I slap his hand away. "Hell, for a while, I thought we'd be friends again someday."

The way my stomach churns takes my breath away.

In public, I can lie to myself that he doesn't scare me.

But not while he's in my face with no one else around to see what he's doing. My phone is inside, and I don't know if I could get the cops to take this seriously, anyway.

Even if I scream and a neighbor hears it, will he just laugh it off?

So many doubts whirl through my head. The worst superpower Harry Jay ever had was shredding my self-confidence.

There's no proof he's harassing me. He's barely touched me.

And the scariest thing of all is that he's a public figure with money and power. People know him. People *like* him.

My breath comes quicker, and I'm cracking.

I hate that he sees it. His inhuman smile spreads, wider and wider, until it's on the verge of devouring his entire face.

Honestly, I'm living a horror movie.

But I'm not about to let him turn me into a helpless deer.

Maybe when I was twenty, when I didn't know any better, and when I was so desperate to be loved.

Not anymore.

Not by him.

"I said *leave me alone*!" I snap, lunging at him. I push against his chest with all my might, and it must be the shock that moves him, because he's taller and stronger than me. "I will call the cops. Just try me." Even if they don't believe me—even if all they do is escort Harry off my lawn—it'll be worth it. I can still get a police report.

If I'm lucky, I can make him leave.

Right now, I'll do anything to get him away from me.

"Big mistake," Harry whispers as he looks up, brushing himself off. His eyes are slitted and cold. Worst of all, he doesn't fucking *move*. "Use your brain, girl. Think really, really carefully about your next move because—"

"Lena!" a rough voice explodes behind him.

I glance over Harry's shoulder just in time to see Brady charging down on him like a raging bull.

Harry might as well be the matador's red cape.

Holy shit!

I barely have time to move out of the way before Brady has Harry's jacket in his hands, whirling him around, slamming him against my house's old shake siding so fast I barely have a second to breathe.

Never mind scream.

With them next to each other, it's obvious who'd win in a fight.

Against me, Harry feels huge, a human tower built to destroy.

But Brady—he's an entire mountain. A dormant volcano like Mount Rainier, and right now, he's erupting.

Holy. Shit.

His shoulders flex and bulge as he leans in toward Harry's face, baring his teeth like a wolf.

Harry tries to shove him away, but that only makes Brady hold on tighter, choking him in a headlock until his eyes bulge and Brady's knuckles whiten.

Harry's jacket is ripped now. Torn down the middle.

Neither man seems to care.

Harry will when he gets home, though. He'll hate the fact that Brady ripped his fancy clothes, and he might press charges.

He's the first to scream to the authorities, even though he'd curse anyone who called them on his disgusting bully ass.

When he was at my doorstep, I knew I'd made an enemy.

Now, with Brady looming over him, I know Harry will stop at nothing to destroy me.

"Stay the fuck away from Lena," Brady snarls as he lets go, watching Harry stagger a few steps back, gasping for breath.

I've never heard a voice like that. Low and destructive, like a mountain lion preparing to launch itself at an intruder.

When Harry stops rasping enough to look up at me, there's such hate in his eyes it stalls my pulse.

"Get moving. Fuck off home," Brady bites off.

"If you ever lay hands on me again," Harry warns, "you'll regret it. Fucking simp."

Enough.

Enough. I can't do this.

My hands shake as I fumble back inside, coming apart at the seams.

I slam the door behind me, not bothering to lock it, knowing I don't need to when Brady is right outside like a bodyguard. But I need space.

I need a minute or two of distance to *breathe*.

The violence splatters across my eyelids in glorious color.

The way Brady's muscles rippled and his lip curled with dark promises.

The two men at war.

And the terrible promise in Harry's eyes that this has only begun.

A sob rips free from me as I press my hands against my face with a terrible realization.

My buyout was supposed to close one chapter and open a new one.

Now, this isn't even close to over.

What have I done?

XII

WORKING DOG

(BRADY)

I'll admit it.

I can be denser than a damn rock sometimes, but I'm pretty sure I'm not the one who fucked up here.

That guy was a catastrophe, and I'm not sorry.

I scattered his miserable ass so he'd stop growling in Lena's face.

He had to go.

And if he wasn't leaving when she told him, someone had to make him. Now he's gone and the danger is over, so why is she coming apart?

I shut the door behind me and clasp her shoulders, urging her back inside and leading her to the sofa.

Her whole body shakes. Some trauma response.

Shit.

I'm no shrink, but is this a panic attack?

Thankfully, I've never had my nerves fried before. The worst of the carnage in Syria that chewed up other guys just left me numb. There are also days when I wonder if icy, detached calm *is* my trauma.

"Hey." I smooth a hand down her back, warming her. "Breathe for me. It's okay. He's not coming back."

She gulps air so fast she coughs, her breath rattling. It's like feeling years of pent-up emotion working its way out.

"You . . . you shouldn't have butted in," she whispers. "Not with him."

Seriously?

That's where she's going with this?

Call me an asshole, but when any dude threatens a woman at her house, I'm not the type to stand there and watch like I'm at a damn petting zoo.

"You asked him to leave. He didn't. What choice did I have?"

"I had it under control, Brady." Her voice hardens, but I can sense the doubt.

"You did the best you could. I never doubted that. But I saw the way he got up in your face. You needed a hand, Lena."

My gaze sweeps around her small house, taking it in. It's a small place in an old working-class neighborhood. A cheap fixer-upper from the 1950s or maybe something she inherited. The kind of home that's no longer cheap at all in a city that seems like it's racing to break new records for eye-popping prices.

It's cozy and clean enough, though. Also, it smells like her—that subtle apple-blossom scent mixed with spitfire that's driving me mad.

"I hate this. *Hate it.* I don't cry like this, I swear." She sniffs loudly, wiping a shaky hand across her face.

Anyone else would say she looks like hell, but to me, all I see is heaven.

Where the fuck is my mind?

If Nancy ever cried—and I'm not certain she ever does for good reason—you can bet she rehearsed being a pretty crier.

Lena keeps trembling.

Her appearance is obviously the last thing on her mind. Not with this fountain of grief overflowing. But somehow, it just makes her more appealing—seeing her so vulnerable.

"Here." I wipe her cheeks with my cuffs. "Are you all right?"

"I'm fine."

"Sure. Now try telling me in a way I might believe."

She gives me a feeble laugh, which still feels like a victory.

"Why are you here?" she whispers.

"I came to meet you. Remember?"

Her face blanks. "I really don't. What is it today?"

"We have plans tomorrow. I wanted to discuss them and avoid any surprises." And honestly, it's getting harder than it should be for a single day to slip by without seeing her.

That's not something I'll be saying to her face anytime soon, no.

It's still a harsh fact I don't want to admit.

But seeing her like this, raw and helpless, when I've seen how fiercely she defends herself strikes fire in my blood.

I don't want to put a name on it, or even think too hard.

I just know if that ugly swaggering peacock fuck ever threatens her again in front of me, I'll be turning his face into a sack of gravel.

Screw the consequences.

He should've thought harder before he tried to put his hands on her.

Her breath steadies a little now. Still coming too fast, still not even, but not the panicked gasps I heard earlier.

Good.

"It's not that I don't appreciate what you did, Brady. I just . . . I don't want you getting involved with him," she says quietly, averting her eyes. "He's not your problem. You're paying me to look pretty and put on a show, not to hold my baggage."

Like hell.

But that's an argument for later.

For now, I need to get her out of this place.

What if he comes back and I'm not here?

I have a sneaking suspicion she won't go easy, though.

"Feel like getting some fresh air?" I touch her back lightly. "How about getting out of here and heading back to my place? I was thinking pizza tonight."

"Takeout again?"

"Or I can cook, but I'm not sure you're ready for that. It's the one skill I didn't grow up with. I've been trying to teach myself the last couple years, but I still burn thirty percent of my meals that don't get thrown in a slow cooker."

"Only one skill?"

"I was a precocious little rat."

To my relief, she laughs again, sad but genuine.

With one hand lingering on her back, I help her up. "Come on. I've got a car waiting out front."

"Luis? Hang on. I don't want him to see me like this . . ."

"Believe it or not, I drove myself. I can operate a car, you know."

"Wow! This must be like your third time now? Promise me I'm not risking a broken neck if I ride with you."

I chuckle at the teasing in her voice.

"Okay, fine. But I need a shower first. I never had a chance, and you'd be surprised how pet smells linger after a full day."

I give her time to clean up, idly checking my phone for emails in her small living room. There's nothing groundbreaking today with my food project or my slice of digital media.

Lena's well-being never leaves my head.

Neither does the impulse to cave her ex's face in.

When she emerges, she's dressed down in a T-shirt and jeans. Her face looks a thousand times better without the tear tracks.

I let out a wolf whistle until she blushes.

"Idiot," she clips, but she doesn't fight me as I take her arm and we head outside. I check around us as Lena locks up behind me.

No sign of the clown who came here barking threats.

My SUV waits on the curb, and I help her in before climbing into the driver's seat.

It doesn't take long to get to my penthouse. We're mostly silent until we're through the traffic and up my elevator, heading into my living room.

"I always forget how big it is." She sighs.

Compared to her little mid-century house, I guess so, but there are days when I'd prefer a smaller space. I don't do much here besides work and sleep, or else brood in front of the firepit on the balcony long after most of Seattle falls asleep.

Call it what it is—first world problems for a man who's learning to carve his name on the world with more than money.

I get her seated and bring her a glass of water.

"So, tomorrow," she prompts. "What are we doing again?"

"That's what I wanted to talk about."

She folds her arms like she's hugging herself, looking so small. She's still not making much eye contact.

She may look more relaxed, but there's no mistaking how guarded she seems after that Salvador Dali–mustache creep crashed her evening.

I don't usually let my anger simmer—growing up, grudges were a luxury. Any resentment had to be abruptly squashed under the stifling blanket of polite civility.

Most people think of rich guys as being spoiled, and maybe we are. But for me, growing up old money, everything about my life was so perfectly planned and conditioned I wasn't free to misbehave.

Not until I started to mutiny, acting out as a teenager.

Guess that rubbed off when I chose a life in the public eye, every movement and word carefully crafted for effect.

There's no room for impulsivity.

Yet here I am.

My mom would call me confused right now.

My dad would throw a fit over laying hands on an intruder instead of waiting for the hired help to do it for me.

That doesn't mean I have any intention of changing a single damn thing.

Lena huffs out a long breath, her chest heaving as she pushes out every last bit of air in a long sigh.

I shuffle closer, taking her hand.

"Forget tomorrow. Tell me about today," I press gently. "Don't mince words or worry what I'll do. Because any guy after you is my problem."

She narrows her eyes. "I already told you he wasn't."

"Listen, Sass. The second I heard you tell him to leave and he didn't, he became my issue. Top of the fucking list. I wasn't about to stand back while he tried to muscle his way into your house."

I stop short of telling her that I'm not going to let her leave here tonight. Not until I know the situation and assess whether or not she's truly safe.

I already know there's more to this than meets the eye. Until today, I've never imagined her truly scared before.

"Think of it as returning the favor after you helped me with Nancy."

"You didn't need my help."

"Sure as hell appreciated it, though. Paying you back, that's the least I can do." I glance at her slowly. "What the hell did he want?"

"He just wanted to talk about the clinic." She closes her eyes and leans back against the sofa.

"Bullshit." I squeeze her fingers. "He didn't just look like he came to talk business."

"He's a cutthroat."

"He's a psycho. That's not the way you look at competition."

Her eyelids flutter. "How did he look at me?"

Like prey.

"Like he wasn't done with you. Like you just broke up yesterday." I go with the second-best answer.

Also, the bitter truth.

That man looked at her like he wanted to devour her, and not in some kind of sadistic, sexual way.

More like he wanted to destroy her. Like her tears amused him. Like he wanted to take her apart, piece by piece, purely for the joy of leaving her shattered.

Too far? Maybe. There's still no way in hell I'm letting that happen to her again.

"Did he ever hurt you? Tell me the truth." It's a heart-wrenching question I hate to have to ask.

Lena's nostrils flare as she drags in a deep breath.

"It's a long story," she whispers. "We dated in college, like I told you. A couple messy years where I didn't know any better. I really lost myself, Brady."

Outwardly, I'm steel. Inside, my blood boils at the thought that the fucking thief stole two years of her life.

I raise her hand softly to my lips and kiss her knuckles. It's all I can do to keep my yap shut.

I'm dreading the rest of this, but I have to know.

This isn't the kind of story that ends well. I just need her to know I'm with her as she walks me through it.

"We were just kids, even if he was a couple years older. I always thought he was brash. One of the popular boys who liked to party. At first, he had a little depth. But he was always hanging out around my mom's ice cream shop in the summer with his friends. Right when I'd take the night shift." She takes a deep breath.

"Easy," I murmur. "Take your time."

"It just happened, I guess. He seemed bright, and he made me laugh. He always tipped ludicrously well. Plus, he had a sweet tooth—what bad guy has a sweet tooth?"

"The real sickos," I growl.

She almost smiles.

"Anyway, yeah, when he finally asked me out, of course I said yes. It was just . . . so much. Our first few days, he spent so much money on me. I was shocked because I didn't have much growing up. My parents didn't either. We were always on thin ice, just trying to get by."

I can't relate.

But I don't need to in order to understand that life is hard without money, and we never choose how much we start with.

"It was a whirlwind. The first few months were magical, as cheesy as that sounds," she whispers. "Like a movie, almost. I didn't know how

I got so lucky. He made me feel small with his money, his mind, and all the folks who knew him."

Jealousy stabs my heart.

I pull her closer, into my arms.

"When did it go bad? I've heard of this before, and the guys who go hard from the start always turn."

She nods. "Yeah. I mean, it was overwhelming for the first year or so. Coffee dates, museums, fancy dinners. His parents even had a—a large boat."

The way she says the words immediately put me on edge.

It also clears some things up for me.

Like why my assets make her leery. Knowing she's been ruined by one rich cock who tore her up and tossed her away like nothing.

"Clueless girl that I was, I fell so hard," she says. "Faster than I've ever fallen in my life. When he started turning, like you say, it was easy to lie to myself. It's hard to spot the asshole if you think there's just sunshine up his butt." Her smile slips. "I was a kid, really. I didn't know any better. So, when he started to show his temper, when he'd yell at me, I just . . ."

I jerk her closer, pinning her to my chest. I'll hold her all damn night if that's what she needs to collect her thoughts.

But a minute later, she looks at me again, her smile so broken now.

"I folded. I never should've done it, I know that now. But I'd let him throw tantrums, telling myself he was just stressed. Nothing a little therapy couldn't cure, someday. And when he'd throw my stuff around and break my dishes, he'd apologize later, and I thought his cooler side would win out. God, I was *stupid*."

"We all make mistakes."

"My biggest weakness was the way I would've done anything for him. And he *knew* that. He took advantage of it, he—" She chokes off.

"Hey, hey." I rub her arms, slowly and gently, feeling the way the tension drains from her. "It's okay, take your time."

"Everyone should know what a scumbag he is."

"Then I'll broadcast it nationwide." When she doesn't smile, I kiss the top of her head. "Kidding. I won't say a word unless you want me to. How long were you with him?"

"Too long. Between him sweeping me off my feet and me believing every lie, he had me wrapped around his finger even when things started to suck. I thought we'd get married one day and find a place of our own. All the fairy tales a young girl wants to believe. When you only have that growing up, you don't know you're with an abuser until he's crushing you. Silly, I know."

"It's really not. You think the only people who believe in smoke and mirrors come from—what did you call it? Folks just getting by?" It's an effort not to brush my knuckles across her cheek. "It's what we all want, Lena, rich or poor. A universal fantasy we'll pay a seriously fucked-up price to have."

The older I get, the more I see it, because that's what I want.

Not to be trapped in a never-ending media circus I have to fight and claw my way out of.

"The next part is the worst." She clears her throat. "Please don't say anything until I'm done?"

"Sure," I promise.

"It happened on his boat, and it was the final straw." Her voice is distant. "Harry was kinda depraved. He always wanted me to let him film us while we were—you know."

I hate that I do.

And the knot of fury in my chest snowballs when I hear it.

Tearing that asshole's suit jacket wasn't nearly far enough. I should have busted his head open.

"At the time, I didn't think much of it, not at first." Her eyes are glassy, staring at the floor like she can't bear to face me.

Like I'll judge her for what happened.

I have to bite my lip to avoid interrupting.

"I just wanted to make him happy. But then he went cold. He took a trip to Florida, and he was barely answering my texts. Then the boys on campus started staring at me. Laughing behind my back. Deep down, I knew, even though I didn't."

Oh.

Oh shit.

I clench my fists so hard my knuckles pop.

"About a week passed with radio silence from him. They started calling me 'boat brat' when they'd whisper, and—it wasn't hard to go home and type it in." Her voice hitches, head dipping as she struggles to breathe through it.

I wrap my arms around her, choking back everything I want to say.

Not right now.

She needs space to speak and feel like she can tell her story.

"Turns out, he had a porn account. Photos and videos of me. And other girls too. Always Harry with a new woman, all recent. New ones I guess he moved on with, if he wasn't with them behind my back." She presses a hand to her cheek. "It was *vile*."

My next breath feels so fucking hot it scares me.

Touching her. That's the only reason I don't erupt.

I close my eyes, pressing a kiss to her temple. She's sitting with her back to my chest now, and I think it's better this way, even if I want to see her face, to caress her and kiss her so hard she forgets that back-stabbing fuck.

But right now, Lena doesn't want me to see, and I can respect that.

She idly brushes my thigh, and I force myself to relax.

"I'm okay now," she whispers.

"Go on." I sound like I've been gargling nails. "What did you do?"

"Cried, obviously. Felt like I'd never stop. Finally, I confronted him when he got back, and I told him to take it down, and he just . . . he refused. For months. I threatened to get a lawyer, but I didn't have the money or the time. He called me on my bluff."

I tighten my hold on her waist. She touches her hand against mine, linking our fingers.

"He took them down eventually, just in time for his graduation. I suppose he wanted to clean up his image for future employers. God knows he never cared about mine."

I'm frozen in my seat, knowing there's a good chance I'm going to wind up a murderer.

"But then these *assholes* kept calling, and then a few of them showed up in person. Stalker porn freaks from the internet who somehow put my name and face to the videos. Wanting to know if I'd treat them the same as Harry. They wanted to pay me like a high-class escort. Called me 'boat brat' in front of my mom. It got so bad—the drama, the visits, all of it—that she closed her ice cream stand and moved away."

"Holy shit. It cost your mom her business?" My nostrils flare.

"That was the worst. Raven Swirl was a seasonal thing for extra cash, but she poured her heart and soul into it. She'd built up a nice local following, too, and we were getting more tourists every summer from word of mouth." She sighs. "Mom never asked for much—just a happy place to churn fresh flavors in the morning and smiling kids with sticky faces at sunset. Her Rainier cherry ripple flavor made people cry, Brady. She was living the dream, and I'm the idiot who went and blew it up."

I'm breathing raw fury down her neck.

"I hope you know," I whisper against her skin. "I hope you *know* that what those bastards did to you and your mom is scum-of-the-earth, snake shit. And there's no way—no fucking way—I'll let that man hurt you again."

She twists around in my arms until her nose almost brushes mine. Her eyes sparkle, wet with tears she tries to hold back.

"How many times have I told you? This isn't your fight. Don't defend me."

"Sass, I don't care if I have to plunk down ten times your check to keep that damn clinic out of his hands."

The corner of a smile touches her mouth, brightening the pain shadowing her eyes.

"It won't come to that," she insists.

"I don't care if it does. *If* it does, I'm game. Whatever it takes. What he did is revenge porn. That's inhuman, and it's also fucking illegal. A goddamn invasion."

"Believe me, I know." She touches my face, a line between her brows forming. "I know."

"Good."

"But you know what's weird?"

I stare at her, waiting.

"I feel safe with you. Even with the growly threats you can't act on." Her fingers trace my jaw. The contact feels like being branded. The sweetest agony. "Which is pretty ironic, knowing this is fake."

"Fake?" I huff a breath and adjust her so she's straddling my lap. "Trust me, woman, this is as real as it can get."

And then I prove it, bringing her mouth to mine with bedlam in my lips.

XIII

DIRTY ANIMALS

(LENA)

Fourth time's the charm.

Pretty sure that's the saying.

Brady's mouth claims mine with a hunger that speaks louder than any soft words and flowery kisses can. The emotion, the roughness—it's like a lightning strike reverberating through my nerves.

How angry he is for me.

How much he shares my pain.

How deeply he wants to soothe it like the tide wearing down pure stone.

I've never felt anything like it before—this honest fanaticism from a man who wants to defend me. It's so far beyond my comprehension in a brain that's been kicked and bruised.

Mom was perfectly kind when I grew up, but she didn't do much to warn me about men. Aside from Dad, I guess she never had much experience with romance, and with him she got lucky.

That's why Harry Jay was my teacher. He scarred me. He made me grow a cyst around my heart.

When Harry hurt me, I told myself I'd never give anyone else the chance.

It was too dangerous that way. Too easy to get hurt.

Your heart only shatters once before you're scrambling to save what's left, chasing the shredded pieces like loose marbles, trying to prevent them from pulverizing and blowing away.

But Brady doesn't try to tie me down with pretty words.

He doesn't undo the damage, because he knows he can't.

He knows I'm not someone you buy with cheap talk and big promises. Maybe once, in another life, but not anymore.

It's just his thick, dark hand in my hair, his mouth on mine, his tongue delving against mine with that savage tenderness he's so good at.

It's him holding me like I'm more precious than anything he'll ever own. And Brady Pruitt owns more than I can fathom.

He has an easy claim to high-value women, goddesses who make me look like a dumpster raccoon—bright-eyed, superhuman freaks of nature who could make his life paradise.

But his kiss tells me he isn't choosing the cakewalk.

He's choosing *me*.

If we ever had restraint, it's obliterated now.

I tug at his clothes desperately, wanting them *off*. He's working at my T-shirt, snarling to get it over my head without breaking the kiss.

It's a little hilarious, but I'm not laughing when I feel his teeth pulling my bottom lip.

One of us will win, sooner or later.

Eventually, there's no choice but to laugh with giddy delight. All the crazy emotion spills over into a haze of pure desire.

Weirdly, after telling him my life story, I feel lighter.

Like he's taken my burdens and locked them away in a dark cellar. Somewhere they can't escape and continue stripping me to the bone.

When he saw Harry, he didn't hesitate. He just charged in.

Then he kept demanding every rotten detail from me, and I gave them up like splinters torn from my skin.

That realization overwhelms me as I win the race to undress, yanking his shirt off over his head. My fingers land on a small fresh bruise blooming on his shoulder.

"Oh no. Don't tell me he—"

"Barely a bump. He elbowed me when I whipped him around. Forget about it, Sass," he insists, kissing me so hard I obey.

I try.

But the visible proof of how he cares makes me a special kind of crazy.

I'm not elegant, and I'm definitely not graceful right now—actually, I feel a little like an elephant playing Twister—but when he looks at me with his hair gloriously mussed, he's laughing.

"Come the hell here," he rasps, pulling me closer.

Skin.

So. Much. Skin.

Obviously, I've seen a naked man before. Not since Harry, admittedly, but I never intended for him to be my last. The few dates I've been on were so meh I couldn't bring myself to go to bed with mediocre men who might hurt me.

That trust thing really got me good.

But there's no nagging voice in the back of my head whispering a warning, telling me to stop right now.

Instead, that heat pooling between my legs becomes magma.

I grind against him like an animal in heat.

He groans into my mouth.

Hearing his desire deepens mine. My pussy throbs so much it hurts.

"Need these clothes off, woman. Now. Don't make me shred them with my hands," he mutters against my lips.

Holy hell, the great Brady Pruitt is impatient.

I guess I'm doing something right.

Honestly, it feels so good I wonder if just grinding alone will get me there. That's not supposed to happen.

I'm normally the kind of girl who needs a lot of focused attention to come. Or maybe I'm just a girl who's never been with a real man until now.

My hand falls between his legs, skimming over his jeans. What he's hiding makes me bite my lip.

Oh yes, he's *huge*.

We're talking tree-branch thick. I've never been a big size queen, but when I have such a small sample size to compare him to, I'm terribly curious.

Brady finally gets a good hold on my shirt and pulls it off over my head. He leans forward, sliding it off my arms.

Then he leans back and stares in awe.

"Fucking beautiful."

Oh my God.

I hate how red he paints me, even as I take the perfect opportunity to check him out.

I'm only human, and this man is *fine*.

His abs are model grade—though I'm half sure he's tensing, just to give me a better view.

They're weapons of mass destruction designed to ruin a woman's sense.

In the wrong hands, this human wall could stop armies. Or maybe inspire a legion of war-crazed women to fight. Think Helen of Troy in reverse.

My eyes follow that delectable trail of pure sculpted flesh leading to that chiseled V plunging down his pants.

"Is that all from the army? Or do you just work out four hours a day?"

He raises a brow. "You think I'd blow that much time in a gym?"

"I think that's the only way anyone could be this built."

He chuckles, and the sound vibrates through me, straight to my core.

But his eyes linger on my breasts. There's a dazed look to his gaze, like he's just woken up from a dream.

I know what's coming before he reaches out and swipes his finger over my bra, where my nipple peaks through the material.

"Glorious," he whispers.

"Underwhelming. If I knew this was happening, I'd have worn lingerie."

"A man always appreciates that, but don't get too stuck on the packaging. It's what's underneath that counts."

"Flattery. You're so terrible."

"It's the truth, Lena." He says it with such a serious look, I can't help but believe him.

Any other time, this is where I'd start having second thoughts. Maybe panicking a little.

But not with Brady.

His thumb glides over my hip, and even though the glazed look in his eyes hasn't fully disappeared, he says, "We can go slow, if you want."

Slow? After he's got me this worked up?

Biting my lip, I shake my head.

"Are you *trying* to kill me? We can do slow later." I roll my hips, watching as his eyes heat with pure blue sorcery.

"Deal."

This time when he kisses me, I feel my leash snap.

Our lips collide with frenzied determination, permission to be uncivilized.

I think he's burning, ready to claw his way out of his own skin just to ravage me.

I know I sure as hell am.

He reaches behind me to unclip my bra. His hands are greedy yet gentle against my skin.

I reach for his cock, loving how he curses, feeling how hard and thick he is. It's enough to make me smile against his mouth.

Then he cups my breast in his hand, and my smile fades.

"Fuck me, Brady," I whisper. I'm worried that I sound a little violent.

"Demolition, Sass. That's the plan, unless you've changed your mind." He gives me a wicked smile. "Last fucking chance."

I squeeze his cock again, and man—*oh man*—he is going to rearrange me from the inside out. I'm not sure I'll ever be the same, and I kinda don't care.

His free hand tracks a hot trail down my side to the waistband of my jeans.

"Lena," he rasps against my lips. "Tell me now."

"No. Absolutely not," I gasp.

"Then show me how soaked you are for my cock."

"Brady Pruitt, I thought you wanted slow?" I laugh against his mouth as I shift onto his lap, rocking my hips again. Just so I get the pleasure of hearing him groan with hellfire flashing in his eyes.

He groans again, and his hands land on my ass, squeezing so hard.

I giggle from the high.

God help me, I giggle.

It should be ridiculous and a little embarrassing, but really, it tells me how different this is. With Harry, sex was always this dark chore anchored in his satisfaction. I was an afterthought.

Sometimes before the breakup, he'd get up right after it was over and leave the room, telling me he had work to do with his internship.

This sweet teasing feels nothing like that.

This is pure revelry.

No man has ever made me laugh so much. Even when I'm so horny I might combust, Brady still has a direct line to my funny bone.

He leans back and meets my gaze, his eyes hot and heavy and dark.

He doesn't ask with words—not when his glance is so demanding.

Holding his gaze, I slide off his lap and stand in front of him. The blinds are down over his enormous windows for evening, but part of me wishes they were open.

Let the whole world see.

Let Seattle know that Brady Pruitt only has eyes for me.

I hook my thumbs under my pants, and his hand covers mine.

"Off," he orders.

My lips quirk up in a smile, slow and sensual.

A challenge?

I never could resist.

This man is about to find out *exactly* what kind of girl I want to be.

I bite my lip as I turn, wiggling my ass as I slowly ease my pants down with his big hand guiding mine. It would be better if I were wearing something genuinely sexy instead of slumming it in old jeans and a faded T-shirt, but from the way he inhales raggedly, I'd say it does the job.

My pussy aches.

I think if we stopped right now, I'd be deranged, tormented by the female equivalent of blue balls.

His eyes are fixed and hungry when I turn around to look at him, still sitting there with a bulge tenting his jeans.

Knowing how big that cock is, there's something even more powerful about the way I see his fingers twitch.

"Touch me?" I circle my nipples.

He licks his lips like a tiger.

Fingers shaking, I slide a finger between my legs, skimming over my mound, just enough to destroy him.

Holy hell, I'm wet. My panties have an annoying weight that makes me want them gone faster.

His gaze brands me from head to toe as he takes in his offering.

Then his hand slides between my legs, rough fingers pushing through drenched fabric, stroking my swollen pussy for the first time.

Stars.

My vision starts swimming with embers.

The shock makes my knees buckle.

"Yeah, baby girl. Just like that." I don't understand what he means until I realize he's holding me up.

He's supporting me, and I'm *grinding on his hand.*

His other hand goes to his erection, and he squeezes like it's physically hurting him. "My turn. Are you ready for this cock, Sass?"

Oh, I like that.

"Say that again," I whisper, stepping forward and kneeling between his legs. "And ask me *really* nicely."

"Sass, I asked if you were fucking ready." His breath skips as I undo his belt, then the top button of his jeans.

The zipper comes next, peeling his jeans open.

I slow down, deliberating, loving the hot need in his eyes.

When I eventually wrap my hand around the smooth velvet of his cock, we both groan.

Like I said, absolute monster.

Somehow, he's even bigger than he felt under me before. Veiny and thick and magnificent, a bead of moisture at the tip, a human battering ram made for punishment.

But have I been bad enough?

Have I made Brady Pruitt want to destroy me?

Bending down, I run my tongue up his shaft, instantly drunk on his taste. Earthy salt and skin.

His hips buck sharply.

"Fuck, Lena!" he rasps. His hand tangles in my hair, taking a handful.

It's intoxicating to have a man this big go boneless, unable to do anything but sit in front of me and take what I'm giving him.

His fingers pull my hair, guiding me down again, and I open my mouth, taking him in.

Or trying.

I'm lucky if I can get halfway down without choking.

My eyes burn from the way he occupies the back of my throat.

But the way he looks at me with feral restraint makes me feel beautiful. And so powerful, too, even if he's the one who's really in control.

I like having him in the palm of my hand.

"When I'm done," I say, spitting and pumping him with my hand. "I want you to bend me over and fuck me into the sofa."

"Careful, woman, or I *will* make you come so hard you forget your own name."

"Is that a promise?"

"Shit." He swears under his breath as I take him in my mouth again. "Solemn as a marriage vow."

The ludicrous thought makes me laugh all over again, and he smooths a thumb over my cheek. A silent reassurance that even though this has devolved into pure power play, he's still with me, willing to give and take.

"Whatever you need," he rumbles, his hips rolling as I run my tongue over his tip. "As long as you let me touch you."

It's been too long since I've been with a man.

As fun as toys are, they just don't hit the mark. But it's been so hard finding a man I trust.

"I think you know what." I rise, wiping my mouth as I go, and start to straddle him before I hesitate. "Have you been tested?"

"Regularly. All clear." He grimaces, one hand coming to my waist. "I don't know what you've heard, but I don't get around as often as people think these days."

"You used to." It's not a question.

"Yeah." He groans as I rub his swollen cock over my clit. I love seeing him like this. "I've cleaned up my party ways."

"Mm." I take his hand and bring it between my legs. "See what you do to me?"

"Fuck, so goddamn wet." With a quick glance to make sure I'm okay, he picks me up and turns me over, placing me down the way I asked.

Face down, ass up.

Waiting for nirvana.

I don't know why this has me panting.

Maybe it's the sensation of losing control to a wild animal.

Maybe I'm just that far gone, dying to quench a thirst I didn't know I had.

Maybe it's because there's something a little degrading in the air, and I love it.

But when I wiggle my ass at him, he laughs and slaps it gently, just enough to sting.

"Patience," he whispers.

"Brady, please. You know what I want."

"But I like my fireworks to last." His voice lowers as he sinks down, his breath hot against my pussy. "Let me watch you explode like a rocket, Lena. Let me hear you fucking come for me."

How can I possibly argue with that?

Especially when his tongue does expert persuading.

I never had a prayer.

He takes his sweet time with me, driving me deeper into the frenzy. Kissing, sucking, all tongue and teeth and varying pressure until I'm a mess of sensation.

When he pushes a finger through my wetness, I whimper.

And when he pushes a second finger inside, I feel the way my back arches.

My loud moan echoes off the ceiling.

Good thing this is a penthouse and we're alone, otherwise he'd have some very unhappy neighbors.

There's no way I can keep quiet.

I hear him growling his approval a second later, feeling the way the noise quakes through me.

His scruff gives the perfect friction as he buries my clit in his beard.

My hips writhe, wanting more, certain I'm close—I must be because my whole body pulses—and he eases back, not quite giving me enough.

"Brady." My voice is hoarse, pleading.

"Beg for it," he commands.

"If that's what it takes . . ."

I can feel his smile.

"Please, Brady. Please. Make me come!" I strain out as his finger circles my clit in this slow, killing rhythm.

"Say my name. I want to hear it."

"Brady," I moan, feeling his need building along with mine. "Brady, *please*."

His fingers grip my hips, my ass, as he licks me again, two fingers working, delving deep, stroking me so hard until I'm—

Coming!

It's flipping blinding, white stars exploding behind my eyelids like new suns.

I muffle my moans in his sofa cushions, gasping needy little breaths, breaking so beautifully.

And I say his name through the rapture.

I whisper it like a prayer, like he's the only thing that keeps me grounded.

My fingers unclench from the pillow as my orgasm fades. Brady presses kisses to every inch of bare skin he can find.

Ass, legs, up my back.

Famished, hot kisses that linger, even though I know he's dying to be inside me.

And even though I've just come, I want it too.

I shift, looking behind me, reaching for him. His cock jerks in my hand.

"Brady." One word. His name becomes a prayer.

There's the harsh sound of fabric sliding as he kicks off his jeans and boxers, and then the hot velvet of his cock presses against my pussy. Just the tip.

Oh God.

Oh God!

"Next time, I'll make you ride me to the damn moon and back," he promises.

I shiver at the implication that this won't be the only time. That he's only just getting started with me.

But after a frantic heartbeat, he pushes inside me with one brute thrust, and I arch my back. I cry out as delirium takes hold.

Holy shit! The fullness is overwhelming.

The stretch burns my inner walls.

And he's going deeper.

Deeper.

Undaunted, he groans, bending down to kiss my shoulders. His arm wraps around my waist, fusing me to him.

I relish the sensation so much I don't care if I have to breathe through the harsh pressure of having him inside me, almost buried to the hilt.

"Easy, Sass," he murmurs.

All it takes is a few seconds before the shock and discomfort turn to pleasure again.

"Do it," I spit, arching my neck. "Be rough with me. Take my hair in your fist. Fuck me like it counts."

The palm of his hand slides up my back, the softest feather caress before my hair finds his fist.

He makes a guttural noise as he pulls.

Yesss.

"More, more," I plead.

He draws back, though, holding my head up, tugging on my scalp and adding another sensation that blurs the line between pain and pleasure.

Then he thrusts back inside me, not stopping until he bottoms out.

Another liquid moan floods out of me.

His dick is everything, and so is that attitude.

Nothing else matters.

I want everything Brady Pruitt has to give me with that pummeling cock.

Just like this, holding me still, obeying the command of my body.

I want to be his undoing.

Judging by his uneven breathing, I wonder if I already am.

"Just like that," I urge as he picks up speed.

Sweat mists our skin.

Soon, the pleasure sweeps in, full and angry and too all-consuming to speak.

There's no sense that isn't dominated by him as he works deeper, faster, harder.

There's no nerve untouched as he makes me feel his power, his lust, animalistic and so intense I come again shamefully fast.

I'm barely coming down, lost in sex, feeling him using me like his personal toy.

There's just his hand in my hair, his cock pounding, and the loud, pained creak of the sofa as we almost break the thing.

No regrets.

As his hips punch faster, his free hand finds my clit. The movements are clumsy but still unspeakably good.

Another orgasm sweeps in, choking off my breath.

Because all it takes is that rough pressure to send me spiraling over the edge.

I spasm, convulse, and sputter.

And he holds me steady, never letting up his relentless rhythm, chasing my climax with more sensation. I hardly know where he begins and I end.

I just know I don't want it any other way.

"Lena," he gasps.

Then he stiffens, his thrusts turning wild, erratic, and I'm holding my breath.

I arch my back with a shuddering scream as he empties himself inside me.

I spend the night at Brady's.

Good thing, too, or I would've passed out before I ever made it home.

That was always his plan, I suppose, but after our sex marathon on the couch and again in the shower before we finished in his bed, it didn't feel right turning down warm sheets made like an Egyptian cotton cloud.

Also, if I went back to my house, I'd have to face Harry thoughts again, and who wants that?

Brady turned my insides into soup, and I was perfectly happy shutting out the world in favor of an escape.

Which he gave me.

Again and again and again.

By the time we finally emerge from his penthouse the next morning, I'm deliciously sore in a way I haven't felt for ages.

He takes my hand like it's a pure flex. And hell, after that, maybe it is.

The scary thing is that it *doesn't* scare me. My brain isn't racing with worries or doubts as I hold hands with him while we enter his private garage to pick up his sleek white custom Range Rover.

No driver today.

Just us.

I'll admit, it's kinda cute.

So is the way he opens the door for me and helps me up into the passenger seat.

"I love that you know how to treat a lady," I say as I duck inside.

"I'd better. The helping hand is part of the experience after I ruined you last night."

I can't help it—I laugh. Mostly because it's true, and he's such a cocky prick. But Brady knows that I know he has the package to back up his talk.

I'm trying so hard not to look like the dumb girl with fluttery eyelashes watching her first crush as he climbs in behind the wheel.

His sleeves are rolled up, and he's sporting that Apple Watch with the opulent gold wristband, but it doesn't bother me as much as it did before.

His money isn't everything. He's a good man, and good people are entitled to a few luxuries. It's a gorgeous watch too.

As queasy as I feel over the gaping difference in assets sometimes, I can't imagine him using his money in a controlling way.

Unlike some people I could mention. Brady isn't another demon in a skin suit possessed by pure greed.

He looks at me as he pulls out of the underground garage into the sunlight. "You're staring, Lena. Everything okay?"

"I just . . . I like you this way." I reach over and rub my knuckles across the scruff on his chin.

He smirks. "You haven't seen me any other way. Watch out."

"I internet stalked you, though. You were clean shaven back when you were busy breaking hearts."

"Mm, yeah. Guilty." He rubs his chin, his brow creasing when I mention his past.

"I prefer this look. Huge glow-up."

"I was planning on keeping the beard." He runs a hand over his jaw like he's considering how it would feel to not have it there. I don't think it's just the lack of facial hair that might bother him.

"You could always grow it longer, Viking boy," I tease. "I had a huge lady boner for Jason Momoa when I was in high school. Only reason why I could speak fluent nerd with the *Stargate* geeks."

"Loved that show. You had me sold before that, Sass." He grins. "I'm not about to crawl through portals to other galaxies, but I think I'd take dealing with aliens over my mother's shit if I walk in straight out of medieval Norway. Don't think she'd appreciate it if I tell her I'm living out the Scandinavian side of the family tree."

I smile.

"So, who's hotter now? Do I have a shot against Momoa?"

"As long as you keep the beard, it's a maybe," I tease.

"You're blushing, Sass."

"No." I scowl at him. "It's a warm morning, dude. That's it."

"Liar." He reaches over and pinches my chin, so effortlessly affectionate it makes my heart sputter. "I like turning you red, woman. Get used to it."

"Fair, I guess, when you're good at that." I look pointedly at his lap, where I can see the outline of a hard-on stirring.

His laugh bellows out, loud and unrestrained, the way I've only heard it when we're alone. None of his many social media clips ever show him laughing like this—free and unfiltered.

It's a shame.

In my opinion, this is his best look, even if I don't mind his darker face one bit when he turns growly and protective.

But as he cracks his window for fresh air as we hit the highway, I'm all butterflies.

This is Brady Pruitt at his finest.

Easy laughs. Wind in his hair. Dressed down with that smile crinkling his eyes.

"Where are we going, anyway?"

"Finsted's Farm. It's a longtime supplier, goes way back with the family company over fifty years. All organic too. Happy place, you'll see." He nods. "They're my go-to for help with sourcing ingredients for my dog food pilot program. They churn out quality and they really care, you know? Reasonable costs, about as fair as you can get. From a business perspective, it's ideal, if we can just get the damn formula right."

The frustrated look in his eye almost makes me laugh.

I toy with the ends of my hair, reading between the lines. Brady likes them because they care, but for his family, it sounds like it's all business.

So many lines drawn in the invisible sand between them.

Us and them.

Him and them.

We're quiet for most of the drive, which takes us over an hour north into the Skagit Valley. Finsted's Farm is a quaint little name for a rustic place dripping charm, not far south of Anacortes and just far enough away that when we pull up in the yard, there's no hint of anything but green country in the air.

I breathe deeply and smile.

A dirt track leads to the farmhouse, forking off toward what look like several big milking sheds. Chickens wander in random paths through the large yard with patches of mud, a huge green space that fades into the vast fields beyond.

The goats bleating in a corral just past the whitewashed wooden house are too cute for life.

Just like he did before we set off, Brady circles to my side of the vehicle and opens the door for me. I give him just enough time to get out of the way before I'm bolting over to the goats for a closer look.

By the time I reach their fence, I'm laughing my dumb head off.

They're munching away on grass and brush. One looks at me with his beady gold eyes like he can't believe I'd dare interrupt his mealtime.

This place feels so peaceful.

I see what Brady means by *happy place*. It's a good farm, old-school looking, not one of those mass factory farms where misery opens a line to hell just to keep modern civilization running.

A fearless chicken walks up to investigate my shoe. It cocks its head and pecks once before deciding there's better food elsewhere.

Brady stands by my side, hands in his pockets. For a long moment, we just enjoy the scenery, taking in the pretty mountains in the distance, shrouded in wispy clouds.

A rough-looking grey-and-white farm cat slinks past, watching us cautiously. I kneel down and wag my fingers, whispering encouragements that make Brady laugh.

"You'll want to watch out for George," a voice says from behind us. "He'll chew your fingers up if you dare show him any affection. He's a mean old tomcat but the best we've got for chasing rats."

We turn to see a middle-aged woman in rubber boots and mud-specked jeans, beaming at Brady at she chews gum.

Guess no one's immune to his charm.

They hug, and she immediately turns to me.

"Wendy Finsted," she says, holding out a callused hand. "Guess you must be the famous fiancée? Hell of a pleasure to meet the gal who could lock down this troublemaker."

"Famous? Oh no, I—"

"Don't play it modest, lady. The whole state knows by now. Half the women at the diner won't shut up about it this week." She laughs and pulls me into a hug. She smells faintly like straw and horse and mud, but it's not unpleasant. "Glad to finally meet you!"

I wonder what Brady thinks now, watching someone who's clearly important to him meeting me like we're really engaged.

There are far more people we're fooling than his parents, in the end.

Does it make his stomach feel as unsettled as mine?

"You guys here for the horses first?" she asks cheerfully, gesturing over her shoulder with her thumb. "They're right this way."

"Um—" I glance at Brady, but he just smiles and nods. There's something pure about the way he looks out here. Despite all the money and class he's been raised with, it's like he belongs to the great outdoors and the mud.

"Sure, let's say hello," he says. "You ridden a horse before, Lena?"

"Oh man. Not for years, but . . . I can give it a go."

"That's the spirit! I'll bring you our best," Wendy says cheerfully. "You two wait here while I bring 'em around. Maybe you can get a few shots in for your socials, Brady?" She winks. "Every trip's business with him."

I have no idea how he's managed to make friends with these folks, but when she leaves, I lean in and whisper, "Does *everyone* just love you?"

"Everyone but my old man. With Wendy, I don't mind. We go way back."

I have to repress a laugh, smothering it in my cuff.

"It's a nice place. The air alone out here is heaven." I lean against the fence, careful not to leave my fingers too close to a goat watching me warily.

"I love visiting."

"I bet." I nudge his side. "Especially if they let you ride around whenever you like."

He smiles, catching my hand and folding it in his.

"Wendy offers riding lessons here. Whenever she puts me on a horse and I post about it, she always sees a bump in bookings."

"Mm, that's cool." I remember seeing the pictures now.

Which means that I also know he looks ridiculously good on a horse. This man is wasted behind a desk, and I'm so glad his ventures keep him out in the world.

"So, really, she's getting more out of the relationship than you."

"No. They can grow organic produce and raise grass-fed beef at prices no one else in western Washington can touch. For us, that means cheaper ingredients, less shipping, and hopefully an answer to my cost-control problem."

I chew my lip, looking at him. This is the most detail I've heard about his new company.

Of course, I know what he's trying to do is difficult. But it's different hearing how hard it's been, how much thought must go into a project that sounds deceptively easy.

"Do you think you're making progress?" I ask quietly.

"Hope so. Last taste trials didn't go so well with the dogs. Too much barley. Let's just say they weren't impressed." He looks behind me and waves as he sees Wendy leading two horses into the yard.

Horses aren't my specialty. I think Pawsome Hearts has only ever had two visits in the time I've worked there, and both from riders passing through and needing a quick checkup before getting back on the road. But from what I can tell, these guys look like good specimens.

Tall, muscular, healthy, they follow along as gentle as lambs after Wendy.

"Here you are," she says. "All saddled up and ready to ride."

I eye the horse she's offering me. It snorts gently.

"This one's Silver. We love her to bits, and she's very docile," she says as I take the reins. The horse's coat is silver grey and beautiful, true to her name.

That bodes well.

"Storm, nice to see you again," Brady says, delighted. He presses a kiss to the horse's soft nose and swings up into the saddle.

It's almost obscene how good he is at this—the way he leaps up like a born cowboy. This is far from his first rodeo, I'm sure.

I wish I was that lucky.

I think I was seven the last time I was on a horse.

Wendy takes the reins and puts a hand on my back to steady me as I try to climb up as deftly as Brady.

It does not go well.

Just when I think I'm almost there, my foot slips, skidding out from under me as I try to find my balance. My other foot in the stirrup immediately jerks free.

Even Wendy's flailing can't save me from falling on my ass.

Right in the big puddle of mud just off to the side, a couple feet away.

And this is good old-fashioned muck, spraying my face and sticking to my side like thick paint.

Brady jumps down to help me up, asking if I'm hurt.

I shake my head.

When I stand up, I'm a sputtering mess of apologies, still trying to sort up from down.

I'm so out of it I barely notice the gate down the gravel road swinging open and a fancy black car pulling in beside Brady's a few seconds later.

"Damn, Lena, you're lucky the mud broke your fall. You could've gotten banged up pretty good."

"Lucky, yeah. I've had worse. At least it's not projectile puppy vomit."

But the smile fades from his face as he lifts me to my feet, and I don't think it's just my little accident. He's looking past me at the vehicle pulling up.

I recognize that face.

That face last showed up right before Nancy Loomer barged into his condo. My blood heats.

Holy hell, if it's her again, following us all the way out here, I swear I'm not above giving her a nice big mud ball to the face.

Brady doesn't seem guarded, though. He just flashes me a strained smile as the back door of the car opens and out steps an elegant foot clad in a black heel.

Then comes the rest of one of the most glamorous women I've seen in real life. She's wearing oversize shades and burgundy lipstick deep enough to highlight her face.

Everything about her seems designed to impress.

But as she stares at me, one hand moving to the arm of her sunglasses so she can lift them to her dyed dirty-blond hair, I have the weirdest knot in my belly.

Brady's hand presses lightly against the small of my back.

Oh no, what is this?

The world starts spinning, even before he speaks.

"Mom," Brady says as she approaches. "I wasn't expecting you this early."

"I can see that," she says, the curl of a smile touching the corner of her mouth.

"Lena, this is my mother, Kerrigan Pruitt." He sends me what I think might be a warning glance. "Mom, meet Lena. My fiancée."

XIV

THREE DOG NIGHT

(BRADY)

Shit.

Shit!

There's no universe where I'd ever choose *this* introduction.

Too bad the universe doesn't give a flying shit and it's made the choice for me.

The worst part is, I'm the idiot who put the wheel in motion.

Originally, I intended for this to be an organic meetup, a way to introduce Lena and Mother, but not like this.

Not with my fake fiancée covered in mud, panic filling her eyes as she realizes exactly what's going on.

One quick glance tells me she's as thrown off as I am by the timing.

She's also covered in muck, painting one side of her body.

To my relief, she manages a smile.

It's the one she uses with her clients—professional and kind, designed to put people at ease.

It's also the biggest guilt-kick to my balls in recorded history.

"Hi, Kerrigan. You, um, you caught me at a rough time." Lena checks her hands before offering Mom the clean one. "Sorry for the mess. This isn't how I normally do my mud treatments."

Mom laughs. Surprisingly, she doesn't hesitate as she squeezes Lena's hand.

"I appreciate your humor. A pleasure. Especially when you're accompanying my son to his favorite place in the world."

Lena gives back a pained smile.

"Still. Sorry about the rough first impression," Lena says weakly.

"Oh, no. Your grace would shame me if I was in your shoes, darling. It never was my strong suit, was it, Brady?" She leans in to give me a kiss on the cheek. "He's the only one in this family brave enough to climb on a horse. Lord knows my father tried when I was a little girl, but one minute in and I'd be a crying fit."

"Just Brady, huh? His father doesn't ride?" Lena sounds genuinely curious.

"Ha! I think Alec would opt for a crowded water park rather than climb any creature that can't read an investment portfolio." Now, it's Mom's turn to laugh.

I'm officially gobsmacked.

This whole situation could've gone down a million times worse. I can finally breathe, rolling my shoulders.

Both women talk warmly, apparently determined to make the best first impression they can under the strange circumstances.

That's one giant fucking disaster averted.

Wendy hands off the horses to a stable-hand.

"Why don't you guys come inside the big house and clean up?" she offers. "We'll get you decent again. Would you like some coffee, Kerrigan? We've got that stuff from Kona you always love."

"You're a dear, but I'll take some mint tea, if you have it. I'm watching my caffeine."

"Of course!"

I slide my hand through Lena's. She grins as I wince at the mud coating her palm.

"How screwed am I? Be honest," she whispers as we follow Wendy through the side of the farmhouse.

"Less screwed than any girlfriend I ever brought around before. You're acting human, and that's the important part."

"*Fiancée*, Brady," she hisses. "That's way bigger than some date."

"Fake fiancée," I growl. "Yeah, shit. Seeing as you're the first woman I put a ring on, you've set the bar pretty high. But don't let it go to your head."

I just wonder if I'm following my own advice when it's too easy to forget this is fake, dammit.

"Holy shit, the ring!" Her eyes bulge as she holds her hand up and stares at it miserably. "Can they even *clean* this?"

I take her dirty hand and bring it to my lips, gently clasping the muddy ring with my finger.

"The jeweler I went to can work miracles. Don't worry."

"That's a relief." She flashes me a laughing look as we step inside.

"I'm sorry as hell for skipping the warning, though. Feel free to murder me later."

"No—what? Are you telling me you set this up? I thought it was a coincidence!"

Guilt slams into my gut again.

"The mud was a coincidence. Meeting my mother . . . I put a little more thought into that," I admit.

Her face heats as she pulls her hand back, then flicks mud in my face. Probably the least I deserve.

"Right. So, setting up a nice surprise meeting between your mom and me was the whole point of this outing? And you didn't think to *tell me*?"

"I knew you'd stress if you found out in advance. Didn't want to put you through a whole thing like the engagement announcement again."

"Brady! I'm stressed *now*." Her face is flushed, but she can't help smiling bitterly behind her scowl.

"I thought it would be better to introduce my mom somewhere casual. Somewhere you can both—"

"If you're about to say somewhere we could both make a good impression, do you even see this?" She waves a hand at the mud she's scraping off her jeans before we head inside. "I wish you would've warned me. I never would've tried to get on that horse."

"How was I supposed to know you'd fall, Sass?"

Her eyes are lasers.

She pierces me with a glare so fierce I chuckle and hold up my hands.

"Okay, fine. If it helps, I'll give you a list of places to dump my body once you're done dismembering it."

Rolling her eyes, she huffs a breath and turns back to the bottom of her shirt, which is smeared with yet more mud on the inside.

"At least it's just mud and not horseshit," I whisper.

She's so not amused.

I sincerely hope the animal smell around here isn't just concealing it, though. I wouldn't be surprised by *that* either.

"Well, what am I supposed to talk about? Tell me," she hisses, rinsing out the hem of her shirt with a nearby hose. "Your mom is . . ."

"Just another human obsessed with her appearance. Pretty old-fashioned. Talk to her about animals. She loves them. Trust me, she's easier to win over than my old man."

Lena grunts. "You wanted real, huh? You've got enough to choke."

I run a hand up and down her spine as she works out more mud. For all her big talk, she's handling this well.

If this were Nancy, or any of the girls I dated in the past, they'd have lost their shit and dialed their freak-outs to eleven.

They wouldn't have even humored staying here to get cleaned up. They'd be demanding to go home, and I probably wouldn't hear from them for two weeks after.

But this is Lena Joly.

She's more rattled by my stupidity than a dirty mishap. Even though she should be tossing my severed head into the stables, she's giving this her best shot.

Once her clothes are clean enough to stop dripping mud, I wrap an arm around her waist and press a kiss to the side of her head.

"Come on," I say. "Let's go inside."

I walk Lena in and show her to the bathroom so she can wash up better.

Later, we find Mom in Wendy's living room, her hands wrapped around a mug of what smells like herbal tea.

Wendy bustles away to make us two coffees and give us a little space.

"So, Brady tells me you work at a veterinary clinic," Mom says, smiling gently at Lena. I warned her before she arrived that she needed to be nice. No claws and zero venom.

"Yes, I'm a nurse there." She looks at the sofa next to Mom. "I'd sit, but . . . I really need a change of clothes."

"Everyone loves her. Pets and humans," I interject, stepping by her side and wrapping an arm around her shoulder.

"Actually, pets love me more than people do. The clients can be rough." Lena shuffles so her shoulder presses against mine. "Or maybe I've just never gotten over my soft spot for animals."

"That's understandable. People can be so difficult," Mom says agreeably. "We always wanted a puppy or a nice cat when Brady was growing up. But Alec—my husband—he's never been particularly fond of having animals in the house."

Huge understatement. I don't think there's anything he likes less than the day he collapsed and he was put on oxygen.

Some people have a wake-up call with a health scare.

Not my father. If anything, the crisis only amplified his worst qualities.

"That's a shame, but it's not for everyone," Lena says politely.

"How many pets did you have growing up?"

"Not a lot, exactly, but . . ." She smiles, pursing her lips. "When I was growing up in my little house, there was this old stray cat who just sort of found us. He showed up one day when I was playing outside, and then he never left. And when I say old, I mean *old*. Only had one eye, so many health problems. My parents warned me they didn't have much money and we'd probably have to say goodbye anytime. We called him Ambrose."

Hell yes, I'm smiling.

I can see it now, clear as day. Little Lena, caring for this ancient, ragged beast the rest of the world would've left for dead. Loving him despite the impossible.

This woman is a treasure, and I hate that her kindness ever allowed a fucking snake like Harry Jay to leave scars on her soul.

"We all thought every day was his last, but despite everything, he kept going. He was with us for five years, and they were so good." Her smile drops a little. "There were a few times when Mom was sure it was the end of the road. She wanted to put him down and end his suffering, thinking he wouldn't get any better. But he did every time I convinced her. In the end, he was comfortable and I—I loved Ambrose a lot."

She's a little choked up at the end.

I pull her in, kissing her head, not caring about a few specks of dirt that wind up on my lips.

"I bet." Mom leans forward, her eyes bright, clearly touched by the story. "Animals are like that, always able to mean so much without saying a word. They get under your skin, and then you'd do anything for them." She smiles at me fondly. "People are like that, too, of course, but they're so much harder to find."

"You talking about Dad or me?" I snort.

"Both, darling. Between the two of you, it's remarkable I don't have more grey hair and lines under my eyes." She winks at Lena. "Not that I'd ever let them show. Aging gracefully isn't one of my virtues. I plan to fight old age tooth and nail."

Lena laughs, and I let her lean against me, both of us relaxing. My hand finds hers and squeezes.

How is this going so well?

Mother doesn't fake her true feelings much when she's not impressed, and if she's already joking about herself, that's a damn good sign.

If Mom's determined to like her, and Lena can handle being liked, I'm confident we won't be derailed anytime soon.

Wendy returns with more drinks—tall glasses of lemonade we sip while Mom peppers Lena with more questions about her work. What she thinks about every cat, dog, turtle, parrakeet, and hedgehog under the sun, and how she got into it.

Casual questions, but assessing.

She might be the more open-minded one compared to my father by a mile, but she's still searching, trying to see if Lena's truly *good enough*.

It's not just the old money factor.

It's that invasive way mothers have when they think they know what's best for their kids. Particularly when their sons have bad habits and a whole history of idiocy to their name.

Even though Mom is pretty decent with respecting my boundaries and letting me make my own choices—and lots of damn mistakes over the years—she isn't immune to checking in, with love.

Once our glasses are empty, Lena frowns and glances around. "I think I left my jacket by the laundry. I'll be back in a second."

"Of course," Mom says. The moment Lena leaves the room, she turns to me. "I like her. She's very authentic. Down to earth, obviously kindhearted. Exactly the kind of centering feminine energy you need."

"Again with the energy talk?" I scoff. "I don't need centering, Mother."

"Regardless, she's good for you, Brady. Don't let her get away."

"Can't argue with that."

"But you should get the poor dear home and truly cleaned up. I feel awful, making her stand here and chitchat while she's soaked to the bone. No young girl should be that dirtied up and stressed out when she's meeting her future mother-in-law."

"This wasn't the plan, Mom." I smile, feeling a success—and also no point in pushing it further. "Thanks for coming out here and humoring me. Lena loves this farm, too, mud and all."

"I'm so glad I got to meet her. I think I'll slip out before she's back so there's no pressure to entertain me. I'm going to that little orchard up the road, the one with the cider your father loves." She rises and gives me a kiss on my cheek. "Now go get your girl."

That's one hurdle down. With Mom on our side, it'll be easier to prod Dad into accepting our arrangement without wanting to strangle me.

He might pretend he's emotionally dead to the world and Mom doesn't influence him, but she's the one who rules the roost.

Mostly because she's become an expert at pushing his buttons over the years, including the ones for logic and whatever little dregs of human emotion he has left.

I find Lena while she's grabbing her jacket, and steer her outside, giving Mom's orchard excuse as a reason to leave.

Mostly, I'm greedy to have her to myself again.

Didn't think sleeping with her would change so much, but I was wrong.

It's not just the harsh desire churning in my blood, hounding me to ravish her again, especially if she needs a shower and she doesn't lock me out.

I fucking wish it was just that.

No. With her, everything feels like a cotton candy adrenaline rush, and I'm chasing that high.

I couldn't control the thoughts that flooded me after we fucked either. The ones still knocking around my head even after the drama today.

"You're sure you want to rush out like this?" she asks, glancing behind me to where Wendy and Mom are still visible in the living room, chatting away.

Mom doesn't have quite the same fondness for this place I do, but she and Wendy have always been friendly.

"I'm sure. She's got cider on the brain, and you'd be crazy to delay her."

"But I should say goodbye."

I rub the base of her neck softly. "Sass, we should escape while we can. No need to push our luck when we're ending on a good note."

"Oh? You don't think I can handle it?" She fires me an arched glance.

"I think we both have to handle this lie like it's made of glass. Why risk a slipup and shatter it now?"

My phone buzzes, and I grab it from my pocket.

Luis, checking in to let me know he's done following up with my nutrition team for the day. They'll have a new report for me by tonight for our next trial formula.

For a second, I hesitate.

Then I look at Lena again, at the uncertainty on her face, and I wonder if I put it there. Or was it there long before me?

That bitter doubt, caked on her heart, just like the mud, by a man who isn't nearly as innocent as Silver the horse.

I need dirt on Harry Jay. Start digging, I text.

On it. His reply comes a second later.

There must be something I can do to pry him off Lena's back. To put her mind more at ease so she knows he'll never trouble her again.

"We need to play it safe when we're just starting out. I don't want to blow it, and I don't want to make this harder for you," I tell her, stuffing my phone away.

"For me?" Her expression sobers, though I don't mention Harry's name. "It's really not that bad. Jesus, Brady. I'm already over what happened yesterday—"

"That pretty face says otherwise," I say gently.

"Brady—"

"Don't fight me on this, okay? And don't try to minimize what happened. That savage fuck doesn't deserve the courtesy." I haven't forgotten the haunted look in her eyes when she told me how he'd posted those videos online—the revenge porn—like she was never anything more than a sick joke to him.

My blood boils like steaming tar.

"You're sweet, but you're testing my patience. I don't need you to fight my battles," she whispers, looking up defiantly.

Those eyes have no end when they catch the light. Prisms of cocoa and amber.

She's so goddamn beautiful it hurts.

"Think of it as me fighting *with* you. Shoulder to shoulder, shield to sword. It's past time you had someone in your corner, Sass. You can fight, but why should you have to do it alone?"

Just when I think she'll argue back, her shoulders slump.

"Maybe. Just . . . don't do anything stupid without running it by me first, okay?"

"Understood."

"Do you still have my address?"

"Yeah." We climb in the car, and I pull up the history on my dashboard screen. Before taking this on, I did some hunting.

I know more about her than anyone should.

Not the revenge videos, and they wouldn't have changed my mind. But her address. Her phone number. Her voter registration.

Scary how easy it is for someone with money and connections to strip people naked.

Scarier because if I have her info, then Harry Jay surely has it too. And there's no damn way I'm letting her face him alone.

It's not that I don't think she's capable—we both know she is.

This is about leveling the playing field.

That's the last time the bastard thinks he can pick on a defenseless young woman, dragging her back to the hell he caused.

The long drive down the highway is mostly silent, and as we approach Seattle, she fumbles around in her bag for her keys.

"It's not the nicest place," she says anxiously. "Nothing like your palace, I mean."

"I've seen it before. You don't need to apologize. It's a nice little house."

"It's just . . ." Her mouth opens and closes. "Okay."

"Good. Let's get you home so you can have a hot shower."

In ten or fifteen minutes, I'm walking through her front door. I notice her stop in the doorway and how her eyes dart around, making sure there aren't intruders.

That makes two of us, and not just because of Harry Jay's shit.

At this point in my life, it's second nature to be wary. Always watching for cameras, for corporate spies from rival brands after Pruitt Ag. Someone always looking for their next viral story, because I turned my face to scratch my nose and it looked like I was fishing for boogers.

Once the door's unlocked, she ushers me in.

Her house is small, a little cramped with books everywhere and scented candles lining small shelves in the living room. I spy a Kindle on top of a small stack of books next to the sofa—all romance paperbacks—and smile a little.

Some of these books look filthy. I've known enough girls to figure out that the dirtiest books hide under the covers with pretty flowers and mountain sunsets.

"Want a beer?" she asks a little nervously, gesturing to her kitchen.

"Sure. We just survived death by Mom, and that's reason to celebrate." I sink down on the sofa, sensing she wants to do this shit herself. "She does like you, you know."

"I still can't believe you didn't warn me. Jackwagon." She gives me a dirty look.

"But you'll forgive me, won't you? You're sugar and spice, Sass. Not a vengeful bone in your body."

"I'll show you vengeful, stupid man." She rolls her eyes, but I see the corner of her cheek curve. "Don't be so cocky."

"Am I wrong?" I nudge a book with my toe. "This is some interesting reading material, by the way."

"What can I say? I like smut." She shrugs so nonchalantly it takes a second to sink into my head.

And when it does, I laugh.

Then I think about her in bed, some toy buzzing between her legs, biting her lip as she comes like a dream.

I also get pissed that I'm not there to push the toy away, to replace it with a dick that brings her off leagues better than any vibrator.

Shit, maybe I need to start reading more.

She smirks as she hands me a beer. "What's wrong? You look like I knocked you over the head with a mallet."

"Just imagining what makes you tingle in those books," I tell her.

"Oh, you know. The usual. Fun times with firefighters and lumberjacks and guys who are *really* good with their hands." There's no hint of shame in her gaze as it meets mine.

I laugh, and she smiles, too, her earlier embarrassment gone as she sips her beer.

I raise my bottle in a toast and say, "Here's to everyone loving you as much as my mom did."

"Pffft, you're exaggerating. She wasn't that impressed."

"I don't exaggerate. She said you're perfect for me, which is basically the best compliment my mother can give."

Lena smiles again, her lips curving, stealing my attention. My bottle taps my teeth. "Only because she thinks her son is perfect. How well does she know you?"

"Your implication wounds me."

"You're the one who keeps coming back to expectations."

"Yeah. Guess she's happy I'm finally settling down with someone who isn't made of drama," I admit. "But she has standards. My mother wouldn't be happy if it was just anyone."

"Minus the fact that she was pulling for Nancy, you mean?"

"Nancy was a political choice, and an old family friend. They never put much thought into it."

"Hmm." Lena traces the rim of the bottle with her lips, thinking. "Do they really not see it? The entitlement on that bitch?"

"It's complicated." I sigh, because thinking about Nancy never puts me in a good mood. "They're just concerned about appearances over everything. They saw an easy solution and ran with it."

"That's a fancy way of saying they either don't notice or don't care."

"Can't argue with that. My parents will never be normal, and I think you know that." I lean over, my lips close to hers. "Happy now?"

"Brady." She eyes me thoughtfully, heat staining her cheeks red.

"Yes?"

"You kept talking about safety first and precautions."

"What about them?" If she's going to fight me on this, she's about to lose.

"What do they involve?"

Spending every second of every day in your company. Preferably with empty balls.

Unhealthy. Stupid.

Yet tempting just the same.

"Why?" I ask carefully.

"Because I thought, if you wanted to—and there's no pressure—maybe you'd want to spend the night here." Her blush strays down her neck. "I know my place isn't fancy, and the bed isn't like imported Egyptian cotton, but—"

Before she can finish the sentence, she's over my shoulder.

If she wants a lumberjack, I will *give* her one tonight.

"Brady! Are you serious?" she squeals.

"So serious, I waited for this all day," I growl.

"Even after this morning?"

"*Especially* after this morning. You think I didn't want to follow you into the bathroom at Wendy's house and clean you up with my tongue?"

Her laugh turns into a gasp as I throw her on the bed.

In contrast to the living room, which is filled with books, her bedroom is small and neat, which makes me smile. For all her bluster about being a hot mess, she's well organized.

I barely give the environment a second glance before I turn my attention back to her.

"I hope you know how beautiful you are." I kiss the skin of her collarbone, pulling down her shirt, and she shivers. "I want to take my time with you."

"I have neighbors. We might as well share a wall with how close they are. And I still haven't showered yet."

"Then you'll just have to shut it, won't you? And I'll have to fuck you again while you clean up." I flash her a wicked smile.

Her nipples are already pebbled, and I tweak them with my fingers. She gasps, fastening it behind her teeth. I scrape my teeth over the flimsy material of her tee.

"You know the drill," I whisper. "You want me to slow down, I will. But I don't think you do."

"Keep fucking going," she pleads.

"Fucking. Right," I rumble into her skin.

"I trust you. Remember that." I reward her by pressing my mouth against the hollow of her throat, practically tasting the flutter of her heartbeat.

"You can trust me. I've got you."

"It's almost too easy. It's scary."

"You can tell me to stop anytime."

"But I don't want you to." She shifts under me as I kiss her again. "God, don't stop, Brady."

That's good, because even though my head tells me to lay off her and give her space, my cock has different ideas.

Appalling ones.

"What sort of smut do you read?" I growl into her ear, resting my body against hers. Gently at first, then with more pressure when she doesn't flinch away.

"Mm. Depends on the book. Sometimes it's funny and adorable. Sometimes it's pure filth wrapped in a pretty cover."

"I've seen those discreet covers. Got to keep your freak flag hidden?"

"Yes," she whispers.

Growling, I lift her shirt with my teeth, exposing bare midriff, and then pull it over her head.

There's so much I want to explore here, so much to kiss and suck and torment with my tongue.

I want her hands on me too. Especially when she moans like butter.

"Your turn. I want this off." She tugs at my shirt now.

"Take it, woman. Take what's yours."

Her laugh comes low and husky in a way that burns my balls.

Her little nails skim my bare skin, caressing my stomach as she takes my shirt and pulls.

I watch her big brown eyes go gratifyingly dark like rich amber.

Her fingers arc down lower to my pants, where she's about to find a hard-on so intense it could drive fucking nails through the wall.

She's done this before, yes, but now it feels less like an exploration and more like we're marking each other.

She's imprinting my body on her mind, and I love it.

"Pants," she says.

I roll off her and lie on my back, hands behind my head.

If she wants to lead, permission granted.

We both know who's really in control.

Hell, there's nothing sexier than a woman removing your clothes like you're a king, especially when she looks at you like you just hung the moon and the stars.

Jeans first.

She presses a hot, hungry kiss below my naval as she unbuttons them and works down my zipper, gliding her fingers over my bulge.

I suck in a breath.

Her eyes find mine, all honey brown past the dark of her pupils, almost gold.

I'm no poet, but even a literary idiot like me could write goddamn sonnets if she asked.

"You like that?" She trails another nail down my erection, featherlight.

My cock throbs violently against her touch.

"You know I do." I smirk at her. "Do it again."

"First, I want to see what it's like when Brady Pruitt gets teased." Still holding my gaze, she removes her light-pink bra. It's another sensible, everyday bra.

How does something so basic make me unhinged?

A little too wild. A lot reckless.

With Lena, I have to stay focused.

Even if it feels like I'm drenched in gasoline and she's holding the match, hovering the flame over me, smiling with delight because she can burn me down in a second.

Fuck.

As I watch her, she takes my hand and places it on her waistband.

She doesn't need to ask twice. Not with words.

I'm lightning—a little too fast, maybe—ripping the sheer material of her pastel pink panties as I yank them down her legs and fling them aside.

I breathe deep, feeling my nostrils flare as her scent fills the room.

Honest to God, I could bury myself in her wet little cunt for days.

Then I twist around, throwing her underneath me in one hungry movement, spreading her legs with mine.

"Open your legs and give it up, Sass. That sweet pussy's mine."

Growling, I plunge my fingers into her.

She's all slick heat. I knew that from the damp spot on her panties, but feeling her silky smoothness against my fingers makes my blood storm.

A second later, I'm damn near grinding against her thigh, but she doesn't mind. Especially when I take her nipple between my teeth.

I bite down.

Not too much, but hard enough so she knows I'm not playing.

She squirms delightfully, whimpering, her body shifting to give me more access, eager for my cock.

It isn't fair.

How did I waste so many years in my prime before I found her?

"You're tight as hell today," I whisper against the damp skin of her collarbone. I rub my thumb against her clit until she shudders, moaning loudly in my ear.

"R-right there. Brady, don't stop!"

"Never. Not until you come so hard for me, sweetheart. Not until you see stars."

Her fingernails dig into my back as I keep going, drawing those perfect nipples into my mouth and sucking hard, one at a time.

This is it.

Absolute feminine perfection.

She tightens around my fingers, her breath ragged and face flushed, brown eyes shining like jewels.

"Not yet," I snarl.

"Brady!" Her voice is a whine.

"Quiet, brat." I nip her skin, then kiss it. "Wait for me."

Her pussy clenches around my fingers as I slow my thumb strokes on her clit to a crawl.

"Wait for *what*?" She shifts again, grinding against me, desperate like she'll blow if she can just find the pressure to tip her over the edge.

"I want you to come on my cock."

This time, she shudders until her eyes roll in the back of her head.

It's the sexiest damn thing I've ever seen.

"I need . . . I need . . ." She moans loudly, her long lashes fluttering.

"Not yet. Patience." I pull my fingers out and suck them, giving her thigh a gentle slap.

She throws her head back and sighs so hard I almost laugh.

Like it or not, I'm training her.

Good things come to good girls who wait.

And I like the thought of unloading deep inside her even more while her hot little pussy squeezes my cock.

The thought sends lust stabbing through me. As fun as this might be, I'm not made of infinite patience.

Definitely not with Lena in my arms, wet and willing and so achingly close. Her eyes take up half the real estate on her face. Her mouth takes up the other half right now, those lush lips slightly parted.

I give her no warning before I shift my position and slide inside.

All the way home.

My thumb slips into her mouth, making her taste herself.

Her entire body tenses. Her back arches.

She's on pleasure autopilot as her mouth closes softly around my thumb and her tongue flicks across the pad.

So damn tight, so hot, so *good.*

No exaggeration, I could live in her for days.

Lena wraps her arms around my neck and pulls intently, bringing my face to hers for a searing kiss.

I give her what she wants for now as I push my cock in, pumping hard, letting rhythm take over, muffling the sounds of her pleasure with my mouth.

Soon, she's tightening around me, her whole body humming as her climax nears.

I push up on my arms to bring this home.

Her legs wrap around my waist, urging me on, but I want to see her when she goes off. I want to see her face breaking with the exquisite chaos I've made.

Call it stupid. Some primal monkey-brain shit I can't control.

But when she comes, I want her looking me in the eye, knowing I'm the man who ruined her.

Permanently, I hope. I'm a jealous, deranged fuck, and the thought of her ever having anyone else makes me insane.

And I need her to know it.

I *need* her to feel me branding her for life.

"Brady." She gasps my name, and I fucking love it. "I'm close."

"Look at me, Sass. Eyes up here." I reach down between us, drawing slow circles on her pussy even as I'm pounding her.

"Brady!"

"Not yet. A few more seconds."

Her lips part, teeth clenched, and she's falling so hard she's about to go to the center of the earth.

But not *too soon*.

Not before I'm done fucking her.

"Brady, I-I can't—" She draws in a ragged breath, and that's when she fractures.

I don't ease up, slamming into her, pressing my hand over her mouth as she cries out. I think her small twin bed is about to break, creaking like hell, but I'm too far gone to care.

Her pussy spasms around my cock, but her eyes stay open, fixed on me, so I can watch her demolished with every sharp flick of pleasure across her face.

I've never seen anything so goddamn glorious in my life.

The second she's done, I ease my hand off her mouth and lean in to kiss her again, whispering how beautiful she is.

My hips keep going, mindlessly driving to my nut, not giving her space to breathe.

"Good girl," I growl in her ear before I kiss her.

Even as her breaths sharpen and her chest heaves and her nails bite my skin, another frenzied release building in her, she doesn't tell me to stop.

I'm not an idiot.

I don't have a magic cock.

But there's something damn satisfying about seeing her body react to mine. So slick, so wet, and already fighting for more.

Christ, is she about to come again?

"Fuck, Brady," she whimpers.

Her mind is gone.

I think she could recite the dictionary during sex, and I'd be into it like it's the dirtiest talk ever.

"Are you going to come for me again?"

"I don't know." She tosses her head restlessly, hair tangled against her sheets. "I can't usually, but—"

"Try."

Her breathing quickens, and she's panting now.

I keep rubbing with my fingers, slowing down a little so she has time to process the sensations. Grabbing a pillow, I push it under her ass, the better to delve deeper, stretching her to her limit.

"There. Right there!" Her eyes go white as they roll.

"Come, girl. Don't hold back," I mutter, fighting to stop myself from coming inside her.

Not yet, dammit.

There's no way I'm about to finish before she loses it again.

Even if it means I have to go over the multiplication table and the ancient Greek I took on a whim at school.

Whatever happens, I don't let up, my hips working like a demon, a single-purpose machine designed to break her.

"I think—" Her eyes snap open. Fuck, I'm losing it, the pressure building at the base of my spine. The moment it moves to my balls, it's all over. "I think I can."

"Now, Lena!"

After a scalding moment, she stiffens, and I know I've won the secret battle with myself.

I've also beaten that greedy ratshit ex out of her brain, making her come like she never could with him.

"Yes, yes," she whimpers. "Brady, please!"

I couldn't hold back if I tried. The second her pussy clenches my cock like a fist, I'm gone.

My electric climax chases hers, turning me pure animal.

I empty myself in her with a roar, forgetting about her neighbors, forgetting about anything except this.

Except *her*.

That's new to me—this feeling of being turned inside out.

I've always enjoyed myself with sex, but this?

This is divine.

This is the music of the spheres made flesh.

This is the kind of spectacular fuckery that sticks under your skin like a bur, soul-deep and always reminding me it's there. As long as I can keep her.

My cock heaves for an eternity, wringing my balls out.

Then I collapse on top of her, into the warmth of her embrace.

We lie like that for a while—me bracing so I don't crush her and her limbs tangled with mine.

I can feel her heartbeat slow, and I'm sure she can feel mine too.

"Wow," she whispers, thoroughly exhausted.

"Yeah," I agree. *"Wow."*

"Is it just me, or was it better than last time?"

I press a kiss to her forehead, glazed with sweat. I want to tell her so many things, but they catch in my throat, so I just say, "Yeah. I've heard that happens when you know someone well."

And I *want* to get to know her.

It's ridiculous and unnecessary for the paid sham we're running, but I do.

She twists around until we're lying on our sides, facing each other. The unnatural flush has left her face now, mostly, but she's still glowing from exertion.

This might just be my favorite look on her.

"Your first time?" she teases.

"What? Do I look like a damn virgin to you?"

"Doing it more than once with the same girl, silly."

Laughter barks out of me, harsh and unexpected, and I brush my lips against hers.

"First time it's made me want to do it again so soon," I say.

She laughs, fingertips dancing against her jaw.

"How long do we have to wait?"

"Give me five."

Her eyelids flutter closed, though it's not that late yet. We haven't even had dinner.

I know the feeling. The whole day's slipped away, and I didn't get much sleep with her in my bed last night.

Tonight, I'm only going to get a few hours again.

Not that it bothers me.

For once, I'm not thinking about work or the dog food formula or my father slumped in his chair, angry and disapproving of every breath I take.

Tonight, it's just Lena and me, and that's all I want in my world.

Tomorrow, I'll worry about the impact—the feelings I shouldn't have slamming into my life like a screaming meteor.

XV

HAVING A LARK

(LENA)

Hello, disaster. My name is Lena.

It's the second time I'm waking up next to Brady Pruitt, and it feels like my heart is doing backflips.

It's official.

I'm *feeling* things.

Warm, gooey, butterfly-kissed things that no self-respecting woman should ever feel over an arrangement that's a total fraud.

This is fake.

Fake!

I scream it at my inner self, but of course she's too busy basking in the sugary afterglow.

That's a problem, isn't it? With his big arms around me and his soft breath falling against my hair, this doesn't seem remotely unreal.

Not even a little.

And the way he touched me last night didn't feel fake.

It felt like the realest thing in the universe.

We have a contract, though.

We have a flipping *expiration date.*

A moment in time and space and heartache where we'll part ways as planned. The more attached I get, the more it's going to break me when that moment comes.

Just because we've had gravity-defying sex and his mother likes me doesn't mean we're meant to be anything more than temporary partners for a very strange deal.

My heart finally gets the message my brain keeps sending. The gooey feeling fades, replaced by anxiety.

Awesome. So much better.

I'm breathing faster, and his arms tighten around me.

Even in his sleep, it's like he's tuned to my mental state with this instinct to protect me—even from myself.

And I remember the way he held me when I broke down and spilled about Harry—the breakdowns I've been having way too often lately—and all the sweet things Brady said.

The way he convinced me it's not my fault.

That sticks in my head like bubble gum to hair. Impossible to separate without hacking it out.

I roll over, pressing my lips to his collarbone, careful not to wake him. Brady doesn't stir, but he makes a soft sound of contentment and slides his leg between mine.

I breathe with my eyes closed until my nervousness fades and the confusion settles, just letting myself be.

This doesn't have to be so complicated.

We can enjoy each other just fine.

We can enjoy the time we have, and at the end of it, we can still walk away as *friends*.

Oh, but doesn't that feel satisfying?

Friends.

That word feels ludicrously pale compared to whatever the hell we are now.

Not friends, but not *together*.

Well, technically we're pseudoengaged. To the world at large, we're a smiling power couple, counting down the days to our extravagant happily-ever-after.

But *technically* doesn't have a smidge of reality, much less a real, heartfelt love story behind it.

I'm not sure what this story means, besides having more money in my life, and that scares me more than anything.

My eyes flick to Brady again. The stubble that left a rash on my inner thigh. The way his eyelashes cast half moons across his cheek.

A proud nose that might be too big for his face if it wasn't for his strong, sculpted jaw.

A strong face, Mom would say. All carved lines and princely features designed to trap hearts.

He rocks masculine beauty in a way that makes my breath catch like a hiccup every time I see him.

That smile too. That ridonkulous smile.

I don't know how he does it, turning it on and chasing the shadows away with every effortless grin.

Smiling certainly comes easier for him than me.

That probably has a lot to do with spending his life in front of the media.

When he smiles for me, it's different from the million-dollar grin I've seen scattered across the internet a hundred times.

A little more genuine. Infinitely warmer.

And yes, I'm a sucker for big blue eyes. Like chips of sky brought down to be windows to a very kind soul. The way they darken when they look at me—

God.

I am so completely screwed. So far in over my head I'm basically a pretzel.

Casual was my thing after Harry. And when we agreed to do this, I never expected it to turn physical, especially not this fast.

What happens if we can't stop? What if we can't—

A knock at the door rips me out of my brooding.

My heart lunges up my throat, adrenaline pumping through my limbs. My brain races through every possibility.

Harry, returning for revenge? Unlikely this early in the morning.

Elle? Nah. She's off in LA this week with billionaire bae for some illustrators conference. Plus, she's never been a big drop-in girl.

Dr. Ezzie? Impossible. She never comes over, though I think she technically knows where I live.

We've never quite touched the *friends* side of colleagues, even if there's massive respect on both sides. Probably the age difference, and she also has her own life to worry about.

Work doesn't leave me much time for a lot of socializing between the long hours and everything it takes out of me. I should work on that, I know.

Another drumming knock sends me out of bed, though, scattering for something to throw on.

I grab a robe from the back of a chair and tie it around my waist as I head through the tiny apartment to the door and open it without looking.

There, standing on my front porch, is the sweetest old lady with the mind of a twenty-year-old master criminal.

Grandma Lark, or just Gran to the world.

She's got a classic yellow raincoat over her flowery blue dress, rubber boots pulled up to her knees, and a steaming plate covered with a tea towel in her hands.

She's in her seventies now, and although she sometimes plays the poor-old-lady card, she's as spry as I am.

She could probably leave me in the dust.

Technically, she's Elle's grandma. We're not blood related or anything.

But we've also been close for as long as I can remember, ever since I used to run up to her door as a kid and she'd bribe me with handfuls of chocolate for helping her pull weeds in her garden. Or the many times my bestie and I fought over coloring books and Gran would make us talk it out over tea.

"Gran! I wasn't expecting you today." I hide my surprise with a big smile.

She gives me a weird look, which—fine, I deserve. It's not like her popping in is a rare occurrence.

If anything, it's a weekly event. We only live a few houses apart, and she loves dropping by.

Mostly to gossip, the shameless old bird.

But I love her.

And I love the plate she pushes at me before she says a word, which smells like heaven. "I brought banana bread for breakfast. And flowers."

I eye the bunch of flowers she's handing over, obviously from her garden. They smell just as good as the bread.

I accept them with my brain ticking, trying to think of a way out of this. Brady is still in my room, dead to the world.

Maybe I can make it quick and usher her out before he wakes up.

Then again, it's a risky game to ever push Gran out *quickly*.

But I can't turn her away, or she'll definitely suspect something's up.

It's a Sunday morning, not a day where I typically need to rush out for work—with the clinic closed.

"Get in here before you drown out there," I say, making a point of yawning as I open the door wider to let her in.

It's still raining steadily outside.

Brady's shoes are still by the door, and I pick them up the second she's turned her back, stuffing them under a cushion.

"Hmm? I suppose so. Time moves different when you're old."

"You're only old in body, Gran! Not spirit." I set her offerings on my small table, then grab a couple plates and a knife as she settles in without being asked. "Coffee?"

"I'm down to two cups a day, and I already had 'em. Anything more gives me rabbit shits."

"Gran!"

"Like you said, old in body. I'll have some tea if you've got it." She cackles as she unwraps her latest baked masterpiece.

"Sure." I put the kettle on the stove and bring out the French press for myself. Haven't splashed money on a fancy coffee maker yet—not like Brady's espresso machine—but I still like my coffee good.

Only the finest Hawaiian-grown brew from Wired Cup in this house—a local coffee chain with a lot of drama a few years back. I'm not sure why Seattle draws eccentric billionaires like magnets.

I only add a splash of cream and sugar too. Nothing like Dr. Ezzie, who drinks hers instant and bulletproof style, so thick with butter and cream the teaspoon practically stands up in the cup.

"Thanks for the goodies," I say as I find a vase in my cabinet for the flowers. "Next thing I know, you'll be asking me for a date."

She gives me a scorned look. "Young lady, if the only folks who ever give you flowers are trying to jump your bones, you're—" Her face splits into a grin. "Well, you're still young, that's what I say."

I wince.

The last thing you need from your adopted grandmother is a lecture on bone jumping.

"I meant to say—" I stop. I have no idea what I meant, and I don't have time to figure it out, because that's the exact second Brady walks out of my room, yawning like a cave bear waking up.

Of course, he's shirtless and magnificent. Washboard abs on full display, jeans slung low on his hips as he runs a sleepy hand through his hair.

Yep, I'm doomed.

There's *no* way I'm explaining this away now.

That doesn't stop me from trying.

"Gran, this is my friend Brady," I say hastily. "He, um . . . he stopped by last night for a chat."

I suck at this so hard.

Brady's eyebrows fly up, and the corner of his mouth twitches as he sees I'm not alone.

If he could stop being so amused, that would be awesome.

"Brady?" Gran's eyes narrow like a hawk, and she pulls out the seat beside her. "Well, don't just stand there, boy. Put some clothes on and join us for breakfast. Lena was just getting started."

He gives a lazy grin and winks at me—*winks!*—and then strolls back into the bedroom to find his shirt, still tugging it over his head as he returns.

"Mm, coffee smells good. Thanks, Sass," he says as he drops into the chair.

Gran gives me a look. The awkward grin plastered on my face might break it.

When she looks away, I fire Brady an evil eye as I work on steeping Gran's tea.

He just grins right back at me again like it's all a huge joke.

Cocky prick.

"So, you're the man who's warming my Lena's bed?"

"Gran, no." I choke on my own spit.

"That's fine and all, I'm no prude, but if you're looking for one naughty night, you can pack up right now. She's a good girl," she tells him magnanimously.

Holy hell.

I want to sink through the floor to India.

"No one-night hookups here." Brady seems to turn his brain on—thank God—but there's no way we're bluffing our way out of this one.

Luckily, Gran doesn't spend much time on the internet, but she'll know the Pruitt name the minute she hears it. And once she does, she'll figure out the rest faster than you can say *time bomb.*

Brady must realize the danger too.

"Not exactly, I mean," he adds.

Not exactly.

"We're together, Gran, full disclosure," I say quickly, eyeing her cup to see how strong it's getting. "Please don't say anything embarrassing?"

"Hmm." I notice she doesn't agree. "Brady, huh? Brady what?"

"Pruitt," he says.

Oh no.

She grunts like she's perfectly familiar with the name.

"Ah, yes. I knew your grandmother back in the day, all that land they used to own past Tacoma? Still in the farming business, are you?"

"Close enough, ma'am. I'm working on my own spin-off brand of affordable organic pet food."

Gran's brows rise.

Oh Jesus, no.

"Your family's done well for generations. How rich are you, then? I'd love to see you give my Elle's hubby a run for his money."

"Oh my God. Gran, you can't just *ask* people that . . ." I sink into a chair after serving Gran's tea and sliding Brady's coffee toward him so fast it almost spills.

Then I take a big gulp from my own cup, wishing I'd splashed some whiskey in there. Or rum. Or maybe I could just skip the liquor and throw myself out the window.

"Now, Lena, you're the last one who should be surprised. If I didn't vet the men my girls are dating, who else would?" She laughs at her own granny logic.

I'm so dead.

But this is the karma train coming home for teaming up with the old lady to push Elle and August along, I guess. It's my turn to get flattened.

"I do well for myself," Brady says.

Understatement of the century.

He doesn't mention he's an heir to freaking billions, but the snide look on Gran's face tells me she can figure it out.

"And what do you think about Lena's job? I trust you're okay with her coming home smelling like wet dog?"

Face, meet palm.

"Can't say I mind a little funk when it comes from helping pets. Besides, she cleans up well. You'd never know, Gran. Actually, that's how we met: through her clinic. I brought in a lost dog, and she was smitten at first sight." He gives me a conspiratorial look.

I whack him on the shoulder. Not so playfully.

That wins me another one of Granny's trademark cackles.

"You like animals, then?" Gran asks.

"Yes, ma'am. I was that kid who always chose the zoo over arcades or water parks. Always loved the tigers and wolves. I could watch them for hours."

"A man with taste. Good." She sniffs with satisfaction. "How old are you, son?"

"Ignore her," I say. "Only answer if she tells you her age first."

"Thirty-five, and not a day over." She doesn't miss a beat.

"Oh, I would never doubt it." Brady hides his grin behind a sip of coffee.

"Charmer." She looks at me and gestures at the plate on the table. "Kindly cut the bread and feed your man, Lena, or we'll be here all day. Now, Brady, how old are you?"

"Twenty-nine."

"Almost thirty. That's a big one." Gran gives him a wistful look while I slice the loaf and plate it up.

Gran goes the extra mile, adding these dried banana flakes on top for added sweetness and crunch. Normally, I appreciate it, but not today.

"It's coming hard and fast, but I'm game."

"Any previous marriages? Messy divorces? Current wives? Children?"

Brady snorts into his coffee cup. "None that I'm aware of."

"A Boy Scout." She leans closer to me and whispers loudly, "You must corrupt him a little, dear." Then she turns to Brady again. "Any vices?"

"Grannn," I moan. "You're killing me."

"Surely, he has a reputation. Any young man with his looks and money does."

"A few I regret. The family name used to stir up a few headlines. My grandfather got me into gambling on dog races for a while. I was a partier back when I could get shit-faced without feeling like I had a tank drive over me the next morning," Brady says, handing this woman ammunition that makes her laugh like a witch over a magic cauldron. "But that's all in the past. You're right, thirty's a big number, and I don't intend to screw it up."

Gran smiles, arming herself. "And you think you're the prince my Lena's been waiting for."

Brady glances between us, bewildered like he's still trying to figure out our connection. I sigh.

"She's my best friend's grandmother. We're basically family. Unfortunately."

"You bet your lucky stars!" Gran chimes in. "And if this is serious, girl, I must make sure he's right for you and spare your young heart from getting mangled."

A little late for that.

Gran doesn't know everything about Harry Jay—not all of it. But she knows enough. She knows we dated, and she knows it didn't end well.

Ever since, it's fair to say she's been a little protective.

Not that I've ever dated much since, much less brought my dates home.

Until now.

I'm still trying to hash that out: what I want—if anything—and if it's safe to want anything with Brady.

"I'll look after her, ma'am. You have my word," Brady says firmly. I guess that's the years of PR skills speaking. He never has to fumble around for the right words, unlike yours truly. They just drip off his tongue, all sugared honey. "That's all I want to do. Make her happy."

"Hmm."

"It's true," I say, desperate for the interrogation to end. "We're very happy together."

Brady's eyes slide over to me, and he takes my hand under the table, linking our fingers and squeezing.

Embarrassingly, I flush.

"So, that's where we are. Judgment time." Gran gives me a knowing look.

"I hope you approve, Gran. I want Lena's whole tribe to like me."

Gran grunts, digging into her banana bread to hide her smile. We don't often get all cutesy and emotional, but I really do see her like family—the same way she sees me as a surrogate grandchild.

Brady winks at me.

"It's been fun, but I should probably get dressed for real." With a kiss on my cheek that's part performance and part heartache, he heads for the bathroom.

The second the door shuts behind him, Gran leans closer with a glint in her eye. "You could do worse, you know. The man's so flawless I could barely get a single swipe in."

"Thanks," I say dryly.

"I like him. If he's good with animals, he won't be mad when you come dragging home from work after dark."

Charlie the corgi certainly seemed to like him too. There's no doubt Brady cares, and he's entirely forgiving.

Apparently, his magic charm isn't just isolated to people.

It feels kinda daunting, if I'm honest.

I've never been a people pleaser, and not everyone likes me. I can't count the number of times I've delivered bad news to clients to save Dr. Ezzie the grief.

Normally, that's no problem when I only see a handful of people socially every day.

But with my name linked to Brady Pruitt, all of Seattle will have questions about me soon, and then they'll have opinions.

Whatever my superpowers are, instant likability isn't high on the list.

Not like Brady.

"The money can't hurt either," Gran tells me. "Hardly the most important thing, of course, if you can find a rich one and he checks the other boxes . . ."

"Gran!" I eye her. "I didn't think you were so mercenary."

"Your *mercenary* is my *common sense*. You know what breaks up a lot of marriages? Money issues. If he's got enough cash piled up to make a rainy day a walk in the mist, you're golden. You two can keep each other happy for the long haul."

"Slow down, Gran. We're not getting *married*."

"No?" She gives me a sour look that cuts through my soul. "Don't you bullshit me, pet. I've known you too long."

Ugh.

There's nothing I can say, though. Not without either letting her in on our ruse or lying more to her face, so I keep quiet, gobbling a mouthful of banana bread.

"You don't find men that good looking growing on trees." Gran grins, her wrinkles deepening.

Brady chooses to walk back into the room that second, his smile turning wicked.

"Thank you," he says with a teasing bow. "I try my best."

Gran just chuckles, tapping the table with one gnarled finger. "Sit back down here, boy. You'll do for our Lena. You'll do just fine."

"Lena tested; Gran approved. That's huge." The worst part is, he sounds like he *means* it.

"I should probably get going and leave you two lovebirds to your music." Gran pushes up from the table with a dramatic stretch. "Mind you, tell Elle soon, if you haven't yet. Or I will."

"Gran, I've been busy. But sure."

She's so relentless.

But yes, why *not* bring my best friend in on the dumbest mistake of my life? Again, it's only fair play, after I had so much fun helping push her into holy matrimony.

"It's been nice with my granddaughter married, but so boring." She clucks her tongue and looks at me. "We finally have something to liven things up around here. Don't let me down."

No controlling that.

Whatever happens between Brady and me, someone's going to wind up massively disappointed. That's what I dread.

"Thanks, Gran. Always fun to entertain you," I say dubiously as I follow her to the door.

She laughs and lifts her face to mine, planting a sloppy kiss on my cheek.

"Look after yourself, Lena girl! Be happy. And if that man gives you a reason to smile, you stuff the attitude."

I glance over my shoulder to see Brady helping himself to another slice of banana bread. It's oddly domestic—the sight of him in this kitchen on a lazy morning, making himself at home.

Weirdly, nicely, deeply unsettling.

I can't get too used to this. But part of me already wants to.

"You know I wouldn't dare waste your wisdom." My smile is slightly forced.

Gran just doesn't know it's for my own benefit.

XVI

FOR THE BIRDS

(BRADY)

"Your grandmother likes me. That has to count for something." I smile at Lena as she ignores me, the wind pushing her loose brown hair from her face.

We're on our way to Bainbridge Island on the big green-and-white ferry, and the sea breeze stings my cheeks.

"Technically, she's not my grandmother."

"Do technicalities matter, Sass?"

She shoots me a disgruntled look, and I laugh, taking her hand.

"What's your mother up to these days, anyway? Does she visit?"

Her face falls.

"Retired. Mostly. I visit her a few times a year. Port Townsend. It's a nice little getaway, even if it's kind of far. After everything that happened, she's not too fond of revisiting Seattle."

She's afraid to show her face here.

That's what she's not saying, and I hate that I can read between the lines.

I ease up, bringing the conversation back to Gran. Thankfully, the old woman's antics spun enough old stories to keep Lena smiling while she tells them.

It's a light crowd on the ship today, and no one else can hear our conversation, but the appearance is still public. Deliberately staged so people will see us out and about together, knowing a few of those bystanders will pull out their phones and snap not-so-discreet pics.

I want it to look natural.

Experience says Lena doesn't perform well if she knows there's an audience, but we also need this to be convincing.

That's becoming less of a problem by the day.

Hell, after this morning, it's no problem at all.

"Stop being a prick, and enjoy the breeze." She twists her hand in mine so our fingers twine.

"I'm just enjoying the fact that Gran called me handsome. And rich. And basically God's gift to Lena Joly."

"Careful, dude. If your head gets any bigger, I'll pop it."

I pull her in, capturing her against my chest, bringing our laced hands to rest on her waist.

"What were the other compliments again? There were so many, I can't remember them all."

"If you like her so much, go fake an engagement," she says, but she leans her head back against me.

Mindful of any cameras, I nip her ear, feeling her shiver as she giggles.

No more.

Not here, as tempting as it is.

"She *is* a catch, age difference be damned. Considering her questions, she's clearly got her head screwed on right."

"I can't believe she asked if you were married. Gah."

"Well, she doesn't want some crazy wife to come out of the attic and start swinging for your head. You'd be surprised how often it happens in my circles. Guys get greedy and think they're invincible, only to get their dicks rammed in the door."

"Like *you* could get married without the whole world knowing." She huffs a breath.

The thought claws at my chest, though I don't know why.

She's not wrong about the attention lavished on my dumb ass. That's the entire point of this whole sham, after all.

Even if I tried some low-key courthouse wedding or eloping to Nepal, someone would get wind of it.

"I dunno," I say. "I could probably go to Vegas and pick up a girl there to marry without anyone knowing."

"Classy. Do they still have Elvis impersonators licensed to marry?"

"Hey, don't blame me. You didn't specify *how* this marriage would happen."

"Theoretical marriage that's never happening," she corrects. Why does she sound so annoyed? "I mean, a big showy thing followed by a real ugly divorce would undermine what you're trying to do here, wouldn't it?"

"Yeah. But it might be fun." I lean in, blowing a strand of loose hair away from her face.

She pretends to hate it, but I see her cheeks bloom red.

Shit, with her body against mine, all warmth and supple curves, it's hard to imagine ever sharing a life with anyone else.

"Do you ever wish you could disappear?" she asks after a second. "Like hire your way into some witness protection thing to assign you a new name and life?"

"What?"

"The publicity."

"That's part of my life. I've made my mistakes—too many to count—but they're mine. No sense in starting over and living a total lie, even if I *could* make it happen." I shrug, not wanting to get into this when we're surrounded by *the publicity* on all sides.

The second we dock on the island and walk into town, we'll be swarmed with attention. Bainbridge is a quiet place with a small-town vibe and basically the same appetite for any whiff of gossip. The summer crowds also tend to be larger and livelier.

"But wouldn't it be easier? You get no privacy, Brady."

"That's what I asked for when I fired up my social media machine. Part passion project and another part trying to reinvent myself. Even when it works, you still pay the price, trading some shitty comments and unwanted attention for awareness that can make a real difference in everything you care about."

I can practically feel her skepticism rising, but she doesn't respond.

"We're nearly there. Ready?" I say instead, nodding at the ferry terminal coming into view. A few lazy harbor seals lounge on one of the nearby buoys.

"No. I'd rather watch the seals and ride back and forth."

"You'll do fine. You're with *me*, baby girl."

"God, you—" Her voice chokes off as she leans against me, her skin so hot.

"What?"

"You have to stop doing that. And fine? That's easy for you to say," she grumbles, but when the ferry docks and we step onto the long walkway gate to deboard, there's a smile on her face.

A natural one.

"Just pretend it's a normal day out of the city. I come here all the time, and I still love it," I say. "Wave at the friendly people when you catch them staring."

It's not a long walk through the small terminal and up the hilly sidewalks into town, walking hand in hand.

The sun is out, and I spot a few obvious gawkers along the shaded streets, already trying to film us.

By tonight, their content will be everywhere.

Like always when there's a performance to put on, I slip back into my show suit, smiling and pressing hands with a few folks who do a double take as we pass.

Beside me, Lena relaxes slowly.

On the ferry, it was easy to forget what we were here for, but the attention we pull as we head down the main stretch of town acts as a constant reminder.

I wave to a group passing by.

"Now I know how it feels being royalty. So ridiculous." She sighs.

"Never spent too much time with royals, and nobody here would recognize them." I peer through the window of a bookstore as we pass. "Do you want to stop and browse? It's a nice, quiet break in here."

"What, to buy something?" She stops beside me, hand tucked in my arm.

"I told you it's just a day trip. So, yeah, if you feel like picking up a new book or some touristy gimmick, why the hell not? Let's look natural."

She huffs, but a little more of her tension fades as she glances up at me, her big brown eyes softening.

"I don't do touristy. Sorry. There's a reason I avoid the Seattle waterfront like a plague."

"Ice cream, then?" I nod at a small place a few more stores down, which sells the good stuff. "I know you've got high standards from your mom's place and all. Never gets old to feed your sweet tooth. Also, it's good for the local economy."

"Well . . ." She blinks, her lips pursing as she mulls it over. "The chocolate cherry flavor sounds interesting."

"Perfect." I steer us toward the store, sidestepping two people who snap quick pictures of us.

Lena's shoulders tighten, but to my surprise, she offers them a goofy smile and a wave.

"There she is. You'll be a natural in no time," I say.

"And you'll drag me into an early grave," she grumbles.

"With that smile? Like hell. If you're not careful, you might start having a good time, woman." I lean in to kiss her cheek as we stand in the shade of the awning, taking our place in the long midday line. "No one's going to look at us and think this is new."

"You think?" She examines our clasped hands like she's just realized we're still linking them. "*Everything* feels new. I can't stop feeling jittery."

It's not like her to be intimidated.

"I saw you face down your ex," I say. "Even though you were scared for your life. That proves you're made of stronger stuff than you think."

"The cameras are scarier," she lies.

"The cameras just want what they can't see—a fairy tale. That's not so bad. They're in the mood for a happy story or two. We just have to serve them like this ice cream shop dishing up scoops."

She fires a glare at me, but it has no bite. "I can't believe you're such a romantic. How does that happen when you're so . . . so you?"

"The same way you misjudged me."

She laughs and allows me to lead her into the store. Although this is a show for the general public, I want her to relax—for her sake and for our watchful eyes.

I ignore the phones pointed in our direction as we decide on our order, taking our sweet time to taste test a few more types with the little wooden spoons they offer.

Soon, we step back into the summer sunshine with our cones, heading up the street.

"I don't know how you stand it. Even the ice cream can't take the edge off," she whispers, deliberately not looking at my face.

"You get used to it."

Her nose wrinkles. "I hope I never do. Is this what it's like every time you go anywhere in Seattle?"

I check my watch. Just a little while longer.

"Not every time. Sometimes, we make sure a place is clear first. Or hire out a venue for true privacy, that sort of thing."

She blinks in surprise. "A venue? What, like a whole restaurant?"

"Once in a blue moon. My father's more prone to pulling that shit than me. He's more allergic to people than ever since his—his condition."

Especially so he can chew me out at will without anyone else listening.

She notices how I stumble at the end. I'm also glad she takes the hint on my face not to dig.

"NDAs go far too. Always important for our long-term relationships," I say.

"Like the one you made me sign."

I nod as I take a long lick of my toffee-flavored ice cream. "It's for your own good as much as mine."

"Somehow, I find that hard to believe."

I find her hand with mine again and link our fingers with ease.

When we pass an older lady not even trying to hide her recording, Lena actually waves and makes a wild face.

"Do it again. Have fun with it."

"Let's not get carried away now."

"Perish the thought." I use our joint hands to check my smartwatch again. "I've arranged a ride to meet us up here by the church in about a minute."

"A car?" She glances around like she expects it to come bursting out from between the buildings, barreling toward us. "Why?"

"What do you mean *why*? Luis has been here since morning. He's going to take us to the nature preserve."

"Nature preserve?"

"Don't tell me you've never been to Bainbridge before."

"I haven't, actually. Not since I was old enough to remember it."

Damn, this girl needs to get out.

I bite back the words that it's only a thirtyish minute ferry ride away. I don't need to remind myself that our worlds are very different.

"One last smile for the cameras, and we're good," I say, grinning at two young girls who are staring at us. "Look like we're in love."

"Oh, I haven't forgotten."

Neither have I. My blood heats every time I touch her, pulsing pure hellfire into my dick.

The hardest part about taking a day trip with her is fighting hours of blinding hard-ons.

Right on cue, Luis shows up in a black sedan with its windows tinted.

"Right on time. The man's never been late in his life," I say, oddly relieved to leave the people staring at us behind.

This is nothing new. It's just my life.

The mindless gawking, the glaring attention, the whispers, the laughter, the sneers, the cruelty, and occasionally even the autographs and spontaneous marriage proposals—it's all part of the fame and infamy I inherited.

But today, it's not the kind of life I want.

Luis gets out, sunglasses fused in place like he's a model secret service agent.

"Miss Joly," he says, opening the door for her.

She glances at me, briefly uncertain, before smiling at him and sliding in. I join her in the back seat.

"So, this is your idea of a casual day out? Having your assistant hanging around?" she teases.

"Nah, Luis won't be joining us later. It's convenient to have him here to keep me updated."

And aware, I don't add. My media errors could easily multiply without his second set of very sharp eyes.

"Don't worry about me, Miss Joly," Luis says, adjusting the rearview mirror. "I have a kind boss who allows me a couple hours of downtime, and this week it's on Bainbridge in the summer."

"A few hours?" Lena turns her horrified eyes to me. "Brady, you—"

"He's kidding." I scowl at Luis's grin. "Drive on, my man."

"Kidding?"

"He has working hours and revolving duties just like every other person ever hired for this role." I roll my eyes at Luis's chuckle as we pull away, winding through the lush green overgrowth to the northern side of the island. "I can't believe you were ready to believe him."

"Eat the rich. I'm on team driver," she says firmly.

Luis mutters something in Spanish, his dark eyes lighting up in a grin.

"I like her," he says.

"Just get us there before I fire you." I lean back in the seat as Luis laughs, shoulders shaking.

"You like me too much for that, boss."

Unfortunately, true.

It doesn't take long to arrive, and I help Lena out of the car before Luis can say another biting word.

"Where are the cameras this time? Will the crowds be bigger here?" she asks as we head down the path.

As always, the preserve looks divine, shrouded in endless rows of trees and snatches of vibrant purple flowers. The gardeners must be some of the best on the West Coast.

Above us, the old white estate house sits looking over the Puget Sound.

I direct Lena down the meadow trail, through the maze of bright-white and supple pink flowers.

I've been here enough times over the years to know where I'm going without a map.

"No cameras," I say.

"Huh?" She stops and looks around like she's expecting someone to jump out at us and fling their phone at her face. "I thought we'd be at it all day?"

"Not here."

". . . But it's a public place and it's a nice day. It can't be that deserted. How can you be so sure?"

"Because I reserved the place for us, Lena. Remember when I told you I do that sometimes?"

"You . . . what?" She stops walking, her eyes dancing. There's something incredibly satisfying about the naked shock on her face. "What do you mean by *reserved it*? The whole park? Jesus."

"Only for a couple hours. Plenty of time to explore and relax."

"But why?" She's flabbergasted.

"Why not? It's summer, and from what I've gathered, you don't get much time to yourself outside work. I want my girl to stop and smell the flowers. Literally." I shrug, threading my fingers through hers and kissing her hand. That's all impulse. I don't give a single, solitary shit if there's no one around to see it. "Consider it a reward for putting up with everything in town—and with me."

"But isn't it *expensive*?"

"Tremendously. Luis made the arrangements. They normally just close down the entire preserve for weddings."

"Holy shit, are you *crazy*?"

"Shhh, you're disturbing the birds." I bite back a laugh at the shock on her face. "Just enjoy it, Lena. I wanted to be here with you, so I splurged for a few hours in paradise. You smell that?" I make a big show of filling my lungs until my chest puffs out. "It's gorgeous out here."

"I—"

"Come on, I'll show you around." With her hand in mine, I walk her over the narrow path winding toward the bird marsh. "Check out the birds and keep quiet."

She doesn't need much encouragement, drinking in the atmosphere in awed silence. Friendly birdsong floats over us, even if we don't see anything more exciting than a heron and a couple small hummingbirds flitting around.

I haven't been here for over a year. Never with a woman worth closing the place down. With no one else around, there's another layer to the majesty, the vibrant wonder surrounding us with every breath.

She's the whole reason we're experiencing any of this now.

Without her, I never would've done this. Likely wouldn't even be here.

We wind up a smaller path snaking off the wider one to the rhododendron maze—an absolute riot of blooming pink and white flowers.

"It's impressive. Like walking through one of those immersive art things, except real," she says after a long moment.

"Yeah, immersive." I don't take my eyes off her for a single second.

I know how bad that sounds.

I know how boned I am, watching her like she's the prettiest thing here.

I also know I don't give a damn.

She looks at me as my phone buzzes, though, and I take a quick look.

There's an email from Luis—no matter what he said earlier, he doesn't really do time off when he's on the clock. He's been working from the car while we've been wandering through our own secret conservatory.

The document attached to the email looks enormous.

I can't resist opening it and quickly scrolling through as we walk, skimming pages and pages of what looks like some very sketchy history regarding Harry Jay's business dealings.

Fucking checkmate.

"Brady?" Lena stops and looks at me. "What's so important?"

I blank my expression and swipe away the PDF. "Just thinking we should do a selfie. It'll be great timing to post it when we're on our way back, after the snapshots in Bainbridge start making the rounds."

"A selfie? Oh, you're serious?"

"It won't kill you, will it?" I smile, opening my camera app.

There's no sense in letting Harry goddamned Jay rot my brain and ruin this. Plenty of time for that later. And for charting ways to send him to hell.

"My hair's a mess. That wind on the ferry did terrible things," she complains, but when I turn the screen to us, she doesn't try to hide.

That's the girl I tell myself I'm not fucking falling for. Bold and determined to push through life.

Just as I'm about to take the photo, my last thread of control snaps.

I lean in.

I kiss her hard, drawing a gasp from her lungs.

One for me, one for the camera—Instagram will love it—and then another for me.

Tongues flowering, all fire, sticky as hell.

I am obsessed.

And I bring her closer, chasing away any question about what was on my phone with my mouth.

Then I forget about her twisted ex, too, because I'm enjoying her that much.

She kisses me back slowly, sensually, her slim arms winding around my neck and her nails digging at my collar.

When I break away, her eyes are amber stars in daylight.

"That was way more than your fans needed," she whispers.

"Hell yes, it was. No regrets." I kiss her again before she can pull away. "But they'll eat it up just the same, I promise. Just don't tell me I'm the only one to blame."

Her face heats scarlet. She doesn't deny it, because she can't.

The sparkle in her eyes tells me I'm not the only one struck with this madness.

Shit, shit.

She's falling, hard and fast.

I can feel our little no-strings agreement ripping apart, and it hasn't been a solid *month*.

How do I convince myself this just make-believe?

How can I ever stop my clumsy ass from trampling her heart?

XVII

PUPPY LOVE

(LENA)

I am scared.

Over the next week, everything snaps into place like a well-oiled hinge.

Any other time, I'd be tempted to think this life is too good to be true.

Call it cynical, but living taught me to be.

But with Brady, I don't have the heart to be all stone and thorns. Not when he's painfully sweet, going out of his way to make sure everything is as easy for me as possible.

Not when there's Ezzie and Pawsome Hearts and the rest of my life to plan.

She's approved of my financials and even agreed to help me interview a new vet doctor looking to buy in and partner up.

Everything is going the way it should, and that's the problem.

Even Harry hasn't shown his ugly, sneering face since Brady stepped in and ejected him from my property.

My pride hates that I needed a big, strong man to chase away my nightmare, but my inner princess adores the freedom. Without Brady charging in, I'd have a ten-ton boulder pressing down on my neck and nowhere else to turn.

"There is something unusual," Dr. Ezzie says as we walk to the boarding building together.

"Unusual how?" Instead of tensing up like usual with doubt, I just glance at her, waiting patiently.

"A letter." She waves a hand and shakes her head. "It's probably nothing, this notice about a plumber who didn't file his permit paperwork right back when we had a pipe replaced. I think it was three years ago."

"Three *years*?" I whistle. "Doesn't this city have anything better to do?"

"That's code enforcement for you—and they're slapping me with a large fine. I don't think it's anything for you to worry about, necessarily." She gives me a tired but genuine smile. "Things are looking up. Frankly, this is the first time in years I've had to turn clients *down*."

I try not to blush, though we both know the reason for this new wind at our backs.

Brady Pruitt.

News of our engagement spread fast, including my entire life story. When Dr. Ezzie hit me with fifty questions about why I didn't tell her that nice young man with the corgi was *my* nice young fiancé, I had to throw together the most awkward lie of my life.

Pathetic.

But it's *weird* knowing my engagement with Brady is the only reason people are beating down our doors.

I mean, it's awesome and all. There's no good reason to get upset over more business. And the newcomers love our personal touch, minting many happy new cats and dogs.

Fine.

What's not fine is having lies multiplying like rabbits.

If that's really a sin, I'm going to superhell.

I didn't think buying Pawsome Hearts would cost me my soul, but whatever.

There's no denying how lovely it is to see Dr. Ezzie smiling and breathing lighter. It's like I can see more light in her eyes, the stress melting away.

Our only real problem today is an adorable black Lab named Queenie whom we're boarding. She's a gorgeous girl, so friendly and loving.

Only, just this morning we got a call telling us her mom died from an untimely heart attack while she was away on a business trip.

The relative on the phone was panicked, saying they couldn't take the dog, not even for a little bit, with a special needs child and an elderly cat in the house.

My heart twists like a rag in my chest.

I know better than anyone how deeply animals feel sudden changes, dogs especially. How deeply they can *hurt*.

To think poor innocent Queenie no longer has a home as she scampers around madly at the sight of us almost breaks me.

She's ten years old, too—not that you'd know it with her dynamo energy.

"Hey, old gal. How are you feeling today?" Dr. Ezzie holds out her hand for Queenie to lick enthusiastically.

The Lab whines with excitement, her thick tail wagging like mad.

"Poor girl," I murmur, stroking behind her ears.

She really is a sweetheart.

There's grey around her muzzle. I wonder who would pick her over a younger, sprier dog, even if Queenie can wag with the best of them.

"We'll figure something out," I vow.

Dr. Ezzie glances at me. "I know you will, Lena. You don't let up."

I also feel too much.

The hum of an engine reaches our ears then, and even though it's only been a week, my heart lurches.

Brady.

Simmer down.

It's becoming a thing, where Brady picks me up after work to whisk me back home or off to his condo.

Oh, Gran can't get enough of seeing us disappear into my house. I caught her smiling and laughing a few times from her front porch. I know she's not out there every day that late just for a little sunset gardening.

The car pulls up, then Brady climbs out of the driver's side.

Screw you, heart.

I hate that he's putting it through acrobatics.

But it's determined to remind me that I have a thing for my fake fiancé, and it's devastating.

When he sees me, he waves and walks over.

"Hey, Lena." He steals a kiss before he glances at Dr. Ezzie, whose hand is still being loved on by Queenie. "Who's this?"

"Our latest crisis." Dr. Ezzie scratches the old girl behind her ears, and Queenie groans happily, her tail smacking Dr. Ezzie's legs. "Her owner died and nobody can take her, I'm afraid. So, we're currently looking for another solution."

"Oh shit. I hate to hear it." Brady slides an arm around my waist as he thinks.

"We don't want to send her to a shelter at her age," I say.

"No way." There's a gruffness in his voice even as he holds out his hand for the curious Lab to sniff. Her bright brown eyes fix on him. "Damn, well, why don't we take her? She can stay at my place."

"What? With everything going on?" I probably shouldn't be so stunned after he stepped up for Charlie, but I can't help it.

Warmth spreads through my chest.

"She needs a good home, and I have the network to find her one. People will line up for days after I post about her a few times." He gives me that cocky grin, and for once I don't blame him.

Dr. Ezzie looks at me, her eyes dancing.

Right. This is obviously *my* decision. She's letting me deal with the little things, a warm-up to the big, scary decisions involving the entire clinic once it's mine.

Fair enough.

I mean, I insisted we couldn't just pack her off to a shelter. I'm also the one who took the call from her owner's relative.

The warmth in my chest strikes a fire as I watch Brady hoist her up on two legs, scratching the Lab's neck until she's in heaven. There's a very good chance I'm going to be burned.

I'm not sure if I care.

"Okay," I say softly. "If you're serious—if you really mean it—you can take her today."

"Awesome. Any paperwork to sign? And if she has any leftover bills, of course, I'm happy to cover them."

Oh, of course.

It's not fair that this man proves gentlemen aren't extinct.

Dr. Ezzie leads him back through the kennels to the clinic building. I linger behind, bending down to bury my face in Queenie's neck, just breathing soft doggy fur.

She makes a low, uncertain grumble.

"Watch out for him, girl. He's too nice, and I don't know what to do about it," I whisper.

Queenie whines.

"I know, I know. It's just a lot." I lean back, running a hand all the way down her neck.

She watches me with those adorable whale eyes.

You think that's a lot? I've got to find a whole new home.

"Yeah, you're right. You've got it rougher than I do. But he'll treat you like the Queenie you are, and so will your new parents, once we find them. I promise." I can't quite bite back the smile.

Queenie dances around in a circle as I work on packing up her stuff: one big grey bed, a few toys with teeth marks, and her bowls.

Nothing else.

No other pieces of her old life.

It's depressing, even if I know she's in good hands.

But we have to move forward.

I shake my head, pushing the dark thoughts away.

If there's anyone in this city who can help her find a loving new family who accepts what she is, it's him. Brady Pruitt, instant best friend to an aging, happy, slightly dopey black Lab with worn teeth, worse breath, and a heart that's overflowing.

When he comes back from reception, swaggering in with his eyes glowing and his stubble neatly trimmed, I'm ready to roll.

"I'll have Luis round up what she needs and drop it off at my place," he says as I help her into the trunk of the SUV. Despite her age, she's still got lift, jumping in easily.

"Luis on pet-run duty?" I tilt my head at him. "I think he's right. You're the worst boss."

He snorts. "If you think the worst I've done is send my assistant out to get some dog food and treats, you're deluded."

"What if he's busy?"

He makes a big show of checking his watch. "It's barely three o'clock. Besides, he can pick it up on the way back to my condo."

"What's he doing now? Bringing your suits back from the dry cleaner?"

"Shopping to upgrade my studio. We're always looking for new tech for better videos." The corner of Brady's mouth twitches. "I told him to bring back Indian food for dinner. I don't like to use the apps when I can just tip my main man with his own meal."

"And then you'll lock him in the basement until you let him out for another day's work, right? Or will he be taking Queenie outside too?"

His penthouse is pretty high up. That's why he had Charlie staying with his parents in that massive Lake Washington estate with the lushest dream backyard.

I can't help making sure he has no second thoughts about what he's getting into.

"He'll be sleeping on the balcony where he belongs," Brady jokes. *I think.* "And no, I'll take her. Takes a little while to get to the park up the street, but I can always use another excuse for some fresh air."

I laugh at the absurdity, like he doesn't go out all the time, though my stomach clenches a little.

"What's that look?" Brady grabs my hand and brings it to his lips.

"*You.* I just don't want you putting yourself out with all the other craziness going on . . ."

"The ruse, you mean," he whispers.

". . . Yeah."

"It's not like taking in an old Lab will blow up anything. We'll find Queenie a real home soon. She's a sweet girl."

The Lab happily confirms it about twenty minutes later, after I've cleaned up and clocked out, by putting her head above the back seats and grinning at us, tongue flopping on the way home.

"She's one lucky pup, with the richest foster dad in Seattle," I say with a sigh.

He smiles at me, the corners of his eyes creasing and those blue eyes flashing like lightning.

No mortal should be actually perfect.

I keep waiting for a land mine, thinking I'll trip on some fatal flaw that will blow my silly crush to pieces.

But so far, there's nothing.

The vortex of Brady Pruitt just keeps spinning, pulling me deeper, and soon the only one to blame for the impending heartbreak will be *me*.

I can't fall in love.

The thought is alarming, but it's there, roots twisting through my brain until they crowd out everything else.

Nice reverse psychology, Lena.

But I'm not sure anything could persuade my dumb heart.

A few weeks in, and I'm dangerously close to catching feelings.

And he's oblivious to the minor breakdown I'm having right next to him as he hands me his phone and tells me to pick out some music for the drive.

With the windows down and a soft summer breeze kissing our faces, this feels like a movie scene.

You know the one, where the jaded woman who's been beat around before by love falls for the jock, and everything is perfect—right before the world comes crashing down.

Brady glances at me and reaches over, resting his hand lightly on my thigh. His long fingers curve along my inner thigh, and—

I'm blushing.

Even though we're in public, at a stoplight in thick evening traffic, with a rescued dog in the back seat, I'm swooning.

Flipping swooning.

And I don't swoon.

Honestly, it's embarrassing he has that power. But the giddy buzz in my veins tells me I want him to keep touching me.

Keep the illusion alive just a little while longer.

His fingers press lightly against my skin until I can feel his pressure.

He glances in the rearview mirror, out the window, and then at me, mouthing along to the song I've put on—Sabrina Carpenter.

I didn't even know he was a fan.

But there's a fire in his eyes, the same way the sun gleams off the mountains as it slips toward the horizon. There's also an ache between my thighs.

Then he gives me that lazy, heart-shredding smile and moves his hand down to my knee, only releasing me when I'm nearly biting my lip through.

He puts his hand on the wheel again.

And I'm left wondering how the hell any girl can ever resist this without losing her mind.

◆ ◆ ◆

It's only Queenie's first night in Brady's penthouse, and they're already inseparable.

She has her bed set up in his room, slumped across it with her head up, looking at us. Every time we look at her, the dog's tail thumps for attention, but otherwise she's content.

That makes two of us.

I'm perfectly happy to stay where I am, nestled in Brady's arms.

He drops a kiss on the end of my nose, which shouldn't make me want to giggle and squeal the way it does.

Thank God my filter is titanium.

"I'm glad you're off tomorrow," he says.

"I know this is a foreign concept to you, but I get days off."

"Brat, that's not what I mean. Tomorrow's important." He smacks my butt, looking briefly distracted before returning his gaze to my face again.

"Is it?" I frown, trying to remember why it's so big.

"The charity event I told you about." He takes a lock of my hair in his fingers and flicks it back and forward.

"Oh, right. Sorry, nurse brain. What's this thing again?"

"An excuse to meet my father."

Queenie looks at us curiously, wagging her tail. She must notice the way my body tenses.

"It's okay, girl," I say.

"The old man softened up after my mother raved about you," he says. "For him, it's a rare public appearance. He doesn't do them often since he had his heart attack. If he wants me to show up with my girl in front of the local money circle, that's giant."

Is he staring through the wall?

I'm actually nervous.

But I also know I can't refuse.

This is his life, and I signed up for it the minute I agreed to the sham and put my name on that contract.

These are his parents, including what sounds like a hard-ass dad who won't be so easy to convince.

I think about his reputation again, and my stomach flips. Not in the cutesy way that means attraction and yummy things.

"If you're game, it'll mean the world for the family business. Lots of big players there," he says, still playing with my hair.

Of course. Networking. Critical to high society.

I try to smile, cursing how weak it is.

"It should be fine. I have lots of practice playing your fiancée by now." I force a smile.

"Don't need you to be anything but yourself, Sass."

"But you do," I insist, leaning forward so he meets my eyes. "You need me to be polished and on point, ready to make your dad love me. Or at least believe we're in love."

That won't be difficult to fake.

My stomach lurches again, and I lock that thought away.

He smiles, though it's not his usual rakish grin. It's softer, lighting his eyes sky blue until I'm a gooey marshmallow.

"Lena, my dad will love you the way you are. Be yourself. He's a beast—always has been—but Alec Pruitt respects strength. You don't have to change shit."

"No, but I should have my shit together." I smile.

He kisses me then, his teeth tugging at my lower lip. "Just the way you are, woman. You won Mom over caked in mud."

"Will you ever let me live it down?"

"Nah. And if you can impress when you're dirtied up, this should be a cakewalk." Another kiss turns me to jelly. So does the way he squeezes my ass. "No buts. None except this one."

I shudder.

There's definitely a *but* that has nothing to do with how his hands make me feel.

From what I've gathered from Brady plus my own online sleuthing, Alec Pruitt hasn't ever approved of much in his life. The *only* reason he wants to meet me now is because his wife wore him down.

That's not being receptive.

That's no guarantee he won't be holding a shotgun to Brady's face, and to mine.

I have to dazzle if we want this to work.

"I'm not sure how these things work, but I've always heard a lot of business goes on between throwing money around. Are you going to be approaching people about your project?" I ask between kisses.

"My pet food venture, you mean?" He pauses and looks down at me. "Yeah, that's the plan. The pressure's less intense to stand in for all of Pruitt Ag with Dad there. I won't big-deal it. A few polite pitches to the people who typically show up when there's enough money in the room to choke an elephant. A few willing suppliers who could help get this off the ground faster, even if there's a long way to go before we get to that point."

Just like I thought.

It's doubly important I'm on my best behavior.

And he knows it, too, judging by the way he asked and the stark reassurance in every kiss.

Seeing Brady nervous leaves my heart in shambles.

So, I take his face in my hands, looking him deep in the eyes so he knows how serious I am.

"I won't let you down, Brady."

"I know. Never an option with you." His smile is all butter, and his hand slides through my hair.

This time, when he kisses me and his hands roam wild, we don't stop until I'm a screaming mess.

XVIII

ANKLE BITER

(BRADY)

I insist on being the one to drop off Queenie at Pawsome Hearts for day care with the other dogs before driving us to the gala.

Honestly, I don't know why it matters so much.

Luis could've done it in a heartbeat.

But with Lena by my side, there's this weird family feeling in the air. Queenie whines with excitement when she senses where we're going.

"Hope all this bouncing around isn't stressing her out."

"No way. She's a runner. She'll have a blast tiring herself out with the other pups," Lena says, toying with the edge of her dress.

We picked it out this morning before getting ready.

She wanted to pay her own way, and I wouldn't hear it.

This damn gala's for my father's sake—and mine. I won't have her shouldering the cost for a dress this fancy.

In the end, she went for a navy silk piece from this boutique shop that does its own alterations. The dress fits her like a glove.

Simple and elegant. Timeless. Blue as the summer ocean.

I try to ignore her dabbing on lipstick in the mirror, along with the raging hard-on from hell.

"You look great. Stop worrying," I tell her.

"I'm *not.*"

"Bull. I know that look, and I'm telling you to lose it. You look like a smoke show." I pull up in the clinic's lot and park. "Stay there. I don't want your shoes getting dirty."

"Dude, we're not at the farm. The lot isn't that filthy," she grumbles, but her eyes flick to the building where I'm dropping Queenie off.

It must be weird, having your status change so drastically in front of your longtime coworkers.

Whenever this insanity ends, it's going to upend her life just as much as mine.

I let Queenie jump out the back, and she immediately tries to go flying to the door before the leash catches in my hand.

The guy manning the kennels runs up to us—a friendly man with red hair and thick glasses. I hand off everything our girl needs for the day, plus bagged meals and a couple new toys, then climb back in the car.

"Let's go." I reach over and squeeze Lena's hand. "Everything will be fine."

"I hope. The only time you ever say that is when nothing's fine at all."

"Ah, but *this time.*"

"This time," she echoes.

"You'll fit right in. Everybody there wants to save the planet and wishes they could fawn all over animals all day."

Which is why it's a perfect opportunity to talk up my organic dog food. Whipping up interest and lining up investors and retailers ahead of time certainly can't hurt.

"I've never been to anything this important before," she says, her voice tight.

"It's not. Just think of it as a cocktail party full of people who like to flaunt their money and wear their hearts on their sleeves for social brownie points."

"Pssh. And you said I'd fit right in."

I smile. "Try not to get too pissed at their egos. The money winds up in good hands at the end of the day, no matter how much they bluster getting it there."

"Right. I'll just have to bite my tongue the entire time, I guess."

"You like me despite the long odds, Sass. You'll be fine. No one's going to look at you and think you're not meant to be there."

"Especially when I'm on *your* arm," she inserts slyly.

"Exactly. Image matters." I nod at her, and after a second, she relaxes and smiles back. "I promise you everything will be fine."

Finally, her shoulders slump, and she doesn't spar with me again before we arrive.

The gala is set up inside this fancy hotel in Bellevue, and it's clear when we pull up that Lena has never been inside.

I toss the keys to the valet and take her arm.

"Watch your step."

"Be honest with me, Brady. How awful will this be?"

"No more than a 6.5 on the fire-breathing-pricks-with-too-much-money scale. Meeting my dad will be the hard part, so we'll try to get that done soon. Then you'll gorge on finger food and drink some expensive champagne while I do the rest. Enjoy the show."

"I'll try. You've got people to wow."

"I know. The champagne helps." I wink at her to hide my inner thoughts, already spinning like a helicopter blade.

We climb the soaring stairs to the lobby, where a man in a tux greets us with a smile and finds our names on the guest list.

"Mr. Pruitt and Miss Joly," he says with a rehearsed smile. "Welcome. The gala is just through the doors."

"No press?" Lena whispers as we stroll through the huge double doors, which have been thrown open wide.

I shake my head.

The hotel is older. This was probably some kind of grand ballroom once, with its huge golden lights spaced at regular intervals on the ceiling and a polished wooden floor underneath.

Now, it's filled with the cream of Seattle high society, chirping like crickets and flitting around like butterflies.

One big happy dysfunctional family.

Lena stiffens on my arm as the smell of money hits her and the glamour fills her eyes.

I pat her hand, searching for my father in the crowd. That's the first hurdle of the evening, and I wonder what kind of mood he'll be in today.

Not one where he'll see through our deception, I'm sure. He'll be fending off his own thoughts, hating every sympathetic smile and whispered comment about poor Alec and his health.

I just hope he won't unload any venom on Lena.

My phone buzzes, and I glance at it, keeping the screen turned away from her.

Luis, timely as always.

Boss, red alert. There's a rep from Harry Jay's RE firm. Probably keeping eyes on you.

Fucking hell.

One more problem I don't need.

No doubt they're still sore about the way I left him limping home. Maybe they're spying because they've heard about the engagement, too, and they wonder if it's my money behind Lena's buyout of Pawsome Hearts.

Plenty of reason to trail us.

And if I'm with Lena, he can assume I also know Harry Jay's dirty secrets and the history he never should've had with her.

The damage that fucknut did still makes my blood churn.

If I had my way, I would've chucked his carcass into the Puget Sound weeks ago.

Not exactly elegant, and very illegal, but hell, it would be satisfying.

Instead, I have to be *civilized*.

I have to settle for revenge by living well—unless he fucks with my woman again.

More than anything, I have to make sure he never has a chance to hurt her.

Never again, even after this contract ends and even if I don't have a clue how the hell I'll keep that promise yet.

"You're texting here?" Lena glances over, nudging me gently with her elbow.

"I'm done. Had to take care of something." I say the words too fast.

I've never been a stellar liar, despite my life in the public eye.

A line appears between her brows as she frowns.

Her eyes skate across my screen, and I turn it away abruptly before she sees anything.

Too slow and too obvious.

Hurt flashes across her face.

Shit.

Let her go nuclear on me later with demands to see my phone, my messages. *Later.*

Because I really am an idiot at deception.

The lines on her face just deepen as she looks out at the immaculately dressed crowd. It's like I can feel her swallowing the grim thoughts and questions on her tongue.

I shove my phone back in my pocket before it causes more trouble.

Seconds tick by like molasses, but she doesn't say a word.

If she knew what I was doing, she'd have every reason to freak. She's always made it clear that taking her creepy-ex problem into my own hands is off limits.

Still, getting Harry Jay out of her life for good is worth a few white lies.

In the end, she'll be happier, and I'm fatally addicted to making this girl smile.

◆ ◆ ◆

Time blurs by as we make the rounds.

And Lena, hugging my arm, demure and beautiful as an angel, looks just as good at this as I knew she'd be.

Only I know her well enough to read the slight strain in her face or notice the way her fingers grip my arm a little too tightly whenever someone looks her up and down with a carnivorous smile.

Especially the older men.

Every time I see that shit, I want to call them out.

But that's the elite for you, where money entitles wolves to wear their hunger like one more designer tie wrapped around their necks.

Everyone here is curious about this girl who's finally gotten me to settle down, and who isn't from their social circle.

Like I said, one big, inbred fucking family.

When you step outside it to date, eyebrows rocket off faces. And the second you step out of line, it's judgment day.

Watching Lena muddle through it reminds me how much I hate these events.

But if it's torture, she shows no sign.

This woman is a patient goddess, always calm and smiling.

The customer-facing role she has must've hardened her. She has that smile down pat as she listens to strangers prattle on about their lives and overachievements.

She handles people better than the cameras.

Somehow, she always knows when to step back and let me take over.

It helps that we're surrounded by genuine animal lovers. People stop and listen the second she says *animal clinic*.

Lena lights up when she talks about her work at Pawsome Hearts. The second she realizes they care—the second she realizes my cynicism was only that—she opens up.

It's like she bends the room's gravity, leaving them wanting more.

And when I finally see my father and lead her over to Dad's perch on the outskirts of the room while he's deep in conversation with a congressman, her smile doesn't falter.

He's scowling, yeah, but that's typical.

I'm not expecting Lena to untangle her hand from mine and march forward the instant the politician moves on.

"Hi, Mr. Pruitt. Lena Joly," she says, extending a hand downward to his level in the chair. "Such a pleasure to meet you."

For a second, he looks past her at me, his eyes glassy and annoyed.

Do not be fucking rude, I warn with a glance.

"Call me Alec, Miss Joly. I've heard so much about you." He takes her hand and shakes it like he means to pull her to the floor.

"Call me Lena."

With a disinterested grunt, he leans in so they can kiss cheeks, and he nods at her. "How are you finding the crowd?"

"So many interesting people," she gushes.

I step up and lay my hand on the small of her back.

Standing by for rescue. The second he breaks character and starts spewing his usual thoughtless, offensive shit, we'll be gone.

I take his insults in stride—I have a whole life of practice—but not if they're aimed at Lena.

I can see his eyes flicking over her as she talks, mentally computing whether or not she'll ever be fit for the Pruitt name.

In the moment, I fucking *wish* that were truly on the table.

"I love the wildlife charities here. Making a difference for conservation is very important to me. All part of the trade," she says brightly, waving a delicate hand up at the large screen above, which displays the details of the many charities looking for donations here today and the amounts they've raked in.

"Yes, animals. Nature is dumb and blind without us, so we'd better try to even the score." A familiar edge creeps into Dad's feeble voice behind the bland philosophizing.

Only, he doesn't sound like he's about to launch into a gutting critique of her. Is that curiosity in his eyes?

It's been so long, I can't tell.

Lena takes his cold glances in stride. No matter what she might think about the excessive wealth concentrated in one room, there's no denying the money *will* go to good causes—and lots of it.

People in our position can afford to be generous.

Beside him, an older lady nudges in, turning to Lena and offering her a huge smile. "Oh my, you must be Brady's vet fiancée!"

Her eyes look a little tired, but she leans down and presses two perfumed kisses on Lena's cheek.

"Vet tech," Lena corrects with a small smile.

Dad wrinkles his nose.

My fist tightens at my side as I near my limit for his passive-aggressive shit.

"You know, I met the kindest vet nurse yesterday." The lady dabs under her eyes, which gleam in the light.

"Oh? What happened?"

"My cat, Gatsby, he—" She breaks off and gives a brave smile. "Well, it was just his time, and they were very kind, seeing him off."

"Oh no. I'm so sorry."

Dad watches with more interest now, biting back something that looks like a smile.

What the fuck? Why are his eyes so sharp?

Why does he look happy when they're discussing a dead cat?

I glance between him and the two women talking. The older lady, Mrs. Hageman, I think, is damn near crushing Lena in her teary-eyed embrace now.

Something just happened I haven't picked up on.

"I'm very sorry for your loss," Lena wishes, glancing at me over her shoulder, tempting me to step in to give her air.

"That's okay, honey. You can't change anything now, and he's in a better place. I simply had to say thanks for what you people do. It's the noblest profession for those of us who love our babies to death."

Lena pats the woman's arm as she finally uncouples.

"No, thank you. The best owners are the ones who care about their pets as much as we do. I can tell your boy was loved."

"Oh, yes! He was the sweetest tabby—just a stray, you know. My gardener couldn't keep him away, and one day I told him to just let the poor thing in for some water. I was so miserable, moping around after my youngest went east for college. That's the way it is with cats, isn't it? They come when they're called—just not with words." Her smile trembles. "My name's Sandra Hageman, but call me Sandy, dear."

"Lena."

"A pleasure. Even more because you've won over the most creative member of the Pruitt clan." She beams at me, and I nod before she looks at my father. "Alec, I'm still surprised. You and Kerrigan never mentioned your son being involved with this lovely creature."

Dad coughs into his hand and inhales, his lungs giving that harsh rattle that's become too familiar. He waves his hand at Freddy behind him, declining the oxygen the nurse always has ready.

When he looks at us again, I'm expecting daggers in his eyes, but he just looks oddly relaxed.

"That's the way it is with our Brady. Always surprising us. Sandra, if we knew, you never would've had a minute's rest from my wife with the wedding planning." He clears his throat again. "My sincerest condolences on your cat. Was he old?"

What. The. Hell.

My old man has never so much as acknowledged pets exist unless they're in his personal space, like Charlie.

Maybe it's the environment getting to him. He hasn't been to an event this big for over a year, and I wonder if it shakes something loose in his miserable brain.

There's no denying Lena looks like a damn knockout.

Chestnut hair swept up in a loose updo, tendrils framing her face. Minimal makeup, the classy touch pretty women carry when they're trying to accent their natural beauty without pinning on a whole new face.

Another contrast with Nancy Loomer and most of the women I've dated before.

I watched in awe this morning as she was getting ready and she only used about ten cosmetic products. It would've been thirty with other women.

With a little color on her lips and winged eyeliner, plus the barest hint of smoky eye, she looks as good as every other woman in here.

Better, because she's authentic.

My attention flicks back to Dad as Sandra wanders away after a few more quiet words with him.

"You can take the lady out of the vet," he says, "but apparently, you can't take the vet out of the lady."

"What's your point, Dad?" I growl.

"Her timing, that's what. She just helped us impress the heiress to the largest grocery chain in this quadrant of the country just as our contracts are coming up for renegotiation. The damn cat, I never would've thought of that," he mutters, barely under his breath.

I want to roll my eyes and say something shitty. God forbid he have a beating heart.

Yet the way he smiles at Lena and nods tells me the ice is broken.

Mission accomplished, I guess, even if it had to happen in the most annoying, selfish way possible.

"Um, glad I could help?" Lena smiles uncertainly.

I squeeze her hand firmly. She might not know it yet, but she's done the impossible.

"Hey, there's Brian Millstable! He finished buying up every midsize chain pet store last year. I should introduce you," I say, naming one of the most influential people in the Seattle business world—at least when it comes to the wildlife side of things, with the large nonprofit he owns. "Catch you later, Dad."

Lena smiles, looking like an old-fashioned debutante.

"It was a pleasure meeting you, Mr. Pruitt," she says, holding out her hand again.

"Alec." Dad shakes it with a ghost of a smile.

For once, what the hell does his selfishness matter?

As long as she's won him over.

Lena's eyes spark, and I know she's picked up the smell of victory.

"Alec. I hope we'll see each other again soon."

"We will," he promises, and we're off.

We're silent as we cut through the thick crowd, my hold on her arm guiding her.

"Why does it always feel like the women are glaring at me more than the men?" she whispers.

In the corner, I see another problem—Nancy goddamned Loomer, glowering at Lena like she's convinced a dirty look can reduce her to ashes.

"She's jealous," I growl. "Can't handle how good you look with a fraction of the effort."

"Oh yeah, but I wasn't just talking about Miss Lemonface."

I shrug. "Like I've said before, money causes an inbred bunch. Half the women here under thirty-five probably hoped to get their hands on me."

She throws me a look.

"It's not like I gave it to them." I clear my throat. "Shit, Sass. Even when the world thought I fucked everything that moves, I was careful not to risk business and pleasure."

I'm not sure she believes me, despite the smile.

I know I'm an attractive guy, especially when I make an effort, but I'm also not blind. People like me because of my name and the wealth behind it.

That's what sets the woman on my arm apart—if anything, the fact that I'm a Pruitt and have money coming out my ears feels more like a black mark than a blessing.

Considering that, along with my history, she's right to be suspicious.

If she still wants to take my head off for hiding my phone later, she's entitled to. Especially when I *am* going behind her back, just not for the reasons she thinks.

Lena tilts her head back, smiling. "Be honest. How many women here have you slept with?"

My eyes scan the crowd. Once in a while, an old hookup marries up and poaches a CEO.

"Not fair. You know my reputation."

"Even if I wish I didn't," she throws back, but she's still smiling. "Kidding, Brady. Let's prove we're madly in love, just to be safe."

Once we reach Brian's side, Lena's smile shifts to the diplomatic one she uses with strangers.

We do our introductions.

"Just wait until you hear about his pet food," she tells Millstable, resting a hand on my chest and giving me the biggest damn doe eyes I've ever seen. "It's going to make a huge difference in health. You'd be surprised how many owners want to feed their babies the best, but they just can't with the cost and the crappy shelf life of the fresh stuff."

His glasses almost shine like mirrors catching the sun—or maybe it's his eyes. Brian Millstable is one of those human androids who lives for new opportunities. Not human.

Batteries between the ears, I call them.

He patiently listens as she rattles off the preventable horrors she's seen with older pets and mediocre food—the joint issues, the early heart disease, the obesity.

I talk up my experiments—hating that we're stuck in the formula stage—but Brian listens patiently, his face an impassive smile.

Like I said, *not human*.

I'm not nervous, though. Not with Lena making this so easy. If we weren't talking to a potential VIP supplier, I'd kiss her breathless.

Maybe it'll convince Nancy that I'm lost forever, and she'll disappear from my life.

Judging by the way she watches the whole exchange from across the room like a jealous cat, Nancy hasn't figured it out yet. She clings pathetically to her date—some former basketball star who's all height. New money who hasn't figured out what to do with it.

I ignore her and turn back to my pitch, vowing we're on the verge of getting this right the same way I've promised a hundred other times.

This might be the first time I've believed it, though.

Brian shakes my hand and says he'll have his people call mine—no empty promise coming from this man.

When we're done, I get us two glasses of champagne and clink mine against hers.

"Time for a well-deserved break."

"Oh, thank God. Does that last guy ever blink?" She drops her smile.

"Nah, he sleeps with his eyes open. You're not a legend without being a little weird," I say.

She laughs. "My cheeks hurt from smiling. How do you do this for hours at a time?"

"Practice and face massages," I joke. "The risk of shitty press changes your priorities too."

"Hmm, I guess. You said we won't do this much, right? I don't know if I can keep up."

"You're doing amazing. Millstable never bullshits or makes promises he doesn't mean. I owe you." When I wrap my arm around her waist and pull her closer so I can kiss her temple, it's not because I'm playing make-believe for an ever-present audience.

It's because I'm fucking grateful.

It's because I truly respect Lena Joly.

It's because we both know this is getting out of hand.

Too bad I don't care.

All I know is when she's by my side, looking like a goddess striking earth, wowing potential partners without really trying, I'm living shock and awe.

"I need to go to the bathroom and touch up my makeup," she says.

A caveman part of me wants to follow her into some secluded corner, shove her dress up, and fuck her against the wall.

The bathrooms are perfectly nice here, not grimy or run down.

I've had sex in worse places.

But as tempting as it is, we're not here for that, and the wrong people might notice.

"Come back soon," I say with a fierce parting kiss.

"I will." She smiles up at me but only for a second.

Her eyes search mine, and I wonder what she's hoping to find. How much did that phone stunt disappoint her?

The ring on her finger glitters in the light, a secret mockery only I know as she weaves through the crowd.

Every step she makes is so graceful, winding through people like a bird through branches.

I watch her for too long, trying to push down the unsettling feeling that something is off.

If it's the phone, we'll talk about it later.

A hand pulls on my jacket, and I turn around.

"Your mother was right. She's good for you," Dad says bluntly, waiting impatiently behind me in his chair with his nurse.

She's useful. That's what he really means.

I glare, swallowing the harsh words he deserves.

"I'm surprised it only took one conversation to win you over," I say.

"There's something charming about a girl who can hold her own with a crowd like this when she's a fish out of water. She lacks the pedigree, yet you'd never know it."

"What can I say? She's a charmer."

"She might be your first sensible decision in years, Brady. Perhaps you're turning a corner."

My gut churns, hating that I can't remember the last time I saw him so relaxed.

"Thanks, but don't get too used to her wasting time at these things. She has better plans. We made an exception for you today." My shoulders itch, and I roll them under my expensive suit.

I know I should just leave it there. Walk off with my father satisfied and no explosive arguments brewing like thunderheads.

Only, I've never been good at accepting easy wins.

"Frankly, I'm surprised that's all it took. Lena showing a little compassion to a woman you need to deal with. If empathy goes that far, you should try it sometime," I say quietly.

He chuckles roughly before a cough chokes it off.

"I fully expected to hate your fiancée. However, you know I've always had a certain respect for people with talents I lack." Dad doesn't look away from the hall where Lena disappeared, his eyes narrowed. "Don't blow this up like an idiot, boy."

"Not planning on it. I'm engaged, remember?"

Until the contract ends and we announce a quiet breakup.

Fuck.

For the first time since we showed up, the lying bothers me. It's harder than I expected with my old man, and not for any of the reasons I would've guessed.

I'm not pissed because it's a big fakeout.

I'm bothered because it isn't *real.*

I suck down the last of my champagne and swipe another glass off a passing waiter's tray, glad that Luis is outside, waiting to drive us home.

"Careful with your thirst. Important people are always watching," Dad snarls, wagging a finger. "Frederick, let's go."

His nurse helps him turn and steer back through the crowd, leaving me to feel the hornets swarming my chest, the anger he's put there my entire life.

I don't enjoy the champagne, and I don't give a shit who's watching. I pound it back in one swallow.

That's the real Pruitt brand coming through. Good old-fashioned ice and dysfunction all wrapped up in paper-thin civility.

After I hand my empty glass to a passing waiter, I head off in search of Lena.

She emerges from the bathroom just as I'm approaching, and I hold out my hand.

"Ready to go? Our work here is done."

"Oh, already? I thought we'd have to put in another hour or two."

"We've been here long enough, and the mood has peaked. It won't get any better. Trust me."

She eyes me uncertainly, leaning in like she can smell the champagne on my breath. "Are you okay? You smell a little tipsy."

"We'll have Luis drive."

"He's here? But you drove us."

"You think he's earned a night off?"

"You're right. How stupid. Where would you be without him bailing you out?" She laughs and slides her hand through my arm, but even though we're back to how we were before, it doesn't feel quite the same.

Something feels flat.

Like she's pretending and not just because we're still in public.

Goddamn, I hate this feelings shit.

"If I'm being honest, I've had enough," I say as we reenter the ballroom. "I've donated six figures, spoken to everyone who matters, let the cameras flash, and now, I want you to myself."

"Queenie might have something to say about that." She smiles, and this time it doesn't look so forced.

"We'll swing by and grab her on the way home, if you don't mind some dog hair on that pretty dress."

"Nope." She glances up at me, then away. Too quick for me to read her expression. "The sooner, the better. I can't wait to pry off these shoes."

"I can't wait to see them on the floor."

She smiles, but just like before, the expression shutters. Wiped clean.

Only for a second, but it's enough to make me ready to leave this circus of posers behind. I grab her hand and practically tow her to the door, firing off a quick text to Luis on the way.

We're not even the first people leaving, judging by how the crowd has thinned out. I make sure to give Lena a wolfish look as we make our exit.

That part's too easy.

What's hard is up ahead—the evening I want with her that I'm afraid I don't deserve.

The one where I watch as she takes off that almost-invisible makeup. The moment where I unzip her dress, throw her on the bed, and fuck her into a sex hangover where we have just enough energy left for takeout.

It's not lust stabbing through me but this weird longing.

Luis lingers by the door, his eyes alert. He nods when he sees me.

"Car's pulled up right outside," he says, holding my eyes. I slide free of Lena, leaning closer so I can hear him. "Not to worry you, but I saw Miss Loomer talking with Harry Jay's rep while you were with your father."

"What the fuck?" I draw back.

"Probably nothing. You know she's a social butterfly. Still, on the off chance they've made any contacts—something to keep an eye on."

No denying that. It confirms the ominous feeling that's been stalking me all evening.

This doesn't bode well.

"Just stay on high alert. I don't want any surprises," I growl.

"On it." He sighs. "This is the kind of shit that can come back to bite you in the ass, boss man."

"Yeah, no kidding." I glance at Lena, who's smiling at the hotel valet as they help her into the back seat of my SUV.

"He knows you're onto him," Luis says quietly.

"I'm sure he figured that out when I chucked him off Lena's porch."

"Be careful." Luis's dark eyes flare. "Your parents will never shut up if there's a police report."

"Then we'd better neutralize this asshole faster." I pat his arm. "Take us home."

As I slide in next to Lena, I feel a persistent set of eyes that make me whip my face toward the window.

Nancy, scowling, standing alone on the curb.

With her purse held too high against her chest, she locks eyes with me and extends her middle finger, flicking at the strap pointedly.

She's like a dog with a bone. An obnoxious little ankle biter.

With Lena next to me and too much trouble in the air, I can't even react to her jealous teeth mangling my life.

XIX

CORNERED DOGS

(LENA)

There's an unpleasant quiver in my belly as we arrive back at Brady's penthouse.

I don't know when we quietly agreed we'd spend every night together, but that's become the norm shockingly fast.

Even more shocking, I never thought to question it until now.

Until he hid his phone and sent everything spiraling.

Worst of all, I feel so *stupid.*

We never agreed to anything.

Not one word about exclusivity.

I have no greedy claim to his body, his time, his secrets. I know that—I *know*, and it still doesn't help.

Just like we both know this is a sham. A glorified production where we stumble into bed together at the end of a day.

Friends with benefits with mammoth responsibilities.

. . . Are we even friends?

Ugh.

The way my stomach flips intensifies as the private elevator opens, and we walk into his penthouse with a furry black cannonball who flies back at us the second she's off the leash.

Queenie prances around like an overexcited deer, getting dog hair and drool all over Brady's suit pants and then my dress.

I'm laughing, though.

He doesn't seem to mind, either, rubbing behind her ears and stroking her sides as she leans against him.

I stare at him, wishing I could run from another happy moment and everything I'm afraid it could mean.

Call me a coward.

Right now, everything feels too raw. Every emotion hits too close to home, and after the exhausting day we've had, I just don't want to deal with it.

Not now.

But I can't afford not to. I never learned to be that socially graceful.

"You've been quiet since we left," Brady says like the mind reader he is.

I shrug, feeling silk sliding over my body like a kiss.

At least we both look incredible while we're saddled with emotions harder to decipher than ancient hieroglyphics. I know something's eating at him, too, and it's not just his usual bottomless appetite for me.

Brady hasn't taken his eyes off me all evening.

I'm petty enough to feel proud of that, even though Nancy kept preening and seething over him from across the room. He barely looked at her.

But it can't overshadow the way he hid his phone, and I don't know why, but it can't be anything good.

I almost want to curse myself for noticing how he flipped the screen away with guilt swarming his eyes.

Almost.

But if he's sexting other women or setting up his next fling, I'd rather know now.

I'd rather stop putting him on a thirty-foot pedestal and wipe the glitter from my eyes so I can see what he is.

Just another rich dude with the world at his feet.

A dude who treats me like gold to my face when I'm actually just another piece of bronze in his machinery.

I take a deep breath. "How did it really go, you think? Did you have any fun?"

"Dad liked you. Not exactly for human reasons, but it's enough." He nods slowly, shrugging off his jacket and tossing it over the back of the sofa while Queenie settles on the floor. "We did good. Tiring but worthwhile."

"I'm glad." I eye him carefully, trying to read his mood.

He's relieved, I think, but also bothered. Unsettled. Restless.

I can't tell if he's feeding off my energy, or if I'm bathing in his. Or even if our minds are close to the same wavelength.

I bend down to unfasten my heels and kick them aside.

Then, with a burst of self-consciousness, I set them upright again. The shoes were almost five hundred dollars.

Better to keep them in good condition. He might be able to return them if they're lightly used, or at least send them to a woman who knows how to wear these things without risking broken bones with every step.

Brady watches me from near the fridge as he refills his water bottle, his tie loosened and a whisper of a smirk on his face.

"You don't have to worry about damaging them, Sass. They're yours, even if you never need them again. And if something happens, we'll just get you another pair."

"Hey, just because you *can* doesn't mean I should be careless. I didn't want Queenie to think they're chew toys."

"Don't be paranoid," he says as the Lab looks up, wagging her tail. "She's a good girl, and even if she's not, shoes come and go."

Oh, okay. What about people?

Hell yes, I'm paranoid.

And I know it's my issues, my scars I've carried over from past relationships where nothing was ever what it seemed.

But he hid his phone. He *lied* to my face.

That's not the kind of thing I can just shrug off and pretend we're back to laughter and spine-shifting sex. But what if it was a fan messaging him and I'm being ridiculous?

A fan, my ass.

I know Brady well enough by now. He doesn't strike up long conversations with randos from his channels.

I've seen the women who come piling into his DMs. They must have their notifications cranked up every time he posts so they can race to comment first and get his attention.

They're obsessed, ready to hook up faster than a right swipe on any app.

Or maybe I'm just so into him I really am bursting out of my cocoon, emerging as a paranoid bitch.

He sips his water as Queenie trots over for a head scratch, his eyes never leaving me. "Lena, let's hear it. You might as well tell me."

"Tell you what?" I bite off.

"What crawled up your ass and died. If you don't talk, we can't do anything about it."

We.

That one little word darts past my defenses and shreds my heart.

My face heats.

"It's just—well, who were you texting?" I demand. "And don't lie to me, Brady."

His face is a mask, impassive, telling me too much without uttering a word.

With a huff, I throw up my arms, shaking my head as I pace to the other side of the island in his kitchen.

"Look, if there's another woman—a sidepiece or whatever—I get it." *I also hate it.*

Why should a man like him limit himself? He didn't want me because he *wanted* me, at least at first.

That came later.

Shit, but here I am.

Standing in front of him, red faced and unraveling by the second. Money aside, I'm not so different from Nancy Loomer, after all.

I'm prone to overthinking, wondering if he ever wanted me at all or if I was just a convenient fuck the minute I wound up under his roof.

"This isn't real. I get that," I say as he stares at me, apparently speechless. "But can you just be *honest* with me? If there's someone else . . . I'd like to know."

My voice breaks, and I bite my lip.

Have I mentioned I *hate* this?

His brows crease. He looks at me like the crazy woman I am.

"What? You think I'm seeing someone else?" he asks softly.

"If you're not, I think you want to. Why else would you lie about texting?"

A hint of telltale redness creeps into his cheeks.

Feeling better yet? Bravo, Lena.

"It's not what you think," he says. Like every man with an excuse ever born.

"Oh, fantastic. So why don't you enlighten me?"

He eyes me like he's thinking of coming closer, but thankfully he decides to keep his distance. Queenie has the good sense to keep her distance, too, flopping down on the sofa with her chin perched on the top of the cushions, watching with worried eyes.

Leave it to a dog to tell you when there's too much drama in the air.

"Fuck it, you want the truth?" he finally mutters. "I haven't been one hundred percent up front with you, but it's not another woman. I have zero interest in that, and I'd have told you if there was."

Shields up.

I fold my arms, refusing to let myself feel the slightest relief. Even though it's there, hopeful and pulsing in my chest, filling my entire body with this unwelcome warmth as prickly as a cactus.

But I haven't decided if I believe him yet, so my body is getting ahead of itself.

He stops and swigs water, his throat moving. The sound seems too loud in this cavernous space.

"Well, what is it?" I grind out impatiently.

"Harry Jay," he snarls.

Huh?

I blink.

"What about him?" I whisper. "Brady, I don't get what you're—"

"Ever since I saw that dickhead and you told me what he did, I knew he wouldn't stand down. I've met his type before. I laid hands on him, I made it personal, and I knew I'd have to keep him the fuck off your ass if I truly wanted him gone."

"Gone?" I'm so stunned I can't breathe. "He's my problem. I thought I told you that? What gives you the *right* to do anything?"

"He's dirty as hell, Lena. I did some digging."

No argument there.

I doubt there's been a time when Harry was clean in any sense of the word.

"You mean his business? His real estate dealings?" I'm almost afraid to ask.

"Yeah. I had Luis help piece it together. I've got an entire report on his recent history and strong-arm acquisition tactics that should be illegal. Hate me if you want, that's fair, but take a look." He holds up his phone and swipes a few times, then shows me a document on the screen.

I don't take the phone.

I don't dare.

Right now, I'm just frozen and confused.

Also, fuck Harry Jay.

When Brady came in guns blazing and Doc accepted my offer, I honestly thought that was a wrap. The end. Time to move on and forget his ugly, cruel face with a mustache I'll never have the pleasure of ripping off.

But now time itself feels stalled.

The very real fear that Brady might've had good reason for playing defense, even if he overstepped my boundaries . . . it's too much.

"Why are you doing this?" I ask with a sigh.

"Because he threatened you. What choice did I have?"

"That's just what Harry does. That's my past and my issues." I step forward, taking another look at his phone, now flat on the island between us. Just waiting for me to see the nasty truth.

God, it's so tempting.

To take the information he's unearthed and behold the nightmares Harry has been weaving all over this city.

But Brady did this behind my back.

He went and sunk his brave, stupid teeth into my mess when I told him point-blank not to.

Especially when he doesn't understand what a loose cannon Harry Jay is, and his retribution won't stop with me.

Last time, he broke my mother's heart and shuttered Raven Swirl. He murdered her dream, and he used her own daughter like shrapnel to shred it to pieces.

Not even deliberately.

I'm not sure if he ever knew about the collateral damage he caused, but in the end, it doesn't matter.

Not when the result was the same.

Not when I can't stand to let him take another shot and hurt Brady in the process.

But I can't tell him any of this, because he won't understand.

Certainly not while he's standing there, bowed up and manly and determined, a human grizzly bear who's ready to charge through anything to protect me.

"I can't stand by while he's out there, ready to burn you down. You can't ask me to do nothing." His jaw tightens, making him look older.

More stubborn than ever.

I can relate.

"But I spelled it out for you," I say sharply. "I thought you understood. I said this was my battle and not yours."

"Why should it be? I have resources you don't, Sass. Hell, if I hadn't shown up that evening, if I hadn't grabbed him when he was up in your face—" He stops, swiping a hand over his frustrated face.

Not cool at all where this is going.

I can read between the lines.

You're helpless. I'm not.

Oh, that bites me, hard enough to draw blood.

The fact that he's *right.*

He's in a position to fight harder than I ever could and protect me in ways I can't.

But it's the principle.

It's the way he rubs his money and power in my face along with my own disgusting weakness.

And it's the mortal terror coursing through my veins that the past would love to rhyme again.

One bad scrap with Harry Jay, and he'll never see the punch to the face that's coming. And Brady has so much more to lose than a cherished summer ice cream stand.

"Whether it's true or not, it's my choice. I can deal with this myself, if I need to," I whisper.

His brows pull down, making his eyes glint like cobalt steel. The barrel of a gun in evening, maybe. Just as dangerous, just as unforgiving.

"Then why don't you?" he asks quietly.

I stagger back a step.

"Um, excuse me? What do you think I've been doing? I won the contract for Pawsome Hearts. He's toast. He lost, and he'll have to walk away." I hate the way my shaky voice echoes in this big room.

No conviction, just anger. Denial.

"And you think he'll just suck it up and go home? You really believe that?" Brady looks at me with pity. "Shit, he ruined your mother's business."

Holy hell.

But maybe I deserve it.

In the beginning, Mom could've made more money if she'd kept her temp jobs through summer rather than going back to the ice cream stand.

But Raven Swirl developed a real following before the bitter end. Plus, it made her happy, even when we were nearly broke, and even when Dad's income disappeared when he died.

Mom realized how short life could be. She decided she wouldn't let it pass her by without crafting tasty treats guaranteed to make people smile.

Elle, my bestie, was always the one with her head in the clouds. A daydream believer from the minute she had her own fake marriage proposal.

I've always been the pragmatist because I *had* to be.

That's called survival, and it's served me pretty well in life.

Everything except—

Harry.

The man who hollowed me out, who left me helpless while my mother lost her final true love after Dad.

"I told you before, it's not your choice. It's my business, and I'm the only one who gets to call the shots." I ball up my hands, feeling my nails biting my palms. "If I stand back and let you swing the sword, where am I? Where's my fight? I have the most to lose!"

"You're safe, dammit," he growls.

"Not really. I'm hiding behind your money and your courage. I'm letting you think you know best."

Just like every other rich guy in this city who's used to throwing his weight around.

Those unspoken words bounce around the empty space between us, as reckless as stray bullets.

Brady takes a step back, pushing a hand through his hair.

"Shit, you've got this all wrong. I'm not stepping up because I want to control you, Lena." His eyes are so conflicted. "I'm doing this to *protect* you. Can't you see that? You told me what he did, that inhuman fuck. You think I should stand back and let him have open season?"

"My past. My life. My clinic. Mine to defend."

For a second, we lock eyes, two distant hearts clashing across a chasm.

"Can we put the damn egos aside? Can you let me care?" he rumbles. "He'll come for blood after I drew his, and so did you, swiping that land out from under him. You've won a battle, yeah, but it sure as hell isn't the war."

I swallow thickly, hating that he's right.

He turns away, glancing at Queenie. His eyes are almost as sad as ours, and it hurts my heart.

"Look, I get why you want me out of the way," he says after a second. "I know you're passionate, you're smart, but I just . . ." He trails off.

I just don't think it's enough.

"Goddamn, Lena. If anything ever happened to you . . ."

I take a deep, rattling breath.

"I know you mean well."

"Take a look at the report I sent, Lena. See what he's been up to and why it's not as easy as you think. Someone needs to stop him before he keeps abusing this city."

"And you don't think I can?"

He doesn't look at me.

His silence is deafening.

My chest tightens until my lungs stall.

Whatever.

At least we know where we stand, walking a tightrope between feelings we shouldn't have and no real mutual respect.

"You know what, it's probably best if I go home tonight," I say. His ice maker kicks on and hums, the only sound between us. "Alone, I mean."

"Yeah." His throat bobs as he nods once. "I'll give you your space. I appreciate what you did for me today, again."

"And I would've appreciated a little notice if you were going to go all secret agent man on my ex." I sound so bitter.

There's no way he would've told me. He knows I never would've agreed to let him be my shield when I'm in too deep. The only reason Harry isn't already lining up demolition contractors for Pawsome Hearts is Brady's money.

Just shoot me.

Right now, I'm not in a forgiving mood. I'm in a ragey, pitiful, hate-you-for-making-me-second-guess mood, even if I know his heart's in the right place.

Even if I care way too much.

The words eat me alive until I'm hollowed out as he approaches, pulling me into his arms.

"Take all the time you need. Get yourself sorted," he whispers. "I'll fucking miss you."

"I . . . I'll miss you too." Yep, I'm stuttering.

My arms instinctively wrap around his back.

It's not even a lie.

For a second, I feel like hot trash for ever questioning if there's another woman.

With all the time we've spent together, he'd barely have a *chance* to see anyone else.

And this here—this isn't for show.

It's a real, organic, heartfelt fight.

A battle for *us*.

Still, the fact that he lied about investigating Harry and went behind my back to play superhero stings.

A betrayal is a betrayal.

Worse, maybe, because I never once said we had to stay exclusive for this arrangement. But I *did* tell him not to fight my battles.

Worse, because I know he still wants me and there's no one else bleeding his attention. Brady freaking cares enough about me to go feral in the clumsiest territorial way possible.

And that's what makes this so dangerous. He can't see the risks.

I couldn't the first time, and neither did Mom.

Not until she lost everything.

With a quick goodbye head rub for Queenie, I leave the apartment with my head down, speeding down the elevator and through the lobby, where there should be an Uber waiting by now.

Brady would've driven me or had Luis do it if I'd said a word, but I'm not making my dependency worse.

Some things a girl has to do herself.

If only to prove she still can, to hold her crumbling self together just a little while longer.

This weepy, uncertain, guilt-ridden girl is not who I am.

I've always prided myself on being stronger than iron and sharp as nails. Ready to take my problems head-on, along with everybody else's, since the day an amoral porn addict ripped my soul in two.

Sworn to never be so weak I let the lightning that ruined Mom and Raven Swirl strike twice.

But what if I'm not as strong as I think?

What if I never really healed and scarred over?

What if Brady's right, and I need him to swoop in and save me?

And what if Harry Jay isn't done with me yet?

What if he's the raging storm I can't stop, and he'll destroy everything I love a second time?

True to Brady's word and my miserable confusion, we don't see each other for a few days.

I throw myself into work and the new adjustments in my life. After we close up for the day, Dr. Ezzie brings me into business briefings, feeding me one bite of management at a time.

The transition has begun.

Soon, she'll be handing me the keys. I won't be alone with Trish and Keith very long once I've found a partner.

I flick the sign to *Closed* and switch off the main lights, heading back to her office, where the sunset spills out in that cloud-filtered gold that makes a Seattle evening.

"Hi, Lena. Come in." She looks up over a stack of papers on her desk.

"You look like you could use some sleep, Doc." I frown at the dark circles under her eyes.

"Someday," she says dryly. I pull out a chair and sit beside her. "Give yourself another twenty years, and you'll know where it comes from. There's nothing easy about running a clinic."

"No, but I'm ready."

"I hope so." With a sigh, she gestures to the paperwork heaped on her desk. "There's been a complication, I'm afraid."

My heart stops. "What complication?"

"The money-and-rules kind," she says, looking down. "Fun new city fines."

"Oh my God, what? Code enforcement again? You haven't broken any laws, right?"

"Right. Or so I thought."

I take the envelopes from the city code department in her stack without asking, rifle through the top letters, and start reading. She's opened them already.

They're just as petty as I thought.

Inspection inquiries. Pages and pages of them—all going back years, like someone just decided to audit Pawsome Hearts under a microscope and slap us for every loose shoelace.

This can't be coincidence.

I flick through the stack, faster and faster, grabbing more envelopes. *So many pages.*

"Holy crap, where does it end?" I whisper. "This is insane!"

She rubs her eyes tiredly. "Well, the fines don't amount to much. Some of them are under twenty dollars for old light bulbs and such. The inspection is a bigger issue. We need to get the boarding center back in shape to pass a modern code inspection."

My heart sinks. That's no easy task.

"When *was* it last inspected?" I swallow.

"Well over ten years ago. I have the details in this mess, somewhere."

Ouch.

She's been lucky to keep the exterior painted and the inside squeaky clean. She doesn't need to tell me how dire a full inspection could be. I already know.

Sure, it's perfectly safe for our four-legged guests, but there are always little things that add up when a building's thirty or forty years outdated.

Another issue Dr. Ezzie never had the time or money to fix, and soon it'll be mine.

But I'm not ready for a total gut and overhaul. Not now.

There's no way this is a coincidence.

I'm not stupid.

Someone has been digging, doing everything they can to chuck a firecracker down our pipes.

"I don't believe it." My fingers tighten on the letters, crinkling them. "Doc, this is bullshit."

"The worst timing," she agrees too calmly. "Regrettably, it means someone may have to put up additional capital before we can progress."

There it is.

The sucker punch I was waiting for.

Normally, before a sale, an inspection might be requested by the buyer, but Dr. Ezzie and I discussed it, and I basically waived my right.

I'm intimately familiar with this place and its quirks like the back of my puppy-chewed hand.

I choke back bile, my nerves knotting.

"Okay, righto," I say. "I mean, I'll see what I can do."

"And the fines."

"And the fines," I echo through clenched teeth. The room feels like it's shrinking down to shoebox size.

Outside, the gorgeous evening sunshine paints the trees a cheerful orange. A couple dogs bark in the enclosure with Keith, getting their last zoomies out before dinner as he throws rubber balls for them.

The phone rings, but neither of us move.

Dr. Ezzie taps the voicemail button a minute later, and a demon talks through the speaker.

"Hi, Dr. Esmerelda," he says, smooth as honey. "I'm just calling to let you know I'm still interested in Pawsome Hearts, and I'm prepared to make a counteroffer. Let me know if you're interested."

Bastard.

I'm seething as the message ends and clicks off. Before Dr. Ezzie has a chance to move, I grab the phone and start redialing.

He picks up almost immediately.

"You *asshole*," I snarl.

"Lena!" Dr. Ezzie hisses.

But Harry just chuckles, the oily sound sliding over my skin like marching spiders.

"Is that LeeLee?" He's amused, like nothing I do will ever faze him.

Old, familiar horror creeps in.

I remember what it's like, feeling trapped.

But I also remember I'm *done* with that. Brady might be right about Harry being relentless, but I can handle this.

I don't need a hero to run him off.

"That's no way to speak to an old friend," he says.

"You're no friend of mine."

"I might be. I *could* be. We both know you're in over your head with this old property."

"*Bullshit.* The deal's off, Harry. Go home. You're never getting your hands on this land."

"Well, it's not up to you, is it?" He sighs. "I'm trying to do this the simple way. So sad that you won't let me be gracious. It would be *so* incredibly easy for me to facilitate a smooth transfer, considering I've been doing this for years. I've seen it all—especially those complicated properties wrapped up in all kinds of red tape."

Red?

Oh, I'm seeing it right now.

"I knew it was you," I bite off. "So, what, you think you can bully me into walking away because you bribe some shady inspectors? That isn't happening. I'm not the same girl I used to be. And you are *never* going to ruin this place."

Not like you tried to ruin me.

He didn't succeed then either.

But that soulless goblin man just laughs.

"Oh, Lena." He's almost singing. I never knew I could hate any human being this much. "You really should have taken my initial offer." He pauses, and I'm on the verge of slamming the phone down when he adds, "If it wasn't for your dearest fiancé, you wouldn't be in this mess. Tragic that his money can't buy everything."

My mind blanks.

This is white noise. Static. The anger washes out in a flood, chased away by a coldness that feels like biting fear.

"What are you talking about?"

"There she is. Finally listening, huh?"

"Harry, I swear—"

"Old problems have an annoying way of resurfacing. Particularly when they're on video. They say the internet is forever, and they aren't wrong." He chuckles, and that chill spreads down my spine, paralyzing me.

Dr. Ezzie stares past me at the window, resigned to the disaster unfolding, but I shake my head.

This is the sort of threat you can't explain to anyone without total humiliation.

I swallow the rock in my throat.

No, my past with Harry is something I'll take to my grave.

Although I have the vicious suspicion I'm about to learn that's harder than I ever dreamed.

"You won't. You wouldn't dare," I whisper.

"*I* wouldn't do anything, of course. It's just like those pesky code issues, I'm afraid. They pop up when you least expect it," he continues. I can hardly breathe. "But I wonder what would happen to Pruitt if your past came oozing up? Reputation's everything at his level. I'm sure you're aware."

. . . Is he bluffing?

My mind races until I'm dizzy.

He can't have the boat clips after all these years.

Surely, he doesn't.

But just because he scrubbed his accounts doesn't mean the clips aren't saved somewhere.

And he's right about one thing—the internet makes terrible secrets immortal.

My eyes sting. I blink hot tears back. Every breath feels like a hacksaw in my chest.

If anything can take him down, it's calm, ice-cold rage. Not blinding threats and bluster.

Brady was right. I need to fight fire with fire and—

Oh my God, Brady.

He's the one who'll suffer if Harry spills my dirt. Being engaged means he's vulnerable too.

I need to think. There must be a way out of this.

There has to be. But my mind skids around like a helpless dog on an ice rink. Zero traction.

"Still there?" Harry prods.

"Don't try it," I clip.

"Not me, again. But as for some brutish little hacker, well, I can't be blamed for that. It happens all the time now. Sometimes those data breaches reach back for years." He pauses. "What will you do, LeeLee? Spend your hard-earned money on lawyers, chasing ghosts? Maybe more of your fiancé's money? I suppose he can afford legal bills for days. Or maybe you'll be smart and let this go. Walk away, save everyone a massive headache." He clucks his tongue softly. I can just imagine him twirling that devil's fork of a mustache. "Don't fret too much, doll. If it turns out I was ever compromised by leakers, you'll be the first to know."

"Shut up!" My voice hitches, exploding into the phone.

My lips are numb.

"It's a lot to take in. I understand. Choose your next words wisely, Lena, and your next move. I certainly don't want this to be messy and needlessly complicated—and that goes for both of us as well as your beau."

I barely hear him drumming his fingers, too much like a ticking clock, right before the phone drops.

"Lena? *Lena?*" Dr. Ezzie shakes me gently by the shoulders, but I'm unresponsive.

All of Brady's warnings sink in like arrows in my back.

It doesn't matter if I'm older and wiser and determined not to break.

I'm still a hostage. Captive to a monster who won't stay out of my life, and it overshadows everything I wish I could be.

LIKE CATS AND DOGS

(BRADY)

Wendy beams at me on the screen.

Her hair looks just as wild and windswept as always, this time with a pencil thrust through it.

That's one of my favorite things about her—and the farm. The fact that she's authentic.

No dressing to impress. No fakery. No minced words.

There are days when I'm jealous of her ability to kick optics to the curb.

I'm in my home office that doubles as a studio. I glance at my phone, then force myself to pay attention to the conference.

"I'll send you the details soon," Wendy says, not seeming to notice my distraction.

Probably because it's totally out of character.

Until now, work was my world.

It still is—mostly.

"Thanks," I say. "That's incredible. Exactly what we've been waiting to hear."

She grins. "Me too."

Finally, we're closing in on a breakthrough. The call outlined a new farming technique they've developed that's producing a greater organic crop yield for heirloom grains and legumes that are appealing to dogs.

A path through the wall we've kept smacking.

Taste and affordability.

I should be over the fucking moon.

Instead, I'm distracted, even as the good news keeps rolling in. Lena keeps invading my brain, making it damnably hard to think straight.

"I appreciate all your hard work at Finsted Farms," I tell her. "I'll have your samples sent to the nutrition lab ASAP to start testing."

"You're welcome, Brady. I really think we've got it this time."

"Me too." I send the email she's already forwarded to me along to the lab, and as another of our investors asks a few more questions for Wendy, I check my phone again.

Nothing from Lena.

Fuck.

Honestly, I hadn't expected much.

She's been distant ever since our argument. We're certainly not lovers pretending we're madly in love, not when we've reverted to something much colder.

Even Queenie seems confused, dragging around my condo and sleeping when it's not time for food or the park runs.

How the fuck do I fix it?

I wish I knew.

It's a relief when the call ends and I log off, flicking through our messages over the last few days. The few evasive ones we've exchanged at all.

I'm not one of those guys who loves a challenge.

I don't believe in playing hard to get or dicking around with tone games over a screen.

When I want a girl, I go out of my way to get her—so long as she wants me too.

Until our fight, I was sure she did.

Which makes this frosty, one-word-answer, back-and-forth bullshit that much more bewildering and maddening.

Something isn't right.

And it's that certainty that has me dialing her contact.

It's a nice evening out there, which means she'll probably be coming home if she isn't out with Grandma Lark, gossiping in the kitchen or helping the old lady tend her garden.

The phone rings, and I think she's not going to answer until the phone clicks and a small voice that doesn't sound like Lena answers.

"Hello?"

"Hey, Sass. Just wanted to check in." I flick the pen between my fingers.

"I'm not dying, Brady. You don't need to worry."

"We haven't spoken for days." I try to ignore the bitter voice in my blood demanding answers, but I can't. "Fuck it, you know why I'm calling? Because I miss you."

There's a shuffling sound, and her breathing sounds heavier, like she was just outside and now she's coming in.

I bet my Grandma Lark theory was right.

". . . I miss you too," she says, but the words feel forced. "But I thought you were working? You said you had a busy week."

"Just finished for the day. What are you up to right now?"

"Mm, just trimming some flowers."

"With Gran?"

"How did you know?"

"My awesome powers of deduction. Also, where else would you be using your green thumb?"

Silence.

"Do you need me somewhere again?" she asks flatly.

My jaw clenches.

"No. I need us to talk about the damn elephant in the room."

"Talk about *what*?"

"What's eating you, woman," I say, no longer trying to be calm. If she needs me to squeeze it out of her like toothpaste, I will. "Don't tell me it's nothing. We both know that's a lie."

"I never said that," she admits.

"What is it, then? You're still sore at me for going after him? For overstepping my bounds?"

"Brady, it's—it doesn't matter." She sighs, the sound crackling through the speaker.

"Like hell."

"I mean it. That's why I wanted space. You still don't get that you don't have to *fix* anything."

"Are you still mad at me? Be honest."

A hesitation. Just enough to feel it in my bones. "No."

"So, talk to me. You're not pissed, but you don't want to talk to me or see me. Is it him? Is that fuck causing more trouble?"

"No," she says sharply. "Not everything in my life revolves around men, past or present. Tricky concept, I know."

I fight back a smile, grateful she's showing a little sass, like her nickname.

"Not him. Then why do I smell it on your voice?" I say. "What's he done now? Lena, be straight with me."

"Dude, this isn't about him, and even if it was, it's not your business. It's my job. How many times do we need to talk about this? The clinic deal has nothing to do with you or—" She stumbles, unable to say his name, and I know.

Total certainty.

Yeah, she might be lying to protect herself or even me, but that doesn't change the facts.

He's still coming for her, and that's an open invitation for me to take out the trash.

I don't like it one bit. The Lena who left my apartment ready to tear my head off would never hold back.

This Lena—she's too quiet. Too unsure. Too afraid.

If this was only about me, she'd have said it to my face. She'd give me hell for breaking her trust and screwing up the sexy chaos we had.

Her silence now tells me there's more to worry about than my own dumb mistakes. And whatever it is, I need to know.

"If it's not Harry, then what?" I demand.

"I'm just having second thoughts about . . . about this whole thing, I guess. The Pawsome Hearts deal."

What?

My chest squeezes.

That's not what she would've said a week ago, and this change of heart has Harry Jay's fingerprints all over it.

What the fuck did he do to her?

"I'm coming over." I clench my fists and release them, trying to push that smarmy asshole's face out of my head. "It'll be easier to talk in person, assuming you're—"

"There's nothing to talk about! God. If you insist, fine."

"I'll swing by later. I want to see you."

"Brady, I—"

"Talk soon." I hesitate, then end the call before saying anything else, like how I'm practically having goddamned withdrawals without her by my side.

I'm no expert on feelings, but I know I need to tread lightly.

I need to be sensible with this, or she'll change her mind about if there's anything to fight for at all.

I pull up Luis's number, swinging back in my office chair as he answers.

"Boss man, what's up?"

"I need the biggest nuke you have on Harry Jay. What has the best case legally to sink his ass to the bottom?"

He pauses, thinking. "Probably the small business cases?"

I flop back, propping my feet on my desk as I think, remembering what I read before.

Harry's firm had an astonishingly rapid rise in commercial real estate by chasing down old, stagnant businesses on the edge of Seattle's Chinatown-International District.

From the witnesses Luis interviewed, the pattern was clear: Harry Jay would show up with a big offer to reel his sellers in. Then he'd shave it down substantially after newly uncovered code violations piled up.

The struggling business owners felt pressured to sell at steep discounts, knowing they couldn't go to other buyers without extensive and draining renovations or brutal disclosures.

"How does he do it?" I growl. "Is he bribing the inspectors, or what?"

"Close enough. My guess is our little friend has his hands deep inside the department," Luis says. "Bribery, probably. Or blackmail. A man like that can't have many real friends."

I smile a little, but I'm still thinking. If Harry pulls this trick with Pawsome Hearts, it'll knock them out and force the doctor right into his hands.

But he'll need to bring some heavy firepower to get his way.

Dr. Ezzie will want what her property's worth, but more importantly, I've seen her passion when I brought in Charlie the corgi. It's partly where Lena gets it from.

If she can, she'll sell to Lena, no question.

Which brings up a bigger one: What the hell will he do to strong-arm Ezzie into a deal she doesn't want?

"It's enough. Go time," I say roughly. "I want you to work our connections to the press. Do whatever you have to—an anonymous leak with the documents, a press release, a public onslaught. We have enough rope to string his ass up."

"Damn, you're really not playing."

"Not this time, Luis. Get it done."

I end the call and sit up as Queenie stretches and comes over for a back rub.

I can see it now—dealing this selfish fuck a mortal wound.

Seattle real estate is always newsworthy when it's scarce and comically expensive. A story where any local mogul pulled all the dirty tricks in the book to get an advantage in an overheated market is basically peak rage-bait for the local press. Guaranteed to bring so many eyes it's irresistible.

And the more eyes on Harry Jackoff, the more we'll find.

That's how it goes.

When people see a moral outrage, they're tenacious. If there's something to find, they will. It's like unleashing the hounds.

I have him in our sights, and I just need Luis to pull the trigger.

With any luck, in a few days' time, Harry damn Jay will be neck deep in his own filth, drowning.

Then he'll never bother my woman again.

Once I finish replying to a few last emails, I head over to Lena's place.

I'm happy to drive myself today and leave Luis with no distractions for his special mission.

When I pull up, the front door's propped open, and I see Lena hauling something outside.

I scramble out to help her. I don't realize I'm pulling a suitcase from her hands until I look down.

A very heavy packed suitcase.

What the hell?

I meet her eyes for a second before she ducks down and looks away.

"Leaving town?" I ask carefully.

"A trip with a friend. Just a few days to clear my head." No elaboration. She just wrenches the suitcase from my hand.

I'm so stunned I let it go.

There's no denying it now. The damage is so intense she can barely look me in the eye. Hell, if she knew what I'm up to, she might spit in my face.

I don't know what the fuck to do so I trail along like some sad kicked puppy as she takes it to her car and lays it in the trunk.

"What trip, Lena? What friend?" I definitely don't sound like a puppy. More like I'm gargling glass. I catch myself and shake my head. "Will you tell me what's going on?"

She looks at me, her big brown eyes turned to desert.

There's no light, no love, no hope.

"Is that part of the contract too? I have to ask permission to leave the city?" She slams the trunk shut and sighs. "Brady, look, I need time to process. We'll talk when I get back."

"We can't now?" I try to keep the thorns from my voice without success. "Sass, is it that fucking bad?"

Her eyes heat, guarded and sad.

"Yes. I have so much to deal with." Her lips tremble.

"I know." And I step in front of her. Years of growing up in the spotlight kick in when my own reason doesn't—but we can't have a scene in a busy neighborhood, right here in her driveway. "Can we just sit down for a minute? Five minutes, then I'll buzz off."

She glances longingly at the car, but then she nods and leads the way back to her open front door, waiting for me.

Thank God.

I shut it behind me, and once we're inside, I glance around.

Her normally small yet orderly environment looks like it's been through an earthquake.

Stray clothes everywhere, tossed over chairs and piled on the floor, like she's just done her laundry and decided to stuff everything clean into a suitcase.

"What's the rush?" I say. "Shit, are you that desperate to get away from me?"

"I have a flight to catch." She folds her arms. "If you're going to try to talk me out of going, don't."

"Don't put words in my mouth," I bite off. "I just want to know what's going on with you. The truth, not excuses to shut me up."

"The truth." She repeats that word like a curse.

Then she shakes her head, her cheeks flaring and her eyes swimming with agony.

Goddamn, I hate this.

She's a candle with its wick burned down, her usual fire leaving her wilted. My gut clenches. I already know that whatever she's got has to be bad.

"Fine. I suppose you deserve that much," she whispers, lifting her chin. "The truth is, I'm not the right person for this sham engagement anymore. I'm sorry it got this far—I really am—but if we keep going through with it, you'll only have a harder time later."

Her words are fucking bullets.

I rock back, feeling them vibrate in my bones.

"What the hell, Lena? You can't believe that. Be serious."

"I am—and I'm *sorry*. You don't even know. I was going to think this through for a few more days and tell you first thing once I thought about how . . . but we're here, aren't we? What's the point of dancing around it? This isn't good for you and your brand. I know I signed a contract—but you'll have your money back, of course. Every penny. I'm not going through with Pawsome Hearts."

I stare at her.

When I walked into this, I knew she was panicked.

I didn't know she'd lost her damn mind.

"Lena, come on. This isn't about the goddamned money. What *happened*?" I'm desperate. I rake a hand through my hair, trying to pull myself together, to keep thinking like a sane man, even though my lungs have seized with panic.

"I'll say whatever you want to explain the breakup," she continues, tearing up now. "Whatever it takes. Blame me. Tell the world I cheated or . . . or . . ."

Her strained voice chokes off.

"Cheated? Fuck! You think I want to announce I couldn't handle a fiancée for thirty damn days? The love of my life?"

Those last words cut deep.

She looks down, sniffing, blinking back tears.

". . . I . . . I know. But it's how it should be."

Wrong.

She's never been more wrong in her life, and I can't believe she's lying to my face.

I fucking know better.

Lena's not melting down and cracking under the pressure. She's too strong for that.

For the first time, anger flashes through my heartache.

"You're walking, then. You're leaving me stranded, and you won't even tell me why." Every word scorches my throat.

"Because I can't do it, Brady!" She flares. "Because this isn't me, and I can't stand to hurt you. I thought I could when we first agreed, but now I know . . . I know better. And I'm sorry you feel misled. All I can offer is damage control. Can't you just accept that?"

"No. Because this isn't about my reputation and we both know it."

She shakes her head fiercely.

"You're wrong. Stop pointing fingers. I said I'll help you make up for it. Just let me go."

I stare at her, beyond bewildered. She doesn't realize she's demanding the impossible.

I'll never let us go, I want to say.

Stupid, I know.

Outrageous, really, when she has the weakest half-hearted lies carved on her face.

There's no negotiating when she's in this state, though. Not here, not now.

For today, the deal's off, and we're becoming strangers again.

What else is there when she won't give me the slightest opening to talk her down from the ledge?

The game just ended with the goddamned table flipped upside down.

"So that's it," I growl, still trying to convince myself to move my legs.

Walk the fuck away while I can.

"Y-yeah. That's it." She nods, but she won't look at me, swiping at her tears with the back of her hand. "But wait."

I turn around, my throat so tight as I look at her, but she's back in the kitchen. I watch her grab something off the counter before she marches back to me, refusing to meet my eyes.

"Here." That's all she says. One word before the ring I gave her, symbolizing this farce, gets mashed into my palm.

I'm a dead man walking.

With my dignity in tatters, I clench my fist around that lying metal and turn my back on the prettiest little liar I'll ever know, marching back to my vehicle.

Her total silence devours me one last time in an eternity condensed into seconds.

XXI

CARDINAL BLUES

(LENA)

I wish I could pinpoint the moment when life became so brutal that I can't even appreciate the loveliest turquoise blue water I've ever seen.

Even Lake Tahoe's beauty can't fill the crater in my chest. It feels like I've been ripped apart with a meat hook, and I'm left with only threads holding me together.

One second, I'm staring out across the unbelievable water, the distant trees visible on the shoreline.

The next, I have to blink through my vision blurring. I see Brady's face for the thousandth time, angry and hurt because he knows I lied point-blank.

What a pathetic ending.

I might as well have given him George Costanza's infamous "It's not you, it's me" speech.

I should've known he'd see through it, but I had to wing it when he showed up in my driveway, determined to talk sense.

The worst part is, it wasn't enough.

I have a rotten feeling he's still trying to piece together the missing bits I wouldn't give him.

I just hope he stays away from provoking Harry, at least. There's nothing left to fight over now that I've basically surrendered.

I blink again.

This time, when I open my eyes, there's a huge smiling face staring down at me, pinched with laughter and concern.

Elle watches me through her blond hair hanging over the sides of her face like curtains.

"What is it?" I ask weakly, glancing around and wondering how much of the day I've wasted in this chair with a romance thriller on my lap.

I didn't know I could feel like I've aged twenty years in one week.

My bestie blinks, looking like she's about to say something. Probably something true and to the point and dusted with optimism like powdered sugar.

That's the Elle I've known and loved since we were kids.

But she just shakes her head, a small frown pulling her lips down.

"Not another headache?" I ask, sitting up. My turn to be concerned, knowing she's prone to migraines from hell.

Actually, that's how she met her superhusband, August. *Husband.*

God, it's still weird to think of her married, especially to him. Even weirder to see them so happy together after they slogged a hundred miles through the biggest drama in Seattle that didn't involve a Pruitt.

That's Elle's luck, though. Marrying the first hot billionaire beast she ever fainted on.

"Nope, they're pretty rare these days, thankfully. I just wondered if you still wanted to take the boat out today? There's time." Her wary smile gives me the impression it's not the first time she's asked.

"The boat," I repeat absently.

It's official. Heartbreak has made me an idiot.

"Don't worry! I won't be driving. It's way too big." She grins mischievously.

"Well yeah, I don't want to drown."

She giggles.

Although sinking in a lake this heavenly doesn't feel like the worst end to the Lena Joly story. It would give Brady a convenient out without any breakup bombshells, wouldn't it?

Could I fake my death and start over at a clinic in Thailand?

I'm being ridiculous, I know.

Elle knows, too, because she snaps her fingers in front of my face.

"Hello, Lena? Is anything getting through?"

"Half of it. But sure, let's go out for a boat ride. I've been wanting to see your latest toy, anyway."

"*Technically*, it's Gruffykins's toy. But he's said I can take it out anytime I like as long as the captain's on hand."

"Aren't you guys married?" I squint up at her. "What's his is yours, right?"

"And what's mine is mine." She grins and beckons to the door leading back inside from her expansive patio. "Also, I'm *so* pumped you agreed, because I already had the captain on standby this evening."

The captain? Holy hell.

There are times when I forget just how rich my once-starving-artist friend is.

Fresh air will do me good, though.

I just got here yesterday, and so far I've spent my entire time in three large rooms, moping around like a soggy kitten.

Three *gorgeous* rooms, in Elle's defense. And mine.

It's not like being here has been a hardship.

Except for the fact that every single room screams Brady Pruitt.

I don't know why. It doesn't make sense, because this place is a world away from his expensive penthouse lording over an urban kingdom.

Here, it's an ultramodern, beautifully decorated lake house suitable for a billionaire power couple. Every room has soaring bookcases and furniture so comfortable I wonder if I'm dreaming.

The place doesn't need a library since that's basically the entire house.

More books than I can count in every room, shelves bursting with the oversize illustration and art tomes you'd expect from a talent who keeps tearing up the world of kids' storybooks. Elle's library is probably worth more than my life savings.

Under any other circumstance, I'd love it here. There's even a basement theater and a heated pool overlooking a white dock so spotless it's unnatural.

It better. I think August must own like three large boats now. *Plural.*

So aesthetically, no, this isn't anything like Brady's place. It's bigger and more natural. It's missing his balmy smile and Queenie's happy licks and a big, warm bed to crawl in with a man who gladly helps me shed my sanity.

Ugh, poor Queenie.

I miss her terribly.

And double ugh, this *house.* Brady would capture some amazing videos here for his Insta.

I can just see him outside, talking to his fans with Queenie's tail slapping his legs, every time I glance out the window.

You want to know the shittiest thing?

I never gave *either* of them a proper goodbye.

The lump in my throat swells until it crowds my eyeballs.

"Okay, missy," Elle says, taking my arm and dragging me up. "That's enough glooming for one day. We're going out on the water, and you're gonna smile and drink wine. Then you're going to *tell* me what's going on in that pretty head."

I snort. "Like you don't know."

"Eh, I know you and Playboy McFakerson broke up, and it was never real to begin with. And you're dead set on a fake romance not meaning anything even though there's a married girl standing right in front of you who started off in the same place." She smiles so brightly I laugh. I'm so lucky to have her—a friend who can do pity gracefully. "But I know that isn't the whole story front to back if you're still this cut up about it."

"Okay, fine. On the boat," I promise.

"Great!" Soon, I'm trapped in her inescapable positivity as she grabs a small basket of snacks and wine and sets off for the dock.

The lake boat seems fairly modest for a yacht, nothing like the Seattle monsters that can have their own ten-person crew and helipad.

It's a different life out here, slower and quieter. I see why they picked Tahoe to get away from Seattle's constant energy. But Elle looks like she's settled into her happy new life, and I'm seriously glad for her.

The wind streams her long wispy hair back from her face as we climb aboard, and the boat starts moving a few minutes later.

While Elle pops into the cabin for a chat with the captain, it gives me another chance to check my phone.

Nothing from Brady.

I mean, I wouldn't text me either. Not after I chucked his heart in the dumpster.

Nothing from Harry, either, and that's no big comfort.

Plenty of frantic messages from Trish and Dr. Ezzie, though, asking me about my snap decision to back out, suggesting I revisit things and maybe consider bringing Harry's firm on as a partial stakeholder.

Fuck that entirely.

By walking away, I'm giving up on Pawsome Hearts' survival and myself.

The clinic is Dr. Ezzie's legacy. Her dream. It *was*, and now she's running the risk of signing over its soul to the devil.

With my breath lodged in my lungs, I scroll through Brady's socials too. I keep waiting for a big announcement about the end of our "relationship," but so far there's nothing.

Maybe he doesn't know what to say.

I don't blame him.

But I know guilt, and it stings me like crawling scorpions.

Did I make the right decision? Running away from *my* dream, my life, from Brady? When I think about it too much, they've become indistinguishable in my head.

Pawsome Hearts and Brady Pruitt, tangled up in an inseparable mess I blew to smithereens.

Oh, scorpions, you don't let up. Your venom makes me feel so shitty, and it's what I deserve.

It's not like I had a choice. Not with Harry holding a blackmail gun to my head.

Sticking around would've meant disaster for Brady, his family, for my business. Any doctor I could've partnered with would've ran away for sure the instant they got a whiff of that scandal.

I couldn't do it, risking a bigger heartbreak for—what, exactly? A not-relationship that was always meant to end?

And if I told him, he'd have gone for Harry's throat. He might've done something unholy for me, ruining the rest of his life. The polar opposite of what this whole dumb fake engagement was supposed to accomplish.

God.

I'm wallowing in self-pity, but I try to stop when I see Elle coming my way, still wearing that permanent cheery smile.

"Isn't it refreshing out here? I love the fresh air."

"Yep. Worry-free," I lie.

We're slowly gliding toward the center of the glassy lake as she climbs into the chair next to me. "We're on the boat now, so what's the story? Do I have to remind you that you would've clawed my face off if I'd been this tight lipped during my drama?"

Touché.

I tilt my head back, staring at the baby blue sky as my stomach knots.

There's no way to avoid the truth—I'm a coward and I'm running. It doesn't matter if I've picked a beautiful place to escape.

"It wasn't fake," I whisper.

"Duh."

I look up and roll my eyes at her. "Girl, come on. You could at least *pretend* to be sympathetic."

"Oh, I'm plenty sympathetic. If I had some tea aboard, I'd be giving you the whole Gran-bleeding-heart tea chat right now. But anyone could tell you're heels over head for this guy. I'll trust you that he's over the playboy stuff—but does he love you back?"

Love?

Oh, shiiiit.

That's a big little word.

I mean, we've been together for less than a season.

Face-to-face, it's more like a matter of weeks.

Magical, life-bending weeks that have turned me inside out and made me wear my own skin like a scarf, but weeks, yes.

"He likes me, I guess." I have to look away when I say it, blinded by the hurt, angry eyes Brady gave me right before I walked out.

"So, he's at home, then, nursing a broken heart. Just like you," she points out.

"He has the best girl for company. I miss that dog so much." I break, smiling at her even as my lips quiver.

"Uh-huh," Elle says incredulously. "You miss them both desperately. What would you say if this was me and August?"

"I . . . I'd make you pick up your phone and call him. Oh my God, this is stupid, isn't it?" I bury my face in my hands. "But do I really have to be the one to call? He hasn't said anything about the breakup. Not publicly." I peek at my phone, just in case anything slipped by me, but there's nothing. "I told him we were done. I said the arrangement was a ginormous mistake."

"He's a dude. I bet he doesn't know what to say." *Now* she sounds sympathetic. "Also, living in the media eye isn't easy. It gets hella messy."

"Yeah, I know." I sigh.

There's no argument there. Elle Marshall certainly has the experience to know.

Then again, so do I.

How many times did I play social media wonder girl alongside him, all so he could get his views in and let his followers peep at his life?

Kind of parasitic.

Except Brady's social media presence is his life. His attempt to reinvent himself with a reputation that ranks above shriveled turkey vulture.

We talk like old times then. I rehash everything, leaving no ugly detail hidden, and the anger on her face is mine every time I mention Harry and his meddling.

"Forget messy. This is a fucking cataclysm." I drop my head in my hands, breathing harshly.

Elle pats my shoulder. "Just a little. But we're not panicking, remember? No freak-outs allowed on the boat. Captain's rules."

I shake my head.

"This doesn't *have* to be the end. You can pick the scab off and let the scar fade over time. Don't let some corkscrew dickhead ruin a good thing," she whispers.

"Only in the universe where Harry keeps his nose out of my business. Not this one. I've already walked and accepted my heartbreak." I stare through her. The longer there's radio silence from Brady, the sooner he moves on and forgets the timid mouse who was never cut out for a relationship, real or otherwise.

Those scorpions in my stomach are turning into rattlesnakes.

"Thanks for trying to clear my head," I say, even though we both know I came along to humor her.

That's the thing about heartbreak, I guess. It poisons everything else.

God. I keep calling it heartbreak, don't I? All while I'm conveniently avoiding what that means.

"You wanna know what I came up with while I was plotting my latest Kiki the Koala book? Blue the cardinal pays her a visit because his wife is pissed at how nice he's being to Polypops the one-eyed squirrel who keeps destroying their nest."

"You named a cardinal Blue?" I smile at the absurdity. "Even though cardinals are—"

"That's why it's a banger to illustrate, okay! But listen . . . so Blue decides to go all manly man to win her back. Next time Polypops comes tearing apart their nest, looking for acorns, Blue tries to talk him down. He invites them to sit down for some eucalyptus tea with Miss Kiki, and of course Polypops laughs in his face because he's a giant asshole. But they make such a racket shouting at each other that Barry Barred Owl overhears and takes things into his own hands . . ."

"Oh no." I blink at her. "Kinda dark for a kid's book, no?"

"Heyyy, it's not like the squirrel gets eaten! Barry just carries him off so he can cool his heels, and Blue spends hours rebuilding the nest. When he's done, it's better than ever. And when his wife comes home, she's crying. Totally happy and apologetic because she remembers how much Blue loves her and how he'll do anything, even when he never really had a chance against squirrel bro."

It's so silly I'm laughing, making these honking sounds that leave my face burning.

"But are you saying there's a moral?" I ask when I can speak again. "I don't think we'll ever have a Barry swooping in on our squirrel."

God, I wish.

"No, but someone's trying to save your nest. Would it really be so bad to let him?"

Knife, meet heart.

Her big, soul-searching eyes nearly drop me on my face. The realization hits like lightning.

I'm in love with my Blue.

I love Brady Pruitt.

And here I am, blowing up and acting bonkers because I love him so truly and deeply and he'll never know.

I've lost my shit—and the plot—because I'm terrified Harry Jay will exploit the past to run him off like he did to my mom.

I don't answer, but I don't need to.

A knowing smile hangs on Elle's face as she gets up to call into the cabin, telling the captain we're ready to start making our way home.

We stare at the pretty scenery a little while longer while rocks bang around my head and Elle tells me about their home away from home.

Woe is me.

The kind of misery that no number of tall trees and scenic rocks and a glimpse of a black bear can fix.

The bear's pretty cool, though, no lie.

And I feel a little lighter as the boat slides back into its dock and my phone *finally* pings.

But it's not Brady.

It's Dr. Ezzie, and her text is just a link to a news story.

A Seattle news story.

An exclusive about big-time developer Harry Jay and some insanely dirty business dealings.

Every drop of blood drains from my body as I read.

The article discusses the myriad ways Harry manipulated property owners to accept his offers: strong-arm sales involving code violations, county fines, sudden liens out of nowhere.

The same familiar shit show he's made us live.

"Oh my God," I manage, taking a seat on a bench by her docks. "Holy shit."

"Holy what?" Elle yanks the phone from my hand and starts scrolling, her eyes flicking with excitement. "Lena . . . this is brilliant!"

"It's something," I grunt. I feel like I need to be coached to remember how to breathe. "It's—"

A disaster.

A death wish.

No *way* in hell will Harry ever let this go.

Everything I thought I was protecting Brady from just sealed his fate. And just like Elle's blue cardinal, I'm scared he's picked a fight he can't win.

But Elle doesn't see it that way, of course, not when her glass is always half full.

"Now you've got him. This is huge!" she whoops.

"This wasn't me. I didn't do anything."

"No, but between you and Brady, you've got that jerkwad's balls in the vice." She leans over the dock and spits like the delicate lady she is.

"He *is* a jerkwad," I agree.

"Think about it, Lena—he doesn't deserve to get away with any of this shit. It's not just what he put you through. The article says there must be at least a dozen people he's screwed over." She points a finger at me. "You see it now? You know what you have to do?"

I know the argument Brady and I had at his apartment. He wanted to fight so bad, and I wouldn't let him.

I ran away.

I bowed out with his heart, and I even left Dr. Ezzie high and dry.

Chickenshit.

I have to admit, Elle has a point, even if she drives it home in the weirdest ways.

I'm so sick of being afraid.

Afraid of what Harry will do to me. Afraid of what he'll do to my clinic. Afraid of what it means if I love another man after he hurt me so much.

One man ruined my past and present, but I *let* him.

Do I really want to hand over my future too?

No way.

No effing way.

I'm not turning over my career, my life, and the only man who's ever treated me better than an annoying cactus.

If I don't want other people fighting my battles, it's time to go home and go to war.

"You're smiling," Elle says uncertainly.

"Well, yeah. I'm about to open up some long-overdue hell."

XXII

RABID DOG

(BRADY)

I won't lie. Punching Harry Jay in the throat feels like a win.

It's past time that eel had to fight for his life.

The only thing I don't know is if it's too late to matter. If Lena will rethink the last few days or decide I'm just another villain in her story.

The condo feels like a mausoleum without her. Queenie aside, I dread coming home, hating how Lena has left her impression on damn near everything.

It shouldn't be possible to miss a woman this much—especially when love was always an illusion.

Still, I can't lie even to myself.

I miss her like hell.

When my phone buzzes, I'm grabbing it desperately, but it's not Lena.

"Luis," I answer. "What's up?"

"I think you've seen the headlines, yes?"

"Yeah. Would you agree it's going well?"

"According to my sources, he's sinking like a stone. The man will be stuck under a ten-thousand-pound legal boulder in days." There's a smug pride in every word.

Can't blame him when Luis isn't subtle about loving the cloak-and-dagger subterfuge.

"Good, fuck him," I snarl.

"The local press is a stampede, falling all over each other to get interviews with him. From what I've gathered, his office is vacated, basically locked up." He blows out a breath. "So many lawsuits, man. It's an avalanche. I guess he's decided to come out with his own, but it won't get anywhere fast."

"He's suing *me*?" I snort. "Desperation. That fuck doesn't have a leg to stand on."

"I know, you know, and the lawyers know, but he's suing for defamation, anyway. Just a rabid dog, lashing out at this point for something to bite."

"I love the smell of panic." For the first time in days, I smile.

"He knows how crushing this is. Even if he can wriggle out of criminal charges—and I'm pretty sure he won't—it's so rancid no one will want to work with him again in this town. There are calls coming to boycott him entirely."

"Perfect," I repeat.

I don't know Harry personally from Adam, but we share one thing in common.

Image is everything.

And now, if he's flailing and chasing his own tail like a deluded beast, hiding from the press while they burn him down—it means he's a broken mirror.

He never expected his illegal fuckery to come to light, and it's busted him into a million pieces.

His threats don't scare me. Empty bluster.

Hell, anybody in code enforcement he corrupted is probably fleeing across the state line by now if they have an IQ above frozen lasagna.

"There's something else." Luis clears his throat, his usual tell when he wants to change the subject—and when he knows I won't like it. "Have you heard from Miss Joly yet?"

"No. After these fireworks, hopefully soon."

But why does it feel so unlikely with every passing hour of radio silence?

"I hate to throw this on your shoulders, but people are starting to notice she's missing, boss man."

Goddammit, I know.

I haven't posted anything new for days.

With a social media presence like mine, I could hand off content to others to fill in the gaps, or just repost old videos. But it's always been important that my fans know they're talking to authentic Brady, and they have a near-daily connection to my adventures.

Of course, that also means I'm front and center, and when I'm not, it's a recipe for controversy.

People are talking. Whispers are becoming a dull roar, asking why my last few posts and live streams had no mention of my lovely fiancée.

And my latest ghosting act just pours fuel on the fire.

A dozen variations of #BradyBreakup hashtags are trending.

Fucking hell.

"Where is she? Any updates?" I growl.

"Nope, but I have a few guesses you wouldn't let me pursue."

"No. I'm not invading her damn privacy."

I've done that enough.

"In that case, I don't think we'll uncover her location unless she decides she wants you to find her, my man."

Damn.

And judging by the total silence, even more than twelve hours after I unleashed the hounds on Harry's ass, that's unlikely.

I scowl at my computer screen, the satisfaction of destroying Harry Jay running through my fingers like fine sand.

I need to find Lena ASAP.

"I hate to add insult to injury, but your mother's been asking about her too," Luis says. "She's wondering when you'll bring her around the house to talk wedding plans. She couldn't believe your father sang her praises after that charity thing."

"Fuck me, I know." I rake a hand through my hair, clenching my jaw. "But what the hell do I say? That she dumped me and ran off into the sunset?"

Luis goes quiet. "You want to give them the truth?"

"Absolutely not. Shit, I need to find her and make this right." Even if it'll take her time to understand why I hit Harry Jay the way I did, and a miracle to ever fall in love with me again.

I'm ready to become a praying man for the first time in my life if she'll talk to me.

If I can prove that her devil ex is gone for good.

"Did you send the article to Dr. Ezzie?" Luis asks after a second.

"Yeah. She said she passed it along."

"Damn. I guess we'll just have to wait until she comes back. Hopefully a few more days. She didn't quit her job, right?"

"Not likely."

I believe that, but I shrug because I just don't fucking know, and that's infuriating.

A few days might be an eternity. That's what Lena said originally when I asked about her plans to run off with a friend and escape from me.

"I don't want to wait, Luis. I need her *now*."

"Don't know what to tell you. If I could summon her back in a maid outfit and a cloud of sparkles, I would've by now."

"Fuck you."

"Fuck you too! Respectfully."

"I could have you fired."

"But you never will," he says, a grin in his voice. "Do you want me to go digging? You figured she's off with that Elle Marshall girl, and there's a lot of material there. A lot of places they could be with her money, unfortunately."

"I've got a better idea," I say as it crystallizes in my head. "Hold tight. I'll let you know if it works."

"What are you thinking?"

"We're going to do this the right way, respecting her boundaries. You know, unlike what happened before and put me in a world of shit. I'm talking to the only person who might tell me anything."

◆ ◆ ◆

Grandma Lark's late-summer garden is bursting with color. Bright flowers, bulging tomatoes and cucumbers, little wooden gnomes, and lush ivy crawling over everything.

I'm no expert on this stuff, but it's a testament to how sharp and active the old lady is.

It's also my first time plodding over to her little house just up the street from Lena's deserted house. When she opens the door and sees me standing on the step, her face creases into a mischievous smile.

What am I in for?

"Brady! So nice to see you again. I've got some muffins cooling—apple cinnamon today—and some nice hibiscus tea. Come on in."

"If you're offering to feed me that good, it's a deal, Gran."

"Boy, I think that smile could get you a hot meal anywhere in this city." She winks and leads the way into the kitchen.

Unlike Lena's apartment, this place is decked out with photos and kitschy decorations on every wall. Living proof of the long life Gran built here.

Still, with potted plants on every surface and the homey kitchen so well organized, it doesn't feel too cramped. I'd call it lively.

"Sit." She waves at the sofa. One half is covered in ample folded blankets, so I take the only free cushion. "Coffee or hibiscus?"

"I'll take the tea, if it's going."

"Of course it's going. You'll drink up, and you'll tell me why you're here with that long lantern look on your face."

"What look?" I call after her, but she just cackles as she heads into the kitchen. When Gran returns, she's got a tray piled with muffins and two steaming cups of tea in blue-and-white china.

"Don't flatter me, Brady," she says before I can compliment her. "I'm too old and too curious why you're here."

I bite into the best damn muffin I've ever tasted and swallow before I say, "I'm looking for a missing person."

"I didn't know you were a cop, Mr. Pruitt." Her eyes sparkle.

"Not technically, but this person means a lot to me."

"Mm, yes. Only the world, I imagine. She would."

"I didn't say *she*, did I?"

Her grin feels endless.

"No, but I see that look in your eyes. You've come down with a raging case of heartsickness."

"Like hell," I mutter.

"Incurable, I'd say. It tends to make a person awfully irritable too."

"And I'm guessing you have a cure?" I tilt my head. "How much do you know, Gran?"

"About what?"

"Lena and me." Those three words feel like chewing broken glass.

"Well, I knew you two tried to wear out the bed." She pauses, and I try like mad to delete that phrase from my brain. "I also know you made her blush and giggle like a prom girl. I've *never* seen my Lena smile so much since she was a kid. But she wouldn't tell me much else, the poor dear. The girl will sit and chug my tea by the liter when it's someone else's drama, but she clams up the second it's hers."

The old woman sips her strong hibiscus brew.

"Somehow, I think you know more than you let on."

"Young man, I told you, flattery won't help you here." The smile slips from her face, and she looks at me shrewdly. "She likes you. But I didn't need to bring you that news."

"I'd like to think so, but I can't find out if I don't know where she is, can I? I'm wondering if you do."

For a moment, she's silent, then she slowly nods.

"You men are all the same when you're desperate." She adds another spoonful of honey to her tea and stirs it, watching the swirl. "Did I ever mention my granddaughter, Elle? My *actual* granddaughter, that is."

"Rings a bell," I say politely.

"She got married not too long ago. She's an artist and a storyteller, and getting out does wonders for her muse. Seattle can be lovely in the summer, but you know how it is after October. Months of grey skies and buckets. The first thing her Auggie did after their honeymoon was plunk down your kinda money for a new vacation spot with clearer skies. Big, fancy house, right on Lake Tahoe."

"Lake Tahoe," I repeat.

Shit.

She holds up a finger. "Now, there's no guarantee, even if Elle and Lena are inseparable. But if you've got the means and you're itching to find her bad enough, I'd start there."

"You're sure she's with her best friend? Not her mother?" I watch Gran's face.

"Her mama's a lovely woman, but she never was the best at mothering her little girl when she needs it. She's the quiet type, deep into meditation and singing to the trees alone when times get rough. Lena always took after her father, I think. Too serious for all that." She sips her tea. "You're a smart man. If I can add it up, so can you."

Yeah, and I need to get the hell to Nevada tonight.

"Thanks, Gran." I stuff the rest of my third muffin into my mouth as I jump to my feet. "Sorry about the crumbs, but I've just remembered some—some urgent business."

"I see," she says dryly. "Shake your tail, then. Lord knows I don't want to hold you up, gabbing about nothing."

"We'll do this again real soon," I promise.

Then I give her a grateful nod and shake her gnarled hand before I gun it out the door. As I'm walking to my vehicle, I text Luis to book me the next flight to Lake Tahoe and keep Queenie company for a few days.

I never got an address, but I can find out where the Marshalls have their property.

In less than an hour, I'm packed and ready.

I'm about to head out the door when my phone starts buzzing and doesn't stop. Not a call, but a fuckload of notifications.

I stop to check.

The first thing I see is a new text from Luis—check Instagram—and I open the app with a ragged sigh.

I'm swamped with tags, mentions—far more than usual for posting nothing new.

I don't have to scroll far before I'm confused.

Tags and DMs demanding if I knew.

If I'm okay with this.

People showering me with sympathies.

A call from Dad comes in, and I swipe it away, heading for a post by a particularly shitty online tabloid I recognize.

But it's not me feeding the scandal mill for once.

It's Lena.

The photos make my jaw drop.

She's on a yacht, looking younger. There's a lot of skin showing, and everything's blurred, but it's obvious what she's doing. And it's equally clear the man in the photos isn't me when he has that ridiculous mustache I want to rip off with my bare hands.

I drop onto the sofa and slump against the cushions. Queenie gets up from sunning herself and strides over, leaning against me with a groan.

The dog is psychic. She knows how gutted I am.

And that's when I realize the idiotic lawsuit was never the real attack. This is how he's striking back, and it's eviscerating.

That gutter rat still had the photos. The videos. *The blackmail.*

Now, a whole bunch of gossipy tabloids and online shit-rakers have it too.

The story spreads like wildfire, splashing across every social media app known to man.

Situation: Fuck.

Fuck!

Another call comes in, this time from Mom. Again, I swipe to decline it, staring at the screen like something will magically change.

I chuck my phone onto the coffee table in disgust, slowly breathing as I focus on massaging Queenie's neck.

It's the only thing that grounds me as she licks my hand nervously.

The only reason why I don't go berserk when I close my eyes.

This beautiful, kind dog disarms the ticking time bomb in my blood. And for the briefest moment, she rips me back through time, to greyhounds and Gramps, to a simpler time when I was too young and innocent to have mortal enemies or a possessive streak.

Every time Queenie leans into my palm with a contented groan, I'm one with the sunshine and the dog races again.

I'm lounging in the back rooms after the races with these dogs built like straw bags and sticks, suddenly the gentlest creatures alive after sprinting around like overcaffeinated cheetahs.

Their owners would let me pet them while Gramps laughed his head off.

His bets didn't matter.

Win, lose, or draw, the old man knew how to have a good time and appreciate life.

He taught me not to take everything so damn seriously—a lesson that feels like ten lifetimes ago now.

As Queenie leans up to slurp my cheek, I smile.

But not for long when all I can see is Lena's naked body and the yellow stars someone pasted over her breasts, right before they pushed her biggest humiliation in front of the world.

Right after Harry goddamned Jay launched the retaliation I invited by murdering his business.

Disgusting, degrading fucking revenge porn.

Lena's worst nightmare come true.

I choke back bile, even as I keep staring at the cityscape and stroking the dog, torturing myself with the evidence that she ever fucked that asshole and *he used it against her*.

My stomach wrenches, and I snap up, flinging my phone off the coffee table. It hits the floor with a *crack!*

To my relief, the screen goes dark.

When I pick it up, I see lines spidering across the screen.

"Sorry, girl," I mutter to Queenie, grabbing her a dog cookie from the kitchen to compensate for the jump scare.

If I'd known he still had this ammo, I would've been more careful.

My hands shake as I run them through my hair, damn near creating bald patches.

If I'd known he'd use her to hurt *me*, I'd have kept my fucking mouth shut.

And Lena knew what was at stake.

She must have if she gave up Pawsome Hearts and me.

That's why she ran.

She knew she was dealing with a mad dog, and I stupidly invited him to sink his rabid teeth into her flesh.

Jackass idiot.

My fault.

It's all my damn fault, and this time, I can't fathom how I'm going to fix it.

Happy memories from Queenie with Gramps and greyhounds can only help my mental health.

They can't tell me how to win a fight with Satan.

XXIII

RUFF DAYS

(LENA)

I should've known this curse was coming.

I should've *known*.

Yet somehow, I'm standing there with the biggest shock of my life flashing before my eyes, my worst fears materializing like a hallucination.

The night is dark as August's private jet cuts through the sky back to Seattle, delivering me to my doom.

Even though Elle told me to put my phone away, I refresh X again, watching the social media carnage unfold.

People from all sides come for Brady, knives out and gleaming, laughing or celebrating the comeuppance of another rich guy they resent only because they'll never have his success.

Every post by Pruitt Brands turns into a dumpster fire.

Tabloids spinning more rumors, more lies, oh God, asking if I'm *still* sleeping with a predator who violated me, who tore my soul apart.

A few people are sympathetic, sure. They know it's revenge porn, but it doesn't help.

Predictably, eighty percent of the internet is absolutely vile.

Apparently, I deserve this and more for being "a boat hoe."

Apparently, Brady could've done a thousand times better than a "vet slut."

Apparently, it's my fault for existing and trusting a man not to be wretched.

The insults fly around my head like shattered glass, finding sharp new places to lodge and cut me deeper.

Whore. Slut. Disgusting bitch.

The list goes on for miles.

The worst part is, they're the same horrors I imagined after Harry exposed his dirty clips the first time.

It took time and a little therapy to reframe the incident as him taking advantage of me. To see myself as a victim.

Now, as the biting hell from strangers stabs me in the face, I can feel all that therapy work unraveling.

Because this shit show right here?

This *feels* like my fault.

Elle stirs and turns over. I watch her turning over on the long lounge seat across from me.

I never thought I could be this sad on a private jet, but here we are.

When she realized what was happening, she sprang into action, of course. Thank God.

Once I made up my mind about going home, she had the jet summoned.

She has a publicist now, and she's offering their help, too, advising me what to do when I return—because I'm done running.

Running isn't possible after you've had one leg gnawed by a wolf.

I just wish some of her solutions didn't involve felony charges.

My days as a free woman are almost over after I *murder* Harry Jay for ruining my life a second time around.

Realistically, I'll weather it like I've handled everything else in life, riding out the storm and waiting for it to die down. But first, I need to give Brady an explanation.

He deserves to know why I ran off and left behind this steaming pile of scandal.

He needs to know I just wanted to protect him. Even if I've completely lost the plot.

If only he'd answer his phone . . .

I scroll through every social platform we've ever connected on, seeing when he was last online. The fact that he's not responding can't mean anything good.

Honestly, I wouldn't blame him if he never wanted to speak to me again.

Hell, *I* wouldn't want to speak to me either.

But I have to explain. I have to do whatever I can to set things right.

Elle stirs and blinks just as Seattle's lights start gleaming below us through the clouds.

"How are you?"

I say nothing. My obvious pain shouldn't tarnish her kindness.

"I can come with you," she offers, but her face is tight, uncomfortable looking. God, I'm probably giving her another migraine, and that makes me feel worse.

I force a smile.

"It's cool, Elle. It's going to be busy, wasting away in lawyers' offices and putting out fires. You're better off at home with August."

Her face softens at the sound of his name, but she frowns.

"He can deal with a little alone time if you need me."

Of course I need her.

I need everyone in my corner I can get.

But I also need to handle this alone.

This is still my problem. My responsibility. My disaster.

"It's fine. Seriously, get home to hubby. I'll call if I need anything else."

She leans across to hug me as the plane drops lower for landing. "I'll come right away. You know it."

"For sure. But anything I need can be done over the phone. It's probably best if you pretend you don't know me for a little while. I'd hate for any of this to rub off on you or Little Key and your books."

She thunks me on the head. Lightly.

"Very funny. You know I'll go to bat for you every chance I get. This isn't your fault, Lena Joly. None of it. Brady knew about this whole thing with Harry."

"Yeah, but it doesn't matter now—"

"You didn't *know* he still had that crap."

The way she says *crap* makes me squirm.

The thought that even after all these years, Harry had it stored somewhere, and why? Was he waiting for a day when he could burn me to ashes if we ever crossed paths again?

"He's fucking disgusting," I spit.

"We hate him! And I'll never be ashamed to be your friend. The only one who should feel any shame at all is that pig. How can people be so *stupid*?"

"No one knows he leaked them deliberately," I say dully. "Only we know. And Brady, too, maybe."

"Lena, for the last time—it's *not your fault*. It doesn't matter what other people say." She eyes me sternly. "Have you been looking at shitty comments online again?"

"Hard not to when you have huge crowds of people yakking about your life."

"I know," she says gently. "The peanut gallery sucks, and being caught in it over something like this? Horrible. But he's *not* going to get away with this, girl. Over my dead body."

She looks fierce enough to make me believe it.

"I'd rather it was over his," I say.

"That's the spirit. How should we torture him first?"

Laughing bitterly, we hit the runway with a bump. I square my shoulders, drawing a deep breath.

Home, sweet home.

Truthfully, I don't know how I'm going to survive this, but I will.

Elle watches me with sympathy, and she knows better than to break into a big teary-eyed pep talk.

"You're going to get through this, boss lady. Spine of steel," she whispers as she hugs me again. "Are you sure you don't want that list of lawyers from Gruffykins? He'll put you in touch ASAP. Give your name, and they'll make room for you."

Ugh, don't remind me.

This is my first foray into the legal swamp, and it's plunging into the deep end. But I nod like it's not overwhelming to save face.

"I'll figure something out, Elle. Love you," I say as the plane rolls to a stop.

"You're sure you don't want to ride with me?"

"I'd better get home," I tell her. "It's just a short walk and an Uber ride. I'll call you later."

"Well, okay. Don't do anything illegal, babe."

With a rough laugh, I stand and shoulder my bag. We head for the exit, where a lady in uniform smiles at me. The flight attendants are almost invisible on these private flights unless you need them.

I wonder if she noticed me trying not to melt down for the entire two-hour flight back to Washington.

"Love you too," Elle calls, staying in place as I exit the luxurious plane.

Back into the real world.

A light rain mists my face as I walk down the passenger stairs. To my relief, no journalists or cameras are waiting on the tarmac, but I guess that's the advantage of flying private.

No gaggle of black cars waiting past the building with the tall fence either. At least no one seems to know where I am, although that probably won't last.

Especially when I need to see Brady.

They'll assume we're broken up.

I try to feel like that's a good thing, but it's really just another nail through my heart. It makes it harder to focus when I get to the parking lot and try to hail a ride with the app.

Despite the fact that I didn't ask, August texts me a brief list of lawyers' names. Take a look at your convenience. Let me know which one you prefer and I'll call.

That hits different.

For a man as outwardly grouchy as August—Elle is like the only one who can make that beast smile—he sure has a kind heart.

Mental note: Thank him properly later. Elle too.

They've been talking about getting a puppy, and you can hook them up.

I scroll through the list, idly flicking through a few of their websites. All of them seem comically overqualified for this, with their Ivy League degrees and impressive records unraveling real cases, but I guess that's the benefit of having rich friends.

Right now, even though I hate, hate, hate the thought of August and Elle spending money on me, I know I'll need a good lawyer or three to put Harry Jay down. Ideally, before I do something really illegal, after all.

Sorry, Elle.

If that means swallowing my pride, I will.

This isn't about me, judging by those articles that told me how many people he's screwed over. I have to do my part to make sure he never gets another chance to hurt anyone ever again.

And if it clears my name while I'm at it, cool. As Mom would say, if wishes were fishes, we'd be eating for a month.

More than anything, I need to be realistic.

I need to fight.

My phone buzzes with an incoming call, and for a second, my heart leaps.

Brady?

Then I remember what that number is, and my heart sinks to my knees.

. . . Luis?

Obviously, there's no beef with the assistant. He's a swell guy and a decent friend to Brady, who doesn't seem to have a lot of them despite his ginormous social circle. Even if he's cashing checks from his boss, he cares.

Still, if it's Luis calling, things are not good.

If Brady wanted to see me to sort things out, he'd call me himself, wouldn't he?

Sending Luis just adds another layer of distance.

Distance *I* insisted on the minute I ran.

Believe me, I *know*. The broken heart pieces rattling around my chest like heavy ceramic are a constant reminder.

"Luis? Hi, what's going on?" I answer the phone with shaky fingers and my breath stalled in my lungs.

"Miss Joly." He sounds the same as always, cool and polite, except—maybe a little frazzled?

I shouldn't be surprised, considering the crisis.

"How are you?" he asks, which is too kind, considering he can guess.

"I'm—" A lie dies on my lips. No point trying to deceive him. "I'm still hanging in there."

"That bad, huh?" There's a softness in his voice now.

Empathy I don't deserve.

"I mean, it's not *good*. But you knew that." My laugh sounds feeble. "I'm sure you're about to tell me it can always be worse." I cringe at my own phrasing. "But how—how is he?"

"Why don't you come and see?" He doesn't wait for my answer. "I've sent Corbin to the airport to pick you up. He should be waiting now."

I blink in surprise. That was fast.

"I'm here, standing on the curb."

"Yes, I know. He'll take you to Brady's, if you'll graciously accept."

My blood freezes over.

"Um, okay," I say slowly. My heart hammers in my chest. "What for? Is everything okay?"

"Brady's been working on the situation," Luis assures me with what sounds like a huge understatement.

"I'm sure he has," I say slowly.

"He'd be grateful for your presence tonight, if you can make it. It's very important."

Oh boy.

I'm sure whatever he's got planned will be super fun. Not at all like being dragged over a frying pan.

"Corbin's waiting. Black Escalade," Luis says gently. "Can you wave to him when you're ready? No hurry, take all the time you need."

I swallow thickly, trying to suppress the fear gurgling up from the pit of my stomach.

But I wanted a conversation, didn't I? And now Brady wants to make that happen with zero inconvenience besides my own mangled heart.

Whatever.

Deep breath.

"All right," I say as I finally look at the black SUV in the lot and hold up my hand. "Anything you need. Anything Brady needs. I'm ready."

"Thanks, Lena. We appreciate you." Luis blows out a long breath that doesn't make me feel any better about the situation. Almost like he's relieved.

Also, *we*?

He can't just say Brady?

That knot in my belly hardens into rock.

I know I'm reading into this too much. I feel like I've been dropped into a trashy reality show with some sinister surprise waiting, but I can't stop.

I have to make this right.

The sooner I see Brady, the faster I stop plummeting to the bottom.

"See you soon," I say numbly, ending the call.

I just hope there's some privacy when I can finally talk to Brady.

By the time I blink, my phone's flashing with the call disconnected and that big black SUV is waiting in front of me.

Corbin steps out to grab my suitcase and open the door, kindly waiting like I'm Cinderella, ready to spirit me away to my moody, doomed prince.

XXIV

A HUNGRY DOG

(BRADY)

The worst damn day of my life is also the loudest.

My phone won't stop ringing off the hook. There must be at least ten frothing-mad voicemails from Dad I haven't played.

No need. I know they'll be nothing but awestruck horror and panicked demands. Plus, cursing me out every way he's ever learned in his long, demanding life.

Too bad I can't write it off as his usual bullshit.

He's right to be fire-breathing pissed.

I've ruined his name. My name. The family name. Hell, the Pruitt brand.

After this, we'll probably need a damn animal mascot, if the PR team doesn't just advise us to ghost media entirely.

I'm sure Dad's spitting demands are brutally simple.

Damage control. Break it off with Lena immediately, then get in front of a screen and tell the world how much she disgusts me.

Like I said, brutally simple—except for the part where I throw the woman I love under the goddamned bus, knowing she's a victim.

Alec Pruitt will never understand that Lena never asked for any of this shit.

Every drama freak eviscerating her online makes me want to break my phone again.

What my father and the rest of the world don't get is that if I go against her, it validates every flippant jackass who's ever sent her a nastygram or talked her up like she's a porn star.

I won't fucking do that.

I won't betray her.

And I also won't stand by without defending my brand and my girl the best way I see fit.

I haven't bothered looking at a single notification on my phone. For my sanity, they're muted, even though I know they're chirping like mad.

Thousands of chattering bees hell bent on making my business theirs because their own lives are so unremarkable. Maybe because so many of those lives have issues that make our drama look easy, and they just want to feel better about themselves for two seconds by laughing at someone else's nightmare.

I'm starting to appreciate how time slows to a crawl as your army of haters grows.

Right now, the whole world feels stalled on a knife's edge while our spectators hold their collective breath, waiting for their next hit of excitement.

It's a toxic addiction.

When will the Pruitts address their public meltdown? They have to say *something*.

They're about to get it.

It's taken an entire day to outline everything I have to say, plus speaking to all the right people to get the logistics in order.

Now, I'm ready to go live with at least a million viewers hanging on my every word.

Even with the entire universe on the line, there's only one spectator I care about.

I had Luis tracking her plane from the very second we found out a jet chartered by August Marshall left Reno-Tahoe International.

It's almost pathetic that I punched the air less than an hour ago when I found out she agreed to see me.

For all I knew, she'd want to hide forever in anger or shame.

Lena must know I'm responsible for this mess. I pushed that asshole so hard, he fired back. I'm the reason he leaked those dirty photos, detonating her life.

Of course, the fact that Harry Jay still had them isn't my fault. Using them to retaliate also isn't a choice I had a hand in.

But nobody can deny that I triggered the duel. I pulled my trigger, and he pulled his.

I fired my best shot over all her objections, over her proud demands for me to let her handle this alone.

If she decides to hate me forever, I won't blame her in the slightest.

If she's coming to see me, though, I don't think she's decided yet.

I still have a chance at a miracle.

Hearing footsteps makes me look up just in time to notice people are moving through my condo, heading for my studio room. Luis enters first, followed by Lena.

For a second, I don't recognize her.

She looks tired, dark lines under her eyes, shadows formed by a thousand tears. Even her walk doesn't look right—it's slower, careful, more subdued.

Her chestnut hair looks frizzed. Not like its usual glorious mess after she comes home from a full day healing animals.

Even so, she's goddamned radiant.

She can't help being the most beautiful candle in the room, even when she's got half the city trying to blow her out.

I'm not the only one who gets an adrenaline jolt when I see her.

Queenie leaps up from beside my desk and goes pounding over, her tail swishing so violently she nearly knocks a lamp off its end table in the corner.

"Hey, pretty girl." Lena's voice is subdued as she kneels down and buries her face in Queenie's black fur for a second. "Oh my goodness, I missed you too!"

Oblivious to the drama, Queenie barks a few times, spinning in circles, before she leads Lena to the sofa facing me across the room.

I glance at Luis as he stops behind the camera tripod, already set up. "Are we ready?"

"If you're sure you want to do it here, yes. Live stream in three minutes."

Not enough time for a proper conversation, but that's what I planned.

For the first time since she stepped into the room, we lock eyes.

"There's something I need to say," I tell her, nodding to Luis and his camera setup.

Through the large window, it's a peaceful day, the sunset gleaming off the city and the ships on Elliott Bay like a fever dream. The shiny silver and glassy water make such a striking contrast you'd never guess the world is falling down around us.

Any other day, it would be an ideal romantic backdrop for my quiet penthouse.

Today, it's just the calm before the storm.

"Brady, what do you mean? You're streaming right *now*?" Lena stares at me, her eyes wide and questioning.

No time to explain.

I can't risk scaring her off.

"Everything's set," Luis says, checking the equipment one last time. I checked it myself three times before he showed up.

Queenie butts her head under my arm, her tongue flopped out with excitement. It's going to be anticlimactic as hell if this dog jumps on me while we're live, but what can you do?

If that's all that misfires today, I'll be a lucky man.

"I don't understand," Lena hisses, annoyance flashing in her eyes. "Can't you just tell me what's going on—"

"It'll make sense in five minutes. I promise. Thanks for coming," I say gently, checking my watch. Sixty seconds to go. "Humor me one more time, Lena. It has to be like this if I want it to come out right."

She clenches her hands, her nails biting her skin as she shakes her head in confusion.

Damn.

I can't begin to imagine what she's been through over the past twenty-four hours, what she's thinking, but there's no time for doubt.

The live stream is about to start.

With the deepest breath, I face the camera. The tablet on my desk shows there are already over ten thousand people tuned in and waiting, with thousands more joining every second.

The counter on the screen ticks down a few more seconds.

I feel the weight of the world crushing me as I try to ignore the beautiful, hurt Medusa in front of me, promising to turn me to stone if I look at her.

Sorry, Sass.

Not now.

Not yet.

Once she's heard me out, I'll let her decide if those big brown eyes are heaven or portals to hell.

"Hey, everybody," I start, without my usual smile. "Brady here, and today it's all business. I couldn't leave you in the dark a minute longer with all the rumors flying, so let me clear this up.

"First, on behalf of my family and Pruitt Ag, I've made some heaping mistakes recently." Off camera, Luis hides his face. Lena looks pale, motionless. I force a smile. "That's all on me and nobody else. Honestly, it hasn't been great for my state of mind. A few hours ago, I even thought about socking a man in the face."

Comments trickle in on the tablet. I glance at them, then at Lena, who's watching with a frown.

Nobody ever said radical honesty was easy.

"Here's some more truth—I'm almost thirty years old. Until this summer, I didn't know I still had a lot of growing up to do. I know how that sounds, so go ahead and laugh. But hell, I've been stuck in the mud for too long. I haven't been growing, not while I've been crashing out, haunted by my past. You know my reputation. That's why half of you are here, I'm sure—you logged on to see a rich playboy punk get kicked in the nads by karma—but I'm going to disappoint you. I'm still a walking mess, just not the kind I used to be."

Lena's eyes brighten. I can practically hear her panic through her slow breaths, her shoulders rising and falling. All the ways she's tensing, silently screaming *no, no, no*.

"Before, I felt paralyzed about my future," I confess. "About what everyone expected from me. What they said my destiny had to be. The public eye is never easy, especially when your reputation is ruled by stupid mistakes you made years ago."

I sigh.

"So, I made a snap decision to spruce up my image. I found a beautiful, smart, outrageously kind woman to get engaged to—to play my temporary fiancée. I set up a master sham." I hold up my hands, but I'm not looking at the camera anymore.

My eyes are welded to Lena.

The whole truth and nothing but. That's what I owe them.

My whole soul. That's what I owe *her*.

"Stupid doesn't begin to cover it, and when you mix ego with stupid and desperate, you get me. I didn't want to deal with my image worries honestly or get tangled up in an arranged marriage with someone I didn't love, so I did the next worse thing. I tried to pull one over on Seattle, my family, and my fans," I growl, watching Lena every second. She's so still she's barely breathing. "I tried to buy myself time, hoping I'd become a real man rather than a wooden cutout. To figure out who the hell Brady Pruitt is supposed to be, because I still don't know.

"That was the mistake I planned for. But the biggest mistake was the one I didn't: falling for Miss Lena Joly *for real* and then falling apart when I let my own reckless anger go wild. I felt like I had to step in and thump my chest when she came under fire from a really awful dude I don't need to mention. You know who he is, if you've been following the news. Turns out, I'm not the only person with a history I hate, but hers was much scarier than mine. And I couldn't stand by and watch hers eat her alive. I had to protect my Lena."

Her mouth drops.

Her lips quiver like she wants to say something but can't find the words.

Understandable.

That was me this morning, figuring out this speech, even if I didn't write down every line. I wound up with bullet points and decided I'd let the words come straight from the heart.

"I'm stating this as clear as day against the advice of my legal team. I'm the man behind exposing Harry Jay's abusive business practices. I'm solely responsible for the leaks, and frankly, I'm proud of it," I continue. "Any consequences, legal or otherwise, should fall on me alone."

Lena shakes her head. Her eyes swirl like melted chocolate, hypnotic as ever.

These aren't big revelations to her.

She knows what I did, but she doesn't know how I feel about it.

I had to breach lines to save her.

I let my ego, my need to protect her, lead, even when she insisted she didn't need help.

Ultimately, though, that's not the point. I could've done it more carefully.

The point is, instead of listening to what she wanted, I insisted I knew better. I caused this mess.

"I regret how I went about it," I say. "Not because he shouldn't have been exposed, but because there are better ways. Also, this wasn't my fight alone, and I'm sorry about that. I'm not sorry I sent Mr. Jay limping to court, because he *deserves* to hurt for what he's done. Only, hurting him shouldn't've have caused anyone else pain—and it did. I'll always regret that."

Luis nods.

Lena almost cracks a smile but not quite.

"But you know what?" I let the loaded question linger in the air. "As much as I've screwed up these past few months—and I know I have—nothing I've done compares to the fatal mistake Harry Jay made. If you don't know, he's behind the leaked revenge porn."

Lena's eyes widen. I smile at her.

It's going to be okay.

"Why did he do it? Why would anybody do something depraved?" I wave a hand. "Because I cornered him, and he wanted to hurt me back. All because he couldn't steal an amazing business opportunity from his ex-girlfriend, Lena."

I look at her, seeing her dawning understanding.

"That's why he threatened her, and that's why he did something so heinous. He tried to use her past and the pain he inflicted to coerce her into handing over a property he wanted. All for money."

I've never seen so many comments landing on the tracker app, and I can't stop to read a single one. But I'm sure a lot of jaws are hanging from people who didn't know Harry and Lena ever dated—and how atrocious it was for Harry to pull that shit.

Revenge porn.

I almost lost my cool when I said it out loud. If it has that power over me, imagine how many angry hornets it will kick up online.

I take a few seconds, collecting my thoughts.

Lena's tears come now, streaming down her cheeks in hot rivulets. She doubles over, hiding her face, sobbing quietly in a way I've never seen.

Shit.

Her agony lances through me. I feel like it's the first time she's really let herself cry about it, and it's been building up forever.

"My longtime fans know I've been keeping quiet. I haven't posted for a few days. I had to sort out how I wanted to handle this," I say, still looking at her. "In the end, nothing seemed perfect besides the hard truth. I knew I needed to stand up for the woman I love. I had to stand up and roar for her the way I should've from the very beginning."

Lena sobs harder, her hand covering her mouth. Queenie trots over, leaning against her knee for moral support, whale eyes fixed on her distress.

"Let me end with this confession—I'm the second biggest idiot in the world," I continue, still watching her. "But I'm just an idiot, and not a monster. I never wanted any of this to happen, to spin out of control. The reality is, I'm not so different from any other bonehead who ever fell in love. I can't stand seeing the woman I love turned into a martyr against her will. And I can't finish Lena's battle when she's the one who's been hurt and wronged. She deserves to end it on her own terms."

Luis slides over, leaning down and patting Lena awkwardly while Queenie noses at her face, licking away the tears.

Out of the corner of my eye, I still see comments pounding in like hail—probably a few people asking about the soft sobbing in the background. Asking all sorts of questions I don't feel like answering.

For me, there's just one that matters, digging at my brain like a hungry dog with a buried bone.

"That's it. That's my attempt to answer your questions, and now it's my turn." I pause until she looks up, staring at me with her tearstained face. "My only question is for Lena, the love of my life. Woman, how can I ever win you back?"

XXV

DOG YEARS

(LENA)

I'm coming apart.

Threadbare.

Torn at the seams.

Everything I've kept inside for so long—since before Brady, since Harry and his filthy videos ruined my life once—comes gushing out in one ugly wail, and there's nothing I can do to stop it.

The dam has broken, and I'm being swept along the current.

So many emotions. So many feels bombarding my heart like diving birds, but none bigger than his rough, naked confession.

Brady Pruitt loves me.

Holy hell.

The words don't feel real, but when he says it, when he calls me the love of his life—

Eek!

I've never seen the kind of sincerity written on his face. And even though there's a camera going, still filming this moment for the world to see, he's talking directly to me.

Woman, how can I ever win you back?

Doesn't he know?

Doesn't he realize he already has?

He didn't need to go out of his way to do it, either, because I forgave him the minute I walked through the door.

I can't stay mad at a man who went out of his way to save me from a monster. You don't go off on a knight when there's a dragon at his feet, thrashing and almost slain.

But it's too much for words. Too much for anything coherent.

I'm not sure if I jump up first or if Queenie beats me to it.

I just know I'm almost airborne as I launch across the room and *throw* myself at him.

His arms snap closed around me just in time.

It's like we were never ripped apart.

His embrace feels warmer and more familiar than coming home.

I don't care how crazy that sounds.

I also don't care about a million online strangers watching us, never mind Luis.

The only thing that matters as I pounce on him, clinging to his neck, is the wall of man under me. The handsome beast who tucks me against my chest with such huge, strong hands that aren't steady.

"You . . . you never lost me," I whisper before reaching up to kiss him.

Sticky as sin and sweet as longing.

His hands frame my face, fingers wavering until he presses them to my temples, smoothing my hair.

His smile could rival the stars.

But my mouth says everything silently. I don't have words, and this kiss will have to do.

I'm here, Brady.

I missed you so much.

And yes, I love you.

"Didn't know if you'd ever forgive me," he says with a guttural laugh as he pulls back.

"You donut!" I whack him playfully on the shoulder, laughing and crying simultaneously.

Harry Jay hasn't won a damn thing.

He can't, not when I've got Brady Pruitt on my side.

So, I bury my face in his neck, inhaling his masculine scent and just breathing until Luis clears his throat.

"Live stream ended," he tells us, breaking new limits in human awkwardness. "If that doesn't get you guys some relief, nothing will." He coughs and shakes his head, smiling. I get the distinct impression he's almost as emotional as we are. "But I'll leave you guys to it. I'm sure you have a lot of *talking* to do."

"Yeah and not for your ears. Shut the door on your way out," Brady orders.

I laugh too hard, reaching across to where Queenie snorts. She's trying to wedge her wet nose against my face. Her tongue laps at my damp cheeks until I'm in such a fit my belly hurts.

"It's okay, sweet girl, I'm back. I missed you too," I murmur, scratching her between the ears.

"It's really okay." Brady sounds almost as relieved as I feel. His hand travels up and down my back.

"I'm sorry for running," I say.

"And I'm sorry as hell for pushing, for lighting him up when I should've known better. I should've listened." He kisses the end of my nose. "Are we even, though?"

"Even." I smile and lean in for another kiss. For a few blissful moments, we're lost in each other's arms, kissing like the ship is going down.

"Sass." He leans back, his sky blue eyes so serious.

"Brady." I trace the line of his mouth with my fingers, loving how his eyes darken from summer sky to winter storm in seconds.

I thought I was hungry, but I'm nothing against the look in his eyes.

"I have something else." His eyes brighten even as his mouth stays almost still under my softly moving fingers.

"Talk," I whisper.

"I love you. Longer and harder than a hundred billion dog years."

My face screws up.

For a second, I'm sure my heart stops.

I've never been great with words unless there's a lot of swearing involved, but I think I can handle this.

"I love you too. I love you so much." When I smile, it feels like I'm throwing my whole body into it.

"All I ever needed." He sucks my finger into my mouth and bites down gently, holding me. From the look on his face, he'd like to do a lot more.

But then he pauses and frowns. Some of the light in his eyes dims.

Oh no.

I know what he's thinking. The pictures.

The disgusting slop Harry kept waiting all these years. The smut I never should've been stupid enough to let him capture on film.

All the ways my naked body has been seen by any creeper in this city willing to take a look.

My body isn't just his anymore, even when I'm offering my whole heart, and it kills me.

"We're working like hell on getting them down. Every picture," he rasps. I don't know who *we* means, but I assume he's got lawyers for days.

"We will. But not now, please." I press my fingers against his mouth. "Right now, I don't want to say another word about it."

"Lena, I just need you to know—"

"I already do. You never give up on me. Even when I totally deserve it." I replace my finger with my mouth, feeling the fight go out of him. "I don't want to wait, Brady. This is my body, isn't it? And I get to choose what I do with it. Today, I'm giving it to you. Harry can't ever take that away."

"Fuck no." His fingers brush my hair back from my face, and his kiss turns greedy.

Until I fell into his arms, I didn't know if I'd be okay with being touched so soon after feeling so violated.

But Brady makes me feel safe again. He makes me feel loved and sexy in ways I never felt with Harry. Not even once.

And after all this, after it's said and done, no one else will ever make me feel like I can't do whatever I want with my body. Right now, I want to offer it to him more than anything.

I'm taking power *back*, yes.

But I'm also taking back control: my love, my life, my destiny.

"You're so damn incredible," Brady mutters against my mouth, and then he's scooping me up, carrying me through the condo until we're racing inside his bedroom.

When he drops me down on the bed, I'm still holding on to him.

He grins wickedly as he bends his head to nip at my neck.

My heart pounds, and my skin goes liquid at the feel of his hand sliding under my top.

"I haven't had a chance to shower since I flew in," I warn.

"You smell like *you*, Sass. And it's driving me fucking insane." He moves lower, hot tongue descending, drawing a line down my lower belly.

Oh God!

My jitters evaporate with every touch, especially when he hooks his fingers into my leggings and tugs them down my thighs.

Now, we both meet sweet insanity. I'm trembling like I have Brady withdrawals, so close to having the gorgeous man I've been denied.

"You okay?" he whispers, his eyes molten.

"Yes," I whisper back. "Never better."

Everything he's doing is a hell of a lot *more* than okay.

When he goes down lower, lower, and presses his tongue against my folds, hot and wet and torturously slow, I'm instantly torn.

"Fuck, Lena, why do you taste so good?" The way he closes his eyes like he's in rapture frays my last senses.

My fingers move without thinking, digging at his hair, anchoring myself to his lips for dear life while his tongue demolishes me.

And Brady's mouth is a masterclass in pleasure.

Every swirling lick.

Every rough suck.

Every hot breath and sugary sting of his teeth.

He grabs my legs and pins me to his face, growling against my center, claiming me like the wild beast he is.

And I just lie there, panting, legs splayed open, his head between them, half naked and wrecked but so relieved that we've finally turned a corner.

The worst really might be over.

There's no uncomfortable ache in my belly anymore. No anxious fear that this is spinning away from us. No more uncertainty.

In this bed with this man, I'm safe and loved.

The thought feels almost as potent as everything his tongue does.

And when he brings me to the brink and stops, teasing me with hot eyes before he sinks a finger into me, my back arches off the bed.

"Holy shit!" I whimper.

"You like that, huh? Sing for me, woman. I'm going to light you up."

I almost laugh, but it comes out breathless.

"You know I do. And so do you." I haven't missed the way his hand disappears, stroking himself.

"Damn right," he rumbles. "You scared me to hell and back when I thought I'd never taste this tight little pussy again."

He adds another finger, and his tongue sweeps my clit again.

I'm gasping his name.

"Brady—don't stop!" Every word scrapes my throat.

"Only if you promise to come for me, Sass. Come fucking wild." His breath heats my clit again, hot and damp, so teasing it's almost fatal.

"Brady, please. I just need—" My voice chokes off. I don't know what I need except for him to bring this home.

The way he smiles and drags his tongue over my swollen pussy says he knows that better than I do.

Then the tip of his tongue flicks my clit, followed by the searing pressure of the flat of his tongue. Sensations merge like black magic.

"You ready to give it up? To remind me what I've been missing too many lonely nights?" His voice reverberates, shaking me to my core.

"Yes. *Yes!*"

"Come for me, Lena."

I'm a lot of things right now. A messy bundle of too many feels to describe, but I'm *not* disobedient.

The moment he commands, my body obeys with delight.

I fall down and shatter, split into a thousand sharp pieces, ripped apart by a white-hot tsunami so strong it strips my soul away.

Coming!

It's never been like this before, this iron grip of velvet that wrings me out.

Blame it on love, sending me into a new zone.

I'm lost in a space between worlds, where my body convulses, speaking and breathing only in the throbbing space between gasps.

I think my lips are moving—probably saying Brady's name again—and I think he's telling me something too.

"Such a good fucking girl. I love you so much it scares me."

But I can barely hear him over the roar in my blood like a waterfall rushing over my ears.

My body glides back down so slow, releasing me from the hottest orgasm of my life.

When my senses return, I realize he's down on his back next to me, one hand drawing patterns across my stomach.

"Welcome back," he whispers, his eyes crinkling as he smiles.

"I love you," I tell him.

He smiles and snorts. "I hope so. Or are you only saying that because I just short-circuited you?"

"Does it matter?" I throw back.

His smile widens into a grin.

"I knew it. Lena Joly only loves me for my skills."

"Shut up and let me kiss you, idiot."

He does, and I do.

Then it's my turn, rolling on top of him and trying awkwardly to remove his pants from the worst angle ever.

With a wicked smile, he helps me and then yanks off his shirt as I finally pull down his pants and his boxers, revealing his glorious cock.

It's a monument to his desire, thick and veiny and pulsing with raw need.

I love how he groans when I dip down, licking the bead of moisture off the tip.

"Tempting as it is to make you come all over my face, I think I'll settle for getting you really, really close," I whisper.

His eyes darken to blue dusk.

"Edge me too long, and I'll nut in under a minute once I'm inside you. No fun."

"Have faith." I grin.

My fingers wrap around his length, and I pull his magnificent shaft into my mouth.

Rather, *I try*.

Mostly head and a couple inches of shaft because he's just that huge, but what I can't get into my mouth, I make up for with technique.

Sucking and licking and teasing as he fists my hair with a guttural rasp.

"That fucking mouth feels illegal, baby girl."

Oh, I agree, because there's nothing better than this.

Teasing my big, overprotective beast until he loses control.

Reminding myself that it's so rare to find this perfect give-and-take in the bedroom, or anywhere else.

Mostly, I just want to see him fight, trying to hold back as my tongue takes him down, as my lips tighten, as I work down lower on his cock until I gag, pumping the rest of him with my hand.

He's at the brink of madness in no time.

I think he's about to rip my hair out as his hand tightens, pulling like reins. The constant snarling curses spilling out of his throat barely sound human.

His cock pulses in my mouth, so hot I try to grin even though I'm full of him.

His eyes could chase off a wolf with a single glance, so heated it's frightening.

"You give me that look again, and you'll choke on my cum," he warns.

Holy hell.

My pussy tingles with evil joy.

I only slow down to prolong his torment, giving him a few seconds of recovery before I start up again.

Honestly, I don't know whether I'd call it teasing, torture, or the best gift a girl can give, but I bring him to the edge three more times before he jerks his cock out of my mouth and brings me up for a kiss.

"No more. Not unless you want that pretty face painted." He takes my bottom lip between his teeth, tugging hard.

His hand finds my breast, squeezing, pinching my nipple with cruel want.

God, he's everywhere, and it's safe to say that I've never seen a hornier man in my life.

"Enough with the opening act. Lie down and spread your legs. I want to see your face when you come on my cock." His thumb brushes my cheek.

I tremble from the hot chill he sends through me and do exactly as he asked.

Once he's settled between my legs, I wrap them around him so tight, quivering as his cock presses against my entrance.

"So damn wet for me. It never gets old." His eyes are glazed with lust.

"All for you."

He makes a low noise then, no warning before his hips move with one purpose.

Brady groans as he pushes inside me, pulling a few noises from me as I remember how big and punishing his dick really is.

So full.

So stretched beyond belief.

So very right.

I throw my head back with a moan that urges him on.

His thrusts come with this brutal rhythm, intense and unshakable, unstopping for anything. I'm not ashamed to say I lose it in record time.

My fingernails dig into his back, urging him on, faster and faster as I rake them down his skin.

Deeper, deeper.

Give. Me. More.

His flesh knows the words I never speak. He props my legs up over his shoulders, opening me fully.

"You are an addiction. A deadly fucking habit I'll never dream of quitting," he growls, driving into me faster.

It's actually crazy how close I am already.

When my hand moves down, searching for my clit, he knocks it away, replacing it with his own. And he's totally justified.

He's learned my body so well he knows exactly how to touch me.

What I need.

When I need it.

And it's not long before I feel the mother of all o's building again.

His pace quickens, an onslaught meant to leave me in burning pieces.

His hand doesn't stop, though. His fingers find my clit and circle in perfect time to his thrusts, fucking one gasp after the next out of me.

Then he rests his forehead on mine, his strokes slowing but coming fiercer.

"Never leave me, Sass. Never again," he whispers.

"Never!" My breath hitches.

"I don't want this to end."

I wrap my arms around him, pulling him against me, skin to skin. Even if he wanted, he can't escape.

"Don't worry, it won't." I bite his ear.

I don't hear the shudder that runs through him, but oh, I feel it.

I kiss him, and his tongue mimics the mad piston of his hips, becoming harsher and more erratic with every stroke.

But this isn't just fucking anymore.

This is *making love*, and I don't care how cheesy that sounds.

I don't even need his hand anymore.

I rise to meet him, grinding against his pubic bone, letting him hit that perfect spot that makes me his, and only his, now and forever.

My orgasm surges like a flood, all angry rapids pulling me under until I'm swept along in its white-hot wake.

Then Brady groans and his cock drives deep, slamming me into the bed.

He pins me down as he stakes his claim, marking me with ropes of fire hurling deep inside me.

With his cock still twitching and his teeth bared, he cups my face in his hands, whispering words that sound too human for this animal fusion.

"Never again, Lena. Never. You're all mine, and I'll never let you go."

"I love you." I'm too awestruck and too exhausted to murmur back anything more.

With my heart overflowing, I pass out in his arms and sleep like the dead.

XXVI

DOGGONE PERFECT

(BRADY)

It's a beautiful, clear day when I find him by the boathouse dock.

If Dad has a favorite spot on earth, it's here, lurking under the sprawling shade of this massive willow tree as he watches the lake rippling in the sunlight. He's alone today like I knew he'd be, no Freddy around, though the nurse is never far behind.

It's a scenario I've witnessed a hundred times growing up, but something about it stalls me in my tracks when I'm still a few feet behind him.

When has my father ever looked so small?

"Brady." Even his voice sounds tiny and faded as he calls to me.

With my nostrils flaring, I walk up next to him. He doesn't bother to look up at me.

No surprise.

"Well, let's hear it," I start. "I'm sure you're livid. For once, I can't say I blame you, Dad. If you want to go off and tell me how stupid and shitty and unworthy I am, now's your chance."

I don't breathe.

Honestly, I probably shouldn't be encouraging him to ragedump with his heart condition, but I just want this over with.

Dad takes his sweet time deciding how to tear my face off—probably considering his options. Then he smiles, his eyes fixed on a sailboat drifting by.

"What's the damn point in rattling off the same script you've heard a thousand times? Especially when it isn't true."

What.

I blink, clearing my throat because I don't know where this is going.

"I don't understand. If you need me to spend the next week with PR, hashing out damage control strategies, I'm ready. If you never want me to meet with them again, I'll do that too. I just need to know what direction you'd like to—"

"No direction," he growls, cutting me off. "You've plotted your path, and I couldn't blow you off course if I was Poseidon himself. I didn't bring you here to spin you around. I want to sit back and watch where the wind blows."

I'm so lost.

When I say nothing, he turns to me, his eyes rheumy and red today.

Christ. Is it his heart . . . or has he been crying?

"Dad, what are you saying?"

"I'm saying you delivered, Brady. We've been waiting for this for years. You made your mistakes, and you took them on the chin like a man. That's massive."

I almost rock back from the shock. His pale-blue gaze sweeps through me.

"You're feeling okay, right? No new health issues?" I ask gently, shaking my head. "No offense, but you look kind of rough."

He chuckles. Low and easy like I haven't heard for years.

That's when I know the person I'm dealing with may look like Alec Pruitt, but I don't know him.

"You know, some days I blamed you for putting me in this damn chair," he whispers, shifting to sit up straighter. "When I had the attack, I was under the gun with that big orchard deal. Your mother told you it pushed me over the edge—and it certainly didn't help. But it wasn't what I was looking at in my office when I had a fit and they found me on the floor."

I swallow thickly, waiting.

He sighs. "I was reading about you. That model blowing her stack when you blew her off—the tabloids ripped you to pieces. And you just carried on posting about dog food."

"Okay," I snap. "What's your point? We know what happened. Are you blaming me for your heart attack now?"

My veins feel like they're clogged with lead, this paralyzing mix of hot anger and disbelief. Just when I think he can't shit on me any harder, he proves me wrong.

"I'm blaming myself for panicking over you, Brady. When that thing with the model came down, I thought you'd never change. I didn't see it in you." He pauses, staring out at the calm water again. "Then you walked into the biggest bear trap of your life. Instead of flailing, you rose to the occasion. I don't say this often, but . . . I'm proud of you."

Holy fuck.

I stand there, gutted, as he smiles at me warmly. I swear there are tears in his eyes as he looks at me.

"You'll continue making us proud, and maybe you'll give an old man a chance to move past his pride," he says roughly. "I don't just mean with Lena, with your projects, with everything. I have to get past the things I never told you. I had a dog when I was a boy. A big white Lab named Klaus. He was my best friend for eleven years."

A dog? I have to pinch myself to make sure this is real.

Only there's no mistaking the warble in his voice, the way his eyes glaze over with a bittersweet smile. His breath rattles.

"I was a jackass to deny you the same joy when you were little, the kind every kid should have. When that dog died, it broke me. I stuffed up my grief, my fear that another animal might remind me of the one I lost. I was selfish as hell, and I'm sorry."

"Dad, shit. You're welcome to meet Queenie anytime. The black Lab we've taken in." I have to fucking cough to keep my throat from sticking. "I think she'd like you."

I've never seen the old man cry, and he doesn't today, but he comes dangerously, dangerously close.

Without another word running through us like knives, he extends a hand.

And my father gives me the lightest handshake of his entire life, free from fifty metric tons of emotional baggage.

By the time I leave him, I've met the man I didn't know he could be, and I hope like hell to see him stick around.

The next few weeks are a rush like one long flight of top-shelf whiskey.

Somehow, while I was busy trying to unfuck everyone's lives, my lab worked a miracle with the latest formula and a little help from Wendy's farm.

The food checks all the boxes for nutrition and costs, and it dominated three similar legacy pet food brands in taste trials.

Now, the secret's out. Every day there's a new influencer, partner, or brand beating down my door to help launch Brady Belly in several different flavors.

It's like I found Aladdin's cave and a genie to turn the biggest shit show of my life into a granted wish. Before, I never believed it when they said "there's no such thing as bad publicity."

But without Lena and the scandal, I never would've tasted this success.

Even so, it's a relief to finally have a chance to breathe. And there's nothing else I need besides my woman, a tent, and our dog.

So much for fostering Queenie. About a week after we got back together, we formally adopted her and had her chip changed over to our names.

No regrets.

No worries that we're moving too fast.

Not when life has never felt easier.

Today, the gorgeous landscape of Mount Rainier National Park sprawls out around us. The ancient lakes up here are a realism painting come to life, so clear you can see straight through them.

It's a clear September day as the golden sun beats down on our heads, giving me the calmest vibe I've felt since—hell, ever.

With Queenie's head resting on her shoulder, Lena tips her head back and smiles. "Feels great to leave it all behind, doesn't it?"

"Seattle? Yeah."

"Anywhere with nosy people armed with cameras. But I haven't seen a single hiker here pull out their phone."

"Aw, you're tired of the photo shoots?" I chuckle as she glares at me, but her eyes are dancing.

"I'm not sure I'll ever be *emotionally* prepared for the attention," she says, absently stroking Queenie's head.

The old girl's tail is a helicopter blade, spinning since we set off this morning. It's probably why she's tired out after one quick run and a hike. That's one reason we're taking it slow, not going too far in one day—giving everybody plenty of rest.

With the shine in the Lab's eyes, I'm half tempted to start taking her fish oil supplements myself.

"It's beautiful here, though," Lena whispers. The lake ahead reflects the grey mountains above like nature's mirror.

No question. I made the right choice.

This is the kind of place where people go to figure out the rest of their lives.

I stick my hand in my pocket for reassurance that I still have my future waiting inside.

It's been burning a damn hole in my flannel shirt since I woke up, but I'm waiting for the perfect moment. You only get to do this once, especially for real.

This entire hike looks perfect location-wise, but it's early fall on Mount Rainier.

People come and go in spurts, winding along the paths. We're tucked away from the buses bringing tourists, sure, but I want some privacy from stray hikers.

My first proposal was a performance.

I want this one to be ours.

Private. Perfect. Intimate.

"You know my favorite part?" she asks.

I look up. "Pretty sure you're about to tell me."

"The phone reception out here sucks, and I don't even mind."

She's right. I haven't checked my phone since we parked, unpacked our equipment, and started moving.

She kicks a rock with the toe of her boot, and it bounces off into the trees.

"The lawyers haven't stopped calling about the case with Satan." She says it so casually. We haven't mentioned him in days.

If I had my way, we'd never mention that fuck for the rest of our lives after his criminal trial ends.

"Of course. You're their gravy train." I take her hand, threading my fingers through hers. "If anybody had a great reason to clean his ass out, it's you. Don't worry too much. The guys Marshall found you should handle everything."

"He's a genius. I don't think the man ever sleeps. But it's not about the money. I just want to make sure Harry will never do this to another woman again."

"You're selfless, Sass. One more reason it's easy to love you."

She smiles. The sun brings out freckles on her nose.

I want to spend the evening kissing every one.

"He'll be behind bars before you know it," I say, serious again. "With all the charges he's facing, there's no chance he'll weasel out of it. Let him blow his money on legal damage control until he's bankrupt."

No exaggeration. Harry Jay faces a deluge of criminal fraud cases, bribery, and yes, revenge porn violations slapped by yours truly.

Lena's case isn't the only one leveled at him for abuse. She just threw the first stone, and once it hit, three other women crawled out the woodwork, chasing him for assault.

He's such a fucking flight risk, he couldn't post bail.

All the better. That means we get to come here and enjoy some peace without the slightest worry that Harry Jay will climb out of the brush with a loaded gun and nothing to lose.

This is Lena's battle, but if I had my way, he'd never see the light of day again. No matter what hit man I had to pay to make it happen.

"Ready for the next leg?"

She nods.

I pull her hand to my mouth and kiss her knuckles, banishing demon thoughts from my head. I help her up, and we start moving with Queenie at our side. The path hits an incline, and she draws in a little closer.

"Enough about the past," I say. "How's the grand reopening coming along?"

She grins. "Pawsome Hearts? I mean, it's more of a gimmick than anything, but it'll help introduce Dr. Vetol to our clients. He's pretty excited to start seeing patients."

"A man likes to know his money's being invested sensibly."

"*My* money now," she reminds me.

"Yours," I agree, squeezing her hand. "I'd say it paid off brilliantly."

"Things are good. Like *really* good. You remembered to thank your parents, right?"

"Yeah."

After my big talk with Dad, he couldn't hold my mother back from beating down doors. She went straight to the mayor and the county board, calling in favors owed from years of large campaign contributions, demanding action to deal with the corruption in the code department.

It barely took a hot minute for my parents to get on board with the new life we're building.

And I'll admit, having Dad on our side is a definite plus. Pawsome Hearts had a flood of donations coming in to fix up their boarding center. The Pruitt name has been around for a long time, and he knows exactly how to throw its weight around.

"About damn time they did something useful with their money." I shake my head.

"Don't be a dick. They've been supportive."

Yeah. And I've mostly forgiven Dad's blistering reaction to the fall-out after the hell video of Lena leaked.

Mostly.

Still, I'll admit, he's been working hard to make up for years of mistakes, ever since he broke down and showed a little emotion and a lot of humility.

For Lena, it's like the old man's freak-out never happened.

"How's the project coming along?"

She beams. "The carpenter just started this week. We're gutting it and building fresh from the ground up. A full remodel. The dogs are going to have a heated *pool*, Brady."

"Shit, that's amazing." I can't help laughing, imagining her chasing after half a dozen crazy dogs splashing their hearts out all winter.

"All thanks to you. Nowhere near as many people would've donated if you hadn't done that live stream."

"Hey, I brought people's attention to it, just like my dad. You won them over." I remember the video she made, where she wears the bravest face as she speaks about the little clinic she loves so much and the heartbreak if it shuts down.

The donations pouring in blew our expectations through the roof.

"You picked a day for the reopening yet?" I ask, stopping to let Queenie sniff at a rock a marmot was standing on as we climbed the hill.

"Mm, it'll have to be October. When we get back home, I'll make a final decision. As long as we're coming back bigger and better than ever."

"You will," I assure her. "No chance you'll fail. Not after you fought like hell to save your clinic."

"Dr. Ezzie still can't believe it." She sounds like she can't believe it either. "When we were in crisis mode, she really thought we'd have to sell and shut down."

"I never would've let that happen."

She leans up and kisses my cheek. "I know. But this is my fight."

"As long as you don't forget I'm always there for backup." When she fake pouts, I lean over and kiss her forehead.

Ahead of us, the trail curves to the left, hugging closer to the sparkling lake on one side with the mountain cast in purple light.

Best of all, there's no one in sight.

It can't get better.

"Let's take a breather," I say, letting Queenie stretch out the long leash on the tie-down and head into the trees for a bathroom break. Never a problem when she has amazing recall. "Your future's bright as hell, Sass. Only question is if you'll let me make it blinding."

Go time.

I pull the box out of my pocket as I drop to one knee, popping it open so the ring sparkles in the afternoon light.

It's the same one as before, though I had it resized for a perfect fit.

When I first gave it to her, I didn't miss the way she looked at it—like maybe it was the kind of ring she'd have picked for herself.

She never asked about it after she flung it back to me in anger.

Of course, I kept it. After the strange bliss of watching her wear it before, my mind was made up. Nothing else will ever be a better fit.

Not when it screams a truth from a lie.

"Lena Joly, will you marry me?" I whisper, clear and sure, even as sharp rocks dig into my knees. "For real this time. Not because we have to pretend, but because we can't live with anything less."

She gasps so loud I swear it bounces off the mountain.

Her hands clap her cheeks.

Her eyes flash like amber gold, all swirling glitter.

"Oh my God! Holy fuckeroo, are you—oh man. You *are*. You're serious." She swallows hard.

For a second, I hesitate. Is this too much, too soon?

"No joke. I fell stupid in love with you before I could even figure out what was happening. There hasn't been a moment since where I haven't wanted to make you mine in every way that matters."

"Y-y-you are serious. Oh my God." Here come the tears, and they're so happy my grin digs into my face.

"I hiked all the way up here with this ring, didn't I?" I push it toward her again. "And I'm asking you properly, like a true gentleman. You can skip hanging the medal around my neck. Just give me a *yes*."

"Yes!" she screams, shaking like a leaf as she throws herself into my arms. The Lena missile knocks me onto my back, and we go down together, laughing. "Get up, get up, you lunk! Of course I'll marry you. I'll pick you every time."

I take the ring as she holds out a finger, then I slide it on.

"Oh, wow. You kept it and . . . did you have it resized? It fits better," she whispers in awe.

"Told you once, I'm doing this properly this time."

And then, because I can't wait a second longer, I kiss my fiancée hard, fingers in her hair. She tastes like salt and the rest of my life, and when I pull away, resting my forehead against hers, I think a few of those tears on her cheeks might be mine.

Tell no one.

"I love you," she says through her tears. "I'm just surprised. I didn't think you'd ask again so soon."

"What's the point in waiting? When you know, you know, and I knew before our engagement ever ended."

She winces. "It never should have."

"It's better this way. You know why I kept the ring?"

I have to wait to answer when Queenie returns, joining our excitement with a flash of leaping black fur. I'm damn glad she's as old as she is.

I catch her about a second before she lands on Lena's head.

But we're laughing like crazy, the dog adding her frenzied yips to our chaos.

When Queenie finally lies down to catch her breath, we stare at the ring in the gorgeous light. The way it sparkles on her hand. Traditional, elegant, and unmistakably Lena.

"Tell me now. Why did you keep it?"

"Because it's you," I tell her. She smiles. "Because I love how it looks, and I love when it's the only thing you're wearing, more than anything in the world."

"It's kinda perfect, I'll admit." She holds out her hand, and I kiss it like the lovesick freak I am.

"Just like you, Miss Joly. Next step, Mrs. Pruitt." I claim her lips again.

My fiancée. My final destination.

Finally, my wife for real.

XXVII

HOTDOGGIN'

(LENA)

Months Later

It's jaw dropping, how fast things move when you have money.

There's no need to have a marriage fund, especially not when Brady's parents insisted on shouldering the cost of our very scaled-down wedding.

Brady didn't want to accept. After growing up under their thumb all his life, he wanted to be independent, and I can't blame him.

It's a nice sentiment. But I understood the gesture too. The apology in the gift.

So that's why I let them splash bills on my wedding dress.

Probably one of the fairest compromises I've ever made.

Six months ago, Brady asked me to marry him for real. Six months ago, I accepted.

Now we're here.

Decked out on a massive rented yacht that gives our big day the perfect fairy-tale touch.

I know Kerrigan Pruitt, my soon-to-be mother-in-law, had this whole extravagant wedding day visualized down to the hour. The social event of the season. The year.

After everything that went down, she thought we'd want to give the world a glimpse of a happily-ever-after it tried to deny us.

But really, Brady and I just agreed to the yacht wedding to get away from the noise, the cameras, and the prying eyes.

Still, Seattle feels like it's a universe away out here. The San Juan Islands are beautiful in the spring, and the day couldn't have dawned more beautifully with clear skies and calm waters.

"Hold still, no fussing!" Gran slaps my hands away as I reach up to fiddle with the fancy hairdo she insisted on giving me.

Elle giggles from her corner perch, where she's curled up on the large sofa beside my bed.

It's hysterical to her, because she went through this with her wedding to August.

"I'm just checking, jeez. The wind will ruin my hair the second I go outside, anyway," I say.

We might have the best kind of day for an outdoor wedding on the ocean, but we're still on a boat. The wind is a given, and these pretty brunette curls draped down my neck will be the first casualties.

"Never underestimate the power of pins," the old woman whispers through a mouthful of them.

I glance at Mom, who flashes me a giant thumbs-up. Honestly, she might be the happiest one here today, awestruck ever since she came aboard the ship.

Then I look through the window, trying to see more of the preparations.

Every woman in my wedding party banded together to keep me inside all morning.

I *planned* this wedding, but I don't have a clue if everything's in order.

If the seats are set up.

If Queenie has her special ring bearer collar on without trying to wrestle out of it.

If Brady's suit is uncreased.

Now *that* will be a miracle.

"Almost there! Just a few more seconds." Gran pushes a final pin in the back of my head.

"Hope your hubby likes puzzles! Brady will have a crazy time getting them out." Elle laughs again.

"What good's a wedding without a little suspense?" Gran snickers knowingly. "It's a joy to keep a man waiting every now and again."

My face heats.

I smooth my hand down my dress. Wildly extravagant isn't my style, no, and this is the most basic sleek white gown Kerrigan Pruitt would let me get away with on her designer budget.

Basic or not, I still feel like a princess. I mean, as long as I don't think about the price tag.

. . . I'm really not going to get used to being rich.

Spending five outrageous figures on a wedding dress feels obscene. Doesn't matter if it's pocket change for a billionaire family.

I could have bought a nice new car instead.

But I also know the usual rules don't apply in this world, and this is Kerrigan and Alec's apology note. Their acceptance and a welcome gift, bringing me into the family.

Every time I get a nice long look at this getup, I remember why I can't complain.

"There!" Gran announces triumphantly, patting my hair and stepping back.

I touch the braids gently as I gaze at myself in the mirror.

Yep, the soft curls around my face will probably blow everywhere, but I have to admit the braids wrapped around my head feel like they're built to withstand a tropical storm.

"You can even sleep on it—but don't," she says with a heavy tone that suggests she thinks that's a distinct possibility.

I can't muster the courage to deny it.

Really, there's only one thing happening the second this dress comes off, and it *will* obliterate my pretty hair.

Nothing about our arrangement is traditional, but Brady agreed we'd abstain for an entire month to make our honeymoon more explosive than ever.

I mean, not abstain from *everything*. We don't have the willpower for that.

Things got creative, let's say.

Just not enough to satisfy the itch that can only be scratched by having him inside me.

I now know true suffering.

I'm so horny we might just leave the pins in and put Gran's handiwork to the wildest test.

I rub my warm skin, almost wishing this dress had sleeves.

It's off the shoulder and elegant, everything I could ever wish for in a wedding dress, but we're basically almost in Canada, and it isn't close to summer yet.

"Nervous?" Elle appears by my side.

"Excited. Just as long as nobody else knows we're here."

It wouldn't be impossible, especially because we're on a very short list of people who can afford to take a yacht this size out of Anacortes. Every gossipy mouth in Seattle and beyond would kill for an exclusive shoot of the Pruitts' big day, even if they have to follow us on a whale-watching ship with high-powered cameras.

"Oh, hush. No one knows the date. I burned the wedding invitation," Elle reminds me.

I snicker, because I know she really went that far.

"It's the honeymoon you'll have to worry about. Or just buck up and smile for the cameras. No creepers today, though," she assures me. "This is your big day, and Brady's. Enjoy it."

"I love you." I smile.

"Love you too, babe. Now go knock your man's socks off." She winks at me. "If I wasn't already taken, I'd be so jealous."

I snort. August is here, too, a hulking bear of a man who only ever seems to smile at his pretty new wife. He comes in from milling around outside a minute later.

I like to think he and Brady are becoming fast friends.

From the way Elle looks at him, one of the smaller islands around us could lift up into the sky, and if August was in front of her, she'd never know it.

It's sweet, though.

Mom pokes her head through the door after grabbing a fresh cup of coffee. Her face breaks into a smile when she sees me fully transformed into a blushing bride.

Ugh, am I really blushing that much?

Sometimes, I forget how much she's been through. But when I see her grinning, with her eyes all glassy, it reminds me of how little she's smiled since Dad left.

It makes my heart hurt in the best way.

To think that I'm *the* reason for her lighting up like this again.

"Lena, oh my God!" She rushes up and grabs my shoulders, holding herself back like she'll ruin me if she gets any closer.

"Mom, calm down. You saw me like five minutes ago."

"But now you're finished. You're a *bride*." She sniffles.

"No crying, Mrs. Joly. House rules," Elle jokes. Then she and Granny Lark head outside with August to find their seats.

As you'd expect, it's a tiny, private affair. Mom will walk me down the aisle with Elle trailing behind as my maid of honor.

"I love you. I love this," Mom gushes, turning me so we're both facing the mirror. "If your father could see you now . . ."

I smile grimly, refusing to let my eyes mist up.

This is a good day. Two generations of Joly women literally sailing into tomorrow.

"Are you happy?" she whispers, her eyes brimming.

"You know I am, Mom. If Dad could meet Brady, they'd be insta-buds. Brady would've loved his old radio-controlled planes, with the drone stuff he's doing for his channel now," I whisper back.

"I know, baby. You chose a good one." She squeezes me. "Are you ready, though?"

"I've been ready since the first proposal. Um, sorry about that—keeping you in the dark. It happened so fast." I watch her laugh and shake her head. "But he's so perfect for me, Mom."

"Yes. I knew something was going on when you wouldn't bring the boy out to meet me until after the drama bomb exploded."

"Something's going on with you too." I look up at her curiously. "You're wearing a new perfume. What is that? Cherry?"

"No perfume, I—" She stops and closes her mouth, her face heating.

"Mom?"

She sighs. "If you must know, Granny Lark pulled me aside after the groom's dinner last night. We were reminiscing about that old bakery in Capitol Hill we loved when you were little. I might've mentioned the ice cream stand, and . . . the woman is relentless." Mom beams me a shaky smile. "You don't even want to know how she tracked down five pounds of cherries in the off season with all the grocery stores closed. It's not quite the old Raven Swirl recipe, but we churned up a decent batch for the reception. Just a fun little extra we thought people would like. Only now I've gone and ruined the surprise, so—"

"Mom!" I just react, leaping up and throwing my arms around her. "I'm proud of you."

I'm honestly trembling, wondering how this day can get any better.

I haven't seen my mother so much as glance at a pint of ice cream in a freezer case since the day Harry Jay wrecked her business.

"Yes, well, my daughter's big day only happens once." She wipes under her eyes, checking to make sure she hasn't smeared her liner. "Let's walk."

I accept the offer without another word. Just grinning because I think this won't be the last time Mom revives her old passion.

I really owe Gran a nice massage gift certificate or a new set of gardening tools. What *can't* her scheming do?

With my arm in Mom's, I take my first step into the brilliant golden sunlight.

Perfection awaits.

Our little crowd turns to look at us as the music swells from the ship's speakers.

Gran has Queenie on a short leash. The Lab barks when she sees me, straining a little to get closer.

She's gotten better at containing her excitement, but it's not easy today with so many people, the sea, and a strange new environment.

Later, I mouth, pointing at my eyes, then back at her, looking as stern as I can. *You'll get hair on my dress, girl. Stay.*

She barks loudly like she understands and lies down with a grumble.

Everybody laughs.

As I blink in the daylight, my chest splits open until it feels like I'm breathing helium instead of air.

It's almost scary, being this happy.

Up ahead, the song switches over, and we start slowly moving forward toward the arch at the end.

Everyone else stands in their seats. Friends, family, the people closest to us and no one else.

And, of course, Brady, standing beside the captain, who doubles as our officiant in his crisp white uniform.

There are so many people as I keep moving forward. So many faces giving me their very best.

Granny Lark throws me a mischievous wink.

Kerrigan beams, maybe the most emotion I've ever seen on her.

Even Alec looks up in his wheelchair and gives me a brusque nod of approval.

Even the hardest hearts are melting today.

Brady chose a wonderful linen suit. He looks like a white knight, glowing in the sunlight, my own wise guardian angel come to earth.

The outfit accents his dark hair and the brightest blue eyes I've ever seen.

His mouth parts as I walk down the makeshift aisle. This isn't a church, no, and although Kerrigan insisted on the traditional "bride walk," all I really want to do is get to my groom ASAP.

Preferably without tripping over the hem of my dress.

He reaches out to me and squeezes my hand when I close in. Predictably, the breeze tosses those loose curls over my face, and I blow them back into place.

"Ouch, woman. You're so beautiful it hurts," he whispers.

"I know," I whisper back, pumping his hand. "You look pretty decent yourself."

With a huge grin, he nods.

Together, we turn to the captain as he clears his throat.

Time melts and starts flowing differently.

I don't remember much about the ceremony or the words we say when the promises are already steel in our hearts.

Oh, but I remember the scenery.

Especially when a small orca pod surfaces in the distance, blowing their spouts, and the ceremony almost pauses so we can all get a good look at them.

A yellow seaplane passes overhead, possibly following the whales for tracking. I actually freak out a little.

One glance at Mom tells me she sees it too.

Maybe it's just a happy coincidence, yeah. But maybe it's my aviation-buff father looking down, giving us a giant thumbs-up from the Great Beyond.

Queenie barks at the whales, to everyone's delight, wagging her tail.

I just hope she isn't too spooled up to forget ring duty.

And I remember Brady's vows when they come, the way he promises to dedicate every second of his life to me, to make me feel supported and loved.

Soon, I echo the same. How I love my new husband more than life and that I accept him completely.

How I'll always want him in sickness or health, anger or joy, life or death.

With Brady, it's so easy, knowing he'll always help me be my own unapologetic self.

Queenie brings us the rings and doesn't miss a beat.

Luis—Brady's best man—unclips the box from her collar, scratching her behind the ears in gratitude as he passes them off to the captain.

Then to us.

The platinum ring feels incredible against my skin, like it's always belonged there. It's a plain band, aside from the slight engraving inside it.

Always, Sass. Forever mine.

I try not to choke up, remembering the words as I adjust my rings.

I'm so glad I practiced *not* crying for a week, or I'd be a total mess right now.

Even Brady's eyes have a shimmer as he looks at me and mouths, *I love you.*

There.

My iron grip on my wedding mask cracks, and my face screws up.

"By the power vested in me," the captain says while I blot at my eyes, "I proudly declare you husband and wife. Kiss the bride."

If I'm falling apart, one kiss seals me back together.

One searing, intense, explosive kiss as Brady holds me, dips me in his arms, and claims my mouth in front of the world.

And as he cups my face, caressing me so gently, I feel myself unraveling, and I don't even care.

Nobody ever said weddings were supposed to be easy.

And no love has ever felt like this before. So complete. So utterly fricking *right.*

"God, I love you," I whisper as he pulls away.

We're both too breathless to say another word, so we just go in for a second kiss.

I think the cheering might scare the whales away.

If not, Queenie bouncing up and down, barking like mad until she's panting, does it for sure.

But all I can see is Brady's smile, heart stopping and gorgeous as he stares down at the rest of his life.

"My beautiful wife," he says reverently.

Smiling, I make a silent promise that I'll never let him see anything less.

◆ ◆ ◆

The best day of my life is also the longest.

I wish I had a degree in physics to understand how weddings warp time. The day crawls by, yet it's also gone in the blink of an eye.

And when I'm done blinking, I'm sharing my first dance with Brady as his wife. Then I dance with Mom and do a quick jig with Elle and Granny Lark.

Queenie finally crashes out from the excitement, sleeping with her paws in the air next to Luis, who brings his Miami energy to the dance floor when everyone else starts tapping out.

Even Dr. Ezzie looks happy as she dances with an older gentleman, an uncle of Brady's in medicine. My heart purrs to see her with a brand-new work-life balance, free from her crushing juggling act.

The sun shines on until dusk. I still feel like I'm walking on air as it gets dark.

I'm certainly dancing on it.

Best of all, the boat only has to dock in Anacortes at the end of our day to let all the other guests off, and then we're alone with nothing but a skeleton crew to keep the ship running.

After a quick refueling stop, the ship backs into the night, moving through calm waters under a laughing, bright moon.

The night sky might be our best wedding present.

We have this yacht for the next few weeks. Our plan is to lazily work our way down the Pacific coast through Washington, Oregon, California, and Baja, Mexico, ending our celebration with a few days in Cabo San Lucas.

So many gorgeous sights to take in.

So much of the world to see.

If we can bring ourselves to leave the boat, I mean.

I tell myself that won't be a problem as Brady unzips the side of my dress, stopping when he sees the corset fit snugly against my skin.

"Damn, Sass. Didn't know you had so many layers," he says as I lie down, content on the sun bed outside our room. There's a heater nearby for warmth, but the cool night feels good on my skin.

I'm so tired I could drift away right now.

"All for suspense. That's what Gran said."

"How pissed will you be if I just rip it off?"

I crack an eye and look up at him.

"If you want, we can have sex with it on. Right here. That'll be a sight for the crew."

"The *crew*, shit. All this energy must've gone to your head." He nips my neck as he leans over and whispers, "Fortunately, they're enjoying a late dinner break, and we're anchored for the night."

"Mm, well, in that case . . ." I tilt my head, giving him better access to my neck. "Just be gentle. This is the most expensive dress I'll ever own."

"We'll change that soon."

"What an arrogantly rich thing for you to say." I laugh under the feel of his hand caressing my bare skin.

"What an arrogantly rich man you married. Worth it, though." His voice drops to low thunder, and I shiver. "Can't believe I'm the lucky bastard who gets to be with you for the rest of my life."

"Um, make your legion of fans understand. According to them, I stole their winning ticket at the Pruitt lottery."

"Bullshit," he says tenderly, carefully drawing the dress off me.

The corset pops off easily, thankfully, and he peels more fabric away until I'm down to what Elle termed my knock-him-out panties, complete with a little pink bow.

He lets out a choked laugh and catches my face, bringing it to his so he can kiss me.

"A word of warning," I say between kisses, twisting so I can undo his jacket and work off his layers. "Don't even try to take my hair down. We'll be stuck here for days."

"That bad? I like it down."

I laugh against his lips. God, I love being here like this.

"Pins." The way his face creases with frustration makes me dissolve into more laughter.

He doesn't seem to mind as he peppers kisses down my neck and across my breasts, rolling my nipples until I gasp.

"A month. A fucking month without my dick inside you," he rasps bitterly.

"Too long, I agree." I push him back, and we walk to the railing, where tiny lights dance on the distant islands. Here, naked as the day I was born, I stand and push my hips toward him.

"Here? You're sure?"

"If you can manage." I glance over my shoulder at him mischievously.

"Fuck, woman, I'd take you on top of the Space Needle right now. I've been dreaming about having you wrapped around me for weeks." He reaches between my legs, his quick fingers rubbing and teasing.

He doesn't need any prep when I'm already soaked.

I bite my lip and lean over the railing carefully. The cold metal nips my skin, a pleasant contrast to the fire he kindles.

There are so many beautiful sights ahead, but I don't think anything will beat this moment, bathed in night, his hot breath on my neck.

He comes closer, leaning over me, pressing me down.

We exchange a quick, feral glance, a question without words.

Oh yes. I'm ready.

In answer, he inhales sharply, pressing his cock against my entrance.

He takes me in one push.

Glorious friction.

For a second, I can't breathe.

Being filled by this man is on another level, the one inhabited by sex gods.

My legs tremble, and he wraps his arms around my waist with a rough laugh.

"I've got you. Don't worry," he says.

Doesn't he, though?

His hand roams my breast, and the other moves down, skating across my belly until he finds my clit. With his thumb adding the perfect pressure, he thrusts deeply, fiercely.

The slowness is delectable—but when I rock my hips back, urging him on faster, it's devastating.

With these rings glittering on my fingers and the rest of our lives coming closer with every thrust, every kiss, every breathless moan, I know how deeply Brady healed me.

He fixed me in ways I never knew I needed.

Everyone at Pawsome Hearts keeps teasing me about the changes the last few months.

I smile more. I make small talk with strangers, and it doesn't feel like a chore. I'm even *singing* along to the radio after close, when we all pitch in to clean the kennels.

They remind me I've defrosted.

And the very hot, heroic beast driving into me is the only reason why.

My hand covers Brady's over my breast, just so I can touch him.

His tempo picks up. He holds me closer, pinning us together with his grip.

Greedily possessive, yes.

But safe. Wanted.

Inseparable.

"So fucking good tonight, Lena," he growls in my ear. The cool breeze skittering over me is the only reason I'm not melting.

I know how risky this is, but my body doesn't care. Technically, some restless crewman could walk out for a cigarette or just some fresh air and look up at our balcony, but when you're on a boat with a billionaire and his new wife on their wedding night, I guess you know the rules.

Don't see it, don't say it.

The waves rock gently under us, adding an extra thrill.

There's nothing gentle as his hips quicken, his cock pounding fire through my nerves.

Another moan falls out of me.

The love, the happiness, the certain forever, and the pleasure that ignites me like a match.

Absolutely no complaints.

A month ago, I would've sworn we have the best sex life. But something about tonight feels different.

Maybe it's the ring on my finger or the giddy afterglow of walking down the aisle and dancing until my feet hurt.

But yes, married sex feels better than I would've believed.

"Don't stop," I gasp.

"Not on your life." He kisses my shoulder, then the other. "Hell, I think you'll condition me to get hard every time I see your hair like this."

I give back a gasping, breathless laugh. "I don't think it'll happen very often."

"Shame. I'd better savor this, then." He plunges in faster, losing control with every thrust, breaking me down.

Then time blurs for the hundredth time today.

I think I say his name.

Brady, Brady.

Over and over until I'm hoarse, but none of that matters.

His strong arms hold me up, and his voice echoes so roughly in my ear, urging me to come.

Vowing to love me forever.

And I love him so much I go off with a wild scream, rocking like mad on his cock as he fills me.

The world falls back into place so slowly, and he pulls out, turning me around and bringing me down on the day bed with a tumble.

"We should get inside. It'll be cold out here soon."

"Eventually. I want to see your face," he says as he pulls me closer.

In no time at all, I don't need to worry about the chill. He's inside me again, and we both groan with relief.

I roll my hips, watching his eyes glaze.

"I want this forever. Can we do that?" I whisper.

"Forever," he agrees.

"Promise me?"

"That's the promise I made today, Sass. Won't break it for anything while I've got a beating pulse." He pauses his punishing strokes to bring my left hand to his mouth, kissing the rings. "Forever, Lena. You deserve nothing less, and you're going to get it."

Chills.

Nobody guarantees the future, I know, but tonight my man sounds like a prophet.

Later, as he drags me inside to the large bed to hold me with my head against his chest, listening to the soft drumming of his heart, I'm stoked to wake up to the rest of our eternity.

Epilogue

DOUBLE DOG DARE

(LENA)

Eight Years Later

Freya perches on the edge of the chair as I work. Ideally, I wouldn't have my seven-year-old daughter with me, but sometimes life doesn't ask.

Her small face is sharp and attentive.

The small, shriveled cat in front of us is clearly a stray. He's missing one ear from suspected frostbite, and he's severely underweight.

Poor little honey.

Even with the lick mat I'm holding in front of his face for a distraction, smeared with tuna-flavored food, the beast hisses as Dr. Vetol administers the first of many shots.

"Is he gonna be okay?" Freya whispers, blinking up at me with Brady's sharp blue eyes.

When she was first born, those eyes were a shocker, but now they're my pride and joy.

Is there anything better than walking around with my husband's legacy, even when he's not here?

"He'll be fine. Just stay back, Freya," I warn, checking the cat for a chip once the doctor finishes.

"What's his name, Mom?"

"For now, it's John Doe." Dr. Vetol chuckles warmly.

Ever since I took over Pawsome Hearts, he's been the perfect partner in business and medicine, bringing an infectious humor and the kindest bedside manner to the wildest beasts who walk through our doors.

"John Doe? That's boring! He needs a better name. Let's give him one, Mom!"

"Let's not just now," I say sharply, biting back a smile.

"But everyone deserves a cool name, even the strays."

I sigh. "Freya, we both know what will happen if I let you name him."

Dr. Vetol laughs again, inspecting the cat's ears for mites one more time.

Freya pulls an innocent look that rivals a cartoon chipmunk.

"What? What will happen?" She whispers breathlessly.

"You'll want to keep him, and we can't."

"Keep him?" She claps her hands delightedly. "Wow, great idea! But you should name him, Mommy."

I look down at the tabby, who eyes me with all the disgust a cat can muster—and for this boy, it's a metric ton.

"I don't think he likes me, honey. He's a little rough around the edges. Who knows how long he's been out there."

"Well, yeah! But John Doe, that's being mean," she says, rolling her eyes.

I mock glare at her. "I knew it was a mistake, bringing you to work."

"But I had to come for school," she says sheepishly.

True, unfortunately.

She's taking after me, growing up camera shy. Every time her teachers give her a project that involves her parents' jobs, it's never any contest who she picks to shadow.

The puppies and kittens only sweeten the deal.

"You," I say, "are your father's girl. You inherited his charm."

She beams wickedly. "I know!"

Coming from me, that's never an insult.

We're almost a decade in, and I don't think I'll ever get over how much I adore Brady. Having a daughter changed things, yes, especially when I look at her and realize I'd die for this little cherub in an instant.

Best of all, I don't have to. Not when I'm married to the hottest, happiest billionaire beast in Seattle.

With Brady, it's been a total joy, showing Freya what a healthy, loving relationship looks like.

"Hey, Mom?" Freya pushes off her chair and comes toward me, head cocked to one side. "You're smiling again."

The cat yowls miserably as the doc finishes looking over a few last scrapes on his legs, and I go back to work, checking the sedative shot we've already prepped. He's going to need to go under while we rinse him off in the big metal sink if we want to avoid getting ripped to pieces.

Occupational hazard of marital bliss. Sometimes you forget what you're doing and start spontaneously daydreaming about getting home to your hubby.

It's almost disgusting how smiley I am with Brady on my mind.

Almost.

And I wouldn't change a single damn thing.

"What about Buttercup? He's got a kinda yellow-tan belly," Freya decides, peering into the cat's eyes. It glares back, annoyed and gold. "Oh, and his eyes . . . Mom, it's gotta be Buttercup!"

I know that look from my little girl. I step in front of her before she can reach for his scraggly fur.

"Careful, honey. He needs a bath, and he's pretty irritable. You don't want to get scratched. We're going to have to sedate him for a bit."

"Okay, fine. But can we bring him home?" she asks hopefully.

At this point, I think she knows I can't resist.

"Tell you what. If his parasite test comes back clean and he looks like he can behave for a few hours—and you promise to keep him in the pet room without visiting unless your dad or I are with you—I'll *think* about it. Now go ask Trish for a sucker. I'll be with you in a second."

Besides the lollipop, Trish rocks at entertaining my little nugget.

Freya prefers me, of course, but Trish has turned into this cool office aunt who listens patiently while Freya talks her ear off about every animal known to man.

Buttercup's tail swishes as he watches us getting ready to deliver the last shot.

"You spoil her, Lena. Careful, or we'll be handing her the keys to this place someday," Dr. Vetol says cheerfully, gently grabbing the cat.

"Yeah, yeah. But we have several dogs and a cat recuperating in observation back there, so I figured taking him home would lighten the load." I grumble, but I already know what I'm about to do.

Luckily, there's a bonus.

I get to see how Brady will react to *another* stray after he's put his foot down with expanding our zoo.

◆ ◆ ◆

I find out the instant we get home almost two hours later with "Buttercup" clean, dry, and groggy in his carrier.

A decadent-smelling seafood alfredo punches me in the nose. Brady just finished making dinner in the kitchen, and he stands against the island with little Noah tucked in his arms.

After greeting our three dogs, who all bound up to lick my face, I'm only in the kitchen for three seconds before Noah sees me and throws up his chubby little arms.

"Mama!"

I laugh, putting down the cat carrier at the entrance to the mudroom and accepting the welcome burden of my second child.

We agreed on two kids. Hard limit.

Don't get me wrong, I love them to death. But having these two precious creatures takes up more time than you can imagine, especially when we don't do the typical rich-people thing where we hand them off to nannies for fourteen hours a day.

While Freya has her dad's looks, Noah takes after me. Snubby round nose, light-brown eyes, and dark hair with chestnut stripes that's just starting to curl. A lot like mine did until I hit puberty and my hair straightened out more.

It breaks my happy heart a little every time I look at him.

"How many fires did you put out today, Sass?" Brady leans over to kiss my cheek, bathing me in his glorious scent, which mingles weirdly well with the seafood pasta.

"Not enough. Little Frey fell in love." I glance back at the carrier holding Buttercup, who's still tipsy and half asleep with the sedation wearing off.

"Oh shit. Again?" Brady blinks, then slaps his forehead dramatically.

Freya giggles, already trying to fumble the carrier door open.

Buttercup yowls a loud warning.

"Freya, wait!" I call. "Remember what we talked about with new animals?"

"Yeah, yeah." She pouts. "Pet room first. No being alone with them. I heard, Mommy."

"It's for your good and his. You scare him. He might run away. Or give old Queenie a heart attack," I say.

Right on cue, the ancient girl swaggers up to lick my hand.

I *cannot* believe she's still with us, but I'm grateful for every day.

She's going on 130 in dog years, a unicorn blessing I'm not sure what we did to deserve.

But that's life in the Pruitt household—and it's as good as it is surprising. It just means we're running more of a zoo than a house, and we wouldn't have it any other way.

Three dogs, two cats—if Buttercup works out—a little pond full of fat, colorful koi, and yes, we even have a rescue goat roaming around in the backyard. There's also an elderly rabbit in a hutch by the side of the house, which is Freya's responsibility to clean out and care for.

She's good about it. *Mostly.*

"Woman, what happened to our rules? We're maxed out on pets," Brady mutters, trying not to laugh as his arms wind around my waist. "I told you if you bring one more fur ball home, we'll need a bigger house."

I bite back a laugh of my own because he's only half joking.

Not long after we tied the knot and found out I was expecting, we moved away from Seattle proper, sprawling into the suburbs like a good dual-income family with ample money to burn.

But this mansion has over two acres and *six bedrooms.*

We've found a place for all of them, plus two true guest rooms that serve us nicely whenever friends or family visit.

I lay my hand on his chest, pushing playfully. "Aw, come on. Three more cats will max out our space. We'd be using it efficiently."

"No more," Brady calls gruffly, loud enough for Freya to hear. "The girl needs time to focus on her homework."

"School's easy! I'll have time with ten cats, Dad!" she yells back, sitting cross-legged, thankfully a comfortable distance from Buttercup. "Just gotta get him to love me first."

"Of course he'll love you. Give it a week or two for him to settle in," I say, kissing little Noah on the cheek and setting him down. He immediately toddles off toward the new carrier, only to be stopped by his big sister as she scoops him up.

"No*ah,*" Freya whines. "Don't get close, he has to get used to us. And Mom said I get to hang out with him first!"

"Be nice to your brother," Brady growls.

"Kitty!" Noah yells, clapping his hands.

Chaos, I think.

But that's the life we chose.

The sweetest chaos with two rambunctious kids and our own private menagerie. Thankfully, two of our dogs are seniors: Queenie and Rufus. Aside from our little dynamo corgi named Liz, the dogs don't pay too much attention to the new arrival.

To them, it's old hat.

No doubt when Buttercup makes his presence known, they'll have more to say.

"He's going to need time to recover and rest. So even when he's nicer, you have to be careful," I tell Freya as I help set the table.

At this point, I don't know if the toy on the floor I'm stepping over belongs to the dogs or Noah.

Probably both.

"With you in charge of his recovery, he'll probably grow his ear back in no time." Brady grins, bringing our food to the table.

I stop and take a second to appreciate his perfect face.

It isn't fair. This man wears age like a designer fashion statement.

Just the slightest hint of early grey silvering his hair.

If I'm lucky, he'll have that distinguished silver fox look his father has, minus the thorny attitude.

The lines around his eyes when he smiles will absolutely slay me no matter how long we're together. He always smiles like he means it too.

Sappy or not, I think I fall a little more in love with him every day.

Before we met, I couldn't imagine crushing on an older guy, but here we are.

"I'll take him downstairs," Freya announces. She has to use both hands to hoist up the cat carrier. No matter how underfed and scrawny he is, she's still just a seven-year-old.

"Easy! You know the rules," I say. "Set him in there and make sure the door stays shut. Do not let him out. We'll do that later, after dinner."

"Fiiine."

She's been scratched enough times to count over the years. I'm going to trust she won't "accidentally" let that door pop open, if only to save her own skin.

I don't put that sort of faith in this cat.

But then again, he's stopped hissing like a cornered snake.

Most animals handle children pretty well.

Freya certainly has good instincts, I guess. Brady insists she gets it from me, but while I've always been there to help, I haven't ever had the same knack for making animals trust me.

There's a difference between understanding the creatures you're treating and having them immediately love you.

My heart unexpectedly brims at the thought of this starved, lonely cat experiencing real love for the first time.

It's a big cruel city out there with a ton of strays around. I certainly wish it wasn't.

Buttercup doesn't know it yet, but he's a *very* lucky boy.

Just as long as he learns to share his heart with a bright-eyed seven-year-old girl who thinks it's her life's mission to save as many forgotten animals as possible.

I don't think it's possible to be this proud.

"I love you," I call to Freya, who's already bounded partway downstairs.

She turns and looks at me with a frown, her blue eyes puzzled and patient and too old for her years.

"Well, yeah," she says seriously, lugging the carrier.

"Do you think she'll be okay with our new friend?" Brady asks.

I wince.

He still remembers the time I brought home our last foster kitten. The little beast scratched his arm and barfed formula all over him the second he took away the bottle.

I kiss his cheek. "She'll be fine. Freya has her father's knack for new arrivals, and we've drilled it into her a thousand times, right?"

"*Are* we really keeping Buttercup?"

"The ship has sailed," I say with a sigh. "You know we'll have a pint-sized mutiny on our hands if we don't."

"Yeah." He chuckles, his eyes twinkling. "If this keeps up, the cats will outnumber the doggos soon. Can't say I like that math."

"Cats are better when you're old, even if we've still got a little way to go before that happens." I grin at him and walk over to start plating up dinner. "Besides, you think we're going to stop now?"

"I'm not joking about moving if this petting zoo expands." He pulls a mock-horrified face.

"I mean . . . little Noah hasn't even had a chance to weigh in yet." We both know what's going to happen when he's older—more animals. Grinning, I hold a hand to my head dramatically and say, "I'm having a vision. I see a hedgehog, an iguana . . . maybe even a house pig in our future."

"House pig? Like hell," Brady grumbles, but he's smiling as I scoop Noah off the ground and take him to the sink to wash his hands.

Freya comes clattering back up to us a minute later, sucking on her hand. I immediately side-eye her.

"What did you do?"

"I just wanted to touch his nose, Mama. But Buttercup doesn't like to be petted," she announces.

"Freya!" Brady's at her side in an instant, kneeling and taking her hand, his sympathy smothering our need to discipline her. Sure enough, two small scratch marks are beading with dark blood. "What did we tell you about touching new animals too soon? Now you had to learn the hard way."

"Dad, he liked it—at first. He let me touch his face until he didn't. It doesn't even hurt!" The tears brimming in her eyes say differently.

"Let's get you cleaned up before dinner. And you're not touching Mr. Buttercup for the rest of the evening," he says.

"*Daaaad!* No fair."

"I'll get dinner on the table," I say, already wrestling Noah into his high chair.

"Kitty! Kitty!" The little boy claps his hands and bounces.

I ruffle his hair with a tired laugh. It's going to be a rough few days when Freya isn't the only one enamored with our new arrival.

Like I said, sweet chaos.

But as I hear Brady talking to Freya about the need to respect animals' personal space, and Queenie nudges my side, already looking for dinner scraps with her big buttery eyes, I remember how much I love this unruly life we've made together.

Brady, the brilliant self-made giant of revolutionary organic pet food.

Me, the crazy cat lady with the best vet clinic in Seattle.

Our wonderful, adorable family.

Who knows where it ends, but there's no doubt about one thing.

This man will keep blessing me with everything in the long, happy years ahead, and I wouldn't have it any other way.

Turn the page to see a preview of Nicole Snow's book *Two Truths and a Marriage*!

Two Truths And A Marriage Preview

SWEET RELIEF

(JUNIPER)

There are days when I wish I was a college girl.

Not often, mind you. And not because I love the thought of having a gazillion dollars in debt on my shoulders either. Because with the Sugar Bowl creaking along on its last legs, the very last thing we need is *more* debt.

But a few more math classes would sure as hell help my brain hurt less with these numbers.

"That can't be right," I spit.

I rub my eyes, squinting at the spreadsheet for the fifth time.

Nobody warned me that inheriting a business means spending more time hunched in front of a computer screen than actually working. My already pale skin practically glows white. I'm ninety percent sure the blue light from the screen is making my hair frizz.

Numbers.

Ugly money numbers.

Numbers with sharp teeth and a ferocious appetite for chewing up my dreams.

Yeah, things aren't looking good.

I take a break from the nightmare on the screen and glance around. The back office looks about like it did in Nana's time.

Same old tall metal filing cabinets propped up against the dusty wallpaper—probably less dusty when Nana ran the shop with an iron fist, of course—and the old, faded photos hanging everywhere.

Same awards plastered to the wall. Newspapers and cards and bronze plaques proclaiming some version of *best in Kansas City!* for more years than I can count.

As I always do when I need a moment to get my wits, I stand up, push my chair back—ignoring that one squeaky wheel that cuts my ears—and pace the room, slowly taking in the wall of photos.

There's Nana, young and bright, standing by the shop with her parents on its opening day in June 1955. The date is recorded at the bottom of the photo, taken at a time when the world would shine in black and white with a certain charm no Instagram filter will ever match.

My gaze flicks to photos of the interior renovation in the late fifties. And again right around 1970. Before 2000, the Sugar Bowl had a stunning redesign every decade or two, and each one generated a flurry of news and happy, hungry customers pouring in for the grand reopening.

Unimaginable now.

I'm surrounded by an entire gallery of reasons to succeed, to keep going, to remember this bakery's greatness. But I'm also buried in the fact that those fond memories and fabulous accolades came to a screeching halt in 2021—the year Nana stepped down.

Glaring evidence of my failure to take flight.

This is my family's legacy, all wrapped up in a store that used to soar.

With me at the helm, it's struggling to even crawl.

It's enough to make my throat close up.

If I was the woe-is-me type, I'd have thrown in the towel a year ago. Instead, I put my hands on my hips and look around. My eyes stop on another photo, Nana and my mother when she was a little girl.

"You better not be watching, Mom," I warn. "This isn't my finest hour. I mean . . . neither was last year or the year before that. Come back in a few. The store will be hopping again or the sign will be swinging in the wind."

I wince at another possibility—we'll keep stumbling along, just like we have been since I took over the place, twenty-two and fresh-faced. Back when I still had a boyfriend and sky-high hopes for the future.

Better times.

Easier times.

I take one last melancholy look around at every sharp reminder of why I need to step it up—and why I suck—before turning back to my computer.

"Hunk of crap," I whisper. The ancient thing was probably on the *Titanic* with its boxy monitor that's big enough to fit Nana's flower garden inside.

One day, it'll give up the ghost, just like everything else here, but I don't dare replace it.

Not when revenue looks so thin I'll be lucky to buy an ink cartridge for the printer next quarter.

My chest swells as I sigh and melt into my chair.

The spring menu's pushing new coffees and light pastries, but they're lower ticket items for a fast-casual customer base.

Two weeks ago, the ovens randomly stopped firing and our accountant retired, meaning we had to shell out big bucks for a new guy with triple the fees.

Not to mention the payroll needed to run this place, cutting deeper and deeper into my skeletal profits.

My projected turnover, if these damn numbers are to be trusted, looks like—

Well, let's just say it's litterbox territory.

Instead of pressing my face into my hands and screaming until my throat rips—totally reasonable under the circumstances—I lean forward until my forehead thunks against the screen.

The very *hot* screen.

Which almost certainly shouldn't be hot enough to slow cook an egg.

"Oh, no. Oh, shit," I hiss, shoving back and almost knocking the giant machine off the creaking desk.

That's when Emmy pokes her head in. *Perfect timing.* "Hey, Junie!" she says, tucking her static curls back with one hand. "There's a guy waiting at the register."

I rub the sore spot on my forehead, grinding my teeth.

A guy? What guy?

The only kind I meet.

Another rude prick expecting the red-carpet treatment and a lifelong discount because his espresso was three degrees too cold.

But it's my store. I'm effectively the boss and I'm expected to defuse every temper tantrum that comes barreling through the door.

I didn't say I was *good* at it. I'm only slightly better at customer relations than I am at math.

My armpits are already sweaty in this heat. Missouri summers always have that merciless phase and we're in the thick of it.

God, if I have to choose between replacing the archaic computer and functioning air conditioning, I'll be in real trouble.

I suck in a breath and step away from the glaring monitor, hoping to leave my nervous breakdown behind with the overheated machine.

Maybe by the time I return, the numbers will magically change.

"Lead the way, Emmy," I say with way more enthusiasm than I feel, fanning a bit of much-needed air up my shirt before following her to the front and the asshat waiting for us.

And what an *asshat.*

Holy hell, I wasn't ready for this breed of scary-hot alpha male to be standing at my counter, waiting to tear my face off.

I expected a scowling prick—and let's be honest, he certainly *is* one—but he's a finalist for world's hottest prick.

Toweringly tall? Check.

Dark-blue eyes flashing with sin? Yes.

Mile-wide shoulders that look like they could hold up the sky? Oh, baby, he's got them.

He's the full Prince Charming package, up to and including the intimidating look etched on his face that's pinched with a thousand demands.

While I take my place behind the register, he glances at his digital watch with the designer gold band and sighs.

Yep, definitely a prick.

But rich as hell, if his designer-brand oxford shirt and bright-blue tie are anything to go by. I don't have it in me today to offend rich paying customers.

So I do the only sane thing a struggling business owner can—I reach down, dive deep, and dredge up a smile from the bottom of my soul.

"Hi there," I say, my customer service voice bright and bouncy, ready to deflect the avalanche of crap he's about to dump on me. "Is there a problem with your order?"

"No. I haven't made one yet," he clips. He's not even looking at me. His eyes are turned up, fixed on the overhead menu.

O-kay.

Good thing I've been doing this for a while.

One prick, no matter how sharp his cheekbones are or how defined his jaw is—and God, what a jawline—will distract me from making money.

"Sure," I say cheerfully. "How can I help you then?"

"Can you execute a large custom order for delivery today?" He doesn't even wait for me to nod before waving a hand at the glass case gleaming with pastries. "I need a sampler of this crap. Tortes, cheesecakes, turnovers, cupcakes, the works. Make it extra sweet."

This crap?

I'm frozen, stunned and staring as my brain tries not to get ragey and defensive.

This is an order, even if he's placing it in the rudest way imaginable.

A real oh-shit-this-is-expensive order that will make good money.

My *favorite* kind of order that only comes up a dozen times a year, if I'm lucky.

I turn my smile all the way up to blinding. "Certainly! Do you have any specific requests for your crap?"

There goes my tongue. It didn't get the memo to be polite.

He looks at me like I'm a crushed bug under his shoe and swipes a frustrated hand through the air. "All of it. Everything you do here. I don't care."

I blink at him, waiting for more, but he stares at the bakery case like it's personally offending him.

"Okay, yes, we can do that," I say slowly, looking him up and down.

So, he doesn't look insane, but maybe he's unhinged in the usual rich-people way. The kind where you walk in and buy out an entire store without even caring what it sells. "I'm sure we can accommodate your needs with a custom package of—"

"Extra sweet," he snaps. "So rich you'll choke."

Oof. I hate the way his eyes flash when he makes me imagine gagging.

"Sure, sure. It's easy to scrounge up our sweetest creations or add a little extra frosting to the lighter stuff."

"Whatever, lady. It needs to be perfect. I'm trusting you." The way he narrows his eyes at me says he trusts me to muck this up beyond recognition.

"Perfect, huh? You're in luck. We've been doing that for over fifty years," I bite off nicely at his assholery, beaming an even wider chipmunk smile that hurts my cheeks.

He hate-glares at the bakery case, then turns his dubious eyes back on me like swords.

Oh, boy.

My hair's probably a worn red ball in this humidity, plus the back office turning into a sauna.

But why does he look so skeptical?

"Sir, trust me, you've come to the right place. This place lives up to its name," I tell him, gesturing to a few framed thirty-year-old newspaper reviews behind me. "Whatever you need, you can count on us.

Cakes, éclairs, apple turnovers, honey-olive tortes, or anything you can imagine. Custom orders, bulk orders, samplers, the lot. You tell us what and when and we'll deliver. Even *today*." Oh hell, I'm rambling. But that's not a bad slogan. "Whatever you need, we've got you covered."

"Right." One dark eyebrow rises and he rakes me over with a look.

It isn't fair.

No grouchy customer barging in has any business making me feel this vulnerable.

"Would you like a few samples to give us your feedback?" I ask brightly. "It'll put a smile on your face, guaranteed."

Somehow, his mouth turns down even more.

"I don't do sweets and I don't have time to *gab*." He spits the word like it's dirty. "Can you have this order ready for six o'clock?"

Eep.

My eyebrows almost fly off my head.

But fine, fine.

If he wants to play bad cop and put us under the gun for turnaround, I'm more than happy dropping the cutesy act and getting to work.

"The Sugar Bowl isn't a Kansas City institution for nothing," I tell him in the same hard-edged tone he just used on me. "We'll get it done. Early."

"I hope to fuck that reputation is as sterling as you claim. Here's the delivery address," he mutters, pulling out a small Post-it Note and slamming it on the counter with enough force to rattle the display cabinets. "Six o'clock sharp. Don't even think about being late."

Then, with one last frigid scowl worthy of a Mafia don, he storms away from the store, the bell tinkling behind him like it's glad to send Satan back to hell.

Emmy and Jake immediately start snickering behind me.

"What a dick!" Emmy whispers, and Jake bursts into more giggles. "Way to go, Junie. You're a lion tamer today."

I don't acknowledge that.

Let them be kids.

I'll be the grown-up professional owner who keeps her shit together, even if I'm inwardly turning into a basket case. I can always beat my pillows at home *after* we get paid.

I tense my shoulders, just for a second, and inhale sharply.

The address he left is a fancy-ass hotel a few miles away. The kind that only lets people in if they smell like money.

Figures.

"Okay, team," I say, turning to the two laughing teenagers behind me with my best boss face. "We have two hours to buckle down and get this done. And the man said extra sweet for—everything, I guess. I'm calling in backup. No matter what happens, we are *not* screwing this up."

◆ ◆ ◆

The engine whines as I ease my foot on the gas, hoping the lights at the intersection don't go red.

I'm making beautiful time, just as long as nothing *else* goes wrong and the late rush hour traffic is kind to me.

Flipping caramel apple tortes.

But I'm the genius who decided to break out the sweetest treat in Nana's old recipe arsenal. It took three batches to get them just right.

I was almost forced to leave without them to meet Mr. Sweet Tooth's life-and-death deadline. Luckily, they came out and passed a quick taste test just before the deadline, but it was *close*.

So much for the promise I'd be early.

Even now, I'm pushing it, grinding through the bustling traffic of a summer evening. I swear the humid nights bring people out like bees.

I really can't afford to be waiting at the intersection, though.

To my eternal relief, I only whack the wheel once before the light turns green, and then I head down by the Riverwalk, passing the Winthrope KC hotel on the way.

The engine's whine morphs into a rattle.

"Oh, no, are you joking? Not now!" I grimace at the windshield. Just another big ugly repair bill I'll need to scrounge up money for. "Come on, baby. You can make it. I'll let you rest as soon as we get there . . ."

The rattle shakes through the seat as I stomp the gas and ease off it again.

Ugh.

I've never been much of a praying type, but I will sell my soul to any deity right now just as long as I make it to this stupid hotel.

This dude's order is big enough to cover several big car repairs and then some. It's so huge that if he didn't reek like money, I'd have worried whether he could pay it.

And if he isn't a total scrooge when he tips . . .

Ohhh, if he tips, I might actually be able to *live* on more than home-baked banana bread and frozen burritos for a few weeks.

But I try not to get my hopes up.

Hefty tips are never guaranteed, but if there's one thing I've learned about jackass customers, it's that they're often halfway decent tippers. Almost like they're trying to buy off their guilty conscience when nobody's looking.

Of course, that hinges on everything going right, and I *have* to make this deadline.

Miraculously, I swerve into the hotel parking lot without the van breaking down.

No time for celebration.

After a quick chat with reception, I grab the first set of boxes and haul them into the conference room. Thankfully, it isn't far from the main door.

To my surprise, Mr. Sweet Tooth stands in the conference room alone, leering over everything like a general surveying a battlefield.

He leans on the ginormous walnut table with his sleeves rolled up to his elbows, his lips slightly tilted and those cutting blue eyes ready to flay me open for the slightest error.

But I don't think he sees me at first.

He doesn't seem to hear the door or my panicked footsteps; he just stares out of the long, wall-length window overlooking the city basking in the sunset.

"Nobody else coming to the party yet? This is a lot for one guy," I joke as I set down the first box.

He starts, whipping toward me with that familiar stormy scowl.

"Unbelievable. You're five minutes late." He taps his watch in case I've forgotten the concept of time. "Your desserts better be goddamned ambrosia. Where's the rest?"

"Um, coming right up!" I say nervously, biting my tongue on adding *you absolute jackwagon*.

It takes him two seconds to realize it's just me unloading the stuff.

To my surprise, he follows me outside to the van and helps grab the remaining boxes, stacking them high in his arms.

"Can't believe people eat this stuff," he growls once we're back in the room, popping open a lid and checking out its contents—Nana's famous strudel bites. "It's begging for diabetes. There are places where sugar bombs like this get a sin tax."

Yikes, talk about opening a can of worms.

"So, what? You think no one should ever be allowed a little sugar?" I ask flatly.

"In any sane world, it'd be a controlled substance enforced by DEA troopers. If I were dictator for a day, I'd ban the shit entirely."

. . . He's mighty serious about a world without glucose, isn't he?

And I wonder how a man this painfully handsome wound up with the world's biggest stick lodged up his ass.

"You're hilarious." I stop what I'm doing and stare at him, trying to brush it off as a joke. He's hot, sure, but clearly a little—okay, a lot—deranged. "Do you hear what you're saying?"

"I know. I shouldn't bother debating the merits with someone who makes a living peddling death salt."

"Death salt? Excuse you?" One second later, I bite my tongue and sigh.

His glare cuts right through me.

For the love of everything holy, be nice.

Remember the money.

"Um, I mean . . . I'm a little confused. Help me out. You're the one who ordered this stuff *extra sweet*, right?" I rip open another box a little too forcefully and frown at the raspberry and white chocolate cheesecakes inside. "Please don't tell me you're some sort of health freak."

"If health freak means I actually take care of myself, then yes, sue me," he snarls.

"Oh, that would be the day," I huff under my breath.

His glare just got ten times hotter.

Putting all the samples out on the tables and arranging them neatly clearly isn't his talent, so after I tidy them up a few times, he gives up and watches me with an unwavering stare that makes me sweat.

Dude, could you let up on the evil eye?

It's a minor miracle I don't drip all over the dessert spread.

When I turn around, he's folding his arms. I hate the way the shirt tightens around his biceps like a second skin. *Nope, not staring.*

"You want to know the truth? If it was up to me, we'd have mandatory tracking and weekly workout times to offset every gram of this stuff," he grouches, looking past me at the treats.

So, he's not just a sugar-hating prick then—but a prick who's anal enough to obsess over the metric system too.

I ignore his insanity and step back to examine my handiwork. Not a bad presentation, if I do say so myself, especially considering the time crunch.

"Well, we're lucky it's not up to you. Too many control freaks already in power," I say with a sunny smile I hope hides my total contempt. "Anyway, sorry about the *five-minute* delay. I'd be happy to knock fifty bucks off the price for your trouble." I lay on the emphasis real thick and his scowl deepens. "But everything is here and customized to your liking." A smirk escapes before I can bite it back. "I mean . . . clearly not to *your* liking. But customized to your order, I should say."

His eyes flick around the room, probably searching for something else he can blame me for.

He looks like that kind of walking horse dick.

Nothing's ever good enough. There's always something to complain about.

But there's nothing wrong with what I've put out—I triple-checked—and after a breathless minute, he nods. Grudgingly.

"As ordered," he admits. "Forget the discount, I'll pay you in full."

Holy crap.

I stagger back a step.

I'm not used to things going right.

"Great!" I shove the paper bill and the credit card reader at him before he can change his mind. He raises his eyebrows at the bulky plastic reader pushing fifteen years old.

Jerk.

I half expect him to make a pointed comment about convenience—and I would've been half tempted to take the cherry pie and shove his face in it—but he just scrawls a signature on the bill and jabs his black credit card in the reader like a knife.

Like he just can't wait to get rid of me.

Righto. The feeling is mutual.

While he stares at the screen and waits for it to finish processing at a speed slower than molasses, I stick my tongue out at the back of his head and that thick dark hair.

Childish, yes, but it makes me feel better.

Then the door opens.

We both look up to witness the Kingpin of All Money swaggering in.

He's a bear of a man, probably in his fifties. Sweet Tooth is built and lean, yes, but he looks almost small compared to this older guy with thick limbs and a penguin belly.

Sweet Tooth immediately stops scowling. Oh, is he nervous?

Interesting.

So maybe Kingpin is Sweet Tooth's boss or something?

Makes sense. Doesn't every shark answer to a whale?

I turn back to face my tormentor with a saccharine smile.

"As you can see, everything's here and perfectly in order," I announce loudly while he gives me a look that tells me to scram. It's kind of delicious, the way his eyebrows sink low above his eyes. They heat with a blue-fire rage he can't indulge, not while he's in front of this other guy. "And extra sweet, just like you asked for. I'm not sure if you have any allergies, but just to be sure, the items with nuts were baked separately and are off to the left, over there, and—"

"Yes," Sweet Tooth clips through gritted teeth. "Understood, ma'am."

Kingpin stares across the spread with raised eyebrows and a shit-eating grin on his face. "Rory, color me impressed! Or should I be thanking our lovely delivery gal?"

Sweet Tooth inhales sharply and glowers at me.

"Thanks," he grinds out without an ounce of sincerity. "This all looks . . . great."

Lame, dude.

You aren't even trying.

I smile innocently.

"You don't think it's too sweet, do you?"

He shoves the bill into my chest and guides me to the door with one big hand pressed against my back.

I don't even have time to glance back at Kingpin and find out whether he's enjoying the cheesecake before Sweet Tooth practically picks me up and throws me out the door.

It closes behind him with a loud *click!*

"Jesus." I turn around, rubbing my arm and yelling, "You're welcome!"

Then I decide not to press my luck and beat it.

I get out of there as fast as I can without running.

It's only when I'm back in the van that I bother looking at the signed receipt.

There's a name scrawled across the bottom in a garish slash. *Dexter Rory.*

"All right," I say, rubbing my face. "Let's find out how crappy a tipper you are, Dexter Rory."

I skim down to the tip line and my eyes nearly exit my face.

My jaw drops.

Well, crap.

About the Author

Nicole Snow is a *Wall Street Journal* and *USA Today* bestselling author. Plotting her great escape from the cubicle, she found her writing groove by hashing out love scenes during lunch breaks. Her work roared onto the indie romance scene in 2014 and quickly multiplied into all the contemporary romance butterflies she's known for today.

Since then, Snow has been creating the very best in broody book boyfriends you can't help falling for, alongside tropes with meaning and swoon storms aplenty. With over a million books sold, she lives for the joy of making two people fight with every bit of their souls for a happily-ever-after.

About the Author